MORE THAN I LOST

TOM BLACKBURN

ARCHWAY PUBLISHING

Archway Publishing books may be ordered through booksellers or by contacting:

Archway Publishing
1663 Liberty Drive
Bloomington, IN 47403
www.archwaypublishing.com
1 (888) 242-5904

Cover design: A. Acorn
Cover moon photo: Nathalie C. Martin

ISBN: 978-1-4808-5891-6 (sc)
ISBN: 978-1-4808-5892-3 (e)

Library of Congress Control Number: 2018901824

Print information available on the last page.

Archway Publishing rev. date: 2/19/2018

. . . battles are lost in the same spirit in which they are won.

— Walt Whitman

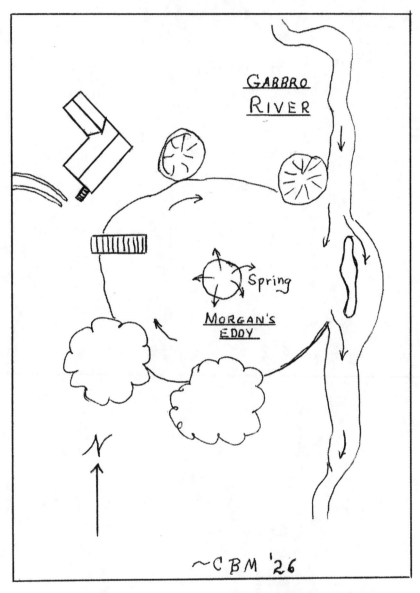

Morgan's Eddy (Sketch by Custis Morgan, 1926)

Prologue

THE OUTREACH INTERN
By M. Faye Bynum

Chapter One.

Faith Blackstone, recent graduate of Our Lady of Luminous Mysteries Senior High School, Class of 1947, stands before a mirror on the top floor of a rooming house – L. Morris, Transients and Long-Term – on Quaker Street in Greensboro, North Carolina. Faith is not Long-Term; nor is she exactly Transient, how that sounds. She is in Greensboro only for the summer. She is dizzy. Sleepy and wide awake, and thus dizzy. Looking back at her is a Depression refugee with a sober face hung in a frame of straight, not exactly stringy, black hair.

Face: pale, intelligent, not homely but no knock-out; pale eyebrows, eyes dark. Chin solid, romantic, 19th-Century; mouth wide, considering, unsure. Nose … well, generous. Shoulders: slumpy, with funny bumps on top. Breasts: present and accounted for. Belly: flat, but soft-looking from neglecting her sit-ups. She will go back to them tomorrow. Hips: narrow but, she must admit, kind of graceful. She bends a knee to cock them slantwise, streetwise, provocative; then straightens up. Legs: long, muscular. Kind of bowlegged, or just skinny? Toes wiggle on skinny feet that have always been kind of fairly big. Grandpa said once it would take a strong wind to blow her off them.

In the mirror, the reflection of a half-unpacked suitcase, a cigarette balanced on the hinge, smoke rising blue and lithe into the lampshade, emerging jumbled and

1.

DAWN; A SCATTERING OF BIRDSONG. HUMID AIR drifts through the screens to curl a manuscript abandoned on the roller of a Remington portable. A jay calls. Small winds stir the ragged leaves of August, pattering to the ground the last of midnight's rain. Across the room, a sheeted form stirs and curls against another. There are murmurs of recognition.

"Happy birthday, Faye, honey. And my sincerest congratulations."

"Yeah? For what?" Creaky with sleep.

"Thirty-seven's a prime number. You're prime again, first time in six years."

"Oh, boy. Like a piece of aged beef. I found a new wrinkle yesterday. Next thing'll be hot flashes."

"You look exactly the same right now as you did when I first laid eyes on you. Which is, you're the loveliest, sexiest woman that ever ..."

Faye Bynum yawned, jaw yawed as commentary, and stretched, shuddering; but pulled his head to her breast and tangled her leg with his. "How sweet, Fordie. But first of all, you're blind as a bat without your glasses, and it's barely light out. Plus, you know I never believe anything you say about how damn lovely I am."

"Yeah?" He cast off the sheet. "Do you believe this, then?"

Later, she wrapped herself in his castoff shirt and wandered to the screen porch to taste the day. And called back to him, "Forde. Come and look. It's something ... amazing. Hurry."

He hurried, stubbing his toe on a pan that Faye had risen at two AM to place under drips from the leaky place in the roof. The water spilled, creating the puddle it had been intended to prevent; and they stood together, watching dawn skim the scalloped blanket of fog above Morgan's Eddy, a spring-fed bulge in the otherwise negligible Gabbro River. Above its surface, the morning mist was touched by sunlight and currents of air barely alive in the hush; in its depths the bones of Confederate dead slumbered and cycled, long since fossilized to fool's gold. Fingers of sunlight touched the mist with peaks of white and gold, a coloristic meringue. The white peaks were edged in orange and blue; the hollows between were like some alpine land that neither of them had visited, cradling worlds in valleys tinged with color from the peaks. It lasted a few minutes more; then glints of water showed, and the fog began to evaporate in the steepening slant of sun.

They lingered, content to rub hips and breathe the mingled scents of pine, mist, and bed. "Well."

"I'll say. Pop told me about that one time, the sunrise mist thing, s'posably saw it when he was a kid. I never seen it, and barely believed in it." His hand traveled the curve of her waist. "Till now."

"I bet it's one of those Stonehenge-y things, where the sunrise only lines up with some sort of break in the woods once a year, and there has to be no clouds on the horizon, and a layer of mist on the Eddy. And then, you have to be up at dawn. No wonder this is the first time you've seen it."

She looked out over the Eddy to see the far shoreline emerging, distant flow sparkling through the fading gold. "And if it's taken forty years for you to see it once, who knows if we'll ever see it again."

"It's the Eddy, giving you a birthday present. Faye, you know how much I love you."

"I do, Forde. I'm very sorry that we're so at loggerheads over all that."

"We don't need to be."

"Sure not, if I'd just give in, I suppose. Is that it?

A very aged border collie heaved herself from a bed on the porch and staggered over to them. Faye knelt to bury her nose in the fur. "Hey, Rosie, g'morning, Hon. Who's a good girl?" The dog nuzzled her in return, panting from the effort of getting out of bed.

"Well. Faye, I can't blame you, now we're, um … where we are. We're getting on, to be thinking about making babies. But still -"

"Look, Forde. You know I don't think it's a good idea for people who work in the same office to marry each other and have babies. Just please think about what life would be like. You would go on exactly the same, except I suppose you'd hire a new associate editor. I would stay home and raise babies, and that would be the end of me as a writer. Next thing, I'd get mad about that, plus out of touch with things you still care about, and either start making your life miserable, or I'd stop being interesting, and start sounding stupid and out of touch, while, guess what, I start losing my looks at the same time." She looked up at him, aware that she had lost very little of what looks she could ever have claimed, wrapped and framed as they were by his pin-striped Van Heusen. "Don't you like just being the way we are?"

"Of course I like it. I way more than 'like' it, I'm the luckiest man in Gabbro County. If I didn't, I wouldn't be here. But it won't last forever. I'm getting on -"

"Pfft. You'll be forty this fall." In fact, Forde was getting a little portly, and his brown curls were graying about as fast as they were falling out.

"Forty's the last decade when I could think about being a father; and I don't like to think about passing some day, and that's the end of it. My Pop may have been an old scoundrel in a lot of ways -"

"He was a sweet old guy … and a little bit of a crook."

"Well, say what you like. He had a son and a daughter, and that means that something of him is going on after he's gone. I will never love anyone but you, Faye, and if you won't give me a son … or a daughter, it wouldn't have to be a son."

"Yes? Very broad-minded of you. But if I won't give you either one or the other … then what?"

"Then ..."

Forde stopped. They turned their eyes back to the Eddy. It was still beautiful, if only in its ordinary way.

She rose after a final ruffle of Rosie's ears. "Then you will either have to defer your dream of fatherhood, or find a nice willing woman, and marry her." She shrugged. "And have your babies."

***

They never left their overnights together, though of course the *Intelligencer* staff had long since learned to read in their relaxed arrival at the office more than a half-hour apart a consequence of having slept together the night before. Still, it was Monday, and Faye's contributions were long since written, proofed, and typeset for the day's edition. With Forde out the door, she could take some time to digest the scene just ended, and consider whether it might appear in some form in the novel. And then stop by Gabbro High School on the way to the office, for a look at their new AV gear.

She put on her housework uniform of gym shorts and a faded and threadbare Mount St. Anne tee shirt, and padded about the cottage, picking up and scooting into place the chair that Forde upset when he leapt up from the birthday supper at her invitation to skip the dishes and come to bed. She mopped the puddle of rainwater, collected and washed the glasses and crockery, renewed Rosie's kibbles and water. Rosie was drinking a lot of water lately; the vet thought it might be a sign of failing kidneys.

Faye felt the settling-in of melancholy that had begun to plague her since Forde began his campaign for marriage and family. Rosie was over a hundred dog years old, and could hardly be expected to last many more; and Faye herself was thirty-seven. Not really her middle thirties any more. Nothing she did could be considered precocious, or promising, or even all that surprising. She was beyond the excuse of youthful folly, even if not beyond reach of its consequences. She should be at the peak of her powers. And where was she?

Well, in truth, she was somewhere. Her salary at the *Intelligencer* had afforded the gradual purchase and domestication of this cottage, including a telephone and propane-powered stove and refrigerator, and to pay the modest taxes on the half-acre at Morgan's Eddy that was about as pleasant a setting as could be found in eastern North Carolina. She supposed it would even stretch far enough to repair the leaky roof. More important, she was resentfully respected in North Carolina as a liberal (she would have said, fair-minded and righteous) thinker and writer. Forde had recognized a really good series of editorials on the impact - or lack of it - of *Brown v. Board of Education* on Gabbro County schools, by promoting her to Associate Editor.

The editorials had been noticed; she was a regular op-ed contributor to other papers in North Carolina, and working on a contract for statewide syndication. A guest column of hers in the Raleigh *News and Observer* had been condemned by Jesse Helms. A collection of "This Town's Times" columns about colorful Gabbro County doings had been published by a Chapel Hill press, which had also expressed mild encouragement for the novel whose first page waved at her from the typewriter in the bedroom. She was, in fact what she had yearned to be from childhood: a published writer, if still a pretty minor one. The Walter Lippmann of southeastern North Carolina.

Did she want to sacrifice even that for the sake of motherhood? She supposed it was selfish of her, but no, she did not. Even if it meant sending Forde into the arms of some Methodist brood mare. *A brood marriage, ha. Save that for when I'm mad at him.* It would hurt, of course, if Forde turned away for the sake of this dream of fatherhood. But the wound would be no deeper than her love for him, which Faye knew was not oceanic. They kept each other company, and that suited Faye just fine.

In fact, 'keeping company' was how Greater Gabbro felt comfortable describing the tie that loosely bound them. Forde and Faye were discreet about what would ordinarily be described as 'carrying on.' In public, they worked together, addressed each other politely as 'Mister' and 'Miss,' and were sometimes seen together at a movie or a social occasion. Once in a long while, Forde would join Faye for Mass at St. Ann's - Christmas Eve, for example - and even more rarely would Faye show up with Forde at Gabbro Methodist for their Welch's-and-Wonder-Bread communion, after Forde had finished with Sunday School. (Faye still found it weird for a collection of grown men to call themselves a "Sunday School," and certainly had no appetite for sitting with the Methodist Women's Circle that met while the men were thumbing their Bibles and arguing about what Jesus might or might not have said, depending on which Gospel you liked best.)

The full sexual dimensions of the company-keeping were a shadowy part of the public narrative of Gabbro County, but so was a consensus that it would be tacky to discuss the matter. Nearly everyone who had an opinion wished they would get married and be done with it, but deferred to whatever was keeping them nominally single. They were not cohabiting and they never carried on in public, so what was there to say?

Faye sighed at the renewed discovery. *I am a loner.* She walked onto the porch, stood at the screen and acknowledged it to the solitude, the morning breeze, and to Rosie and the scattering of birds and squirrels who were close enough to hear a conversational acknowledgement. "I am a loner." She wrote it in the pine pollen on the sill: *LONER. The difference between loner and lover is a single line; but a line of perilous crossing.*

She gave that smart-shit wordsmithing a Bronx cheer and rubbed it out. She did love Forde, of course, if in an absent-minded, slightly maternal way. Well, she was very fond of Forde. He was a satisfactory sexual partner, and she had taught him all he knew about sex - at least, she was pretty sure he had nothing else going. She controlled the rhythm of their dates, and the means of contraception. What could improve on that?

She turned and saw the Remington on the desk, abandoned when Forde emerged from the dusk last night with his bottle of Blue Nun and his awkwardly wrapped microflask of Silken Rain. And his eager loins, celibate for the past month. Faye looked over the bare, interrupted beginning of her manuscript; and allowed herself to be distracted enough not to answer her question.

Most of the start was OK, she supposed; she added 'gray' to the last line to complete the symbolism. "Faith Blackstone" was stupid and too obviously derived from Faye Bynum; she ran the roller back, penciled a line through it, and scribbled "Mercy Greylock" as a placeholder in the space above it. Wondering whether she could leave in a mention of breasts, in a narcissistic episode in the life of a young girl, even in this relatively daring era, and still get the thing into print in North Carolina. They were in there now, unavoidable in the scene if she didn't want to sound like a prude. And without the scene, her baby novel would shrivel to about two sentences.

She walked through the kitchen and down two steps to a grassy place at the back, where she worked through the ground exercises that had kept her acceptably tight and graceful this far. They were getting a little harder the last years; when she finished, speckled with twigs and sand, she turned in the kitchen door to let her breath and pulse come back to normal, and to feel the effect of the workout on a body that she considered pretty good for a woman starting to push forty. She inhaled deeply, held it, and traced the line of obliques down a tight belly to solid thighs, and a still handsome butt with no sag to it. Blood coursed through it all, singing at its work.

Last night's rain had brought clarity and freshness to the air. A few sumacs and a bald cypress were showing fall colors. The scrub oak leaves were still green, but they were bug-spotted and leathery, with a jaded look to them, as if the summer had worn them out, along with its welcome. Faye Bynum, 37, took her towel-wrapped self and a cake of Ivory down to the Eddy to clean up, to wash away sweat and the traces of Forde Morgan, and to begin her 38th year in its brisk and tannic embrace.

***

She walked into the *Intelligencer* building at ten, greeted by a smirk from Sharon the receptionist; having wasted an hour admiring and making notes about Gabbro High's new Webcor intercom and school-wide CCTV that would let Principal Romer intrude into any class- or rest- or boiler room at any time of the school day. The presence of cameras and monitors in restrooms struck Faye as a guarantee of rebellion and disrespectful graffiti. But she let it go, recognizing the limits of common sense when up against technology.

"Mr. Morgan in?"

"Yes, Miss Bynum. Been waitin' for you."

"I was at the High School. He knew that."

"Yes'm … *Just bet he done.*" Sharon muttered the last when Faye had sauntered far enough not to quite hear it.

Faye entered her office and heard Forde's extension ring next door. Announcing her arrival, no doubt. And sure enough here came Forde, ushering ahead of him a coltish, solemn-faced girl of mid-teen years with dark hair, dark eyes, and a remarkably straight, just charmingly off-line nose.

"G'morning, Miss Bynum," Forde said, in formal tones. "Like you to meet my second cousin once removed, Lee Forsythe. Lee, Miss Faye Bynum."

"How do, Ma'am," the girl said, not offering a hand.

"How do yourself. Not sure I ever met a second cousin once re-moved. That I knew of. How can we help you this morning?"

"Lee is Pop's cousin Ralph's daughter Eloise's girl," Forde said. "Think that's the way it goes. Anyways, she's showing some promise as a writer, thought we might take her under our wing, like, give her some practical experience to go with her English Comp she'll be taking starting next month. She'll be a sophomore at Gabbro High, see."

"I do see. Are you old enough to work, Miss Forsythe?"

"I'll be sixteen next month." Contained, sure of that much. "I read your book, Miss Bynum. I enjoyed it very much."

"Did you. That makes you one of a very select group."

"Yes'm, I specially liked the pieces about the Gabbro County School Board. I about had to laugh out loud, sometimes."

"No more than I, sitting there and listening to them. Mr. Morgan, when you say 'we' will be taking Miss Forsythe under 'our' wing, I suppose you mean 'I' and 'my,' respectively."

Lee Forsythe blushed and looked at the floor. "I don't mean to be a trouble, Ma'am."

"Well, I would, in your place. Apprenticeships - in which I am a great believer - almost always mean trouble for somebody who was doing fine before you showed up. Mr. Morgan, leave me alone with Miss Forsythe a while so we can get acquainted. Have a seat, Miss Forsythe."

When the door swung shut behind Forde, Faye turned to Lee Forsythe. "Now, tell me -"

"Ma'am, Miss Bynum, I'm sure your time is valuable. I did not ask to be tooken under your wing, and I do not wish to be a trouble to you. I would a great deal rather learn what I can on my own." Lee bit her lip and blushed deeper. *'Tooken,' for God's sake.*

Faye held up a hand. "I was just giving Mr. Morgan a hard time, and I did it at your expense, for which I apologize. And I can't believe I'm about to say this, but here I go: you remind me very much of myself at your age. Which I guess means that you are already on your way to becoming a professional writer at a three-a-week paper in a hick town, at the very least. Also and by the way, only Mr. Morgan and I address each other formally. Toward everyone else, we all use first names here, across the widest age differentials, unless outsiders are present. Now, Lee, sit down and let's hear about this promise you're supposed to be showing."

***

Forde Morgan returned to his office to reminisce about the previous evening, night, and dawn, merged in his memory to a rainbow of bliss like previous occasions, and like the promise of those to come. Why wasn't that promise good enough for anyone, damn it? And yet it wasn't. The prospect of seeing himself merged with Faye in a gurgling infant who bore Faye's dark eyes and linear eyebrows, her cute little ears and her delicious mouth; and his own - well, his ... Well, in fact there was not a single aspect of Faye's features that he did not consider superior to his own. OK, his dick, then, if they had a boy. There.

Still and nevertheless, a baby - <u>their</u> baby - would be a mixture of the two of them, a sign and seal of their union that would outlive them both. Maybe with Forde's calmness and even temper, to name a character in which he felt he did legitimately excel over Faye. God above, what a woman, though. Why couldn't she see what a joy it would be to create that merged being, out of the bliss of their own merger? He was reliving last evening - the moment when Faye put down her glass and rose to saunter around the table and loom over him, perfect fingers popping his shirt buttons while her Blue Nun breath purred, *Why don't we leave the dishes for morning, Fordie?* - when his phone buzzed. Forde sighed, and picked it up.

"Yes."

"Visitors for you, Mr. Morgan. Mr. Merrydown and his boy."

See? Even a jerk like Mason Merrydown had a son to follow him, to take with him on business errands. "Send him back, Sharon."

Mason Merrydown owned everything worth money in southeast North Carolina including Gabbro County's only actual industry, a towel-and-sheet factory named River Mills perched at the headwaters of the Gabbro River. Every so often, when a run of beach towels was in progress, the Gabbro would run crimson, blue or purple, to Faye's great annoyance, since she couldn't go into Morgan's Eddy until the color had washed out, a matter of at least a day.

Merrydown, the perpetrator of this annoyance, was fortyish and lean, a busy, snappish fellow who removed a gray homburg to reveal a busy, snappish haircut, bristly salt-and-pepper brushed straight back from his forehead as if he were leaning into a Category 4 headwind. He directed his ten-year-old son to a corner, and brushed aside greetings and small talk to lean over Forde's desk.

"Listen, Morgan. I never ask for help, but once in a while I do get a chance to show people where their interests and mine lie in the same direction. This is one of those times. So listen up."

***

Lee Forsythe's promise as a writer was bound up with a phenomenon called the Gabbro County Fox Hunt. Gabbro County farmers and sporting types greatly enjoyed the Hunt, a downscale bucolic echo of Virginia's hunt country that Faye had once - maybe ten years ago - attended, and written off as a bunch of drunken yokels riding fat horses across the cotton fields and tearing up gardens. Lee's high school essay on the same event managed to be enthusiastic, ironic, and insightful, all in the same thousand words. Faye looked up from it with respect.

"But, Lee, this is just wonderful. How did you make it sound like hero-worship and satire at the same time? And wait, look here. That fella Uncle — Uncle what?" Faye flipped through the essay's four pages.

"Uncle John McNair?"

"That's the one. Is he some kind of grand patriarch, or just an old Falstaff? You made him both, in a way that defies analysis. Are the horses really glad to be tearing across the country, or spavined old plow-horses hoping not to break a leg? Or, I guess, plow-horses who are thrilled - I can't believe I'm even entertaining the notion - thrilled at a chance for some fun? The, the dogs … the foxes, the farmers, the landscape! They're all in here, and you got them all to a T. You don't need mentoring, for God's sake. You need an agent."

Lee blushed, and her eyes lit. "Thank you, Miss -"

"Faye, if you please."

"… Miss Faye. I don't know, see. When I was just a little girl, six or so, Uncle John just reached down and scooped me up, took me with him on his lap, sort of - in front of him on his saddle, really - all around the Courthouse Square, where the Hunt was forming up. I was ever so thrilled. Next year or two, he took me with him right across country, on the real hunt. I reckon that stayed with me, and helped me write about it. None of my other school stuff seemed to come so easy."

"Hm. You mean, he … Hm. So, is the Hunt the only thing you can write well about? I can't believe that; writing is writing, seems like. Most of the time."

"I don't know. I reckon that's the best piece I've done."

"OK, well, I think we just figured out your internship here. When does school start?"

"Fifteenth of September."

"Little over a month. Tell you what, I'll give you some assignments on different topics - very different, I think - and we'll see. If all of it is as good as this, hell, we'll make you Associate Editor, and you can give me assignments. If not, maybe you and I together can figure out how to make them so."

"Well, I would be thrilled to work with you, Miss … Faye. But what about Mr. Morgan? Would he go along with it?"

"He dumped you in my lap, so he's pretty well bound to agree with whatever you and I come up with, don't you think? I'll handle him."

***

Forde leaned back in his boss chair. "Well, come on. You don't mean to imply -"

"Picture it. Here's a little girl, not a baby, mind, but half-grown. sitting in the same saddle right in the crotch of an old goat, both of them straddling the same horse, which is going jiggety -"

"Whoa. OK, I admit, it's a … mm, well." Forde fought to suppress a smirk. "A questionable picture. I don't believe they done that but maybe two - three times at the Hunt, and he never done it with any-one else after she got to be old enough to ride her own horse, which was when she was about ten, I guess. Almost 6 years ago. Whatever kicks he might have got, she's perfectly OK from it, from what you say. Maybe a bit, I don't know – inspired. Little girls love horses, that's all."

Faye snorted. "Inspiration sometimes known as molestation."

"Naw. I read her essay, she wouldn't be half so eloquent and frank about it if there was any … you know. Residue. But I bet there's a lot of more pressing things have come up since then, and here's one: Mason Merrydown come in here this morning with his kid, to tell me we need to help him out against the unions."

"Unions? There even is one in the whole state?"

"More to the point, apparently there's a organizer been buzzing around River Mills, talking union, trying to get the ladies there to organize around brown lung and work safety, strike for better working conditions."

"Well, good for him. Is brown lung a problem down there?"

"You won't get any such talk out of River Mills. Hear Merrydown tell it, this fella wants to do for mills in the South what caused the ones in New England to go broke. One way of looking at it." Adding the last when he saw Faye's brow darkening. "Hard to get facts on it, even people sick with it want to keep it quiet so's they don't get fired. Anyways, Merrydown figures he'll try and fight unions aboveboard before he brings in thugs."

"Fight it by buying ads in the *Intelligencer*? Fine with me."

Forde shook his head. "Mason Merrydown won't pay for what he can get for free. He wants us to run some anti-union news and editorials."

"Oh, does he? Well, I reckon you can't write about what you don't know the first thing about. Sounds like somebody needs to go down to River Mills and do some fact-checking. Talk to this organizer too, get both sides."

***

Faye had, under duress of extravagant repair bills, finally given up on her 1936 Chevy coupe with the rumble seat in which Rosie had taken so many happy rides - tongue lolling, ears blown inside-out by the slipstream - and bought herself a new car. Dealers of all kinds had smiled politely when she asked, in the summer of 1963, about rumble seats. Now, Lee Forsythe sat beside her in a yellow Beetle as it clattered down the long paved drive to River Mills.

"Ever been out here, Lee?"

"No'm. Kind of scary, in't it?"

"Well … " No, Faye did not find the River Mills scary; a little repulsive, maybe. A squat metal building with a brick office wing bumped out on the front, hunkered behind some kind of protective berm. A parking lot held a few dozen cars baking in the sunlight, the nicer ones parked close to the brick section, the rest of the lot dominated by fatigued pickups and unreflective Fords, Chevys, and a blue TransAm with a maroon fender. Three or four 18-wheelers were backed up to loading docks. Beyond them, the low jungle of gum trees and live oak that made up Indian Girl Swamp and the headwaters of the Gabbro River stretched to the east. A complex roar came from the open loading bays, as if the building was full of donkeys and hungry lions, and cattle that needed milked before the lions got to them. The whole thing was fronted by a cyclone fence topped by a kind of barbed wire Faye had never seen, the usual barbs replaced by shiny butterflies of sharp steel. There was a gate with a guardhouse; the driveway led to it. An awkward kid in a size too-large uniform - totalitarian peaked hat and all - stepped out and stood by a lift gate worthy of East Berlin.

"Afternoon, Miss. Hey there, Miss Bynum."

"Hey y'self, Tucker. Got yourself a job, I see. Uniform and all."

"Yes, Ma'am. Police school starts next month. See your pass?"

"We need a pass to get in? Land, Tucker, they making A-bombs in there? We just wonted to drop by and talk to whoever's running things. Mister Merrydown wants some free publicity, which I suppose he'll get if we can get in and talk to some folks. Get quotes about production goals, community benefits, all that."

"Yes'm. Let me call in."

"Do that. We'll wait."

Tucker Pardee had spent the summer of 1961 at the *Intelligencer* under Faye's tutelage. The internship had been a complete success, in the sense that it demonstrated clearly to Tucker and to Faye that he had neither aptitude nor interest in journalism, and so freed him to pursue his real dream, law enforcement. Faye was amused by the sing-song 10-4 rhythms with which he spoke to the hidden authorities:

"Why, we got us some civilians out here't the gate, wontin ta visit ... Sight-seeing, interview, get to know the place ... Community ben'fits, yes, sir. Hold own."

He turned to Faye. "Y'all not representin' no union, are you?"

"Nope. Would that be the kiss of death?"

"Pretty much."

"Tell him Mister Merrydown was looking for some news coverage, and we're from the *Intelligencer*."

Tucker relayed the message, listened, interjecting "Yes sir," and "No sir," at regular intervals; and turned to Faye.

"That was Mister Barnett, that's the plant manager. He says one or th'other of you can come in, but not both."

So Lee Forsythe followed Tucker to a white door in the brick management wing of River Mills. The door was set in an antebellum-looking entrance, all brilliant white millwork and a polished brass handle. Tucker kept lagging, trying to get her to walk next to him, or even ahead, someplace he could put an eye on her, and keep it there. She, with the instinct of an adolescent girl who had already been eyed plenty, lagged more expertly, holding a steno pad to her chest, and remained a step behind. At the door, Tucker ignored the brass handle, knocked and held a badge to a peephole that was the only other feature in the white-painted steel. After a sweaty wait in the reflected glare, they heard a key scraping, and the door opened three inches. Lee assumed a bland face.

She saw that the edge of the door bore no latch hardware, so the brass handle was a decorative fake. The door was held shut by a Yale lock a foot higher. *Lord, they don't trust nobody, even themselves. Sure hope they got that key handy if the place ever catches fire. What's so classified about towels?* She lined up mental notes to write in the steno pad when she got a chance, and tucked them next to what Miss Faye had coached at her, about doing her first interview.

Tucker tipped his face into the crack of the door and said, "Miss Lee Forsythe, the Gabbro *Intelligencer.*" His voice broke on the first syllable of 'Forsythe'. Tucker blushed, the door swung farther, and Lee peered into the opening. A gush of cool air washed across her ankles. A gnarled little guy in rimless glasses, sleeve garters and suspendered trousers, who outweighed her by no more than 30 pounds, confronted her.

"C'mout of the heat, Miss," he said. "Virgil Barnett, I manage the plant here. That'll do, Pardee."

"Yessir." Tucker Pardee wheeled and disappeared. Lee stepped into the air-conditioned fortress, steno pad at present arms.

2.

FORDE MORGAN SCRIBBLED "GABBRO'S BUSINESS Bedrocks" at the bottom of a page of crossed-out scribbles, and then crossed it out in turn, and chucked the paper. It made Gabbro's entrepreneurs sound like numbskulls. Rockheads. Forde didn't have Faye's effortless way with words, and he knew it. Certainly not enough to kiss Mason Merrydown's ass in print without looking like he was doing exactly that. But he couldn't hand the project to Faye without having her type out twenty column feet of sarcasm before she produced anything printable.

The actual business bedrocks of Gabbro, North Carolina consisted of the River Mills towel factory; a quarry that produced less rock at higher cost every year, and would some year wink out entirely; a little college that had been taken over by the state college system and was past the first flush of enthusiasm and running up debt, with enrollment that was good enough to keep it hovering somewhere above the brink of a death spiral; the surrounding cotton farms and the gin that served them; a radio station and a newspaper that lived on the advertising of all the others; and the patience and good will of its denizens. Scraped together, it made up just enough of an economy to support a town of a thousand or so, but not enough to grow it, or to keep its kids from moving to Raleigh or Charlotte in search of more money and fun. And if Gabbro continued to stagnate, so would the Gabbro *Intelligencer.*

A lot would depend on whether River Mills went ahead with a

contemplated expansion of its product line of domestic linens to industrial cord and canvas. Mason Merrydown was dangling the prospect in front of the mayor and council, and appeared to enjoy the way they leapt and pranced to grab after it. Forde tossed his pencil onto the desk and decided to take the rest of the afternoon off.

***

Lee Forsythe looked up from her steno pad, in which she had been scribbling and scratching out things halfway back NC 71 to the *Intelligencer.* "Yes, Ma'am, Miss Faye. I just wonted to get some things written down before I forgot." *Wait, 'written,' or 'writ?' One of them has to be redneck, but which? The moving finger writes, and having –*

"Take your time and get it right. I can't tell you the times I wish I'd written something down, even a word or two."

Lee smiled. "Yes, Ma'am. Well, I can say, it was a very scary experience. You ever read that *Divine Comedy* book? About Hell, and all?"

"Yes, I have. They giving that to ninth-graders these days?" *What about Francesca and Paulo?*

"Found it up at Chapel Hill, my cousin Billy's a sophomore there. College sophomore."

"I see. Did you like it?"

"Some, I guess. Not very comical. Some of it was funny, I guess, but most of it was sad. What brought it to mind, this Mister Barnett took me down in a elevator, come out on what he called the work floor, down at one end. He showed me some of the machines up close, where it starts right from bales of loose cotton, to where they make the different kinds of thread from that, and take that to a fancy loom and make sheeting and terrycloth out of it. And from there to where they make towels out of that, and so on. He walked me all along the line from one end to the other, where the sheets and towels are all boxed up to ship out. Ever one of those machines is noisy enough to curl your hair, though I guess the loom was the worst. Then he took me up on this balcony that the supervisors use, looks out over the whole floor, you can see bales of cotton coming in at one end, and bales of towels getting put on trucks at the other. And in between the two ends … " Lee made a hopeless gesture.

"Yes?"

"Well … in between, there's all these folks sweating away, like the souls of the sinners. 'Course, not nekkid, like in regular Hell. But looked like maybe they wished they was, sweating and coughing in the racket and uproar, air full of cotton dust, doing the same thing over and over and over."

"Uh huh. Such as?"

"Well, such as taking bobbins of thread off the thread machine and running 'em over to the looms. Or on this one machine, slinging big sheets of terrycloth onto these cutter forms, where big ol' knives come down and make … " Lee consulted her steno pad. "Six bath towels, sixteen hand towels, or forty washrags out of it. Then the operator sweeps them into separate little rolling bins, one for each size. They use a air hose to blow the little threads and dust off the cutting table and then it's time to sling the next sheet. The knives are automatic, so the lady that stands there has to get the cloth ready and get her hands out of the way quick. Every … hold on … every eighteen sheets, the bins are full, and somebody better get over there to roll them on to the next step, which is, they put the edges on; and bring in empty bins, 'cause here comes the next big sheet."

Faye stopped at the intersection with East Church to check for traffic. "Is that safe? What if they don't get their hands out of the way?"

"There's this warning horn, goes off every time, right before the knives come down, and there's a foot pedal that stops them, for example if they didn't get the cloth squared up right on the cutting table, and it holds up the knives. But it also holds up everything that comes after that, so Mister Barnett says there's a counter on it, and if it happens more than five times in a day, that's a demerit. Three demerits in a month, you're fired. Same sort of thing with the other machines.

The idea is, run the place as fast and efficient as possible, so they keep labor cost per towel as low as possible, 'cause they pay by the hour, and not by the towel."

"My lord, why do they put up with it? It sounds horrible."

"You'd think, but the folks that work there say not. Mr. Barnett tooken me into a break room, they get a ten minute break every two hours, and let me talk to some of the ladies. All the folks that work on the floor were ladies."

"And all the managers were men, of course."

"There was a couple ladies in the brick part, but I think they were just secretaries and like that."

"Mm hm. And what did the floor ladies say? They loved working there, am I right?"

"Yes, Ma'am, how'd you know? You could of knocked me over with a washrag."

"Was Mr. Barnett there when you talked to these ladies?"

"Yes'm, right - " Lee broke off and put a hand to her forehead. "Oh. I get it."

"I believe there's some kind of scientific principle, says that asking the question changes the answer."

"Well. Depending on who's there when you ask it, I guess. Am I stupid, or what?"

"You catch on pretty fast, seems to me. You mentioned coughing. Was there a lot of that?"

"Mister Barnett called it 'Monday cough.' Seems like coming back to work after the weekend bothers some folks, and then it goes away as the week goes by."

"Uh huh. You also said 'sweating,' but -"

"Perspiring, I guess I should have said."

"Sweating's fine. But didn't you say the place was air conditioned?"

"Just the brick part. It's hot, down on the floor, and the dust and little threads stick to their skin. While I was watching, one of the ladies passed out and fell over. Her face was as red as ... well. You know."

"Oh, go ahead. A beet."

Lee nodded earnestly. "Cliché, but I need to tell all this, so I cain't stop and think of something original. Wait, OK, a brick."

"Lovely. Go on."

"Well, there was a couple sort of spare worker ladies setting on the sidelines, and they raced over and tooken up the work so nothing would, you know, pile up. It was like a footrace, and the one that got there second set the one that fainted up, and fetched her a glass of water, while the one got there first kep' the work moving along. I asked Mr. Barnett about it, and he said the spares got paid starting when they took over the work, and otherwise 37 cent an hour for cleaning up and waiting for somebody to need replaced, so the work can keep flowing, he called it. You get there second, you get nothing but to take care of the one on the floor. And your 37 cent, of course."

"And what about the one that fainted?"

"He said she won't be paid for lying around and drinking water that the company supplied for free. She was off the clock until she could get back and take her job back over from the sub."

"My Lord. I guess they have to pay standbys, because they can't have production stopping when somebody works until they drop. But when they do, River Mills saves 37 cents an hour, because the standby person is getting the regular worker's pay instead of her usual 37, while the regular gets nothing. That's quite an incentive to keep conditions where workers pass out, isn't it?"

Lee looked thoughtful. "Wouldn't you think it'd be cheaper to put in fans or slow things down so people <u>didn't</u> faint?

Faye snorted. "I bet some expert did an analysis and found out they come out a nickel a year ahead, doing it this way." She shook her head. "Well. When you talked to these ladies in the break room, how did they look?"

"Look?"

"Yes. I'm not going to coach you on this, but it's close to the heart of the matter. How did they look?"

Lee Forsythe said nothing while they rolled to a stop in front of the *Intelligencer,* but looked straight out the windshield for a space of a quiet breath. Then she turned to Faye. "They were smiling away just fine, and they all had on River Mills tee shirts. But what they <u>looked</u> like was, they was in Hell for all eternity."

***

Forde Morgan slammed the door on the brown Fairlane that Faye amused herself by calling "Mad Ox" and drove himself to the place he often went when out of sorts: his half-sister Annie Godfire's place. Annie lived a mile upriver from Faye's cottage, in a meadow that was isolated from even the desultory traffic of East Church Street Extension, the road known to most of the world - if at all - as Gabbro County 3C. Annie's lane took off from 3C at a bend just below the Gabbro River bridge, and followed the river for a while before it plunged into pines and scrub oak that had always felt free to run their roots across Annie's two-track and slow any traffic there to a jouncing crawl.

Annie had put a new signboard, "Annie Godfire/Personal Counseling/Finance/Love/Family," surmounted by the usual palm-reader's red hand, out by the road. Though her clairvoyance did not depend on palm reading. Forde concluded that the income stream from word-of-mouth drop-ins had finally become too slender to sustain Annie and her life project of completing the Spirit Catcher; and thus this modest advertising might help.

The Spirit Catcher was a grandly conceived piece of Outsider folk art begun seventeen years ago by Annie's mother. It was a circular structure of welded scrap iron a hundred feet in diameter and at this time just under thirty feet high, aspiring to 110. It was made of boxcar couplers, iron gates, sewer gratings, barber chair footrests, gnarled lengths of rebar that Annie had pulled from demolished buildings; transmissions, cutter bars, tractor seats, and a thousand other pieces of iron and steel, every ounce of which had served for years in some useful way and - according to Annie - absorbed the life, joy, sorrow, and tears of the humans with which it had come in touch. In the whole graceful, lace-like structure, there was not a single piece that had not worn itself out in the company of humans who were in the process of wearing themselves out. Annie believed - and so did her clientele - that in bringing these remnants together, it would become irresistibly attractive to free-ranging spirits. And that they, in turn, would repay their delight in the growing structure by helping Annie with her counseling. Those who have seen it, even in the incomplete form of that time, will confirm that there was already something a little spooky about it.

Even without the assistance of spirits, Annie was herself a skilled counselor and a formidable woman. At 33 years old and 180 pounds, she was as strong as three interior linemen. She had an uncanny gift for reading a client's innermost thoughts and reflecting them so accurately that those who consulted her about "Finance/Love/Family," or any other troubles, revealed themselves not only to Annie, but - for good or ill - to themselves. Because self-knowledge can be painful, or even fatal, Annie had learned to distract and jolly her clients while the truth dawned on them.

Luckily, her feelings toward Forde were so affectionate – they were half-siblings, and Forde had been very kind to her when she was small – that she had learned to let that fondness override her gift of insight. She took much the same approach with Faye Bynum, whom she adored and considered a sister by fiat and mutual acclamation; except that Faye's self-knowledge was keener than Forde's, and so needed less chaperonage. Annie greeted Forde with a careful embrace.

"Hey, big brother! When's the last time I seen you?"

"Road runs both ways, Annie Laurie."

"You know I cain't stand that town."

"Can't say I blame you." Forde scuffed his shoe on a pine root.

"Uh huh, well, hold on. Something givin you hard times? Wait, Faye?"

"It's nothin."

"Is not. Thought you loved her. I know she loves you."

"I reckon she does. Love's one thing, I don't got to tell you, Annie."

"But? Oh. Babies."

"Man. Put you on a assembly line, you could counsel the whole County in five minutes."

"Well, you know why, I reckon."

"Sure, you got this gift …"

Annie said nothing, just smiled at Forde.

Forde nodded. "OK. Well, I know what she <u>says</u> is why. About her career and how we work in the same office, and all. Also, I'm pretty sure she's not so head over heels in love that she'll give up the career to change diapers and wipe noses. Apparently."

"Faye loves keeping company with you."

"That's about the size of it."

Annie said nothing this time, because she could not have put it better herself. Faye's love for Forde, in Annie's eyes, was something graceful and pleasant, about the size of a breadbox. She pulled Forde into a walk down to the Gabbro River, where a river's-edge path led upstream to the bridge and Gabbro County 3C, and downstream to Morgan's Eddy and Faye's Eddy-side home. Forde was reluctant to go either direction, so he sat on the bank and tossed pebbles into the water while they spoke of his yearning for issue. He told Annie of this morning's splendid dawn apparition of golden mist mountains.

"See, our Pop told me he'd seen that when he was a little kid. Wouldn't it be fine to tell my little boy or girl about it, and have him see it some day and say, my Daddy told me about that forty years ago? I would love to know that I'll be mixed together with Faye forever, in a real person that Gabbro old-timers would know, and say things like, you know, She's got her Daddy's chin and her momma Faye's b … beautiful … Ah, shit, Annie."

Annie gathered him to her shoulder. "There, Fordie. There, my sweet big brother. Sometimes, you just have to … Woop, Jesus."

Forde lifted his head to look at Annie. "What?"

"Well, what's that coming down the river? Don't it look like a body to you?"

"Where - oh, Lordy. Wait, no, I think it's just trash. Wish people wouldn't ... Oh, no, dang, that's a shirt. And a face. It's somebody, all right."

Annie waited until the tangled object, which presented leafy brambles and human features on a bed of scrap wood, was some ten yards upstream; then waded effortlessly into the current. "Used to be, anyways." She grabbed the corpse by the collar and started to yank brush away from it with the other hand, then yipped, and waded it back to the shoreline, sucking on her thumb. "Ow, dang. Forde, reach my gloves outa my back pocket here, and get some a these brambles off him."

She heaved the sodden tangle of vines and humanity onto the riverbank and clambered up next to it. "Looks like that piece of pallet kept 'im floatin, but I think he's gone, all right. He's cold as a codfish."

The face showed blue-white, all but obscured by a tangle of vines and brambles. Forde pulled at the tangle and raked a thorn across the nose, which appeared to be broken, and crusted with old blood. A bright streak of crimson followed it.

"Whoa, Annie. He's bleeding. Maybe he's still alive."

"That's what I'm getting. Let's get him loose and see can we bring him around."

Annie took another pair of gloves out of her bib pocket and picked up the tangle of vines and brambles, held it at shoulder height, and shook it. The corpse – or possible survivor – dangled upside down from the vegetal mess, eyes rolled back to the whites while blood seeped from the scratch into auburn hair that was plastered and smeared with mud. An arm flopped free to the ground in an ominously limber gesture, and the body convulsed; Annie knelt and ripped apart enough vines to free the legs, which wore ragged jeans. Forde fumbled with a wrist, looking for a pulse. The motion drove air and river water out of the victim's mouth in a croak that was followed by a hoarse scream.

"Holy … sir, are you OK?"

The corpse spoke in a hiss of pain. "How'd I look?"

Annie knelt on the grass. "Sir -"

The eyes came into focus. "Morons. Nora Lundy, T - Agh!" (Here a bout of hacking coughs that curled Nora Lundy into a comma of agony and ended in a sob.) "… TWUA. I'm s'posed be fookin' dead, and here you gits set me bleedin again. Either of you got a band-aid?"

"Lie still, Nora. Easy does it. Where does it hurt?"

An attempt at laughter, bringing another gasp of pain. "Le … lemme see. Tonsils feel OK. Right ear, not too bad. Ev'thing else hurts. Bahssards pounded the shit outa me, left me in the swamp for dead."

Annie ran back to the scaffolding around the Spirit Catcher and brought a length of 2-by-12 on which they balanced Nora Lundy as gently as they could, and from which they slid her onto the back seat of Forde's car while she keened in distress. Annie slipped under her, and held her steady against the jouncing of pine roots on the way to County 3C. She lost consciousness twice on the six-minute trip into town, and again when she was lifted onto a gurney at the emergency entrance of Gabbro Memorial.

There, she was found to be suffering from a broken nose, some cracked or freshly missing teeth, a broken left arm, right collarbone, and right fibula; cracked ribs on both sides of her chest; seven broken fingers and toes, a dislocated shoulder, a sprained ankle, and extensive bruising, including in the area of her kidneys. Both eyes developed livid shiners while doctors and nurses inspected, winced, and set about shoring up the main areas of damage.

When she was patched and re-set as well as possible, she was gurnied to Intensive Care. Annie settled into the waiting area while Forde sprinted up the street to report to Faye and look up "TWUA" in the office encyclopedia. He thought it might have something to do with transit workers, but that made no sense in Gabbro County; the nearest public transit was a hundred miles away except when the two-car Raleigh & Southern interurban swept through town, usually without stopping.

Nora Lundy almost died that evening, and again the following afternoon, when her temperature, driven by toxins from her multiple sites of injury, spiked to 105, and one of her kidneys shut down. Her urine was the color of Beaujolais. She spent no more than a handful of minutes conscious in that time, though not in a coma, as evidenced by nurses' ability to rouse her to profane resentment when they touched her or her bed. Forde spent as much of that time in the Intensive Care waiting area as he could, consonant with editing a newspaper. Annie came and went, as did Faye, when Forde needed a break.

At eleven the second evening, Annie and Faye together dragged him out of the waiting room and persuaded him back to his house to get a night's sleep. After their usual three-way crunch of affection, and when they heard Annie's truck starting up outside, Faye turned to Forde.

"What's going on with you? She'll get over it, or she won't, whatever you do. OK, you feel some kind of ownership, I guess, you were there when she washed down the river. But … ?" Faye raised a hand and an eyebrow in bafflement.

"I don't know. I guess I feel something … not ownership, f'Pete's sake. Responsible, maybe. I was having a talk with Annie about my troubles, and here comes this, we thought it was a dead body, floating down the river. And when we pulled her out of the river, bad as she was beat up, and half drowned, she had the guts to call us morons and ask for a band-aid. Person like that, I want to hear her story."

"Hm. Well, you can bet her story will get told as soon as we hear it."

"I want to discuss that before we print anything. She's a union rep for the textile workers. We could be putting her in more danger, we make a fuss."

Faye's eyes rolled. "Well, if that isn't just like you, Forde Morgan. By all means, let's not offend Mason Merrydown by -"

Forde slapped his thigh. "No, it is <u>not</u> 'just like me,' damn it. I don't give a flying fuck about Merrydown. I'm talking about not blathering everything we know and getting his thugs sent after her to finish the job."

Faye blinked, and said nothing. They parted, a little bruised.

Faye, not one to miss an implication, reviewed as she drove out to Morgan's Eddy. Forde, including this outburst of profane prickliness, had not been himself lately, but she decided not to worry unduly about the juxtaposition of his confessional about 'troubles' with Annie, - the nature of which was clear to her - and whatever irrational attachment he might feel to this half-dead but still wisecracking stranger who had appeared out of nowhere, broken and needy.

Forde did not understand either; just that it was nothing as pedestrian and self-centered as 'ownership.' Nor was it responsibility, or even curiosity about Nora Lundy's story. Somewhere below all that, she felt to Forde like a messenger, like those who appear out of nowhere in fairy tales and legends bearing fateful news or impossible tasks. Or possibly was herself the message; one who embodied the idea that there could be more to Forde and to Forde's life, than the single-minded pursuit of Faye Bynum to mother his children.

Sponging sweat and mud from Nora's bruised forehead on the river bank, he had felt that the broken nose, the black eyes and the facial swelling were as if some ignorant vandal had sprayed graffiti over a Renaissance painting of … well, not necessarily an angel or the Virgin Mary; maybe some minor sybil. He had no idea what might appear when the image was restored. It might not necessarily be a beautiful one; under all the damage, it appeared that Nora Lundy might be handsome, all right, and trim, with a sweep of freckles to go with the deep auburn hair. Not as graceful as Faye Bynum; but she had a look, that Faye did not. The look, maybe, of someone who bore … well, all right: a message. He was certain only, because it is folk wisdom, that you don't shoot messengers.

3.

FROM THE GABBRO *INTELLIGENCER* FOR AUGUST 19, 1964: :

Beating Victim is Union Organizer

Nora Lundy, 34, a field organizer for the Textile Workers Union of America (TWUA), based in Washington DC, was severely beaten by unknown persons and recovered from near drowning in the Gabbro River downstream from the East Church Street bridge, by local residents Annie Godfire and Forde Morgan, Editor in Chief of the *Intelligencer*. Miss Lundy was treated at Gabbro Memorial, and is currently still in intensive care from numerous injuries suffered during the assault. Gabbro County Sheriff Lyle Rathbun reports that there has been no report of union activity or worker unrest in Gabbro's only textile plant, Merrydown Enterprises' River Mills, and speculates that Lundy may have been brought here from some other locale and thrown from the bridge in the dark of night. "Union organizing is a very risky profession," Rathbun said. "Lucky for us, our workers have been happy...

OUR TOWN'S TIMES
by Faye Bynum
Associate Editor

The recovery from the Gabbro River of a savagely beaten Textile Workers Union organizer was a lucky accident, occasioned by chance when *Intelligencer* Editor Forde Morgan and his sister happened to be sitting on the river bank when Miss Lundy drifted past, insensate and half-dead. Sheriff Lyle Rathbun's assessment of the labor situation in Gabbro County and at River Mills in particular is pretty cheerful, given the nasty working conditions at the River Mills plant. If there was ever a workplace ripe for unionization, River Mills is it.

GGC will beautify the Wye

Gabbro Garden Club chairwoman Berrit ("Bertie") Lang informs us that GGC is developing a plan to beautify the "Wye", where Marley's Cross Road splits to meet NC 71, by planting azalea bushes on the triangular knoll formed by the two legs of Marleys Cross and the highway. "We do believe there is something missing there, and GGC is just the (Continued on p. 7C)

***

Faye was sure that her column would stir things up, and it did. An hour after Dimmy Maron the half-wit distributor puttered off with the day's run, Sharon was buzzing Faye.

"There's a Virgil Somebody at the desk here for you, Miss Bynum."

"Virgil who?"

The phone transmitted the silence of a covered mouthpiece, and then Sharon's voice. "Mister Virgil Barnett, Miss Bynum. Runs River Mills, he says."

"Bring him to Mr. Morgan's office, please, Sharon."

"Mr. Morgan is still at lunch."

"All right. Send him back to me." Faye regretted Forde's absence - probably back at Gabbro Memorial mooning over Nora Lundy again - not because of any strategic cogency she thought he might bring to bear, but because this Virgil Barnett character would be more effectively confronted by any male than by Faye Bynum alone, however articulate and however the facts of the case supported her.

But, here he was, and here she was. He had put on a rusty suit coat over the suspenders, but he was still scrawny, seven eighths bald, asymmetrical, and sour looking. He was carrying a copy of the *Intelligencer*, which he waved across her desk.

"What in hail you think you mean, 'nasty conditions, ripe for unionization,' Miss Bynum? What kind of thing is that to say about the biggest employer in this godforsaken dump?"

"What kind of thing is <u>that,</u> to say about a town that houses your workers and gives you more tax breaks than it can afford, for the dubious privilege of hosting your Dickensian sweatshop, Mr. Barnett?"

Barnett paused. "You got no witnesses to my saying that."

"No? Voices travel pretty unhindered in this office. Just a moment. Rob? Jenny?" Barely raising her voice.

"Yes'm?" from beyond.

"Jenny, could you step in here a second? Bring Rob, if he's here."

"Rob's off interviewing Coach Lorain, Miss."

"OK. You'll do. C'mon in. Did you happen to hear what this gentleman called Gabbro just now?"

"Well, you mean godforsaken -"

"Aw right, fine. The point is, our employees are not 'ripe for unionization,' never will be. They are happy to have the jobs. It is not no sweatshop."

"Hm. Thank you, Jenny, that'll be all. You can leave the door open, thanks.

"Let me tell you, Mr. Barnett. When Miss Forsythe came back here from visiting your plant, I could not credit the description she brought me. Poor kid, I thought, She's never been in a real work environment. So I went out myself, as you recall, just to see how bad it was really. I expected a reasonably normal industrial scene."

"Spying on us under false pretenses, I'd call it."

"Nonsense. I told you at the door I wanted to verify a few things, to be sure she'd got them right."

"Not what it sounded like to me."

"I can't help what things sound like to you. It was not a misrepresentation. Miss Forsythe said, in so many words, that your employees - tee shirts, smiles, and all - looked like they'd been sent to Hell for all eternity."

"They so miserable, they can quit, and there's plenty lined up behind 'em looking for work."

"I know that, Mr. Barnett. If the pure economics of it was all that mattered, you'd be as right as rain." *Why is rain supposed to be right? About what?* "And nobody could breathe a word about it. They need those jobs, and they need them so bad, they'll go through Hell to keep 'em. Are you a church-going man, Mr. Barnett?"

"More so than you, Miss Bynum. And don't bother to talk to me about Christian kindness to my fella man. Women, in this case. I do not have a free hand in setting the working conditions out there."

"Huh. No, I was going to talk about what Hell was like. Eternal fires, Outer darkness, Weeping, wailing, all that. I do think I heard teeth gnashing behind those ladies' smiles, even with all that deafening racket. You ever had your workers' hearing checked?"

"It's good enough. You need to be a little deaf to work on the floor."

"And if you're not, you soon will be. All right, let's talk about Christian kindness, then. What brought that to mind, Mr. Barnett? What did you mean about not having a free hand?"

"Just that. Nothing. Religion don't come into it when you're running a business. What I hear, you hardly never go to church anyways."

"Touché, for what it's worth. That doesn't mean I don't think Christian ideas about fairness and kindness might be useful in everyday life. I suppose it was your thugs who beat up that union organizer, wasn't it? She didn't sound to me like such a threat, you have to haul in bullyboys to beat her to a pulp. My land, two of 'em on one woman. If the folks that set the rules in a workplace can't treat their employees like Christians ought to, then seems to me, the employees have a duty to bargain for better conditions. Slow down those machines a little and hush them up. Clean up the air and ventilate the place so it doesn't run ninety, a hundred degrees on a warm afternoon. Spend some time down on the floor yourself, so you feel what they feel, instead of standing up on that balcony outside your sound-proof, air conditioned office like Satan's army of tormentors. What are you scared of?"

"Good, very moving, I'm sure. I spent plenty of time on a shop floor, working my way up. I wonder if Satan provides air-conditioned office space for his pitchfork army? It has been a pleasure talking to you, Miss Bynum. Nothing you have said here is news to me."

"But you don't have a free hand, is that it? Who does, Mason Merrydown?"

"Mister Merrydown looks out for himself and the dictates of the marketplace. Good afternoon, Miss Bynum. Merrydown Industries will expect a retraction of this union talk in your next column."

"Or what? Else?"

"Some form of Else, I suppose. Maybe writing lessons. Good afternoon."

"Wait ... " Faye bounced a pencil on her desk and scowled at the wall. *Writing lessons.* Virgil Barnett had changed his tone about half way through that argument, from aggravated hick bully to amused sophisticate. Even stood up straighter to add inches to his stature. Like there might be two versions of Virgil Barnett. And if two, how many more?

Version Barnett. But which?

***

Nora Lundy, after the fever crisis was safely passed, graduated from Intensive Care to hopefully named Recovery, to make room for Uncle John McNair, who had woken with what seemed to him and to the ambulance techs like a mild heart attack, but turned out to be gas and rib-cage arthritis.

On Thursday afternoon, Forde Morgan slumped in a chair in the Recovery waiting room, a 1961 issue of <u>Southern Living</u> ignored in his lap, and tried to think about an editorial stance in regard to unions. The workers at the *Intelligencer* were unionized, and it was a pain in the ass. Still, the earful Faye had given him about River Mills, and about collective bargaining to improve conditions all seemed to make sense. It would kill circulation for the *Intelligencer* to seem pro-union, and probably cost it ad revenue as well. He supposed they might pick up some liberal readers over at Gabbro State, but try and sell those bozos any ad space. He was circling the drain of a doze when a gurney emerged from Recovery, bumping the doorway as it came.

"Agh! Clumsy fooker!" The patient was swathed in bandages and casts, but the mop of auburn hair looked familiar.

"Miss Lundy?"

The gurney-pusher grinned. "Providing it ain't Barnacle Bill the Sailor, guess it must be. Never been cussed out so bad since Ol' Miz Laffler had her appendix out."

"Is she out of Recovery?"

"Miz Lundy, you mean. Tha's right. Takin' her down ta 106, you wonted to visit some. B'lieve she's awake just now. That true, Miz Lundy?

"Wasn't, till you slammed me into that door. I am now, I guess. Where are we going? I already had every kind of X-ray you guys got here."

"Takin' you to a room of your own, Miss."

"Man. Just like what's-her-name. Who's that you're talking to?"

Forde cleared his throat from behind her head. "Me. Forde Morgan."

Nora Lundy lifted her chin to peer upside-down past the orderly. "Oh, yeah. You the guy's been hanging around, wiping mud off my face?"

"Some, I guess. The nurse let me in because I was the one ... you know."

"What, like finders keepers?" The slight roll on the *r*'s extracted the sting, and replaced it with charm.

"Well, I just ... I don't know. Wanted to see how you were doing, I guess."

"Uh huh. Nice of you. All that."

"That's OK."

"Better be."

"Well ... Well, would it be OK to visit you again from time to time? Now that you're recovering?"

"Free country." But she said it back over the headrail of the gurney, smiling upside-down at Forde, who took what salve he could from that, noticing the gracefulness of her throat. Not as graceful as Faye's, but nice enough. Shorter neck, he guessed, trying to remember what it had looked like rightside-up on the Gabbro River bank.

"Uh huh. Well, 'bye, then, I guess. Hope you're feeling better before long." *'From time to time,' for God's sake. Who said that any more?*

"'Bye." And - muttered when the gurney was half way down the hall - "Hurra back."

***

On Friday afternoon, Faye knocked on the frame of Forde's office door and heard the silence of an empty office. She sighed. Off to the hospital again, presumably; meaning, it was up to her to cobble together assignments for Monday's paper. Well, let's see. The Jaycees. The Library Board monthly meeting. More deferred maintenance and deterioration at the Middle School. Time to give the new intern some real drudgery, after her spate of glamorous investigation; Forsythe could safely be given the Jaycees and the Library Board. She could count on Rob Stoker for his usual on-the-one-hand, on-the-other analysis of the Gabbro Quarrymen's potentialities for the football season looming, and with the first game coming up in two weeks, this might be a good time for it. She didn't worry that she was giving Rob short notice; he would pull out last year's version, change a few names, and have it done in an hour. She herself would write up the school piece, and end it with some rhetoric about what the School Board thought they were going to do about the building deterioration, short of dumping another bond issue on the groaning backs of Gabbro taxpayers. In a half hour, she was finished, and assignments distributed. She ruffled her hair, found it longish, and headed down the block to the Salonnette for a trim.

Ginnie Freeman, at seventy, had slowed physically, but her mouth was as spry as ever. She bumped her walker on the linoleum when Faye entered, and crowed, "All rise! The judge is in the building."

"G'morning, Ginnie. Feeling better today, are we?"

"Honey, any day I can clap these eyes on She Who Ages Not, I count as a day redeemed from time's reaper. Who you sleepin' with nowadays?"

"My little dog Rosie," Faye said. "If it's any of your business."

"Thought we had an understanding on that. Since I got where I had to drop out of the cakewalk, my business is made up of ever'body else's."

"That would account for it. Well, nothing for you this morning."

"What I heard, you and 'Mister Morgan' arrived for work an hour apart on Wednesday, which I understood was a sure sign."

Faye smiled, said nothing, and turned to Pearlene, the artist who had done her hair for years. "Got room for me this morning, Pearlene?"

"Set down, Miss Faye."

"Welcome words. Now: got a question for you ladies. Who fixes roofs in this town?"

***

When Forde Morgan's head edged around the door frame of Room 106, Nora Lundy's eyes were closed, and her face slack within its habit of bandages. He pulled back the flowers he'd bought in the gift shop downstairs and looked around for a place to sit.

"Back again, are we?"

"Um. Yes. Didn't mean to bother you."

"No bother. Come on in, I'm bored to tears."

"How are you doing?"

"Well, Christ. You know how they say the second day is worse than the day you first get hurt?"

"Um. I guess."

"It goes on from there."

"Oh. Gosh, I'm sorry."

"Not your doing, I hope. Unless you were lurking behind those ratshit thugs with a lead pipe."

"Nope. Did they make any progress figuring out who did it?"

"Not hardly. Sheriff Rat-buns came in this morning and asked a couple questions, made faces like he didn't believe anything I told him, and left. Apparently, nothing I say makes any difference 'cause I didn't go to the same high school he did. Done, sorry."

"Excuse me?"

"Same high school he done. Done went to. Trying to fit in, here, so you'll believe me."

"I edit the local paper. I don't believe much of anything anybody says, till I have another source confirm it. Are we interviewing here, or just chatting?"

"Which would be preferable to you?"

"Chatting. Then I can turn off the bullshit detector."

"Chatting it is. Nice weather, I hear. Think it'll rain?"

"Some day, surely. Rained early this week, probably what flushed you down the river like that. I mean ... swept. Swept you."

"OK, this is boring. Let's interview."

"Fine, long as you know I'll do my best to check everything you tell me before it goes into print, if it ever does."

"Don't bother to check; I don't want it in print. What do they call it, when we're just chatting, but with intent to inform?"

"Well, 'off the record,' I guess. Sometimes they call it 'On background.' Who beat you up?"

"Off the record and on background, I think it must have been a couple of goons in the pay of River Mills."

"What makes you think that?"

"They kept telling me I'd never talk union at another factory in this life. Guess they figured me for an organizer."

"You are, I thought. Didn't you tell us 'TWUA' when we pulled you out of the river?"

"I must have been delirious."

"OK, fine. How long were you lying around with every bone in your body broke?"

"Don't ask me. It was first thing in the morning when those goons jumped me and drove me out into the swamp to explain how they felt about the TWUA. I listened for a while, but when it started to hurt real bad, I must have dozed off. When I came to, they were gone and I was face down in the mud. I think I was supposed to die like that, but I managed to crawl to where I could see the plant through the trees. Took hours. I was hurting so bad, I passed out again when a fly landed on me. Come to again, it felt like afternoon. Dragged myself through the vines and brambles to the river. Found some scrap wood to float out of the neighborhood on."

"You're not with the textile workers' union?"

Nora Lundy looked at Forde, wide-eyed. "I never said that. I am, but I don't go around blathering it to every stranger that saves my life."

"OK. You're with the union. What are you doing here?"

"What makes you think I didn't grow up here?"

"You'd of gone to my high school, for one thing, like Lyle Rathbun done. Also, you sound like you grew up in Scotland, somewhere. And not Scotland County."

"My parents brought me over here from Glasgow when I was ten. I've always had a trace of it in my talk. OK, I'm getting tired from all this verbal tiptoe, and a nurse is going to come in to give me pain pills and shoo you away. So I'll just say this, on background and off the record. I'm with TWUA, but I'm not an organizer. I came here to talk to the organizer about progress."

"Who is the organizer?"

Nora yawned gingerly, trying not to stress any joints. "Gosh, I'm tired."

"I'll leave. Who's the organizer?"

"Think I'll ring for the nurse. Thanks for the flowers. They're grand."

"Can I come in tomorrow?"

"Still a free country. My turn not to interview you, so get your story lined up before you come in."

"Story about what?"

"Och, come on. What is it with you? Why are you hanging around like this, moppin' my brow and bringing flowers, chatting me up?"

"On the record, or off?"

"Which is more likely to be true?"

"Oh, off. You can hardly ever believe anything people say on the record. The down side is, it's an implied promise not to quote the person."

"Off, then. Be off with ye." Laying on the brogue.

"Well off the record, just for background, I find you a very interesting and appealing person. Fascinating, even. Anybody who can wisecrack when they're beat half-dead is somebody I might want to get to -"

"Lord love a duck. You always throw down all yer cards like that, first crack out of the box?"

"Hardly ever. I don't know what's got into me."

"Well. I can't say it's not flatterin'. Let's keep talking, seeing there's nowt o' the physical I'm like to be up to for some time. What about this Faye that's rumored to keep company wi' you? One a the nurses made sure I heard the name after the last time you were here."

"We keep company."

"And? But? Thus?"

"We have our differences."

"Differences that wad allow ye to chat up a different lady?"

"I can't discuss the nature of the differences, but I can say, it would depend on the lady."

"Well, here's what this lady would warn you, my lad. Being beaten within an inch - nay, a hair - of your life affects a person. When you find out you've survived after all, life seems a great deal more in earnest. So dinna chat me up with intent, unless ye have reason to be in earnest yerself. Off the record, mind. Agreed?"

"Oh, aye. Off the rrecord."

"Dinna make me laugh, now, it hurts too much, and I got no time to give lessons in proper Scots. So, off the record, you're on; but on the record, be off wi' ye, ya triflin' scamp."

Back behind the wheel of the Mad Ox in the hospital parking lot, Forde paused a moment before turning the key, drumming the steering wheel with his thumbs. He glanced in the rear-view, and found that he was grinning.

***

"OK, she's not an organizer, but there is an organizer, not her, and she won't tell you who it is."

"That's right. Not yet, anyways."

"Well, there you go, a perfect reason for you to keep hanging around, huh? Maybe next time she'll tell you more. Or maybe she'll keep on teasing you about it, or about something else. Sounds like a long-term thing."

"Whoa, Faye. Are you ... Does it bother you that I spend time with her? She's a complete stranger, and -"

"What does that have to do with anything?"

"Um ... well, I mean, I don't know her, or where she's from, or who her folks are."

"True of me when we first met. And here you just spent the night with me."

"Well. That's hardly the same thing. I'm just curious about her."

Faye tossed a hand. "Fine, me too. What else did you find out?"

"That's it, pretty much. Her folks brought her over from Glasgow, Scotland, when she was ten."

"Guess that might account for the foul mouth. Otherwise, not very useful. Let's think a minute. Why do we care, anyhow?"

"Well, she's a crime victim."

"Mm-hm. She's also a source. If there's union organizing going on at River Mills, that's news. If River Mills is hauling in thugs to stop it, that's more news. Policy question for you, Editor-in-Chief Morgan: what's our editorial position in regard to unions and thugs?"

"We're gonna have to be careful, but I think we are cautiously on the side of the workers, from what you say about conditions there. We are certainly against settling questions like that by violence."

"Me too. Here's another question, then. What do you know about a handyman named Terry Morgan? Kin of yours?"

"Heard of him, don't know him. Different family, and much younger than me and you. Where'd you get the name?"

"Ginnie Freeman. I'm going to get that roof fixed right this time. Only thing, I never quite know whether to trust Ginnie's word on anything."

"Huh. Was she on the record, or off?"

4.

TERRY MORGAN LOOKED YOUNG — BARELY OUT OF his teens, really - but muscular and competent, with dark curly hair and a smooth, V-shaped face on which amusement sat easily. He played a flashlight and frowned at the ceiling over places Faye showed him, where she had to put pots and buckets on rainy days; took a ladder from his van and climbed onto the roof. She heard him moving around overhead while she ducked into her bedroom and changed into her housecleaning outfit. He returned after fifteen minutes, looking serious.

"Looks to me like a bunch of shingles are cracked and leaky, plus a lot of your sheathing's shot to hell, 'scuse my French. It's the consistency of wet cardboard under there. I can patch them places you showed me, but what you really need is a whole new roof. Give you prices either way."

"Hm. What kind of prices?"

"Which way?"

"Both. I'll decide when I hear the numbers."

Terry Morgan glanced at the intersection of the gym shorts and tee shirt. "Yes, ma'am. Well, anyways, just the spots it's leaking now, I could do for, oh ... I guess two-fifty, three if I find more. Whole roof, more like fifteen."

"Talking hundreds, I guess."

He grinned. "Yes, ma'am. Two dollars fifty cent might get you a tarp to go over the worst leaks, I reckon. Hafta pay me extra to put it up there, though, that'd run you right up to the fifteen bucks." He shrugged. "Thing is, though, there's no sort of guarantee your sheathing is any better where it's not leaking right now, than the places where it is. Be pretty surprising, actually."

"Yes?" Knowing what was coming, making him say it to give her time to think where she could put her hands on $1500.

"Meaning, I fix those spots for you, and next year some time, a couple new places open up, and it's another couple-three hundred. Wouldn't take you too long to work up close to fifteen hundred, and then you still got a patchwork roof. Place was mine - which by the way, I'd give my left nut for - I'd go ahead and get the new roof, twenty year manufacturer's warranty on the shingles, and you're good for quite a while."

"If I went for the whole new roof, could I pay you over time? The whole thing at once might be a little tough."

"Well. How about half up front so's I can buy the materials, and the rest by Christmastime?"

"OK, fine. When can you start? You're not one of these contractors that works for one day, and goes away for weeks, are you?"

"I got nothing else on right now. I could start tomorrow and get it finished up by ... Oh, let's say end of next week at the latest."

"All right. I can't give you the seven-fifty until Friday, though."

"That's OK. I can run a tab at the 84."

Faye extended a hand. "I think we got a deal, Mr. Morgan." *Hope he knows what he's doing. Butter him up by calling him Mister, maybe he'll take it seriously.*

***

Saturday evening, August 22, saw a full moon rise over Gabbro County. Annie Godfire was glad of the long twilight and the extra light; she was almost finished with the eleventh circle of the Spirit Catcher, which would bring it to nearly 35 feet high. The twelfth circle would continue a graceful inward bend in its profile toward a vase-like neck, before soaring outward nearly to its original diameter of a hundred feet. Progress would be faster for a while, as the diameter shrank, requiring fewer pieces to complete each circle, all the way up to the eighty-foot level. Annie tried to avoid thinking about what would come after that as the form flared outward, increasing the steel to be found and the work to be done for each circle. Keeping the whole thing balanced and strong, lifting the steel higher with each circle.

With the last weld cooling, holding the tricycle frame that completed the eleventh circle, Annie shut down her torch, peeled the sweaty mask from her head, and looked out over the wetlands of Gabbro County, and murmured to the rising moon.

"There ya go, Mama. 'Bout a third of the way up, now. Still think it's OK?"

A small warm breeze ruffled the live oak at the center of the goat meadow, and one of the smallest kids from this spring lifted its head and blatted. Annie grinned. "OK. If you're happy, I'm happy. I'm headed over to Faye's for a skinny dip. Wanta come?"

***

At midnight, light fell vertically from the moon, 400,000 kilometers up, into Morgan's Eddy, and plunged straight to the bottom, triggering sepia fluorescence from the dissolved tannins and wrapping the swimmers in chill and uniform glory. It made of the water an all-engulfing world of light in which they dove and sported, never losing sight of each other across the luminous bowl while the rippled surface sent weightless bars of gold across their bodies. When it happened that both of them broke the surface for breath at the same time, they stared at each other in wordless glee that such delight could exist in the wide and used-up world. The greatest enchantment was the one they always saved for last, when they joined hands and sank themselves to smile at the elastic dance of the moon-image on the surface, the chill touch of the spring on their backs, while the petrified bones of Confederates tumbled fathoms below.

Sated at last, they were reluctant to leave it, to take back the burdens of time and weight. On the dock, they wrapped in a pair of fluffy robes that Faye had bought for this purpose, stumbled to the steps and mounted, exhausted. Still, they tarried side by side on the old glider to listen to the nightworld and watch the moonlight yellow and slant and finally fade into the woods behind the cottage. At a predawn hour - too dark to read the Grandmother Clock over the fireplace, and who cared, anyhow? - they fell into the embrace of Faye's bed; joined hands, and slept.

**

Wednesday, August 26, marked the deepening of a period of remarkable unproductivity at the Gabbro *Intelligencer*. Forde Morgan began it the previous week, when he took time away from his professional duties to spend with Nora Lundy; to, as he told himself, see that she was properly cared for at Gabbro Memorial, to explore the mystery of her presence in Gabbro County. To enjoy her banter and rasp. He pretty much dropped the reins of management and planning for the *Intelligencer*, leaving them to Faye or no one to pick up. Faye responded by taking matters over, resenting having to do it while Forde footsied around with this stranger; and then by dropping them herself.

As one example out of a multitude of nonfeasances, the Jaycees jelly-sales fundraiser went entirely unannounced, and fell thirty percent short of its dollar goal, reducing substantially the number and quality of wholesale light bulbs the Jaycees could afford to stock for the bulb sale; resulting in turn in an aggrieved subscription-cancelling letter to the editor from old Beachum Prothroe, still a Jaycee power at 81; and the non-replacement when burnt out, of light bulbs county-wide. Gabbro Memorial recorded a blip in minor sprains and contusions suffered because of failed illumination of the county's dark corners. What toppled these dominoes of ill luck?

Faye Bynum left the *Intelligencer* early on that Wednesday to pick up greens, Rose's lime juice and chicken thighs at the Piggly Wiggly, and drove out to Morgan's Eddy, feeling righteously peeved at the way things were going to hell around the office. It was a blazing hot day, and she was looking forward to a cool-off in the Eddy, followed by thighs, greens, and a gimlet or two.

The sound of hammering greeted her as the little VW tiptoed down her washboard lane; and as she cleared the trees, she beheld Terry Morgan, bronzed and sweaty, naked to the waist and straddling the cottage's ridgepole while he banged the new underlay into place. Faye nearly ran the Beetle into a pine tree; then turned blushing to her business and got parked next to Morgan's truck. She took her attaché case and the bag of groceries from the seat beside her, and emerged.

"Hi."

"Ma'am."

"How's it going?"

"Comin' along."

"Uh huh, well, it must be awful hot work." Morgan was in fact gleaming with sweat, making his slender torso into something godlike out of the <u>Time-Life Treasury of Italian Art</u>, which was the extent of Faye's education in erotic sculpture. A skinny trickster-god, but still.

"Used to it."

"You want some lemonade? Or something stronger?"

"Maybe later. Don't want ta get myself dizzy up here."

"Feel free to take a dip in the pond when you're done, you want to cool off."

"Yes, ma'am. Thank you. Be done for the day direckly."

Faye climbed the steps and onto the porch, careful not to trip and scatter groceries, and look like a fool. Inside, she found about half of her house open to the sky as the rotten underlayment gave way to fresh exterior plywood. She unloaded the groceries and got herself into - well, Jesus, she couldn't change clothes with no roof overhead. She heard bronze Terry Morgan banging and thumping overhead, and glimpsed him through the steadily narrowing window of open sky. *Definitely have to get into house-cleaning when he's done. How about a bathing suit and a wrap?*

She was still in her office clothes a half-hour later when Morgan knocked on the screen door. His hair was wet.

"Come on in. Done?"

"Yes, ma'am, thank you. Done for today, uh huh. You're water-proof again, case it rains tonight. Got another couple days yet, put the shingles on. Hey there, little fella."

He wore cut-off Levis, boots without socks and, she was a little sorry to see, a thin cotton shirt that covered the Renaissance torso. It was darkened with water from his cooling-off where it touched him. He had left it unbuttoned, swinging free, and his taut belly and a prominent sternum lay in shifting shade behind it. He stopped at the doorway from the porch and leaned on the frame, backlit by the brightness of the Eddy. Faye introduced Rosie. There was polite talk, a drink offered, beer accepted, no glass.

The polite talk began with whether he was related to Forde Morgan (no), had grown up in Gabbro County (yes), and whether Faye might want him to give her an estimate for replacing the screens on the porch which, with summer now in full cry, were admitting biting bugs through the rusted-out holes. A wistful but polite refusal on Faye's part stopped the talk for a while; when it resumed, it drifted a little toward banter, and the banter toward flirtatious ambiguity by degrees. Faye knew it was stupid to allow it, let alone to participate herself. Still, he was good at banter, clearly not a yokel, but quick with puns and associations. She wondered if he could really be from Gabbro, or perhaps from someplace where people were a little more sophisticated and less straightforward. Still, it was nice just to talk with a clever, funny man, a pleasure she had not enjoyed since the disastrous affair with Travis Wayland. She certainly never came close to it with Forde.

Terry spoke of people whom she might have met in the course of her job, relating construction and repairs he'd done for them, and adding remarks about them that were perceptive, sometimes generous, almost always funny. And hilarious when the subject was Ginny Freeman. After another beer, Faye offered supper, which he accepted. He volunteered to fix the chicken if she would do the greens. While he was doing that, she slipped into her bedroom and, refusing to think about it, changed into shorts, a tee shirt, and bare feet.

After supper, they sat on the glider with gimlets and a citronella candle, to watch the daylight fade over Morgan's Eddy. Frogs, crickets, Rosie snoring in her bed; Faye certain that this was not going to end well. Or, what <u>would</u> be a good ending? She was a responsible adult, and in charge of herself. They were both adults, so why not? She wouldn't mind seeing if his butt lived up to the promise of his torso, but ... In a last-ditch effort to get things in hand, she stood and spoke of a need to rise early.

He nodded, yawning. "Long day tomorra, with a kind of wrinkle to it, I wondered if I could ask you about."

Uh oh. "Yes?"

"Uh huh. I got this extremely interesting, kind of sophisticated lady I'm puttin' a new roof on for her, which she sure's heck needed. Thing is, folks tell me she's fast an' loose. You got any recommendations?" He stood too, cushioning the glider with his calves to keep it from swinging against her.

His head was back, cocked a little, smiling. *Proposition me, you punk? Or did I?* She was pleased to find that she was nearly as tall as he. Up close like this, he smelled of sweat and tar and sunshine. Some kind of vital hum seemed to echo from the tautness and shine of his body. She wanted him, and couldn't see why she shouldn't have him. "Yes. Yes, I do. I don't think you should listen to gossip like that, Terry. Sophisticated, I wouldn't know, but she might not be all that fast."

He put a calloused hand on her arm. "You mean she might like it better if I took it slow?"

She slid her fingers under the cotton shirt. *His body feels like warm steel pipe.* "That is exactly how I would go about it, yes." Her fingers circled a nipple. "If I were you."

5.

THE OUTREACH INTERN

Chapter 4.

Faith Mercy stared into the darkness of her garret room and gnashed her teeth. How could she have been so stupid? All right, he was charming, muscular, and so very eager to make love to her. And the loving had been lovely exquisite, really transformative, almost. No comparison to the fumbling encounters she'd endured with Chad. But honestly. Really? To allow a sweaty kid barely out of high school into her bed, into her life and into her body – stupid, stupid, stupid. Randy, however captivating a lover, was a huge mistake, and she would be so lucky not to come away from this fiasco pregnant or, God, infected. She was as certain as could be that Randy was right now sitting in some bar or locker room bragging to his friends – his jock pals and his bricklayer buddies – about how "hot" she was, how she'd gasped and cried out as the great crashing bright waves of pleasure washed swept over through her.

6.

AUGUST PASSED, AND HALF OF SEPTEMBER.
Lee Forsythe handed in her final story of the summer, an account of a ride on the cash-strapped Interurban from Raleigh through Gabbro to Myrtle Beach that was not half bad, Faye decided, but hardly qualified as precocious. Apparently, the Gabbro Hunt somehow unplugged springs of creativity in Lee that nothing else so far had.

Nora Lundy healed well enough to be discharged on crutches, with casts on an arm and a leg. A check arrived from the Textile Workers Union Medical Fund covering half her bill at Gabbro Memorial. Nora's finite bank account covered most of the rest, and Forde Morgan paid the balance, subject to repayment over time. After a parting conversation in which they discussed plans for repayment of her debt, she mentioned, through subjunctively pursed lips, that he might conceivably wish to visit his nation's capital some time. Should the notion take him, he would be welcome and gladly hosted. She returned then to Washington to report on the dire state of labor at River Mills, and to set in motion a small-bore investigation into the perpetrators of her beating-up.

Terry Morgan finished his work on Faye's roof on August 31. She got through his daily presence with only one further adventure: which was, unfortunately, spectacular. It began with a trip up his ladder to admire the new shingles and the handing-over of a check for one quarter of the remaining cost; which seemed to call for a celebratory gimlet on the screened porch, and watching a gibbous moon clear the forest across Morgan's Eddy. A condensed bantering session led them to the Eddy, its grassy verge, its shallows, and its depths, before coming to a conclusion at midnight on the dock.

Faye was willing to overlook Terry's leanings in the direction of dirty talk and play-acted rough sex, because the whole experience was to her monthly overnight with Forde as Salvador Dali is to Grandma Moses. And besides, his bad behavior licensed her to mistreat him in her own way, with her own weapons, and that was liberating too. She gave as good as she got, and she was pretty sure that her finish outclassed his by several furlongs. Dimly from her sleep, Faye heard Terry's van pull out in the dawn twilight of Tuesday, September 1, and castigated herself anew.

She spent that day in a shamefaced fog that even Forde noticed. He appeared at her office door with a draft of This Town's Times in his hand. "Miss Bynum, are you OK?"

"Huh? ... Why, yes, of course. What makes you ask?"

"Oh, nothing, I guess. Just ... well, you've been kind of absent-minded, I guess. Your column covers the School Board and the Jaycettes bake sale, which I guess is what's going on this week. Usually, a dull week, you've found somebody interesting to interview, some angle. But this makes it sound like the Jaycettes took over the Middle School. And you got Ellice Laffler chairman of the School Board, that died in 1958."

"Hm. Well ... let me see."

Forde handed her the manuscript, and she pretended to read it, knowing damn well what was in it, and what was not. "I see what you mean. I'll get you a revision before the deadline. I have to take Rosie to the vet over lunch. What's the latest with the Textile Workers?"

"Thought that bee was in your bonnet, not mine. Listen, though, our esteemed Congressman Blanton is holding a press conference up'n Washington, claims he's got a major revelation to make, something about how the Beatles was in on the Kennedy assassination. I'm gonna go there with a recorder, because I think it will amount to a public display of senile dementia that could be the last straw for folks."

"Mr. Morgan! You, doing investigative journalism? Are we living in the Last Days?"

"Never you mind, smart-mouth. I'll be taking a little vacation for sight-seeing, be gone for the week. Can you keep things going for me?"

"Of course. Might have to let some bees out of my bonnet, you understand."

"Try not to get us sued, OK?"

"Do my best, but some folks, when you confront them with the truth, they go a little crazy."

Forde grunted, wondering if that was meant for him. "I know you'll do a fine job, Miss Bynum. I'll be back Sunday a week."

One of the sights Forde planned to see in the Nation's Capital was of course Nora Lundy, who'd called him about the Congressman's theorizing and the news conference; and renewed, casually, her offer to put Forde up, if he was of a mind to stay over and "see the monuments."

For her part, Faye's dalliance with Terry Morgan brought home to her how far she had settled into the quicksand of Gabbro culture as Forde's special friend, and how bored she was with the ersatz respectability of "keeping company." People probably found it adorable of them. Gabbro culture seemed prepared to accept just about any deviation – which elevated it far above St. Louis in Faye's mind – as long as its keepers were given license to name, define, and patronize. Faye supposed they might even become used to her as something between a predatory libertine and a no-charge prostitute, which was where she seemed to hover. She even wondered for a time whether going to Father Kenneth for confession might be the thing to jar her out of it; certainly the humiliation of it would be properly cauterizing. But social pressure or the whole Vatican was not going to help her with this; if she were ever to lift herself to respectability again, it would have to be by her own frayed shoelaces. She blushed, sitting by herself over the errant School Board story. *Just that lame cliché tells you all you need to know.*

Still. During her last don't-mention-it date with Forde, he made love to her by the book that she herself had written for him, omitting no technique in which she had instructed him and introducing nothing she had not. It was all over by 8:30. Faye knew that what she was doing with Terry Morgan was stupid, destructive of herself and of him; predatory, and wrong. *Not liberated, not "new morality;" just damn wrong.* Her creature Mercy's self-loathing over her bricklayer lover Randy was a pale echo of Faye's in regard to Terry Morgan. But compared to Forde's erotic oatmeal, to be gently slapped and called a "crazy twat" while being ravished by a naked barbarian on the clattering boards of the dock under a waning moon was almost … She sighed. *Lyrical.*

Which raised a blizzard of un-answerable questions that always sounded in the voice of Sister Rose Penitentia, scourge of Mount Saint Anne High School and of Faye's conscience: *OK to be the town floozy of the county seat of the smallest county in goddamn North Carolina? What about romping with the roofer is so great as to justify that? Can't there be lyricism without either sluttishness or respectability? How about we just drop out of the sex game for a while? Or for good? How many times around that mulberry bush is enough for a lifetime anyhow?*

Come here, Mercy. Ever tasted a mulberry? Let's have a little talk, just us girls.

***

Her re-write accomplished, with a more normal helping of loving irony in connection with the School Board, Faye drove back to River Cottage to collect Rosie and the urine sample she had coaxed at dawn. Rosie, Faye was reluctant to conclude, had not looked good for weeks, and she had lost weight. She rose with some difficulty when

Faye came up the porch steps calling out cheerfully. Rosie came to the screen door wagging, but her back was humped painfully, and she was alarmingly light, just fur and bones, it seemed, when Faye picked her up. After a quick sandwich and a granola bar, she carried Rosie over her shoulder down to the Beetle, to let her sit on her favorite towel in the passenger seat. Rosie did not, as once, hang her head out the window and grin into the rushing air; but curled up and went to sleep.

Elvis Cromartie, DVM, was an oldish guy who'd been middle-aged when Faye brought Rosie to him for a puppy check-up. His smile was sad, and he shook his head, a fond hand massaging Rosie's neck. "Classic kidney failure symptoms, it's one of the main ways we lose dogs, they get to be her age. I can go ahead and send the urine off to the lab for you, but I wonder if you mightn't want to save your money."

"No," Faye managed. "Let's not miss any chance it's something else, that could be fixed."

"Sure, Hon. You can bet I'll tell them, be extry careful, check it twice. I'll give you a call when I get the results. Get you at the paper, or at home?"

"When would this be?"

"Oh ... Before the weekend."

Faye was reluctant to handle emotional news in the company of her co-workers, but she also didn't want to be alone when word came. "At the office. I should be there most of the time, Forde's junketing to Washington."

The first thing that greeted Faye at the *Intelligencer* office on Friday was a dust-up between Sharon the receptionist and Jenny McCall the Society and Lifestyles editor, about whose turn it was to clean the lunch fridge, and whose cup of yogurt had gone all furry on the bottom shelf over the weekend, infecting whose baloney sandwich, the greasy stench of which had ruined whose appetite for lunch in the first place. By the time Faye had established uneasy peace, she was already missing Forde.

She had about finished sketching out assignments for the period of his absence when her phone rang. It was Cromartie, the vet.

"Afraid there's no room for doubt, Miss Bynum. Her urine is way down, so she's accumulating toxins in her blood stream, why she's lost s'much weight, and drinks so much water, I think you said. I'd give her another month, maybe, before any joy she takes in being with you is not worth the pain and nausea she's feeling. I could give you some low-protein food, would take some of the strain off her kidneys, and I suppose that could make her feel better, give her another couple-three weeks. Sooner or later, we need to be talking about a humane way to help her out."

"Help her ... Oh. I see. To help her all the way out."

"Yes, ma'am. Comes a point, you're not doing her any favors, keeping her going."

"No, I see. Oh, this is so hard. Rosie is the only dog I've ever had, my whole life, and she's so dear."

The vet was gently unhelpful. "Some folks find it's useful to pray, this situation. Not that you'd be saving her life or nothing; just getting yourself ready. Miss Bynum, she's over a hundred dog years. She's a very old lady now, and she's ready to rest. Still, however many dogs you've loved, it's never easy."

"I'll say. Well, let me stop by and pick up your special feed this afternoon, and I'll get her started on that, maybe she'll feel a little better."

"Yes, Ma'am. We're open to six."

***

On Thursday, Faye was at her desk, reading a pale and semiliterate press release from the Jaycettes when she heard the street door burst open. Sharon's "Hey there Miss ... hey!" floated down the hallway, pursuing rapid light footsteps, and Lee Forsythe skidded around her office doorway, shining with earnest sweat, her hair flying.

"Miss B - Miss Faye," she gasped. "Something awful."

"Lee? Thought you were registering for school."

Lee stamped her foot. "Faye, listen! It's a horrible accident at the mill, one of those floor ladies got her *hand* cut off."

"Oh, my God. When?"

"Just this afternoon, a little while ago. 'Bout bled to death, right there on the floor, wasn't nobody heard a thing, till the bin boy come back and found her passed out."

"What about these sideline ladies, the 37-cents-an-hour folks that are supposed to step in for people who faint?"

Lee was silent. "Huh. I don't know. Maybe they were all busy."

"How'd you hear about this?"

"Tucker Pardee told me. He'll get fired if anybody knows he let it out, so don't tell nobody."

"Anybody. Don't worry. Was this on that cutting machine you told me about, five bath towels, all that? Or one hand, I guess."

"Yes'm. You 'bout cain't imagine the blood, Tucker says, who they got him to drive her to the hospital."

"Did he say if she's going to make it?"

Lee looked solemn. "In God's hands, they said at the hospital."

"That's what they always say, it's how they wash their own hands of it. Oh, Jesus, how terrible, though."

"I was thinking maybe we could ought to run over there, see if there's a story to go in Friday's paper."

"Well, good idea, but they'll never let us in, with this fat in the fire."

"I got a plan for that."

"Really. Do you want to share it, so when you get killed or beaten up like Nora, I'll know what it was?"

"You'll see. We going?"

"Of course."

On the way out to River Mills, Faye glanced at Lee. "Your plan for getting into the plant, or at least past the guard shack. Does it have any connection with Tucker Pardee giving you information that would get him fired, if they found out about it?"

Lee blushed. "Well. Indirectly, I suppose. Tucker seems to be sort of interested. You know."

"In you."

"Yes, ma'am."

"I see. And what in God's name did you have to promise him, for him to compromise his whole future in law enforcement, in order for you to get this scoop? Or wait, no, that's probably none of my business, is it?"

"Well ..."

"Good Lord. Well, take the advice of an aging libertine, and get good value for what you're giving away."

Lee blushed again. "Getting the story wasn't but a kiss on his cheek, and a promise of a date."

"Hm. And how was he?"

"Sweaty."

Faye laughed. "<u>That</u> takes me back!"

Lee giggled. "Wait'll you hear what he's gonna take to give us visitor passes right into the plant through the loading dock. But are men just generally this dumb?"

"You bet. Look, here we are, and I don't want to come across to you like I'm this goddess of wisdom. I don't have a clue about love or sex, in spite of my years of experience. I guess I have learned one thing which, mind, you should not necessarily build your life around, and that's this: virginity is <u>way</u> over-rated. It's something men invented to puff up their delicate egos, and so they can have all the fun. I was exactly the same person afterward as I was before." *Except I was pregnant, of course.*

Lee blushed, and Faye held her peace until they were at the guardhouse.

"Hey there, Tucker."

"How do, Miss Bynum. How do you do, Miss Forsythe."

"How do, Mr. Pardee. You got 'em?"

"Yes. C'mon back here."

"Won't be but a minute, Miss ... Faye."

Faye shut off the motor, and Lee got out and disappeared behind the guard shack with Tucker Pardee. There was a brief silence, during which Faye heard a mockingbird calling and a few cicadas whirring in the grass. The noise of the towel factory seemed subdued, but determined to carry on. Then voices were raised, at first only forceful and then angry. Faye popped open her door and prepared to intervene, when Lee re-emerged, glaring over her shoulder.

"Nothing doing, Tucker Pardee! That wasn't what we agreed, and you cain't change it now. Miss Bynum, he -"

"Why, it most certainly was, Lee Forsythe. That was just very definitely what you agreed to."

Faye raised a hand. "Perhaps I could help?"

"Hesheagreednoabsolutelyesyoudidnot!"

"One at a time, please; ladies first. Lee?"

"I told him he could put his arms around me an' kiss me twice. But mouth closed."

"Hm. And Tucker?"

"Well, she ... " Tucker stopped, red-faced. "Excuse me. It was my definite understanding that we would be kissing for real. Mouths whatever. We're talking a very serious, firing offense here."

Faye smiled. "I see. Well, we do not want anyone to compromise her control of her own body, nor do we want to get anyone fired. It sounds to me as if we might better withdraw and take another approach, don't you? Both? Lee, I advise you not to get into the business of ... well, let that go for now. Tucker, same to you, except we're talking about your principles, including loyalty to your employer and your own career. There may be other occasions for you two to negotiate kisses. Meanwhile, it occurs to me that we're likely to get more and better information from the victim herself than from anybody in that brick anteroom of Hell. I think you said Tucker brought her to Gabbro Memorial?"

"Yes, ma'am."

"And what name did she give, please, Tucker?"

Tucker scuffed the gravel outside his guard house. "I am not at liberty to -"

"Rather than have even the slightest hint about your role as an informant see print, though, I bet."

More scuffing. "Well. Y'understand, it's my a - it's my neck if they find out I told you."

"Understood. Lee, notice this: journalists protect their sources, always. Not a peep, Tucker."

"... Yes'm, OK. It was a lady name of Sedalia Baley."

"Oh, no. Not one of the outcast Baleys?"

"Well, I believe that would be accurate, yes, Ma'am." Behind him, the guardhouse telephone jingled.

Faye hid a smile. "You'll go far, Tucker. Come on, Lee."

Lee dawdled around to the passenger door, smiling guardedly at Tucker, who picked up the phone. "Guardhouse ... Yes, sir ... Couple journalists, but I ... Yes, sir ... Certainly not, sir ... I told 'em I didn't hear of no accident. And no visiting today 'cause of, of machine rutenance. Routine machine maitanus. They're leaving now." Through the window, Tucker twirled a finger in a cranking motion, and Faye started the Beetle.

After she finished giggling about 'machine mutants,' Lee seemed pensive, and finally turned to Faye. "I have known all my life that Baleys were outcasts, but nobody ever told me why. Do you know?"

"I know what was told me, though who knows if it's the real story. People here have a way of telling you about half of any story, and expecting you to fill in the rest. What the ladies at the Salonnette said is, they are of mixed blood. Derivation, I should say. Both the Lumbees and the Negroes consider them to be half-breeds and beneath consideration, to the point where they even have their own schools, which are pathetic. Don't even ask about white folks, of course. All this started centuries ago, so they're pretty inbred by now, which doesn't help."

"You think that's why nobody jumped in to help her and take her place when she got hurt? 'Cause she was an outcast?"

Faye sighed. "I hate to think it goes so far that they'd just watch her bleed to death. I suppose nobody was keeping an eye on her, and maybe that has to do with her being a Baley. If you're invisible, nobody can see you bleed."

Lee was silent, digesting this. From the corner of her eye, Faye saw her wiping her eyes, but she didn't want to too obviously check to see if it was empathy, or road dust. At length, Lee sighed.

"Wasn't that blackmail? Back there, when you said that about, you know, 'the slightest hint about his role,' and so forth."

Faye's turn for silence; then a shrug. "Yes, it was, or at least pretty dark brown. So I guess I was guilty of ... Well. Not a crime, certainly, at that level. He was already compromised by giving you that information this morning; I just offered him a way forward that would let him avoid compromising himself more by giving us fake passes. A small sin, I suppose. But speaking of that, what's the difference between kissing with mouths closed and kissing 'however?' I bet your Granny kissed you a million times when you were growing up, cute little thing like you."

"Well, goodness. He's not exactly my Granny, so mouth kisses from him are, well, you know... " Lee frowned and adopted a starchy face. "Already intimate. When I kissed him before, it was on the cheek, and strictly hands-off. He'd have to come up with something a lot bigger than phony passes, which I looked at them, and they wouldn't fool a baby."

"Uh huh. But what do you call it when a woman offers a man access to intimate parts of her body in exchange for value?" She grimaced. *Good one, Faye. The difference is, I don't get any tangible value from my no-charge whoring.*

Lee clapped a hand to her belly, and the other to her mouth. "Oh, Faye, I never ... But ... Oh, shit!"

Faye pulled over to the edge of the road. "There, now, Lee. Remember, our purpose in getting the unfortunate Miss Baley's name is to publicize the real-life human consequence of the inhuman conditions at River Mills. Maybe the upshot will be that they'll have to improve things for all the workers. You know they wouldn't if they could hush the whole thing up."

Lee was silent until they pulled up to the hospital parking lot. "Isn't there a thing about means and ends, that goes ... oh, you know. I can't remember it."

"Yes, there is. 'The end does not justify the means.' But people have been struggling for centuries with when that's true and when it's not. If it was always true, you could never so much as sharpen a pencil." She waved a hand. "But so far, we're nothing but a couple of blackmailing hookers until we follow our questionable means to some good end. So we'd better get cracking."

***

That night, with the story of maimed Sedalia Baley written, typeset, and printed, Faye carried Rosie, who was too old any longer to make the jump, onto the wide, cool bed with her, and wept quietly into her fur. *Stupid. I'm just upsetting her by showing that I'm upset.* Rosie turned and gently licked the tears from her face. Faye wiped her eyes and managed a shaky smile. "Thanks, Rosie. I feel much better now, but salt is bad for you. Let's go to sleep."

7.

FROM THE GABBRO *INTELLIGENCER* FOR FRIDAY, September 18, 1964:

RIVER MILLS WORKER
INJURED

Sedalia Baley, 41, was severely injured this week when a cutting machine she was negligently operating lacerated her right hand, resulting in the partial loss of ...

THIS TOWN'S TIMES
By Faye Bynum
Associate Editor

Sedalia Baley lies in a Memorial Hospital bed this evening suffering from major blood loss, her right hand reduced to most of the palm and part of a thumb. The official release given the *Intelligencer* by River Mills manager Virgil Barnett and printed as received on Page A-1 doesn't quite give the whole story. It might leave a reader wondering how a prudent worker could leave her hand in such danger, when the knives that cut terrycloth into towels and washcloths are devilishly sharp and flash down only after a warning horn sounds. And therein lies a tale of sweatshop practices that beggar belief. ...

... can't hardly believe how tired you get, running that machine eight hours a day. And I'd already tripped the Stop pedal four times that day, plus I had two demerits." Miss Baley clarified: "You get five times on the Stop pedal in a day, that's a demerit. Three demerits in a month, you're fired, and without that paycheck..." She closed her eyes and shuddered, because she now will go without the paycheck that stood between her family and poverty, possibly homelessness. Nor should the reader ask about Workman's Compensation, health insurance, retirement benefits, or even first-aid kits. Merrydown Enterprises offer none of these civilized gestures of care for their workers; rather - think of this - they have docked Miss Baley's final paycheck for the piece of toweling that her life's blood ruined. I doubt that Simon Legree at his worst ...

***

Terry Morgan's truck bounced down Faye's lane that evening. She was wary to find herself glad to see him, heartsick as she was about Rosie.

"Terry, come in. I'll get your check ready for you."

"Fine, if you want, but that ain't why I come. I got something for you too, Faye, and I don't want to hear ... Whoa! Somethin' bothering you?"

Faye sniffed. "Nothing for you to worry about. Pollen."

"Yeah? Middle a September? Whatever you say, ya little liar."

Faye burst into tears, hating it. "Please don't, Terry! I can't take -"

"Hey, hey there. Come on, what is it?"

"I done told you, it's nothing, ya stupit redneck, why can'tcha just ... just ... " She fell against his chest and stamped her foot. *Must've picked that up from Lee Forsythe. Great.* "It's nothing."

"Silly broad, thought I told you not to lie to me. Now, what is it?"

Faye pushed back from him, sighing. "Oh ... Rosie's dying, is what it is. No big deal to a tough guy like you, I suppose you slaughter seven dogs a week. But I've had her for fifteen years, and she's just so sweet, and now ..."

"Oh. No, I can't stand to see dumb animals suffer, you oughta know that by now. What's the trouble? Are you gonna have to put her down?"

"See, I can't even stand to hear that phrase. But, yes. Doc Cromartie gives her a month, maybe six weeks, from kidney failure. And then he's got what he calls 'humane ways to help her out.' Kill her, he means."

"Uh huh. I could do that for you, you want. Be cheaper and quicker, and she knows me. It wouldn't mean hauling her to the vet's, which I bet she hates."

"She does, always has. Yeah, she knows you're the guy that made a lot of noise on the roof, where nobody's supposed to go; and then kept me up past my bedtime." She sighed. "How would you do it?"

"Really want to know? Shoot her in the back of the head. She'll be dead before she knows anything's happening."

"Jesus. She doesn't like guns."

"Well, she's smart. Guns never done nothing good for any dog, 'less you count a quick death. I'd clean it good and keep it hidden, though it's tough to hide anything from a dog. But that does bring me to the other thing I need to talk to you about. Which I know you're not going to like."

"Let me guess. You're pregnant."

Terry snorted. "Never tell you if I was. Nope, I read that column you wrote about this dummy at the mill that got her hand cut off -"

"Don't call her that. She's as smart as you or me, but she worked in that hellhole of a factory, and she was under a lot of strain."

"More now, I bet. Not talking about her, though." He put a hand in his pocket a drew out a small, starved-looking pistol. "Talking about this."

"What on earth?"

"This, my friend, is a small .22 pistol, sometimes called a roscoe, ideal for use by the ladies. Meaning, it is lightweight and an easy trigger pull, but with hollow-point twenny-two shorts, it'll stop the hell out of the tough guys you know damn well Merrydown is gonna send calling on you for writing what you put in today's paper."

"Oh, right. Sure, sure, so good of you to think of me. Can you see me standing like Wonder Woman, blazing away at guys in purple suits?"

"If you'd wear that hot outfit of hers, I'd see that all day."

"No, seriously, Terry. You're very sweet to be concerned, but I hate the very thought of guns. If I kept one around the most likely one to get shot would be myself, if it wasn't Rosie."

"Not gonna argue with you. It's loaded, but the safety's on. Gimme your right hand, and shut your eyes." He slid the grip into her right hand. "This here's the safety. Like that, it's on, which is how we'll leave it. But push like this ... it's off. On. Off. On. You want to threaten the guy, you push ... eyes shut! ... you push the safety till it clicks, like that. Now – yikes, careful – just a little touch on the trigger, Bam! Open your eyes."

He slipped behind her in the classic flirtatious-instructional position. "Now, if you actually wanta shoot the guy, point like you're pointing your finger, squeeze firmly, and Bam! again. Got it?"

She pivoted away, sighing. "I suppose."

"Good for you. Now, you're not gonna get into a long gun battle with nobody, so I'm leaving one chamber empty for safety. You squeeze the trigger once, the first round will come into position to fire. That's it. Don't bother to practice, 'cause we don't want you actually killing nobody. Five shots oughta scare Merrydown's punks shitless."

"Yeah, fine. In the most extreme possible circumstances, like King Kong's climbing up my stairs, OK. Otherwise, I'd rather interview anybody than shoot them. I'm more dangerous that way."

"Yeah, fine to you too, dragon lady. You'll thank me when some punk's wettin' his pants, stumbling out through the porch. Speaking of that, though, I gotta go give a lady a estimate for haulin' her ashes."

"Two-timing redneck trailer trash."

"Two? I never get down under four or five. Need your chimbley swabbed out, call me for a estimate. Where you gonna put the roscoe, you can get it in a hurry?"

"In the bedroom, I guess. They wouldn't come in daylight, I don't think. They won't come at all, you ask me, but anyway, you're sweet to think of this."

"Make it someplace, you can get it quiet. And listen, Faye?"

"What?"

"I really do have an appointment with a lady, but it's for a new front porch, and she's sixty years old. And ugly."

"Pants on fire."

"Well, don't that make life a lot more interesting?"

When he was gone, Faye found her mood elevated. A little wistful that he'd not stayed and let them seduce each other again, but somebody had to call a halt to it, the sooner the better, so maybe now was as good a time as any. She fed Rosie, and herself; and was pleased that Rosie seemed to like the low-protein feed. Maybe things were not as desperate as all that. She pictured a mellow Rosie, gliding into contented permanent sleep in her lap, maybe after Christmas some time. She put the roscoe in the drawer of her bedside table and thought about a swim, but decided to wait and see if she woke at midnight and was moved to cool off under the nearly full moon.

***

It didn't work out that way. She slept, woke, slept again, woke at a dark hour to find the moon hidden by a deck of clouds, and slept again until dawn. Rosie, beside her on her towel, wove in and out of her sleep, by turns puppyish and elderly, and once disguised as a middle-aged librarian; but always happy. She opened her eyes to cloudy light and lay with her arm around Rosie, waiting for something to motivate her to rise.

Eventually a bird, fooled by September's springlike temperature and length of night, started to warble outside the window. At that window the Remington crouched, holding her stalled novel where she had left it. She rose, peed, and put on her Mount Saint Anne tee and shorts, ready for a Saturday morning of housekeeping. Rosie slept on, no longer up like a dervish the moment Faye's feet hit the floor. Holding a mug of tea, she walked out the kitchen door. Sipped, placed the mug on the porch rail, and walked onto the grassy spot as she watched frontal clouds race overhead. The wind off the Eddy spoke of a change in weather. Faye Bynum bent slowly from the waist to touch the ground.

Twenty minutes later, sweating and limber again, she paused in the kitchen door to sip tea and look back on the woods, seeing their progress toward autumn; and to enjoy the feeling that the rabble of arms and legs that had hauled a sleep-sodden bag of cells out of bed were part of a functioning animal again. The centipede grass of her exercise spot was beginning to brown, though the weather was still warm and muggy. Another year hinting toward its end. A Carolina wren tuned up, invisible in the yellow woods, and started singing about Richelieu. Faye brushed little spikes of grass from the backs of her legs, and paused to feel the blood humming through them. At the creak of a board behind her, she turned and dropped the mug, which broke and splattered warm tea on her feet.

8.

THE GUY WITH THE NORDIC FLORAL PATTERN ON his mask spoke. "You Faye Bynum with the Gabbro *Intelligencer?* We come to give you some writing lessons."

"Really." *Virgil Barnett.* Faye felt her heart jumping behind the Mount Saint Anne tee shirt, and was sure these thugs could see it slamming around through the thin cotton, which they were watching pretty closely. "Could I see some ID, and maybe we can talk about your credentials." Her voice shook in spite of her best efforts, and she spoke past the ticking of pulse in her throat. "Wouldn't you be cooler if you took off those ski masks?" In the woods, the wren changed his tune, and began a song about teakettles.

The Nordic guy and his helper in the plain black ski mask were wearing what looked ominously like butchers' aprons over their clothes, and they pulled thin black leather gloves from pockets in the aprons. Nordic guy turned to the guy in the plain black mask. "Plucky. I like that."

"Yes?" All she could think of.

"Plucky makes it more fun," black-mask said. He held up one of the gloves. "Watch closely now." He tugged and wiggled his fingers to get the glove snug over his hand.

Faye, emerging at last from the paralysis of terror, ran into the kitchen, screaming for Rosie. One of the thugs jumped after her and tackled her. She fell face down with the thug on top of her, knocking her wind out. While she tried to get her breath, he yanked her to her feet and hauled her back toward the grassy spot. She got a knee into his groin; he slammed a black-gloved hand across her face. As she pivoted upward and back from the force, she glimpsed an arcing spray of blood.

...nose...

Falling, she banged her head on the porch rail; orange light burst across her vision, and she fell to the steps, wondering how she had been transported so quickly to the depths of Morgan's Eddy, watching bones coated with fool's gold dancing in the updraft of the spring; and the moving bars of refracted sunlight.

Then, without interval, she was on the exercise spot, being held off the ground by someone, the Assistant Thug she guessed. His arms were hooked under her armpits from behind, while the Boss Thug, the one with the floral pattern, got to work, slapping and punching from belly to face, and she could only hang there gasping and crying and trying to kick his crotch with her bare feet, while blood continued to drip and spray from her nose to seep into the sand and caterpillar grass, and the Nordic flowers wrenched from side to side, and the black gloves flashed, and Faye wailed and panicked at the sudden taste of blood in her mouth; and the wren sang on, *teakettle, teakettle* while ribs cracked, until one of the gloves found her solar plexus, and there was no more breath to wail with. Desperate for air, she sagged against the Assistant Thug's arms. Another thunderous slap, and the wren song faded to black silence.

She was on the floor by the fireplace. The Boss thug was yanking at the gym shorts, and the bloody Mount Saint Anne tee was up around her neck. Someone – presumably the Assistant – was holding her arms above her head, driving lances of pain into her cracked ribs. *The roscoe. Why didn't I put it in the kitchen? Fat lot of good...* Then the Nordic mask was rubbing against her breasts, a tongue hanging ludicrously out of the mouth hole and leaving a trail of stinking spit. She heard a belt buckle drag across the floor. She struggled to turn her hips away, to cross her knees, but it hurt her cracked ribs too much, and he was too heavy and too strong. *Oh, please, St. Anne...* She spat some bloody saliva into the ski mask, and that delayed the violation. The Boss slapped her face absently, backhand, while he fumbled at his crotch. And then he screamed.

"Agh! Christ! My eye! Get him off, gah .. ahdammit, get him ... Aaah!" His weight lifted, and she felt a splash of hot blood across her belly, and there was Rosie, *good old Rosie, wonderful sick little dog,* attached to his face.

"Good girl, Rosie! <u>Good</u> girl, bite him good!" Rosie snarled acknowledgement while she clamped and chewed at the face behind the mask.

Gloved hands reached from behind her and pulled at Rosie. With each pull, more blood spilled down the mask and onto Faye. With her arms free and with the benefit of the distraction, Faye crawled as fast as she could toward the bedroom while the thugs yelled and Rosie snarled and furniture toppled in the living room. She stood to run, and fell face-first against the door frame, and no matter how she tried to limp straight, she couldn't hold a course to the bedside table, sitting there cockeyed up a dizzy slant of floor. Finally, she fell against the bed and worked her way on her knees toward the nightstand, and snatched open the drawer. Roscoe in hand at last, she stood and zagged back in time to see the Assistant Thug hold Rosie in the air like a football while Rosie snapped at his wrist, and hurl her against the stone fireplace. Rosie uttered a small cough and fell to the hearth, unmoving.

Furious, outraged, Faye tugged at the trigger twice before she remembered the safety, and pushed it off. The Boss Thug was kneeling by the fireplace with his hands clamped to his face, blood pouring through his fingers. *Good. I'll give you some more leaks in a just a second, bastard.* She fired off a shot at the Assistant, as the greater threat.

As promised, the first trigger pull dropped the hammer on an empty chamber. The Assistant spun at the snap, and began to run toward her. Shakily, she pointed the roscoe like a finger and pulled again;

and was rewarded by a satisfactory report. She missed, of course, even at a range of fifteen feet, but the spray of rock chips and the yowl of ricochet from the fireplace galvanized the pair of them. The Assistant yanked at the Boss's arm and hustled him staggering and screaming to the porch while Faye blazed away behind them, knocking a piece out of the door frame and putting another hole in a porch screen. *You'll thank me when some punk's wettin' his pants.*

They slammed out the screen door and down the steps, leaving a blood trail. Faye followed, and stood at the head of the steps while Assistant pulled Boss to his feet and ran him toward a Rust-Oleum orange pickup that was parked at the foot of her lane, heading outward for a fast getaway.

"Run, you bastard pieces of shit, run," Faye screamed, and shot at them twice, not expecting now to hit anything but pine needles and sand. A hole and a spider's web of cracks appeared in the window of the pickup, unfortunately well before they were close to it; but then Faye was thrilled to see the Assistant lurch and grab at his arm. She stumbled down the steps in a killing frenzy while the pickup roared to life and headed for the two-track lane. She adopted a two-hand shooter's grip, planted her feet in the centipede grass, sighted carefully on the back window of the pickup, and squeezed off ... a dry click. Out of ammo, damn. She pulled the trigger twice more; expecting, and getting, more futile clicks. The adrenaline fury drained away, leaving her with the trauma that had fueled it. She fell to her knees and retched a little bloody foam onto the grass.

***

Forde Morgan walked downhill on Lamont Street in the Mount Pleasant neighborhood of Northwest Washington, DC, marking addresses and gawking at majestic three-story row houses. Land, you could fit the population of most Gabbro County towns into one block of those things, and the entire population of the county would rattle around lost in a four-block area. Forde had spent a whole summer in Charlotte, North Carolina, and had passed through Raleigh and Richmond on trains, so he was not the biggest bumpkin a person could find in Washington. But still: the Nation's Capital!

He came at last to 1746 Lamont Street and stopped, heart pounding. At the critical moment, he turned and kept walking down the street, not ready to confront what lay behind that numbered door. Of course, the whole trip would be a stupid waste if he didn't, so he turned left at 18th Street, left again at Kilbourne Place, and circled the block. At his second approach, he forced himself to climb the steps and twist the old-fashioned bell set into the door. There, damn it.

A period of what passed for silence in this noisy place was followed by the clump of shoes. The door opened.

"Awright! It's the Morgan hisself. In the house wi' ye."

"Hello, Nora. You're looking good."

***

Three stories up on the Spirit Catcher, Annie Godfire heard the last two shots, and they confirmed an uneasy intuition that all was not well at River Cottage. She extinguished the torch and climbed down from her perch dropping the last ten feet to save time. She jogged toward the head of the path along the river that led to Faye's house, and with every step her anxiety grew. After ten steps, she burst into a run.

Faye dragged herself to the foot of the cottage stairs. From where she sprawled, they looked like an Amazonian ziggurat, receding into the steaming over-story. But Rosie ...

" 'osie," she croaked through swollen lips, and began to crawl up the stairs. Brave, great-hearted Rosie, tackling the Boss Thug in her pain and illness, now lying on the hearth, broken and alone. It was intolerable. Faye crawled upward, calling Rosie, the empty roscoe clonking every other step.

"Rosie ... Ro-osie! Rosie, you good, good girl, I'm coming, Mama's ... coming."

She reached the screen door, pushed it open, and crawled through. In the living room, Rosie lay on the hearth, still as death.

It took Annie Godfire six minutes to cover the mile between the Spirit Catcher and the cottage. She mounted the stairs three at a time, calling Faye's name, wincing at the sobs she had begun to hear when she was still on the river path. She found Faye crouched by the fireplace, holding Rosie to herself and pouring wrenched guttural sobs into Rosie's fur.

"Faye, honey, sister, my big sister, what is it? Did Rosie pass?"

Faye looked up, crazed, and returned her face to Rosie's still warm fur. Annie went to her and knelt, placing a gentle hand on Faye's back; it only caused Faye to shrink away and redouble her wailing. Annie sat back and watched, listening, crooning sisterly comfort. After a few minutes, the sobbing became less desperate, more long-winded; as if after a sprint, settling into a marathoner's pace good to last for hours. Annie knelt and picked up Faye, Rosie and all, and carried them back to the bedroom, depositing Faye and Rosie together on the bed. She gently pried the roscoe from Faye's hand, seeing now for the first time the blood on her shirt and belly, and the swelling bruises of the beating.

"What? Who done this?"

There was no change in the level or pace of Faye's sobbing. When she had quieted a little, Annie found a towel, dampened it, and sponged away the blood. When she saw that there was no wound under it, and no evidence but the bloody nose that it had come from Faye herself, she relaxed a little and settled next to her, holding, stroking, and murmuring comforts in a language spoken by no one in Gabbro County for over two hundred years.

Annie lay next to Faye and Rosie all afternoon, listening as the sobbing exhausted itself into troubled, and then quiet, breathing still interspersed by moans of pain and sorrow. At midday, a chill rain sent her in search of a blanket for the three of them. When the rain stopped, she rose and ran up the dripping river path to feed the goats and stow her tools. Returning to the river cottage, she brought balms and liniments that she used when women whose husbands beat them came to her for advice and comfort. She found Faye sitting up in kerosene light, holding Rosie across her lap. Her face was swollen and purple, still stained with brownish blood. She began to stand when Annie appeared, but gasped and clutched at her cracked ribs.

"Annie, thank you for coming, you're a life saver. I hope I didn't alarm you with ... my hysterical behavior."

"Don't be silly. Whose blood was that? Who beat you up?"

"Some of it's mine, but not all of it. A couple of guys in ski masks. Sent by Virgil Barnett at the towel factory, I expect. Or straight from Mason Merrydown. Because I dared to tell the truth about River Mills. Anyway, most of the blood was from the one who was trying to rape me. Rosie stopped him."

Annie put a hand under Rosie's head. "And Rosie's passed?"

"Gone. She saved me, Annie, and they killed her."

"Stand up here and let me look at you."

Faye grasped Annie's arm and stood, meekly flexing shoulders and knees and elbows for Annie to judge the damage. "Seems like you got off easier, compared to that Nora."

"No broken bones, I guess. I'm not sure about my ribs."

Annie probed and gently squeezed Faye's ribcage, and found two cracked, a third possible, but no outright breaks. "Why do you suppose they let you off easier?"

Faye shrugged, gingerly. "Beating me up was so much fun, they got the idea to rape me, so they cut it short to get on with that. But that's when Rosie ... oh, Annie, you can't believe how brave Rosie was, she went right for the guy who was yanking my shorts off, and sick as she was, she bit the bastard in the eye. That saved me long enough that I could get my pistol and chase them off."

"Well, good for her. Since when have you had a pistol?"

Faye ignored the question. "She gave her life for me, but see, here's the good part of that: she was dying of kidney failure anyhow, she had maybe a month to live, and instead of slow and painful, and then either being drugged to death by the vet, or shot by ... a, a guy who offered, instead of that, she got a quick, heroic death. She was saving me from harm, which was her life's ambition. I praised her while she was doing it, and she heard me, thank the merciful God. I will sing her praises to the end of my days, and God help me, I will write a poem about it that will make Rosie famous forever. I hope."

Annie saw the suffering, and the brittle crust of determination that held Faye over a cauldron of despair, and embraced them both. Faye struggled out and limped to the mantle, laughing and wincing.

"<u>And</u>, not only that, Annie, get this. See this?" She took from the mantle a bloody, pale and curly scrap about a half inch across. "It was in Rosie's mouth, kind of sticking out one side, and I thought she'd bitten the end of her tongue off when that subhuman asshole threw her against the fireplace. But look. What do you think it is?"

Annie turned it over, testing its hard-boiled consistency, and made a face. "Not the sort of thing I see very often."

"Oh, I think you do. I'm pretty sure this is part of an eyeball."

Faye passed the rest of the day in a brittle fever, skating over a frozen surface of panic, while the bruises and humiliation released their toxins into her blood and soul. When darkness came at last, Annie carried her down to the Eddy and walked into the shallows with Faye in her arms, gently lowering her into the water while she crooned ancient healing songs. When Faye began to relax, the tears came again, this time of resignation at what had been lost, perhaps never to return. She woke wailing twice in the night, first fighting off Annie, then clinging to her and trying to describe the black-gloved demons who had stalked and invaded her. Annie nodded, and sang, and rocked.

***

In Mount Pleasant, DC, Forde occupied the first two days of his visit with Nora Lundy in monument visiting and museum strolling. Nora accommodated him on a couch in the living room. Matters between them progressed briskly beyond the initial stirrings that Forde felt, to something that augmented his "messenger" feeling while still respecting Nora's warning not to trifle with her. And – after a sweaty-palm blurt in which he confessed and tried to explain about the messenger – the regard became approximately mutual. Halfway through the third day, strolling with Nora past the "Netherlands, XVII C." room at the National Gallery, Forde declared himself touristed out, and asked about the possibility of an afternoon of rest. Nora was agreeable, and put him to nap in her bedroom, saying that she had matters to conduct that would disturb his rest if he napped on the couch. She spent the next half hour pursuing union business by phone in the kitchen; then tiptoed up the stairs.

At 5:18 pm that afternoon, late sunlight crossing Rock Creek and the National Zoo found Nora's bedroom window. Nora raised herself on one elbow, bringing the auburn hair into the beam of gold. Forde was dazzled, and offered a dazzled smile. She reached for him across the rumpled sheet, ruffled his hair, and laid on the Bobbie Burns:

"Well, that was quite a luvely doin', Fordie, verra sa'isfyin' an' aw. But a bit bland, don't ya think? Like guid porridge. Sticks to the ribs, surely, but it could use a pinch o' salt, maybe some raisins or cinnamon on top. Or both. We'll just slip into the shower now, you and me, an' get our breath back. We can run down to Adams-Morgan for some dinner, and maybe when we come home I could show you a few wee things Scots have invented to keep us warm o' nights."

***

On Sunday morning, they dug Rosie's grave in the soft sand under the cottage steps; to the distant peal of church bells, Faye gently lowered the furry corpse, wrapped in her favorite sleeping towel, to the bottom. When it was filled in, and Rosie's water bowl dug into place as a marker, Annie gave Faye a drink of the pale blue Lumbee cordial with which they sealed every important event. It dried her tears.

"Now, back to bed."

"Yes. Stay with me?"

"Of course."

"I will remem' Rosie every time I ... " she gestured at the steps overhead.

"Yes. Good. Come along, now."

9.

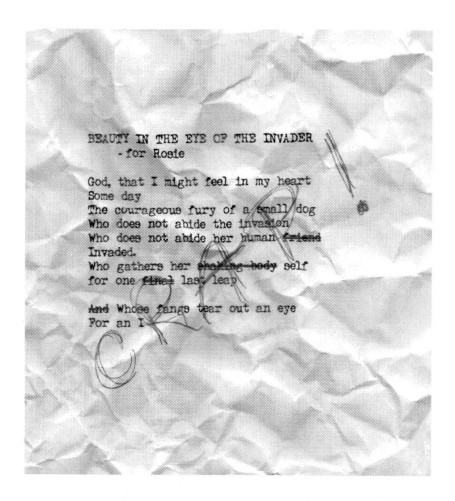

BEAUTY IN THE EYE OF THE INVADER
    - for Rosie

God, that I might feel in my heart
Some day
The courageous fury of a small dog
Who does not abide the invasion
Who does not abide her human ~~friend~~
Invaded.
Who gathers her ~~shaking body~~ self
for one ~~final~~ last leap

~~And~~ Whose fangs tear out an eye
For an I

10.

F ROM THE GABBRO *INTELLIGENCER* FOR WEDNESDAY,
September 23, 1964:

THIS TOWN'S TIMES
by
M. Faye Bynum
Associate Editor

On Saturday morning last, two representatives of
Merrydown Industries called on me to suggest editorial changes in last week's column about the misfortunes of Sedalia Baley and the inhuman working conditions at River Mills. I am still recovering from their
suggestions; the bleeding has stopped, my cracked
ribs are taped, and I suppose my black eyes will fade
back to normal in a week or so. I was saved from
being brutally raped only by the heroic intervention
of my brave little dog Rosie, who gave her life to save
me. I have reported the assault to Sheriff Rathbun,
and endured his skeptical questioning about whether
my provocative behavior might have brought on the
"alleged incident." Thank you so much, Sheriff.

Naturally, River Mills and Merrydown Industries
deny any connection with this brutal thuggery, which

is of a piece with the recent savaging of the union organizer Nora Lundy. No one with a grain of sense will believe their denials.

***

Faye spent the rest of Forde's absence managing the *Intelligencer* from the cottage at Morgan's Eddy or from behind the closed door of her office. Annie Godfire lived and slept with her for that week, ignoring the Spirit Catcher to take on the more pressing job of rebuilding Faye Bynum. They swam together in the Eddy, at midday when the sun struck deep into its slow rotation, and at night under the stars. Afterward, exhausted from pain and exertion, Faye would lie quietly on a towel before the fireplace while Annie rubbed away the pain and horror with liniments that left her body as cool and aromatic as a spruce forest. When the demons had come and gone, she began to dream of Northern forests, Northern Lights; clean, chilly birch woods in Canada or Maine, while the liniments carried the pain into the air and the herbs they brought soaked into her body. Afterward, Annie carried her, wrapped in flannel and drugged by the fumes, to the bedroom to sleep and heal.

Faye loved the sensation of being lifted in Annie's arms and carried like a baby to the cozy bed, to lie with Annie and murmur and drowse. "This is heaven, Annie. I can't wish for you to get beaten up, so I could do it for you, but some day I will, regardless."

"Shut up. It's as good for me as it is for you. I was getting kind of lonesome out there, you an' Forde so took up with your newspaper. It's a treat to be so close to you, Faye."

But Annie's magic was powerless to keep the demons away. They came every night, sometimes standing in the shadows beyond the bedroom door and watching her, or stalking and trapping, pulling on their black gloves to send her into darkness from which she would wake, whimpering, while Annie held her and sang the ancient songs.

But on Friday morning, feeling ready for combat again, she called Virgil Barnett to confront him about his thugs - and, she supposed, to gloat over how she and Rosie had maimed and defeated them. Barnett claimed no knowledge of any thugs, and was only mildly indignant about the Sedalia Baley interview.

"It's a lucky thing that we had nothing to do with your alleged roughing-up, or we'd be bringing an action against you for discharge of an unlicensed firearm. As it is, word has reached me that you have been seeing a fellow who is known to enjoy rough sex. Are you sure your unfortunate injuries were not suffered quite late at night a week or so ago?"

Faye slammed her desktop. "None of your fucking business, you slimy bastard!"

"Indeed not; I was referring to yours."

She started to yell at him, but had to laugh, which pretty much lost her the righteous high ground of indignation. "Mr. Barnett, you are an unscrupulous bastard, but a quick wit. I take back the 'slimy'."

"The fact is, as I'm sure you can figure out, Miss Bynum, there is not a damn thing anyone is going to do about Miss Baley. We have no retirement or workmen's compensation program here, or anywhere in the Merrydown Organization. We provide legally adequate safety measures, and we have broken no laws of the State of North Carolina, or of the Federal Government. We can ignore your muckraking be-cause no one can touch us."

"Least of all Sedalia Baley. Her hand is gone."

Barnett chuckled. "Unfortunate; but not our fault. Her machine was - speaking off the record here - equipped with a warning device, which she evidently ignored, on her own responsibility."

"Because she'd been worked ragged, and one more use of the stop pedal would have cost her the job. Why are we off the record, suddenly?"

"Because <u>on</u> the record, there was no accident. Miss Baley has abandoned her position with River Mills by the fact of not showing up for work the morning following the alleged accident. We had no choice but to hire a replacement so that production can continue, and the rest of the workforce be paid this month."

"<u>Alleged</u> accident? You put out a press release on it!"

"I saw it in the *Intelligencer*. Believe me, no one in this office has any knowledge of that alleged release. For the record, our theory is that it is a fake, fabricated by some third party, possibly TWUA."

"Oh, I can't believe this. The release came to our office in an envelope that bore the return address of River Mills."

"Did it really? That would imply that someone here is circulating false information. Or, possibly, someone stole some letterhead. But we have long suspected that TWUA had a mole in our work force. Was there a name associated with the release? An information telephone? Did anyone examine it for fingerprints?"

Faye demurred. "I cannot release any information that may - I stress, <u>may</u> - have become associated with your press release. Meantime, do I understand that you deny that Miss Baley was injured at your plant? Have you seen the remains of her hand?"

"As I said, and on the record now, I have seen no part of Miss Baley since last week. If - I stress, <u>if</u> - she was injured, it was not at River Mills. There is no record of any accident here this entire month."

"I bet there isn't. When did you have your last accident, if ever?"

"Let me see ... according to our records, River Mills has operated without a work stoppage due to accident for 3652 consecutive days. Today will be the 3653rd."

"Goodness. Must be about ten years."

"Ten years to the day. Thank you for reminding me. I'll make an announcement."

Public response to the Sedalia Baley story was limited to a Letter to the Editor noting that after all, the victim was a Baley, and thus likely to have been negligent in some way, because what else could you expect from one of that worthless bunch? Faye crumpled it up, uncrumpled it, and borrowed Stoker's lighter to set fire to it on the front steps of the *Intelligencer* building.

***

From the Gabbro *Intelligencer* for Friday, September 25:

THIS TOWN'S TIMES

(Associate Editor M. Faye Bynum is away. Her column will resume when she returns.)

***

Forde Morgan returned to the *Intelligencer* on Sunday, September 27, to find a note from Faye:

9/26

Forde -

Welcome back. While you were gone, I had some difficulty that you can read about in my column for 9/23, in case you were unable to find a newsstand copy of the Intelligencer in Washington.

Annie has been helping me heal, but I estimate it will take me some weeks to recover fully. Thus, I will be away from the office for a medical leave of absence, effective the day of your return. I have enough vacation time accumulated to last me until some time in the 21st Century. You might want to bring in second-cousin-once-removed Forsythe to help out in my absence. She is at least as competent as the rest of the staff, and will work harder.

Best wishes. I will be on the road Northward like Stuart

Little, so I doubt you will be able to reach me. I'll call in when I can. The edition for Monday the 28ᵗʰ is ready to go. Follow up on Rob's coverage of cross-country at Douglass - something fishy there.

Thank you for your kind understanding.

Faye

Forde, oppressed by guilt about his tarriance in Washington while Faye was recovering from her beating and holding the *Intelligencer* together until his return, had no objections and made no demur. While Faye's yellow Beetle droned north on I-95 in search of birch forests, he sat in his office, dreaming of sunshine and auburn hair, more or less involuntarily reviewing his new store of carnal knowledge, and trying to sort things whose nature and labels changed every time he looked at them.

***

As she drove, Faye twice caught motion in the corner of her eye: the wag of a tail, the lolling of a Rosie tongue. Her head snapped to the right, and each time, the empty passenger seat mocked her. She was tempted to stop for a hitchhiker - there were many, and one of them was small, solitary and female - if only to fill the seat with someone tangible. But she was still jumpy and fearful even of solitary girls, and wanted to be alone with her thoughts while she fled northward.

Those were not cheerful. Her columns about Sedalia Baley and her own beating as a reward for them drew almost no reader response or anything from the *Intelligencer* staff beyond a stop-in to her office by Rob Stoker the sportswriter, who wanted to see just how black her eyes were, and a handwritten comment from Sharon the receptionist at the bottom of Faye's copy of her carefully typed "Notice," in which she stated her intention to leave the paper on October 15 in order to prepare for wedding her long-time boyfriend Ellis Peavey, the associate pharmacist at Rexall.

Sorry to learn of your unfortunate mishap. Best wishes, Sharon

Faye left Sharon's notice on Forde's desk, with an attached memo recommending in the strongest terms she could muster, that the position be offered to Sedalia Baley.

***

Worthless bunch. Not the Baleys; though, sure, as a group they might or might not be a cut below the mediocre Gabbro average in the way of education, achievement, and general gumption. No, the whole damn population of Gabbro County. Nothing that special about Gabbro, either, so ...

Faye's glance, tricked by a passing billboard, shot to the passenger seat, and found it empty again. *The whole state of North Carolina. South Carolina too. The whole sucking Southland can take their Dixie Charm and shove it.*

Over her years in Gabbro, Faye had come to see that the place had charm galore when it chose to exert it, and a human warmth that she did not recall experiencing as a high school girl in St. Louis. The place was filled to saturation with a kind of inarticulate spirituality that expressed itself in unexpected ways that seldom involved any of the host of churches that crowded the Services page on Friday. Her little cottage on Morgan's Eddy would probably rank high among salubrious locations in the continental United States; and her company-keeping friend Forde was good-hearted; surely one of the best-hearted people she would ever know.

Nevertheless (Bold face, italic; red print, if her mind had access to a bicolor ribbon): **Nevertheless**, there was that undercurrent of lethality.

The Southland was a fatally dangerous place, a place where the surface kindness and good manners by which people reconciled themselves to the poverty of their situations could break through and drop you into a hell of violence, callousness and ignorance that would gag Satan himself. You could see it in the mask-like affect of people who were in the very process of wishing one well; in the meanness, the lagging educational statistics, and the indifference to human suffering — as long as that suffering was confined to a stratum below one's own in the manifold strata of Southern life. And, of course, in the impunity with which anyone with a lot of money could send thugs to beat, humiliate, and rape whoever stood in the way of their getting still more money.

Faye supposed that losing the Civil War had something to do with it, not to mention the soul-rotting effect of living in a slave-owning society or, worse yet, owning some. But goodness, the Civil War was done with a hundred years ago; there were surely none left who were conscious of those things - *a hundred people-years, that is. People as old as Rosie might still remember.*

Faye passed through Richmond *home of the Confederate government!* and a direction sign to the site of the Siege of Bermuda Hundred. A toll booth loomed out of the haze and shimmer of I-95. *PASSENGER CARS .35¢. Fine, that's a third of a penny, you ignorant crackers. Keep the change.* She fished in the ashtray and came up with a quarter and two nickels. *Thank you, Ma'am. Don't mention it, Honeh.*

No, but you didn't have to remember the sieges and slaughters, or have fossilized Confederate bones circulating in your front yard to have that memory passed down to you by helpful neighbors who have kept it fresh for a century. She remembered Horatio Haney, the Negro intern at the Charlotte *Star-Dispatch*, murdered by the Klan for the sin of writing in a "white" newspaper; the Jim Crow management of Gabbro County public schools; the whites-only plush seats on the bus that had brought her to Gabbro in the first place. Southern society, "Our Heritage," to quote the Gabbro Jaycees, was diligent in keeping fresh the resentful memory of the sins and suffering of the past.

But why? Why on earth clutch to your breast the humiliation of being so spectacularly wrong and so thoroughly defeated and occupied? What possible joy or gain could there be in that, beyond sullen and graceless defiance of the Yankee-contaminated Civil Rights movement?

What it was, she concluded with a sense of doom, was that Southerners lived an unspoken and unacknowledged conspiracy to Southernize each other, to seduce their neighbors with Southern Charm and Southern Comfort to the point where they could ignore the ugliness of Southern Life: the violence, the lethal diet, the expensive and soul-rotting racism, the prideful embrace of ignorance and callousness, the selling-out of Southern communities to Northern industries with the promise of low taxes (stingy public spending) and cheap (ignorant, illiterate, and hungry) labor; and the dependence on Northern productivity to keep filling up the Federal treasury with tax dollars for Federal welfare, farm, and health programs that it was the accepted norm to disdain and reject with one hand and stuff into one's pockets as fast as possible with the other. In the trauma and devastation of Reconstruction, Southerners had invented Our Heritage as a consolation and pain-killer. It turned out to be as addictive as heroin; and once you were hooked, it was nearly impossible to get clean.

Well. Faye looked out on the smiling sunshine of the Southland and admitted that it was easy to get carried away with cynicism about the South, because the South took so much trouble to make it easy. What could she call Gabbro's tolerance of sexual "company-keeping" and her libertine reputation, but a kind of social Christian acceptance mostly unknown in the North? Not that it went so far as to shelter her from thuggery and rape, which most of Gabbro would have agreed she was courting with that reputation and with her free-thinking editorials. She pressed north up the map, not sure what she was seeking, but clear about what she was fleeing.

The coastal plain of Virginia, full of small rivers, toll booths and wet ground, passed by and she crossed the Potomac into the District of Columbia. She thought vaguely of stopping to look up Nora Lundy, but decided against it. She was tired of driving. Her butt and ribs ached from the way the Beetle pummeled the sores and bruises of her beating, but she wanted to get out of the South before she quit for this first day. She followed the Interstate numbly, thinking of New England or nothing by turns, and at sunset she found a little motel north of Baltimore that at least did not mention Dixie in its name. Crab cakes, coleslaw, and a glass or two of Moselle improved her outlook; she fell into bed and - when the night demons had finished with her - dreamed of little town squares with flaming maple trees, white steeples, and rocky coastlines. In one of them, a monument listed the names of a hundred men who had died a hundred years ago at Bermuda Hundred. At dawn, she filled her tank, sniffing with glee a Yankee nip in the pale air.

With refugee traffic from the Bronx, she met the leading edge of fall colors in Connecticut, and they intensified as she drove up Connecticut 15 (*"Road Legally Closed" but full of trucks; what the hell is that supposed to mean?*) into Massachusetts. Signposts morphed into quaint ogee'd shapes, and lo, in Saltannic, Massachusetts, hard under the New Hampshire border, she found a village green with a white-steepled church surrounded by blazing maples. She parked by a drugstore and bought a cheap camera with which to record it all, maybe to rub the Forde's nose in how pretty the world could be, if you got your butt in gear and went out to find it. She was surprised when the thought of Gabbro people made her feel lonely.

She went back into the drugstore for late lunch and got a plate of fried clams that was heavenly, and terribly unhealthy, she supposed.

"Sumpna drink widdat? Frap?"

"Uh ... coffee, please."

"Regula?"

"Sorry, what's that?"

The waitress looked martyred. "Regula means cream and suga, honey. Where you from, anyway? South somewheah?"

"North Carolina. Regular's fine."

"Watcha doin up heah? Leaf peepin?

"I'm on vacation. I'm sick of mint juleps and sweet tea and fake smiles."

"Won't find none a them here. Real smiles, neither."

"Uh huh. This town have a newspaper?"

A mug clattered onto the counter, and was filled with pale coffee. "Next the tawnics."

"The ... ?"

"The tawnics. By the daw." Vaguely flipped hand.

Faye turned toward the door and saw a rack of Saltannic *Examiners* next to a coke machine. "Oh. I meant the office. That's what I do, for a job."

"Lucky you. Two streets ova, Beech Street."

The *Examiner* office smelled - printing ink and hot newsprint dust - exactly like the *Intelligencer*. The setup was enough different that Faye was a little disoriented, blinking in the dimness, from which another Yankee voice emerged.

"Pahssonals close out in ten minutes, Miss."

Faye smiled. Why didn't the *Intelligencer* run Personals? Bet we'd make a mint. Julep. "Well, I can't think up anything that'll save me in ten minutes, so never mind. No, I came to chat with the editor, if he's available."

"Mista Bahnwell's with a visita just now. Have a seat?"

"Thank you."

Faye picked up a copy of the *Examiner* and pretended to read it ("*Hub Cops Crack Fake Sox Tix Pact*") while she asked herself what she was doing here, besides shunning more driving in the now torturous Beetle. Well, she was being on vacation, but not just buzzing through places. She was digging beneath the touristic surface. And besides ...

"Miss? No openings this month." A dumpy little guy with a comb-over and a pipe, the ashes of which dotted his pinstriped blue vest.

Half-glasses. Blue pants, brown shoes that were unevenly worn, as if from some orthopedic misfortune.

"Oh? No, I'm not looking for a job." *I could never write your kind of headlines.* She stood and offered a hand. "Are you the editor? Faye Bynum, with the Gabbro *Intelligencer.*"

"No, really? *The* Faye Bynum?"

Faye allowed herself a momentary fluster. *My God, I'm famous. All from that piddly ...* "Well, yes, I ... Oh. You're kidding, aren't you?"

The guy grinned, charmingly for a New Englander, Faye supposed. "Oh, pretty much. Your name does ring a very faint bell. Wait, don't tell me ... " He looked at the ceiling, then shrugged, a little crookedly. "Nope. I give up."

"Well, I don't know that there's any bell to ring. I'm the Associate Editor of a little three-day-a-week rag down in North Carolina, and I do love small-town papers. I just wanted to -"

"Wait, I know. You have a book of columns out, don't you?"

"So do half the editors in the South. We're a colorful bunch, and civilized people just adore reading about colorful Tobacco Road do-in's. You're probably thinking about Harry Golden or Sam Ragan."

The handshake became a tug. "Come with me. Ted Barnwell, Editor in Chief here, 'cause there in't but one editor in the whole place. You got two, do you?" He limped through a door behind the reception counter and down a dim corridor that shook with the rumble of presses knocking out another edition.

"Yes ... Well, one point about six, most weeks."

"Unh. We got one of those, too, in Sports. Here."

Faye glimpsed a metal brace on his ankle as he swung around the door to an office - the place his hand grabbed the door frame was worn to bare wood - and pulled from a bookcase ... Well, Faye would be damned. *This Town's Times,* by M. Faye Bynum; Southern Lights Press, Chapel Hill, NC, 1959. Faye's eyes prickled, and she thought she might faint.

"Oh. Oh, my gosh. Oh, if this isn't the biggest thrill of a dull life, I ... Can I kiss you?"

"Alice out there'n reception a'd never shut up about it." He shrugged. "You wanted to get together for a drink after I get this run out the door, you tell me what you're working on next, how come you're so young, I'd be open to that. You sure don't fit my mental picture of the woman that wrote that book."

**

After an afternoon of leaf-peeping and covered bridges, Faye entered the dimness of Sal's Grill with her guard up. She was already kicking herself for agreeing to this rendezvous. It was just the kind of thing that winds up in some ratty motel, or in groping, wrestling, slapping, and fleeing, and hard feelings all around. She had been as good as raped a matter of days ago, and she needed to rebuild and reaffirm her sovereignty over her own body. She very nearly turned around when she saw the dive Ted Barnwell had chosen for their drink.

But when he stood to welcome her — if there is an emotion that is a hybrid of relief and slight indignation, Faye experienced it. Seated at Barnwell's table was a handsome woman with real-looking blonde hair, half-glasses, and a perilous neckline, whom he introduced as his wife Marlene. Faye groped for a chair and sat.

"Faye wrote that book about the little town in North Carolina you liked so much, Honey." He turned to Faye. "What was the name of the town again, Miss Bynum?"

"Gabbro, you dope," Marlene said. "I never lahfed so hod in my life. I just have to come down there and meet some of those folks. That Salonnette bunch is just a hoot. What are you drinking, Hon?"

"I ... well, I guess a glass of white wine."

"Oh, I don't think so, do you, Teddy? You ever try Massachusetts wine, Faye? We mostly use it to kill rats. Here, let's see ... " She picked up a drinks menu. "Mmm ... here you go. Evva had a Sledge Hamma?"

Faye never quite got straight what goes into a Sledge Hammer, but it was well named. Some time during her second one, Ted Barnwell produced his copy of <u>This Town's Times</u> and insisted on a signature on the title page. Marlene plucked it out of her hand when she had finished a scrawled benediction and signature.

"Now then, dear, I think you'd better let us drive you back to your motel, don't you? Not that we're tired of your company, but I can see that you're just exhausted."

Faye nodded, and stood. "Oh. But."

Marlene raised an eyebrow.

"But I don't have a motel. I meant to be in New Hampshire by now. Maybe you could suggest?"

"Pooh. Ted, take the Dot, and I'll go with Faye. You're coming home with us, Hon."

It was while Faye was looking for a place to hang her skirt and blouse, and Marlene was putting sheets on the bed in their spare room — airplane models hanging from the ceiling on black thread, ripply cutouts of Ted Williams and Carl Yastrzemski pasted to the walls — that Marlene interrupted a song of praise for someplace called Sebago Lake, in Maine; stepped back and frowned at Faye.

"Honey, get rid a him."

"Who?"

"Don't be cute with me. Whatever boyfriend gave you all these bruises, and the rib tape. I thought that was a funny shade of mascara."

Faye shook her head. "No boyfriend. Couple of company goons worked me over after I criticized their work envir'ment in a editorial."

"Oh, deah. Speak out on anything in public, pay the price. I worry about Ted all the time. What company?"

"Oh ... Little two-bit towel factory. Air full of cotton dust, hot as the hinges, almost no break time, deafening noise. A woman running a fabric-cutting machine got her hand sliced off, and I din't say it was her own fault. So Merrydown sent a couple of thugs to rough me up. But my little dog -"

"Merrydown? Would that be Mason Merrydown? Oh, never mind, of course it would." She sat back on the bed and looked at Faye, evidently weighing what she would say next. "Listen, how old would you say Ted Barnwell is?"

Faye shrugged, wanting to get on with singing Rosie's praises. "Dunno. Fifty-something? But my little Rosie -"

"Ted will be forty-one in November. Twelve years ago, he criticized Mason Merrydown in print."

Faye stared at Marlene, one foot in the air, a thumb hooked into the waistband of her pantyhose. "And got beat up?"

"He was in the hospital for two months. Both legs broken. His knees will never work right. He was a half inch shorter on one side by the time they finished screwing his ankle back together." She sighed. "Ted was a halfback in college. He looked seven feet tall to me, and he was smot and handsome and funny." She shrugged. "Still is, far as I'm concerned. But you have to know where to look now, to see it."

Sober suddenly, Faye sat on the bed, making a board rattle. "That mean, lowdown son of a bitch. Marlene, why didn't he sue them, or something? Couldn't the police ... " She tossed a hand. "Oh, listen to me."

"Uh huh. The cops jumped right in an' caught the guys that beat you up, did they?"

"No, of course not. I was lucky - we're too little to have cops, we have a county sheriff, but same thing. I was lucky he didn't arrest me for defamation of character."

Marlene smirked. "The goons that beat up Ted wore U.S. Ommy uniforms, in case anybody happened to see it going on. Nobody did, of course."

"Wait a minute. What was Merrydown doing up here? thought he was only North Carolina's problem."

"Have you seen our mills?"

"I'm kind of taking a break from mills, while I put myself back together."

"Wouldn't matter. The big Saltannic Mill is now Saltannic Mall. Chamber a Commerce tries to make it nostalgic cute by keeping the overhead shahfts and pulleys, turning the lights down, to look like kerosene. It's full of used book stores, balloon-and-ribbon outfits and antique co-ops, which one or another of 'em goes belly-up every other month. Mason Merrydown bought Saltannic Mills for a song, 'cause it wasn't competing with sweatshops in Mexico and Singapore ... and *North Carolina,* honey. He fired all the union employees and declared bankruptcy so he could get busy with what the point was all along, taking out what he could use, some machinery the old owners bought after the War when things looked promising, and shipping it south. He sold the shell back to the city for the same's he paid for it, which was a little wrinkle he'd put in the purchase contract while nobody was looking.

"Saltannic - the town, I mean - went flat broke. Whole families moved to Boston or Hotford, looking for work like Okies in the '30's. Come to think, a bunch did move to California. What we got now, we got retired folks drawing Social, we got a little plastics plant with headquarters in Lowell, that employs a quarter of what the mill did, and could be shut down any time Lowell gets the sniffles. We got a couple banks that employ total a dozen people, most 'em knocking down five - six thousand a year for paperwork on loans that are killing the rest of us. Oh, yeah, and we got the *Examiner,* which has learned to look on the bright side and print wire stories a day late, which is killing Ted. The rest of us make a living by teaching school and taking in each other's laundry."

Faye sat on the edge of the bed and tried to scratch itchy places under her rib tape. "Sounds awful familiar. You might have been talking about Gabbro."

"I suppose. Except you got our mill."

Faye sighed. "True. Lucky us."

When Marlene had pointed out the bathroom and brought towels,

Faye lowered herself warily into the bed. The Sledge Hammers were no protection against night demons who had morphed from men in ski masks to animals - badgers or bears, no telling - with coarse, shaggy pelts, one of which was in a floral motif. She woke shouting at them in darkness the color of their gloves. At breakfast, no one mentioned the shouts, but Ted and Marlene seemed cordially wary, as if they were afraid of being stuck with a raving cripple indefinitely. They again sang the praises of Sebago Lake in terms that seemed to imply that she might find it therapeutic. Faye left as soon as she could, smiling hard.

11.

THE WEATHER TURNED DRIZZLY AND GRAY AS SHE entered Maine. Packing in a hurry to shake the dust of Gabbro from her mind, Faye had brought some cool-weather clothing, by Gabbro standards; toiletries and the Remington rested on the back seat with a ream of paper that she was determined to fill with creative writing; but she had not thought to include a raincoat. North of Portland, she spotted a Goodwill shop, and got herself a waterproof shell with a hood, and a zippered sweater that seemed to have been made out of raw lamb's wool and old ski socks. It was a little repulsive, but warm, and the zipper worked. She put them on the counter, and smiled at the lady behind it.

"Land, this is nice stuff, for the price."

"Summa people."

"Pardon?"

"Oh, listen to you, Honey. Summa people is what we got ta live on hereabouts. Come down and buy themselves Maine-lookin' geah, and then find out they don't got room in their luggage when it's time to go back to New Yahk."

"Well their loss is my gain, I guess."

"They can affahd it, easy. That be all?"

"Ye — No. Is there a working mill around here?"

"You mean sawmill, grist, wool, what?"

"Clothing, I guess."

"One or two, mostly woolen. Hahf what they do, they dress up and re-enact Down-East Yankee life, dippin candles, shoein horses. Lobstah fishermen in authentic-lookin sweatas like you got there. Don't know if any of 'em's open this late. Lorenzo?"

"Eah?" A weathered-looking man stuck his head out of a back room.

"That woolen mill ovah Sebago still open?"

"Ayuh. Closin up this weekend."

"Ayuh." She turned to Faye. "Sebago's fifty miles west. Pretty place."

"Very helpful of you. Thank you, hear?"

"Y'all hurreh back, Honeh."

"Ayuh."

***

Forde Morgan reached a Kleenex across his desk for Jenny McCall. "And I'm supposed to fix that exactly how?"

"Fire him, Forde. He grabbed my ..." Jenny clouded up again at the memory. "My p - private parts, right in front of the press guys. His behavior is a firing offense."

"I'll have a serious talk with him, and get him straightened out. But you gotta understand, Gabbro's four an' oh this season, undefeated and unscored-on. This could be the year for a state single-A championship. Circulation's going through the roof, because Rob has finally found something he can write about decently. We got to leave him, just 'til the season's over. It's the first of October already, and we don't have time to break in a new sports guy."

"Yeah, and then guess what, it's basketball season, and goddamn Rob will get inspired again, and you'll let him keep it up."

"Aw, Jenny, c'mon. All the good seniors graduated, basketball's gonna stink this year."

Jenny stared at him, and Forde blushed and raised a hand. "OK. Give me five weeks, to the end of football. I'll haul Rob in this afternoon yet, and put the fear of God in him, keep his hands to himself. I'll move his desk down to the hall outside the press room, you won't even have to see him. If you don't vouch personally for his good behavior from tomorrow morning on, I will put him on terminal leave."

Jenny spluttered. "Terminal leave? Fire the stupid bastard!"

"That's what firing is, since we got the new labor agreement. I can't make him go in five minutes, he's got to have a week's notice."

Jenny shrugged. "I guess. I suppose you'll tell him it was me that -"

"No, of course not. 'Course, if you're the only one he's been grabbing, it won't be too hard for him to figure out who complained to me."

"No, Sharon too, but she's leaving, so she doesn't give a darn. I don't know about the cleaning lady, but she's the only other woman around, with Faye in God-knows-where, Alaska."

"Maine. Anyways, you can't complain about him and stay anonymous. Life doesn't -"

"When's she coming back, anyways?"

"She'll be back in due course. She's still getting over all that, what happened."

"Well, she needs to toughen up. The place is a squalid mess when she's not around." *Squalid* had been the Word of the Day on Jenny's calendar last Tuesday.

"I'll be sure to tell her."

Forde was trying to focus on football standings when Sharon buzzed his phone. "Mr. Morgan, Mr. Merrydown is on his way back."

***

Faye Bynum lay face down on a towel on a rubber float in a cove on the western edge of Sebago Lake. The strings of a bikini top scribbled on the float beside her. The rainy weather had given way to a warm, sunny spell, and she was taking advantage to get some vitamin D into skin she had freed last night, tediously with polish remover, from rib tape. She was getting a little cool as the afternoon progressed, but the sun was warm on her back and her dark hair, and she did not fancy moving enough to tie up and wrap in the towel. Not yet. She breathed in, and felt only a slight objection from the worst of the cracked ribs. The others, along with her soul, were very content to be as they were.

Small waves licked the float in a drowsy rhythm. Aged-looking dragonflies skimmed the water, browsing the surface for a snack. The air she inhaled smelled of lake water, rubber, and toweling, a scent she associated with lazy afternoons as a small girl, napping while heroic Daddy earned money flying yokels around in his Gilmore Racer. *I am out of the South at last. I am in New England, and it agrees with me. If it knows what's good for it.* She closed her eyes, gently smacked her lips, and dozed, making up for sleep the demons had stolen. A breeze dawdled out from the slowly receding shore, murmuring about balsam and charcoal starter.

***

The face that peered around Forde Morgan's Venetian blind was not that of Mason Merrydown. A chunky guy in a tight dark suit scowled at Forde, sidled in, and took up a position beside the door. He was followed by a skinny thug wearing shades and a sling, who occupied the other side of the door. Mason Merrydown was next, scowling like the others. Things did not seem very merry with them.

"Good morning, Mr. Merrydown." *How did you wake so soon?* "Would you like to introduce your associates?"

"No. I'm here to put before you a proposition you might find attractive."

"Oh, come on. Isn't that supposed to go, 'An offer you can't refuse?'"

"Mister Morgan, do not think you can get smart with me." Merrydown smiled one-sidedly. "Though in fact, I believe you will find this proposition both attractive and difficult to refuse. I am talking here about Gabbro Labor Appreciation Day."

"GLAD. I already like it. Which particular laborers do you see us appreciating?"

"Our interest is in celebrating the loyalty and hard work of the good folk down at River Mills. You want to chip in your little crew here, or if any other enterprises in the county want to, why, they're welcome, of course."

"I see. You might want to chip in this fella with the sling, for example. Line-of-duty injury, was it? Gunshot, by any chance?"

The guy scowled, and Merrydown snapped, "None of your bidnis. Merrydown Industries will underwrite whatever costs may be associated with the parade. The *Intelligencer* will provide publicity and favorable editorial commentary. We are strongly concerned that the Bynum woman will be on board, and that her column in particular will positively glow in its endorsement of the civic benefits accruing from River Mills. Am I clear?"

"Perfectly. Miss Bynum is on leave for an indefinite time, following an incident that Lefty, there, can probably fill you in on better than I could. It is beyond belief that she would wish to lend support to any event that is connected with Merrydown Industries."

"Her wishes will prove immaterial in this and other future matters." He turned to the thugs bracketing the doorway. "Getting into some touchy financial stuff here, fellas. Wait for me on the sidewalk."

***

Faye screamed and jerked awake as a gout of icy lake water landed across her back. A mocking kid face stared at her and launched another fistful of lake water at her face.

"Jesus, you little brat!"

"Ha ha, saw ya titty."

"You little blister, get the hell out of here or I'll drown you like a rat."

A ten-or-twelvish kid with a sunbleached crew cut and bronze skin that reminded her unhappily of Terry Morgan's, dove under the float and heaved upward to tip her into the water. As she struggled to the surface, she saw the bikini top settling gently into the depths and dove after it. She caught it, surfaced, and trod water until she had it snugly tied; then looked around for the kid.

No kid; but a foamy disturbance heading for shore. She was far out from that shore; the float was behind her, drifting toward mid-lake with the persistent mild breeze. She realized that she was suddenly in a fix. She could let the float go, and try to swim to shore, which looked maybe, or barely, possible; or she could pursue the float toward mid-lake, where it would save her if she caught up with it, or leave her to drown if she didn't. The longer she waited to decide, the more surely she would fail and drown in either case. Going for shore had the advantage that the shore was at least not fleeing her; but the disadvantage that she would be swimming against the breeze and the chop that it was now raising. The float was still no more than a hundred feet away, with the towel dragging in the water like a sea anchor; and if she lost them, she would have to pay for them. She turned and struck out toward mid-lake in pursuit.

***

"Tell me, Mr. Morgan. How are things going along, financially, with the *Intelligencer?*"

"We're doing OK."

"And whose money is keeping this failing enterprise afloat?"

"Is that part of Merrydown Industries' need-to-know?"

"In fact it is. What you meant to say, I believe, is that Gabbro Prudent Savings and Loan holds a substantial note dated January 2, 1960, that will come due five years from date, which is to say January 2, 1965. A matter of three months or so from today."

"Yes. So what? Benny Willingham tells me there won't be a problem with renewing and extending. We're making regular payments."

"I bought Gabbro Prudent this morning. I own your note, Mr. Morgan. I see that the regular payments you have been making cover very little more than interest. If you fail to cooperate in this very simple civic gesture that I have outlined, I may have to conclude that the Gabbro *Intelligencer* is no longer a viable enterprise, nor relevant to the health and well-being of the County, and that it has come time to liquidate it entirely, sell off its assets, and relieve its staff of their duties."

***

"... she comes. Think she's coming around, hey." The kissing mouth returned and continued its invasion. Faye recoiled and vomited.

"Agh! Ge'way. Ow, 'at hurze. Hurts! Ow!"

"Yep, sorry about that, lady. Couldn't help crackin' a couple, or I'd a lost ya for sure."

"Awreh ..." She retched, painfully. "Awready -"

Faye looked around at a circle of curious faces. The float! The damn float, that kept drawing near, and then dancing ahead toward midlake, out of the wind shadow of the shore and into a hearty breeze; drifting, teasing and snatching itself away while she got more and more exhausted, and her arms ached, her ribs started killing her, she was drinking more lake water with every breath; trying to rest by floating, but the chop kept pushing water up her nose; trying to tread water, when everything was heavy, and all the time the float slipping away ... Cramps in her left leg and her ribs; her face barely above water, then not; the dark water, the receding glimmer of sunshine above.

"Uh. Ohh ... Oh, my God!"

"Ayup."

"I about drowned, didn't I?"

The kissing guy - buck-toothed and, well, homely, really, his face an assembly of ungainly angles that looked like the aftermath of a 36-wheel wreck on the interstate, but with kind eyes and a streak of wet corn-silk hair over his brow, sat back in his soaked clothing and grinned at her. "Prob'ly. Whatcha, trying to swim the lake? Picked a good day for it, that west breeze and all. Still, not too many folks ever done that, first try." His voice was kindly quizzical, Down-Easterly floating on a texture like sturdy linen or corn muffins.

"No, I was trying to catch my float. Some ..." She lifted her head, setting off protests from her ribcage. She was on boards, some kind of dock, surrounded by a circle of dark faces with wide dark eyes. "Hey! I was taking a nap, and some brat of a kid -"

"Ayah. Saw that. His folks got him in hand now, on their way back to New York, Darien, somewheres. Don't suppose you want to pursue the matter legally?"

Faye subsided. "Guess not, if it means dragging him back here." She heard leaves rustling, saw them passing overhead, blithe and crimson. "How did I get here, anyway?"

The circle of watchers melted away, now that it seemed that no-body was dead. A volleyball was produced and served into the lake, followed by a dozen screaming girls. The guy who, Faye now real-ized, had saved her life with CPR, sat back on his heels, and looked thoughtful. "Well ... depends where you came from, to some extent. But you are at Camp Nokoma in Standish, Maine, USA, more or less. Specifically, you are in the middle of Sebago Lake, on what we call the Long Island, because it is a whole mile long. The camp takes in high-risk girls from Spanish Hahlem, and I'm a volunteer. Teaching tough girls how to sail, which was how we spotted you. Are you OK now? Can I help you sit up?"

"Of course. Frankly? I feel like hell."

"Ayah. Tryna drink the lake will do that. Where are you staying?"

"The ... The, lemme think. The Harbor Buoy."

"Oh-ah, ova the fah shore."

Faye grinned at him. "Ayuh. You folks certainly have a way of talking, don't you?"

He grinned back, looking like Bob Dylan's homely brother, maybe named Orville. "That's the sperrit. You do right colorfully yourself, Scahlett."

Faye extended a hand. "Faye Bynum. Apparently, I owe my continued life to you. Thank you very, very much."

"Peter Standish. Think nothing of it, happens couple times a season here'bouts. Rare when it's a lady in a bikini, but not that it never is."

"Uh huh. Well. If we could put the bikini aside - I mean - what I'm asking is, what's next? I suppose I will have to invent a whole new life, now that you've saved it. But frankly, your respiration technique -"

"C-P-Ah. Stands for cahdio-pulmonary -"

"Heard of it, never experienced it. Anyway, it's left me sore and dizzy, and I just want to lie down. Still, I do want to do something more than just say, 'Thanks, hear?' but I hate clichés. Is there some kind of clinic around? I suppose I should see a doctor."

"You ah. Seeing one. Left my white coat at the office, but appears to me, you made a pretty good recovery up t'now. Fah as the new life goes, that might be fun, but not required for a full recovery. You certainly should go back to your motel and lie down, and stay there for the rest of the day. I could give you a lift, I don't expect you'd care to swim back. But you should be feeling better tomorrow morning. I could do a follow-up in a couple days; how long will you be here?"

"No real plans. I'm on leave from my job to get over being beaten up by industrial-strength goons. I'm a newspaper editor down south."

"Ah. Hazardous duty these days. Let's get you back to the Hahba Buoy. Still got your key?"

"I had to leave it with the float rental guy, thank God, or it would be at the bottom of the lake. As it is, I suppose I owe him -"

"One of the kids found it and your towel, it's right over theah."

He took her back to the Harbor Buoy in one of the camp's dinghies. She traded the float for her key; he walked her back to her cabin, shook her hand, and wished her well.

"Here's my number. Call LouAnne and make an appointment for a follow-up, oh, Friday or so, if you want. You start feelin' bad - dizzy, palpitations, vision loss - you call right away, any time day or night - it rings at home, nights."

She nodded, reached up and kissed his cheek. "I wouldn't want to disturb your family, and it looks like I'll be OK. Thank you for my life."

"Think nothing of it. No family but Julie, and she's a bahdah collie."

***

"Oh, Forde, that's terrible. Would he really do that?"

"Sure sounded like it. So I'm going to play along with his silly GLAD parade for now, and we'll work on thinking how to get out from under his thumb. How are you doing?"

"I was doing pretty well, but I had a bit of a setback yesterday - almost got myself drowned in the lake here."

"Huh. You OK now?"

"They had to give me CPR, so my cracked ribs cracked again."

"Really? CPR?"

"Yep."

"Huh. Well. Look, you take care of yourself."

"I'll be coming back soon, Forde. You have to get beat up and humiliated to understand, I guess."

"Yeah, I said, take care of yourself."

"OK ... I will. G'bye."

"Thanks for calling. We miss you here. G'bye."

Faye hung up, feeling vaguely abused by the fact that Forde had problems as big as her own, and began to face the question of when, if ever, she was going to take herself back to Gabbro. Just the fact that it was going to be a long drive was dispiriting; but it was clear that she had no reason to linger here, or to go farther from Gabbro. She was far enough north. The Harbor Buoy was thick with birches, and she had conversed with four – no, five New Englanders, all of them pleasant. She rather thought that she might, though, just go ahead and make a follow-up appointment with Doctor Peter Standish before she started back South.

When she slept that night, there was no rescue and no CPR. She sank into bottomless dark, and was met by a legion of the drowned, every one of them fossilized to fool's gold. When she looked down at herself, her skin had started to harden and glister.

***

"Breathe in ..." He moved the stethoscope. "Uh huh, good, now out as fah as you can ... How does that feel?"

"Well, it's pretty tender, here and over here. I can breathe deep, but it hurts."

"We probably better tape you up again. Any nausea, chills, night sweats?"

"Um, no."

"You drank a lot of lake water, and it's not always the cleanest, see. But if you'd got a bug from it, you'd of felt it by now." He hung the stethoscope over his neck and sat back on his little rolling stool, looking judiciously medical. "I think we can say you got off fairly easy, considering, and release you into society."

"Paid my debt, is that it? But no, I haven't, at all. Would you – " She took a breath, and plunged ahead. "Would you consider having dinner with me this evening? I'm about to head back south - troubles in the office - and I'd very much like to ... well, to I guess acknowledge how much I owe to your skill and bravery in rescuing me."

"You don't owe me a thing."

"Maybe not, but I owe a lot to your skill and bravery. I want to take them to dinner, and I guess you'll just have to tag along."

"Well ... All right, then. How if I pick you up around six, we can go to Falmouth and eat some lobstah? Nothing much in Standish but a little pizza place."

"Wait a minute. Standish?"

"Oh, well. Way back, bunch of my folks, descendants of old Myles Standish, jumped ship looking for warmer weather, got mixed up about which way was south, wound up down here in Maine. There's a few of us around, yet. The town of Standish is more of a concept, really. There's no downtown, or business district, for example. Just some houses around."

"Still, a whole town, goodness. There never was a Dr. Gabbro, I bet. Anyway, someplace nice for supper, OK? My treat."

"Dutch."

"I was not speaking to you. I was addressing my guests, your skill and bravery. Let's table the question until tonight around six. Looking forward to it."

***

Faye finished laughing and wiped her mouth. "I couldn't stuff down another bite. Gosh, lobster's a lot better here than it is in North Carolina. Fresh makes a difference, huh?"

"You picked a good one."

"They were all waving their claws, trying to get picked, poor things. I think they thought I was picking one to throw back into the ocean."

"Stop. I can hahdly stand to contemplate what it's like to sit in that tank, waiting for somebody to pull you out and eat you. Doesn't stop me, mind, I been eatin' them since I was two."

Bet you were a cutie, in your little lobstah bib. "Want some coffee, dessert?"

"Don't believe. But I did very much enjoy our acknowledgement dinner. Ready to go on with your recovery by getting a night's sleep?"

Faye grinned, and it turned into a yawn. "Reckon."

"Good Southern girl."

I'll give you Southern girl, Doctor Hick. "Ayah. Getting back in practice."

"Ayah."

Dinner talk had been vivacious. Now, their voices were softer, their glances more hopeful than their minds had caught up to. They settled the bill - Faye got her way by telling Peter he could cover the tip - stood and exited, a little unsteady from the beer. In the parking lot, Peter turned to her as he held the passenger door open on what Faye rather thought must be a Jaguar.

"So, you're leaving tomorrow?"

"Yes." She was suddenly sorry at the thought of leaving this smiling man. He looked less homely now, more … she groped for a better word than 'authentic,' and gave up. "I'm awfully lucky and glad to have met you, Peter. I just have to get back and take up where I left off."

"Ayah. Well, if I don't ask you this now, I'll kick myself for a month. Would you - " He broke off, and ran his fingers through his hair. "Well, I wondered if you, ah, you would be at all interested ..."

Faye smiled. *So he's kind of homely. I'm not going to marry him.* "Oh, good. I mean, I hope. I'd love to stop by for a nightcap, if that was what you were about to ask. If so, the answer is, 'Ayah.'"

"Get in the cah then, smahty."

On the way to Peter Standish's house, Faye talked about the South, its hazards and charms, about her honorary sisterhood to a genuine mystic prodigy. Peter mostly listened, nodding, asking questions that followed up on some of the South's famous weakness for high-octane religious ecstasies, and responded with some anecdotes about Santeria belief among the families of his campers. He seemed very dedicated to the camp, enough that it began to sound to Faye as if he was more than the camp doctor and sailing instructor; maybe also a financial backer. That pleased her.

"But what sense does it make to teach slum kids sailing? They'll never see another sailboat."

"Well, first of all, of course, the sailing is only a part of what they do at the camp. And it isn't really sailing I'm teaching, it's courtesy - which serious sailors are drilled with from the first time they go out - and cooperation, sportsmanship, and so forth. Respect for your boat, your tools, and for the other sailors. Also, not to minimize the uniqueness of your event, there is the occasional swimmer who gets in trouble out there. They are learning to look out for other people who need their help. It wasn't me who spotted you, it was a tough little thing named Rosa Mejía."

Rosie, my guardian angel. "Well, will you give Rosa my very deep thanks for her alertness?"

"Already did, she got the day's prize for helping others. But I will add your personal thanks as well."

There was a little self-conscious shuffling at the front door as Peter invited her in. Once in, she admired his house and otherwise wandered curiously while he opened a bottle of port. The house - belonging, presumably, to one of the <u>Standish</u> Standishes, and to a well-established and charitable doctor at that - was large, comfortable, and cozily furnished. Windows overlooked Sebago Lake, where a streak of moonlight evoked Morgan's Eddy. Bookcases full of novels and politics and a series of elderly National Geographics. There was a smattering of comfortable furniture, and worn nice rugs. A globe with sepia oceans and obsolete nations occupied a corner behind a piano. Off the living room, what appeared to be an office or study, with a massive desk and a typewriter. Bookcases full of what looked like medical treatises, but Faye didn't want to intrude far enough to read titles. The walls of the study held diplomas and a scattering of sailing photos, including Peter and a slender woman flanking a line of dark-haired girls. Next to the window that overlooked the lake, the piano held a silver frame with a portrait of the slender woman. She was handsome, maybe a little haggard; about Faye's age.

"My late wife, Julie," Peter said, entering with glasses and upscale crackers. "Pahssed away with ovarian cancer five years ago."

"Oh, Peter, I'm so sorry. So Julie the dog is named after her?" Faye, determined not to cry and carry on about Rosie, had already greeted the border collie.

"Well, yes. Hate to think I'm keeping Julie's memory alive with a dog, but it isn't that. It's just a name I like. Old fashioned."

Me too. What a nice man. "You want to tell me a little about Julie? Did you have children?"

The early, anxious vivacity coasted to a gentler tempo. They sat side by side and talked quietly about things that people talk about when they encounter a new friend; and, after a comfortable but slightly tachycardiac silence, things that men and women might talk about when it begins to appear that friendship might not be the end of it. The upscale crackers washed down with soft, dark port, they retired to the kitchen. Faye admired the countertops, which resembled leopard skin, but made of stone.

"What the geologists call a gahnet skahn, you see it a lot down along the coast."

"A ... what? Ga*rr*net, I got that. My mother left me a garnet ring. Is that what those are? Goodness, they're huge. And pretty. But a skahn? A scone? A scorn?"

Peter laughed; nicely, Faye thought, but a little ruefully. "Not so easy to translate backwards into standard American, I guess. It's S-K-A-Ah-N. Skahn. It's a kind of metamorph ..." He broke off and pulled a paper towel off the roll over the sink, to blow his nose. Faye saw that his eyes were bright, and didn't know what to say, if anything.

"Are you OK?" The dumbest possible choice.

He smiled, nodding, wiping his nose. "Eah. But, Faye, when you said 'Ga*rr*net' like that, you ... it just made me a little sad."

"Oh. I'm sorry."

"Don't be. When Julie wanted to tease me about being a Mainiac, she would talk about this 'garrnet skarrn.' " She said '*garrnet*' just like you did, and her mouth would puckah just the same way ... " He broke off and smiled. "I think this line of talk might be out of bounds in the rules of dating."

Faye looked up at him, and was - had she been a man - unmanned. OK, he was no movie star by a long shot; his nose was large and a little crooked, and his mouth was probably too "sensitive," over the prominent teeth; but, God, his eyes; steady and kind, with square corners. Collaborating in the smile, killing her when they widened, mirroring her own.

Oh, look at this. Wobbly knees. How long has that been? "Well." Her voice was husky; a cliché, but there was nothing she could do about it. "It's late." (The smile evaporated.) "I bet the dating police have called it a day and punched out, so we'll have to make up our own rules. That could be kind of entertaining, though. Don't you think?" The smile reappeared, eager, a little frightened. She closed her mind to the night demons and to Terry Morgan, and her self-castigation about loose behavior; and backed her hips against the garnet skarn countertop. "You want to see puckah? C'mere."

***

"Ayee. The ribs."

"Remind me which ones?"

"This one, and then up here, a little bit hidden by ... you know. By the curves."

"I'll be careful. But Faye, you know, before this goes any fahther, you don't have to do this, just because I rescued you and all. Also, I wasn't, you know, planning on this, and I'm afraid I don't have any birth control in the house."

Faye started on his shirt buttons while she looked into his pale, killer eyes. "I'm not 'doing' anything, Peter. I'm being charmed, have been for hours now. And I'm on the Pill. But I don't want to intrude on your memories of Julie."

"Ah. Julie was a generous person, and she wanted me to meet other women after ... after she was gone. But I was thinking of your being beaten up. Did they - " His voice softened, as if he were addressing the survivor of a civil disaster. "Did they also assault you sexually?"

"Yes. Not successfully, but, yes. I managed to escape with the help of my dog. Who was a border collie, too."

"See, all the more reason for me to ... I mean, not to take advantage of the, the situation here."

"Well, thank you, Peter. That's very generous, because I can, um, tell that you're pretty interested. I have had some bad moments since that. Sleepless nights. What you're calling the 'situation here' if you want to know, is a very pleasant and welcome contrast to all that. What I think might be the best, would be for us to be very, very gentle. Can you do that?"

"Certainly. But please feel perfectly free to stop matters at any point. And I do mean any."

"Fine, then. I'm sorry about all the rib tape, but there it is."

"Well, I'm the one who made it necessary and put it on, so if there's anyone to apologize, it's me. I'm pretty confident we can work around it, though."

"Oh, please do. And listen, there's not a speck of gratitude or pay-back to this; for saving me, I mean. I just plain like you; well, not 'just plain.' I think I like you a great deal, and I'd like to be close to you." She reflected for a moment, while she began to untuck his shirt. "Of course, saving a person's life is in itself a likeable trait in a fellow. I'd just like to see what others might come forth, given the chance."

He let her slip his shirt off, and led her to the stairs. "I like you, too. In view of your ribs, and your recent history, would you prefer to be on top?"

"There, see?"

Afterward, drowsy and murmuring: "You know, I never noticed what kind of a doctor you are."

"Gyne … hr'm … gynecologist."

She stretched and smiled. "You know all about women, then? You sure seem to have done your homework."

"Literally, one who knows woman-words. Still, it doesn't hurt to be a little familiar with the terrain."

"Hasn't yet, anyway." She folded against him to breathe in his ear. "Very much the opposite. The terrain is just dazzled."

"Your terrain seems very complete and cared-for. A chahming little belly" - laying a hand on it - "and I don't know when I've seen a healthier-looking vulvar vestibule."

She laughed and traced his mouth with a finger. "What a handsome compliment. Maybe we'll have time for you to explain what exactly that encompasses. But before we get into that, I just want to say that this has got to have been about the most … <u>considerate</u>, I guess, sex I think I ever experienced. It was gently ravishing, if that's even possible. It never stressed my sore places, but it sure paid attention to the places that aren't sore. Even at the end, it was not this great explosion of … you know. Howling at the moon."

"Ahgasm?"

She snorted. "Funniest name for it yet; but perfect in this case. 'Ah-gasm,' yes. It felt like a thousand tiny, gentle firecrackers going off all over. Did you manage that? Is it something gynecologists learn in school?

"Well. Not entirely; quite a bit of it comes from experience with, er'm …"

"Oh. With Julie? Oh, Peter, of course, and I'm sorry to intrude."

"No, it's fine. Julie was always very open about what made sex good for her, and I took note. Well, mental notes, of course. I'm very pleased that what was good for her, was nice for you, too."

"'Nice' doesn't begin to do justice."

"There are certain neural centers and networks that can modulate your response one way or another. We spent a little time on that in school."

"Uh huh. And did you put your knowledge of those neural centers and networks to use? I didn't see you doing any measurements or calculations."

Peter kissed the corner of her mouth, making her smile. "I could blow it here, by saying something like, All women are pretty much the same, couldn't I? You happen to be a particularly handsome and responsive example, and it is a pleasure to explore your responses." He gauged her response to that. "Had I just as well shut up here?"

Faye smiled, and wondered how she could ever have considered him homely. A silly snap judgment that probably lots of women made about him, leaving him - gloating here - free to be taken for dinner and to bed. His body was lithe and handsome, and his face was, well, uniquely lovable. The notion that a man, during sex, might care about and pay attention to her own response was a novelty. No previous partner - certainly not Terry Morgan; or Forde, whom she regarded as more a pupil than a lover in any case - had ever seemed to care about much beyond his own pleasure, and when they could go around again. Here was a man - and an expert at that - who not only cared how things were going for her, but commanded the knowledge and means to act on what he learned. *Literally, a fucking miracle. I should write an editorial about it.*

"You can talk all night, if you want. If I get bored, I'll change the subject."

He smiled and nuzzled. "Well, anyway, I was trying to be careful of your injuries. And I was circumspect with regahd to Gräfenberg's Locus."

It was all too perfect; she laughed helplessly. "... Ow, ow, ribs! Oh, Peter, you are one in a billion. Maybe we could drop down to Gräfenberg's Locus for a beer some time. Can you stay with me, just for a little longer?"

"Of course. Give me a few minutes. When you lahf like that, it helps."

"Ayah." She brushed away tears of affection, pain, and laughter. "I just bet it does." She yawned carefully, luxuriously, and husked, 'But it hurts when I lahf, so take your sweet time, you hilarious gynecologist."

The second was like the first, but within a sleek profile of dark time-lessness that convinced Faye that it had happened in sleep. The third time, at dawn, the gentle firecrackers were surrounded and cushioned by a million tiny pearls. Lying with him then, both of them gleaming with bliss and effort; and when her breathing and voice seemed trustworthy again, Faye took his head between her hands and kissed him fondly.

"God, Peter. Now I owe you more than just my life. We'll never get to the end of this."

"Nonsense Faye. You think I was suffering here? Just doing my job, giving you pelvics?"

"I hope not. And I hope you're as surprised and pleased as I am by this. Not meaning your expertise, which I find as amazing as if I'd ... I don't know. Won the lottery. By 'this,' I mean our friendship, how we please each other. Not to mention, I hope you don't see me as the kind of woman who will just jump into bed with the next guy who saves me from drowning. You seem like ... I don't know, you just enchanted me all evening, talking about the camp, and the town, and the world - why I was so quick to take you up on the after-dinner invitation. But then, when you clouded up about 'garrnet,' it just plain undid me."

She reflected a moment. "So I sure hope that's not a line you use on all your dinner partners ... Oh. No, I guess it's not, is it? Damn, Peter, you are such a sweet, sweet man ..." She cradled his ungainly head against her breast and kissed his ear. "I have to go back now, and I don't know if we'll ever meet again. And I owe -"

"Absolutely nothing but another kiss. Or two."

"All right, fine; here ... No, but here's what I do owe you, and I think it's going to be a heavy debt to live with. I never imagined sex could be so ... oh, goodness. So lovingly expert, I guess. Want to come live in Gabbro, North Carolina? I do have a chahming little house. To go with the belly."

12.

THE OUTREACH INTERN

Chapter 6

Mercy's eyes blinked open to the sunshine of the isolated beach; she heard the cry of gulls. A shadow passed over her and a powerful force thrust at her body; she convulsed, and a little sea water shot onto the sand next to the knee of Chad's cousin Peter James, his brow furrowed with effort and concern.

"Ah you all right, Miss?" he asked, hesitatingly.

"Oh, James. I thought I was a goner gone for sure. How did you ... Oh! Ow! My rib! ..."

"It was nothing, Miss. Though it was a near thing indeed! You had gone down for the second time, and I knew there was no time to lose. As for your ribs, as the Bible says, 'Whatsoever thy hand findeth to do, do it with thy might; else, CPR availeth not.'"

She smiled, admiring his lean torso and the fatherly handsome head and capable hands that had saved her life. "I love Ecclesiastes, James, even when you supplement it to please yourself. Please call me Mercy. I am so grateful; I owe you my life."

13.

THE SWITCHBOARD AT THE NUTMEG INN IN ENFIELD, Connecticut seemed to be made of nutmeg or some other nonconductive spice; Faye could barely hear what Forde was saying. Still, things seemed to be satisfactory at the *Intelligencer* office.

"That ///// Baley come in for her inter/// today. Quite the occasion in her life, seems like. She about broke d/// ///ing when she found out she'd /// /// own desk and all."

"She what? She cried?"

"When she /////// wasn't a stand-up job. Like at the mill, I guess."

"Well, for Pete's sake. Sharon always thought she ought to have her own office, as if that would work, for a receptionist. So, how'd the interview go?"

"Oh, ///////, I guess. She don't have /////////cation."

"Vacation? Oh, education? No, I suppose she went through the Baley schools. They don't even give a high school degree. Dang, I didn't think of that. Can she even read and write?"

"Well enough. //////// night school in /////, got a equivalency cert/////, what that's worth."

"Oh, Forde, that's worth a lot. She did that while she was working full time at River Mills? That's worth a PhD, in sheer determination."

"Reckon. She starts //// week."

"I look forward to being there for it."

"///////."

***

The next afternoon in the District of Columbia, Faye found an untampered-with pay phone whose hanging directory still included the pages containing the Textile Workers Union of America. She plunked in a quarter and dialed.

"Textile Workers."

"I was looking for Miss Nora Lundy."

"So are we, half the time. I think she's in this afternoon. Can you hold?"

"Long as my quarter lasts."

Faye looked at traffic and sleek interns for a time long enough to make her nervous about her quarter. She only had another dime in change.

"Lundy."

"Nora, hi! It's Faye Bynum."

"... Oh, yes. The editor."

"Yes. Look, I know I didn't have much time for you when you were in Gabbro before, but we've got something in common now. Can I see you this afternoon?"

"Sure. Where are you?"

"Well, in Washington, anyhow. I'm on Wisconsin Avenue in, I guess, Georgetown somewhere. Almost down to the river."

"Lord. We're on Rhode Island Avenue, in Northeast."

"Is that far away?"

"Almost clear across DC. Look, ask for directions to Mount Pleasant, 1746 Lamont Street Northwest. Got that? Wait on the front porch. I'll be there in an hour."

***

Nora Lundy shuddered and shrank into the porch rocker. "The gloves were the worst of it, for me. To protect their hands and make it hurt more, you just knew."

Faye knew. The gloves had visited nearly every night. "That and the ski masks, made them inhuman. Like demons."

"Mine didn't wear masks. Too hot in the swamp, I guess. Also, I wasn't supposed to survive, so no harm if I saw their faces."

"You did see their faces, though? That's great!"

"Whoopee. As nondescript as you'd want, a couple of tough-looking guys in gloves and meat-mongers' aprons. Plus, after a few wallops, I wasn't keeping much track."

"Jesus, poor Nora. God, yes, the aprons, to keep our blood off their nice clothes. I suppose they burned them after."

"No doubt. It would be nice to nail them an' aw, but it's Merrydown we truly want to nobble."

"Yes, and anyhow, they're wounded, both of them. My little dog -"

"Aye, I heard. That one will be out o' business, being as wi' one eye, he'll have no depth perception, be tripping over everything. What about the other?"

"I shot him."

"What?!" Nora Lundy grinned with delight.

"I did, I was staggering around, half-dead, but this guy I know had given me a ros ... a pistol, for just this situation. I got off one lucky shot, hit the Assistant Thug in the arm."

"Oh, aye, the Assistant. Same deal with me, one of 'em holding me up, the other slamming me around. Except the guy you called the Assistant it was, that stomped my leg an' broke it. That was after, when I was lyin' in the swamp all beat ta shit, half-dead for real. Glad to hear he's hurt, if he's the same bastard broke my leg. But with all respect, I believe they left you off easy, no broke bones an' all. I'm a bit put out, they didn't see me good-looking enough ta rape, it might have held their hand a bit on the beating."

"Don't be. The beating was like a transaction, almost. No hard feelings, Miss, we got to do this, you got to take it. Almost friendly, next to being raped, which …" She broke off to shudder and cover her eyes. " … which was another thing altogether. But after all, you were much more of a threat to them, representing a union; and there was no dog there to save you. All I did was say in print that their factory is a hell-hole."

Nora placed a hand on Faye's arm. "Aye, so which of us is the worse threat?"

Faye looked across the porch at brown oak leaves scampering down Lamont Street before an east wind. "We both are, Nora. Two beat-up women with no money between us, and yet they're scared sick. So let's think about this: What are they so afraid of? What could we do to hurt them?"

"Easy enough. Organize their workers."

"Easy to say, at least."

"If I did not think it was possible to do, I'd be doin' anything else wi' my time, you can bet."

"So, you think we could pull it off?"

"We, who? Is it the … what? The *Informer*'s business?"

"*Intelligencer*. Is it our business when Gabbro County citizens get exploited, abused, maimed, and beaten to pulps? And their factory fouls our water and cheats our citizens and uses our utilities and police and fire, and pays no taxes for it all? You damn bet it is."

Nora whistled. "Bravo. Don't know when I've heard it put better. So why are you cooperating in this GLAD foolishness?"

"Merrydown bought a bank that holds a note that's about to come due on us. If we don't cooperate, he'll foreclose, buy the *Intelligencer*, fire us all, and shut it down. Or, he'll extend the note as long as we toe his line, starting with boostering GLAD. And on from there, I suppose."

Nora sighed. "Aye, the old story. And that's not … Wait, though. Tell you what, the union has money, a PR budget, that could … could, mind … be used for such things. How big is this note?

"I don't know. I can find out. Oh, God, do you think?"

"I'll ask. Find out how much, minimum, you'd need to get clear of old Mickey Mouse."

They rocked, and contemplated cars in futile search of parking; and Faye sat up suddenly. "And I'll tell you what else: You heard about that Sedalia Baley, got her hand cut off?"

"Heard, oh, aye. She was my contact there."

Faye stared. "<u>She</u> was the on-site organizer?"

"That's another yet. Baley was a go-between. There was no way I could be contacting the organizer, who's under surveillance constant, like everyone there. Sedalia was an outcast, that nobody thought was capable of anything, so she was practically invisible. She'd meet me at a hovel of a bar in a town called Shannon, an' give me reports, carry messages."

"Huh. You're that organized; and she's got that kind of guts. Good. Anyway, she's working at the *Intelligencer* now. Maybe there's a way to ... I don't know. Use that."

It was Nora's turn for silent contemplation of Mount Pleasant. At length, she turned to Faye with a half-smile. "There's another expeerience yet we have in common, you and I."

***

Forde Morgan sat at his desk and stared at the ringing phone. After seven rings, it stopped. Forde looked at the door with the Venetian blind, and sure enough, a faint tap came from it.

"Come in." It was answered by a flustered-sounding squeak from the hallway.

"Oh, Mr. Morgan, I beg your partin. I thought you was must of been away."

"Come on in, Sedalia. I'm here, but not exactly, if you see what I mean."

Sedalia Baley, who saw nothing of the sort, pushed open the door, careful not to let the blind clatter. Her dark face, framed by stringy black hair that continued to waist level, emerged. "If you didn't want to be disturbed, I could wait. Only except, not exactly. If you see what I mean."

Forde smiled at the small show of spirit. "Good for you, Sedalia. What was it? Merrydown again, I suppose."

"Yes sir. He called to ast where you was, the parade startin' up and all."

Forde sighed. "Yes, yes. Is he still on the line?"

"No, sir. He told me tell you, get a move on. Except I just cleaned it up a little."

"I bet. Well, Miss Baley, then the least I can do is go sit in his damn stupid convertible in his double-damned stupid parade, isn't it?"

She blushed. "Reckon. Thank you, Mr. Morgan."

When Forde got home that evening, he drove out to Morgan's Eddy to wash off the sweat of a hot day, the moral stickiness of being seen in public with Mason Merrydown; and the literal stickiness of Mason's ten-year-old kid Stevie, who'd sat between Forde and Mason, slurping Dreamsicles and reading a comic-book Bible the whole way. And by the way, to see if there were any sign of Faye.

***

In a pair of stirrups at DownEast Surgical Associates in Lewiston, Maine, Elaine Burckel was getting a little achy and impatient. These doctors don't give a damn how uncomfortable and embarrassing their damn apparatus is, *Just a few minutes longer, This might pinch just a little*; and then they leave you sprawled out like a chorus girl. She should have waited until the much better-looking Dr. Rysgaard was back from vacation, instead of taking anything with this homely ... "Doctah?"

"Ayah?" Peter Standish brought himself back to the here and now;

unlatched and and eased out the speculum. "Just making sure of one or two lahst things, Mrs. Buckle. About finished now."

While Mrs. Burckel was recovering her dignity and clothing, Peter stared out at the darkling streets of Lewiston. He would do it. He must, or he would live the rest of his solitary days looking up Maine ladies' tushies by rainlight. While LouAnne was busy writing up Mrs. Burckel's charges and scrawling her a next-appointment card, he sat at his desk and ran a piece of office stationery into his typewriter.

***

On Saturday at sundown, the little yellow Beetle jounced down the lane to Morgan's Eddy, getting in some last licks on Faye's aching butt. At the foot of the cottage steps, she shut off the engine and opened her window to let the humidity and frog-songs of the Southland wash through. The Eddy lay quiet in the twilight, its silver troubled only by a few water-striders and a faint bulge of turbulence from the springs far below. The year being now nearly at winter, she saw a pair of wintering coots navigating across, looking comically adept. One of them dove, instantly gone. Faye opened the door and got out, letting the relief wash through her legs and butt while she stretched and touched the grass. She kicked out of her shoes and walked slowly down to the dock, feet greeting the chill centipede grass and the sand below it, eyes waiting for the diving duck to reappear. Far to the center, it did, as suddenly and thoroughly as it had disappeared. Quicksilver drops skittered from its back. *I suppose there's a lesson there. What would Sister Penitentia preach from it?* In the wavering reflection of the sunset, she could see Sister P smiling and waving an admonitory ruler: *Grace is invisible. You may think it is gone forever, but it will reappear, shedding glory where you least ...*

Yeah, right. She stripped to her underwear and stood on the end of the dock in the twilight; slowly, she allowed herself to fall backward into the water, rendering herself to the Eddy. As she fell, her long-untrimmed hair blew up into the edges of her vision like dark flame, pointing to the first bright star overhead. *Oh God, thank God, I am home again and safe.*

14.

FORDE MORGAN WAS RELIEVED AND A LITTLE MIFFED. Wasn't there something about not kissing and telling?

"Fordie, goodness, don't be upset or embarrassed. You and I are still just as much special friends as we always were. 'Keeping company' is hardly a sacrament of eternal fidelity." *And besides.*

"Does that mean you don't consider yourself eternally fidel - uh, faithful either?"

"What kind of silly question is that, Forde? I no more than you. I thought the topic here was your little fling - *Uh oh, stupid* - with Nora." She held a hand up to Forde's scowl. "Sorry, I didn't mean to demean your … Your relationship, I should have said. The point is, I consider you perfectly free to explore relationships with other people, and I am not at all upset, or … Oh, I see. Would you rather I were?"

"No, of course not. I'm glad you're not upset, I guess." Forde grinned. "If I was honest, I'd say, if you <u>were</u> upset, I could read that as that you assumed we were exclusive, and we'd have a problem that it turns out we don't; but reading it the other way around, I see you don't think we are, and thus - " He fluttered a hand, and Faye grinned back.

"Thus, that I don't consider *my*self unavailable to other relation-ships. Goose and gander, looks like. Let me put it this way: I still enjoy keeping company with you, Forde. But I consider your life outside our keeping company none of my business. I'm a little surprised Nora saw fit to tell me about it, but not sorry, since it gave me the opportunity to make myself clear on that to her. I do believe I have long since made myself clear to you, about my wish to keep parts of my life to myself. Now: can we discuss what we are going to do about this Merrydown mess?"

Forde sighed. "Mess is right."

"Well, how big is this note that he's holding over our heads?"

"Not millions, or anything. Fifty thousand, about."

"But way more than you, or we, can come up with."

"Exactly."

"Nora told me that TWUA has some kind of fund that might be brought to bear for purposes like this. I suppose it would be a loan, at best, but I have no idea if it would cover something that size."

"And then we'd just owe all that and more - closing costs and all - to somebody different."

"OK, but they wouldn't be Mason Merrydown."

"True. Well, do you think you could ask her about it, now that you know the amount? Seems kind of awkward for me to. As if, you know ..."

Faye smiled, and murmured, "*Just a gigolo* ... I had a rather stuffy conversation with Lee Forsythe about that, a while back."

"Lee? Really?"

"Don't jump like that. She exchanged the promise of a kiss or two, to Tucker Pardee for passes into River Mills, the day Sedalia got hurt."

"Huh. Good for her. Well, still."

"Oh, yes, she got quite pink and flustered when I pointed out that she was exchanging access to her body, for something of value. But the devil showed up in the details, and it never worked out, so it's moot."

***

Nora Lundy whistled. "Lordie. I don't know that the Board would sit still for something that big. But I can ask. I know we spent a'most forty thousand on a renovation of a union hall in Texas somewhere. I'll get back to you."

Forde leaned into the speakerphone. "Thanks, Nora. Um ... how soon do you think it would be possible to find out?"

"No telling. I'll get right on it, though."

Faye spoke up from across the room. "Be sure to remind them this wouldn't be money down the drain, like their renovation project. We'd expect it to be a loan, with reasonable interest."

"Aye, that might help. Still, I fear it's a long shot indeed. I'll try an' be in touch by the start of next week."

"Wonderful. Thanks so much, hear?"

"Never mind. Now, Forde Morgan, if you and I could have a word or two in private?"

Faye stood. "I'm gone." She winked at blushing Forde, wiggled her eyebrows, and blew him a kiss as she slipped out.

The un-severed remainder of Sedalia's right hand was enclosed in a purple cotton glove that she had evidently stuffed with cotton, so that the half-thumb was supplemented but still opposable, while the stiff finger surrogates stood out as if someone had applied a tourniquet to her wrist. Faye came up on Sedalia from behind, putting a hand on her shoulder, saying, "Hi, Sedalia, I'm Faye," as if they had never met at the hospital, and looping around the hand on Sedalia's shoulder to finish off a welcoming hug. Sedalia gasped; the stuffed glove rustled behind Faye's left ear.

"Ma'am, Miss Bynum, you tooken me by surprise. Used to some-times Mister Barnett would come up behind on some of the ladies, pat their behinders, like. You'd never?"

"No, I wouldn't, Sedalia. Had my own behinder patted plenty, thanks. It won't happen in this office, I don't think ... though keep an eye on Rob Stoker."

"No danger there. He don't hardly look at me."

"Huh. Well, all to the good, I guess. Look, I was going down to the Salonnette over lunch, wonder if you'd care to join me? I've let my hair go while I was on vacation, and it needs a trim. If you were interested, I could introduce you."

Sedalia blushed furiously, and seemed to be in doubt how to answer. Finally, she looked at the top of the Reception desk, and muttered, "Truly an honor, Miss Bynum. What time was you fixin to go?"

Faye looked at the clock over Sedalia's desk. "How about in half an hour? I've got a little piece to write, then I'm OK for a while."

"Yes'm."

When Faye entered the Salonnette with Sedalia in tow, Ginnie Freeman's usual greeting cut off after "All Rise! The honorable ..."

Silence descended like a stone.

"Hey, Ginnie, old thing. Cat got your tongue?"

More silence, broken at last by Sedalia. "Ma'am, Miss Bynum, I will wait outside. Or, I guess, see you back at the office."

"What?"

The front door opened and shut.

"What on earth is wrong here?"

Ginnie drew a sigh. "Faye, honey, didn't you know no better than to bring a Baley in here?"

"Oh, come on, Ginnie. Pearlene? Mary-Deane?"

Mary-Deane Gaines shook her head in silence. Pearlene patted the back of her chair invitationally. "We don't generally have much to do with Baley folks here, Miss Faye. Can't hardly believe that would have been news to you after all the time you been living here."

"I see. No, it's not, but I did think ... Oh, dear. Well, Pearlene, you have been a very good friend, and you have stood with me against Ginnie's worst impulses. I will miss you terribly. Goodbye, all of you. I will miss you all."

"Oh, for God's sake," Ginnie Freeman snorted. "Don't tell me you're getting on a high horse about one of the Baleys. They're decent folks, I suppose. Just, they pretty much stick to their own kind."

"Can't say I blame them, when ... well. I was about to say something mean to people who were very kind to me when I was a rookie and new to Gabbro ways. So, thank you for all the many kindnesses you've shown me over the years. But I don't believe in castes, and I specially don't believe in outcasts. You know what I believe about the value of all God's children, so remember that it applies to you, too. I'm off to give Miss Baley a hug."

When she was gone, Pearlene wiped her nose. "All God's children are infinitely valuable. Said that nun friend of hers. I doubt that could be right, don't you?"

Sedalia Baley was back at her desk when Faye returned to the office. She kept her eyes on the desktop and the nameplate (Miss Sedalia Baley), of which she was very proud, while Faye stood before her.

"Sedalia, I apologize. I certainly apologize on behalf of my so-called friends at the Salonnette. I obviously underestimated their potential for ugliness and stupidity. And I apologize personally for subjecting you to that horrible, humiliating scene."

Sedalia looked up from the nameplate. "Don't give it no thought, Miss Faye. It was my fault I didn't stop to think that not everything is changed, just because I got a new job. Here, a letter come for you." She held it out, pinched between her partial thumb and the purple glove.

Faye fought back tears. "Thank you. Sedalia, so help me God, some day we will see the end of stupid bigotry in this town."

Sedalia Baley smiled. "In the day of Jubilee, which I doubt has been penciled onto nobody's calendar just yet. Thank you for the good wishes, all the same."

After a detour to the supply closet to pick up some Kleenex, Faye sat at her desk and slit open the envelope whose return address had set off a gentle firecracker in her belly.

Wednesday, Nov. 11 1964

Dear Faye -

Well, this is about the tenth draft of this note, written over the past week, and I can only hope that it has not been revised, reviled, and edited out of all sense. Let me put it as simply as I can: I would very much like to see you again - and, to be honest, to sleep with you again. When you kissed me good-bye and took off for your Southland, I thought then that it had been a very pleasant and enchanting encounter, and that I would remember you fondly for a long time. Well, that is certainly all true, but as this month has passed, the certainty has grown that you mean much more to me. I could talk about the way your face comes between me and my work, but that might not be all that flattering (still, it does...). I could say that I cannot look at the garnet skarn without hearing you saying 'garrnet' and getting ready to pucker. And most fatally, I cannot pass the picture of Julie on the piano without hearing her telling me, as clearly as if she walked beside me, "Don't let her go, dummy."

Faye, I do not claim that I have "fallen in love" with you. I do not consider you an angel fallen to Earth, or any sort of goddess. I am too old and jaded (fair warning: I will be 48 years old at Christmas) to talk that way. Also, though I meant every word of praise that I offered about your lovely, healthy body, I am not besotted with you as a sex object. No, it is simply this: it is your clear, honest intelligence, your simplicity, not to mention your poetry and humor ... well, to be honest myself, it is all those, resident in a lovely, healthy woman. In 47 years and counting, I have not encountered a more fascinating person than you. It shines from your open countenance*, your evident capacity for joy, the goodness of your outlook, and your sense of meeting the world more than half way.

If there is any way in which you could imagine continuing to see me in the future, I am open to it. That could include anything from occasional trysts, through cohabitation, to marriage and children, any and all of which I now offer you. I will welcome you as and however you see fit to offer yourself. If you should be willing to consider marrying me, I should say that I am pretty well off financially, and I could offer you a comfortable life either here in Maine, or in any other place that interests you.

And if none of those, or any other future eventuality appeals to you - if, for example, you are already committed to someone else - then it remains only to wish you as much happiness every day of your life, as you gave me in three days in October.

But if you could consider it, then as Walt Whitman wrote, "I give you myself, before preaching or law; Will you give me yourself? Will you come travel with me? Shall we stick by each other as long as we live?"

Very sincerely yours -

Peter

(Peter A. Standish MD)

*'Countenance' refused to be edited out. It muscled its way into this lame prose, and there it sits.

***

Faye carried the letter around for most of the week, waiting to see how it held up, and then realized that she was being thoughtless. After supper Wednesday she sat on the screened porch with pen and paper and stared over the Eddy for a half hour while frogs and crickets made risible suggestions as to how she might answer him. Was there anything left of "keeping company" with Forde, to which she might owe allegiance, now that Nora Lundy was so much in the picture? Yes, she would be glad to be with Peter Standish right this minute, out of bed or in, but could she really either marry or maintain a long-distance relationship with a man whose life was so different from hers? And who, by the way, was over 10 years older? All very well, now; his maturity was one of his strong points, and there certainly was no question of his vigor. But later? *When he is 70, and I'm … well, hell, 60? We'll be over the hill, both of us.* It struck Faye for the first time how unfair it was that women, aging out of sexiness earlier but living longer, spent so much greater a fraction of their lives as "old." Maybe a relationship with Peter would be less that way, since he had that decade head start.

The gods laugh when men talk about the future. Women too, I bet. It was not until she undertook a silent and internal interview with her personified conscience, Sister Rose Penitentia, that the right question was asked and answered: *How would you feel if you refused him?*

***

Wednesday evening, November 18
Dear Peter -

Thank you for your highly Peter-like and very welcome letter. I do share your fondness for the memory of our brief encounter, and yes, I would love to see you again. Maybe we can find the right place for us somewhere on your spectrum of arrangements from trysts through marriage. I warn you, though, the latter would be a very hard sell with me, even if things get that far. I have always considered myself a loner who is a poor prospect for marriage. I am very dedicated to making something of my writing, and marriage has a way of grounding such flights of female ambition. I would prefer in any case to focus for now on the short term, and leave any long term considerations for later. (But be assured that in the _very_ short term, I would be very happy to be with you, right this second.)

Right now, my work with my little newspaper is overwhelming, and since I have just returned from leave, I am not a good immediate bet for anything more elaborate than perhaps a weekend somewhere close to here, and at that, probably not within the next month. I need to sleep on this, and I promise to write again tomorrow; I just wanted to get back to you sooner than I could reasonably reason about your ... well, your proposals. Please stand by while I give it some thought...

Warmly,
Faye Bynum

Having slept with her letter on the table (in the drawer of which the empty roscoe still slumbered) she woke, read it again, sealed and mailed it without allowing further debate. That evening, she sat again on the screen porch, and, still with no inner debate but with a smile of anticipation, she wrote again:

Thursday, November 19

Dear Peter -

What might your availability be for some kind of get-together over Christmas weekend? Could we celebrate your birthday? Is it actually on Christmas day? Since we don't publish on Christmas, it could afford me a little elbow room for a long weekend.

As for your 'fair warning' about age: I was 37 in August. We are neither of us children any more, and so much the better, I believe. Maybe we can celebrate the honest enjoyment of each other without worry about whether this is _IT_, or whether it can possibly last, or if we will go to Hell if we persist. I am relaxed and open to eventualities, if you are.

Peter, I think we should be cautious in going into this, and plan no further than to get together for a long weekend as a first step. If that goes well, we can consider next steps, still taking it one step at a time. Maybe a long-term friendship with - well, erotic dimensions (Oh, listen to me! I mean a regular affair, of course.) can work out, even if, as I think, marriage may be a step too far. But we'll never know until we try. So, to Whitman back at you, "Allons! The road is before us!"

In hopes of something wonderful -

Faye

15.

LEE FORSYTHE, HAVING PASSED HER 16TH BIRTHDAY, continued to work at the *Intelligencer* on weekends; Faye worked out an arrangement with her English teacher for her articles on Gabbro doings to be counted for school credit. So it was that she was alone in the offices on the afternoon of Saturday, November 21, writing up notes that would lead to a one-year-ago essay on Gabbro reactions to the Kennedy assassination.

As it happened, that Saturday was also the day of the North Carolina Class A football championship, and Rob Stoker was in Lumberton to follow the Quarrymen as they sought their first state-wide title. Rob had waked mid-morning from a very promising dream in which a bunch of hard-looking guys with steam hammers and dynamite had demolished the State House in Raleigh. Guided by this vision, Rob had taken a flyer and put down $250 - half his life's savings - on the Gabbro Quarrymen to similarly demolish the Webster, NC, Statesmen and carry away the trophy.

This was a cruel joke on the part of Rob's wishbone. The Quarrymen were outclassed from the beginning, and limped off the field losers by five touchdowns and a field goal, 45 - 7. Rob drove back to Gabbro in a black mood, miles over the legal limits of speed, alcohol, adrenaline, and testosterone, muttering contemptuous headlines and lead paragraphs past the knuckles on his steering wheel.

***

Converging on the *Intelligencer* offices from other points of the compass were Faye Bynum, who had an idea for "This Town's Times" that she wanted to get sketched out before she lost it; and Terry Morgan, to whom Faye owed another quarter of her roofing debt. Faye had fended off his suggestion that he come to the cottage to collect it.

"I won't be here after first thing, Terry. I got interviews and shopping to do, and I need to get my column done. Wont to meet me at the *Intelligencer* office? I'll bring your check, and the roscoe, which is kind of useless, now I'm out of ammunition."

"Yeah? You think Merrydown is going, (*falsetto*) 'Oh my, I see she's too tough for us, no more rough stuff?' Better idea, I'll bring the rest of the box and reload you. Don't argue with me."

"I'm not, I'm not. It did make a big difference, in fact. Did I tell you how Rosie saved me?"

"Nope. Eight other people did, that I expect you told at least half of them. She bit the guy's eye out? Good for her, she died a hero. Must of been a sight."

"Sore eyes, ha ha. Anyways, you wont your check, you'll find me at the *Intelligencer* this evening, oh, say four thirty?"

"See you then. Still, I wish I'd been there to pound him into dogshit, the rat bastard. I'm the only one that's allowed to rape you, you know that."

Faye let that go, for the sake of ending the conversation. Her motivation for transferring this meeting to neutral ground was the undesirability of being alone with Terry Morgan at the cottage; the two previous payments had occasioned perilous badinage about exactly what was being paid for, and on one of those, in the week before the Merrydown beating, the afternoon had ended in a rough twilit bedding. Liberated, Faye considered herself free to do as she pleased in sexual matters, but after the Merrydown thugs and after Peter Standish, the charms of roughhouse sex with Terry Morgan evaporated, leaving a residue of embarrassment at her own desperation.

Rob Stoker slammed into the office at a quarter after four, having cooled only a little from his initial fury at the stinging loss. He was uncharmed to see the little high school bint there, but he ignored her and sat at his desk to pound his typewriter (Headline: **Quarry, Yes; Men, Not Much**.)

Lee Forsythe, after offering Rob an unrequited Good Afternoon, refocused on her interviews. She had begun them with the assumption that everyone was as crushed by Kennedy's death as she was; and was shocked that this was not necessarily the case. (Headline: **Some Gabbro Voters Unmoved by Assassination**). After getting all of her main points into the first paragraph, she rewarded herself with a trip to the water cooler; which in turn suggested a trip to the Ladies'.

Rob Stoker's muse had abandoned him in view of the Quarrymen's ignominy. He had ripped from his typewriter and crumpled - knowing that they would never get past Forde Morgan - four fuming lead paragraphs when Lee walked past his door; and that further flummoxed him. *Little honey has got some shape on her, the last few months. Grown-up ass already.* The flushing sound was the last straw. He rose and leaned on the pressroom wall to which his misbehavior with Jenny had exiled him, and smiled at her on the return to her own temporary desk outside Faye's office.

"Y'all remember to wipe your piece?"

Lee turned crimson. "I <u>beg</u> your pardon?"

"I said, Ya'd all September to write that piece."

"No, you did not, Mister Stoker." She walked on.

"Calling me a liar?"

"You heard what I said."

Rob walked after her. "So I did. Sounded to me like you were calling me a liar. You want to apologize, or you want to kiss my ass, little girl?"

Lee looked around. No help in sight. She began to back toward the street door. "Mister Stoker, I do not appreciate this kind of talk. Please stop it."

"Oh, come on. You know you like it, you little bitch. Am I right?"

"Not in the least. Please stop."

"Called me a liar again. We gonna have a reckoning on that talk one of these days."

"Mister Stoker, just please calm down and let me be."

"Calm down? You telling me, calm down, you little pussycat? I'll calm you down." And he grabbed Lee, spun her around and lifted her skirt to get a hand on her crotch, and clamped another on her breast. Lee screamed. The hand on her breast moved to cover her mouth. Lee bit it. He started to knead her crotch and force his mouth over hers. She took advantage of the relative freedom of her mouth to scream again, and the street door burst open.

***

Saturday delivery was usually pretty late in Standish, Maine, and Peter Standish was home assembling a meatloaf sandwich, having biopsied two suspicious cervixes and delivered a boy to the County Supervisor's wife - probably assuring himself of a dry street all winter - when the mail slot rattled. He put down the sandwich makings and walked with deliberate calm to the wire basket where the day's mail rested. Against all reason, he had begun to look for a response from his damn fool letter to Faye Bynum two days after he had mailed it.

Bill, bill, bill, four charity flyers, and at the bottom, an envelope - no, by God, <u>two</u> envelopes - from Gabbro, North Carolina. Peter took a deep breath and walked on shaky knees into his office to sit at his desk. *She said yes, and then changed her mind, damn.*

He peered at the postmarks, and made out which had been mailed second. He opened that one first, because he couldn't stand the thought that hopes raised by the first letter were going to be dashed by the second. *Give me the bad news first, Doc.* How many times he had heard that? His turn now.

***

Terry Morgan pushed Faye aside and tore Lee out of Rob Stoker's grip and shoved her weeping into Faye's arms; then turned and undertook to pummel Rob into - as he had recently put it - dogshit. Ex-athlete as Rob of course was, he put up some defense, and actually landed a pretty good left hook on Terry's nose. But he was unskilled and out of shape. Terry was fairly unskilled too - what he was doing was not carpentry - but not at all out of shape, and well-supplied with the righteous fury that arose from the impact of Faye's beating and the subliminal realization that she had lost interest in him. Rob Stoker paid the price for that, as well as for his assault on Lee. After the lucky left started a trickle of blood from Terry's nose, it was all downhill from there.

Finally, tiring of shielding delicate Lee Forsythe from the awful sights, Faye intervened.

"Terry! Stop ... Hey, stop, Terry. He's licked. Stop hitting him!"

Terry turned toward Faye, still holding Rob upright with his left hand so he could more conveniently belabor him with his right. "Thick so? Oh, all right. You hurt, Biss?" He dropped Rob to the floor and knelt before Lee, concern heavy in his face. Without taking his eyes from Lee, he held out a hand with snapping fingers; Faye figured it out and gave him a wet paper towel from the stack by the cooler.

"Thaks, Faye, hear? You all right, Huddy?"

Lee sniffled into her hanky. "Yes, sir. Thank you ever so much."

"Thick dothing of it, Biss ...?"

"Forsythe."

Faye, against her better instincts: "Terry Morgan, meet Lee Forsythe, our intern. Lee has been working with us since August. Terry is a contractor here in Gabbro." *And a real problem child, Honey. Please, please do not give him those big wet eyes, or you'll be sorry.* "Terry, you and I had some business to transact."

"Huh? Oh, yeah. Hag on, let's get Biss Forsythe settled in - whoa, where'd shithead go?"

"Slunk off, stage left. Lee, was that scene as bad as it looked to us coming in the door?"

Lee blushed and wiped her eyes. "Well, Ma'am, Miss Faye, I'm afraid so. First of all, he spoke very insultingly to me, and when I asked him not to, and to calm down and let me alone, he ... he, well, he grabbed me ... my - " She gestured at herself.

Terry spoke up, helpfully. "Grabbed your kooch and your left hooter, looked like to me."

"OK, Terry, could you leave the verbal part of this to me, please? You're upsetting Miss Forsythe."

"Huh. Can't talk about -"

"Terry."

"Yep, yep, got it. Sorry."

"Did he in fact put his hands on your ... your private parts, and your bosom, Lee?"

"Yes, Ma'am, he done. Didn't just 'put his hands on,' neither. He hurt me."

"Well. I am sorry as I can be. I will see to it that Rob is dismissed immediately, subject, I guess, to our regular procedures in dismissal for cause. If you should choose to bring legal charges, which you would certainly be entitled to do, Mr. Morgan and I could offer a certain amount of corroboration, though our view of it was limited. Are you nearly finished with what you were working on?"

"Got the headline and the lead."

"Could you reasonably take those and finish it up at home?"

"Yes, Ma'am."

"All right." *I'm going to regret this, but* ... "Terry, would you be willing to accompany Miss Forsythe to her home, just to be sure nothing further happens while she is on *Intelligencer* business?"

"You bet."

"Fine, then. Please do so, while I get a little bit of work done here. Hurry back, and I'll have your check ready for you. Check that desk down the hall to be sure Rob is gone for sure. And Lee, maybe you'd like to go into the Ladies' and polish up your face a little, so you don't upset your folks, OK?"

While Lee was off stage, Faye beckoned Terry closer. "Listen, Terry. Please don't let me hear of any untoward behavior toward Miss Forsythe. You are on your honor. And for God's sake, don't you dare ask if her kooch is feeling better, got it?"

Terry grinned. "Yes, Ba'ab."

***

In Standish, Maine, Peter Standish leaned back in his swivel chair, raised his hands, and laughed giddily at the ceiling. Five small pages of Faye's neat handwriting swooped and fluttered to the floor beside him.

***

"Rob, what the heck? What made you think you could do that to anybody, let alone a fifteen-year-old girl?"

"Sixteen."

"Well, so what? And don't tell me it won't happen again, because I already know that. You're gone. Clean out your desk."

Rob looked shocked. "What? You cain't do that. I get a probation period, and listen, I'll clean up my act, promise, Forde."

"Stop and think. You're already on probation, because of ... of that previous complaint, that you and I discussed last week."

"Anonymous hearsay. Carries no weight."

"Where'd you get that idea?"

"I got a right to confront my accuser. It was that little bitch Jenny, wasn't it?"

"Well, maybe you can figure it out, Rob. Who else have you been assaulting?"

"Just - Nobody. It's all a fairy tale. Your Daddy woun't of carried on like this."

"Sorry, Rob. I hate to see you go, you been here longer'n me, and you're almost the last holdover from Daddy's day."

"Bitch Jenny been here from then."

"OK, fine. But it's a different day now, and as long as I'm running this newspaper, men will keep their hands to themselves around women. Go on, pack up. You got a half hour."

"You're one to talk, you been prongin Bynum for years, what, no hands? I'd like to see how that -"

"Shut your fool mouth, Stoker. Don't make me mad, or it'll go downhill from here."

"You're gonna be sorry."

"I'm already sorry. That don't change anything. And don't threaten me if you want a decent recommendation."

***

The tray held two glasses of Blue Nun, one of Southern Comfort, one of apple juice, a cylinder of reconstituted potato chips, some downscale crackers, and an expanding crepe-paper turkey, in view of the season. Faye steered it from the kitchen out to the screen porch and distributed to Forde, Annie Godfire, and herself; and to visiting Nora Lundy, who had come to say something that "needs face to face," as she put it. Faye settled carefully into the wicker chaise, which was, Forde thought, roughly seventy years old, and could no longer be flopped onto as he used to when he was a kid.

"So, Nora? You have good news and bad news? Give us the bad first."

"Nope. The bad won't make sense unless you know the good.

Which is, hang on ta your bonnets, you're a shoo-in for a grant of up to $60,000 from TWUA. That's a <u>grant</u>, mind, not a loan. Yer troubles with Mister Merrydown would seem like they're about to be over. There's just a few little conditions, which is where the bad - well, the other, news comes in."

Faye and Forde exchanged looks. "Well, Jesus, hooray, huh, Fordie? C'mere, all of you, for a big group hug. You too, Annie; I know you don't care one way or another about unions, but you do care about Forde and me. And down the hatch, and we'll go spring for some real champagne. Or, wait. Maybe we better hear about the little conditions?"

Nora nodded. "They are various, so I'll start with the simplest. First, ye've got ta write out a proposal, no longer than ten pages, that explains how you're goin' to advance the cause o' unionism in the textile industry. For a newspaper, that would mostly mean editorial pieces in favor of it, and a certain slant to what you choose to call news, which will likely raise some blood pressure here in North Carolina."

Faye shrugged. "I do that for a living. I'll have a draft on Forde's desk to sign off on by ... oh, by five, tomorrow."

"Grand. Second, it will be some weeks after you get the award letter, before you'll see a check. Nothin's ever simple, least of all, the paperwork machinery of a big outfit like a trade union. You'll have to figure out how to bridge whatever gap might come between when your note comes due, and when you've got the funds in hand. Maybe go to Fayetteville, Charlotte, somewhere and take on a short-term loan. I can have an award letter - Pleased to inform, congratulations, sign here, aw that - in your hand before then, that you can take to the bank.

"Third, of course, you'll have to actually follow through on the editorial support of textile unionization, and publish at least two pieces a month for the next two years that show strong support for the workers. Some of that could take the form of advocacy for better working conditions in general, regardless of unionization, mind, but some would have to be flat-out support for collective bargaining, and

TWUA as agent in particular. So, you may want to hire some thugs of your own. Counter-thugs. For bodyguards, ye know. As we all know, Mister Merrydown can play pretty rough. I think the office will be OK if the hardest editorials don't start until after your finances are settled."

Nora puffed out her cheeks and blushed. "Here comes the tricky part. This fund is restricted by charter to benefit Textile Workers' Union members and employees, and their families."

Thoughtful silence. "Well, but ... ?"

"Aye. The Gabbro *Intelligencer* is none o' the above. The only such is mesel', both a member and an employee." A nighthawk cried, intensifying the silence. Then Annie spoke. "But you are carrying Forde's baby, I think."

More silence, and deeper. Then, "Yes, she is. And she's going to marry me, aren't we, Nora?"

"Well, that's it. Rather sounds like I was holdin' a shotgun in one hand, and a bag o' gold in the other, doesn't it? I'd die rather than ..."

Forde did the needed thing: he knelt at Nora's feet. "Nora Lundy, in the presence of these dear friends, I ask you to do me the great honor of marrying me and serving as the mother of my child. Will you? And will you be my wife for the rest of our lives, grants or no grants?"

All the women present teared up, though the tears of one passed gritted teeth on their way to the hanky. But, "Aye," Nora whispered, nodding, as Forde looked up at her. She extended a hand to raise him to his feet, and sang, "I will, Forde Morgan, <u>verra</u> gladly."

The cheer that rose from Annie and Faye and the uproar that followed irritated the nighthawk, who flew into the forest after depositing a comment in the middle of Morgan's Eddy. Among the rejoicing humans, it occurred to no one to wonder how the long-shot hope of a loan of forty or fifty thousand dollars had transfigured to an outright grant of sixty.

16.

PETER'S LETTER CAME ON THE AFTERNOON OF December 1:

11/27/64

Dear Faye –

Your letters about knocked me flat, they were so – oh, I don't know. This note is strictly first draft. Yes, I would be very happy to spend Christmas with you. Are you familiar with Asheville, NC? There are some very nice hotels there, and a great many things to do, When could you get away from Gabbro? Since you ask, my birthday is 12/26. The idea of a "long term friendship with erotic dimensions" is amusing and exciting. Let's plan to celebrate our LTFWED soon.

Yours,
Peter
(Peter A. Standish, MD)

***

12/1

Dear Peter -

Thanks for your letter. I hope you have managed to rise and un-flatten yourself. I am <u>very</u> happy at the thought of spending Christmas with you, but there is one problem I feel I must raise.

Some years ago, I spent Christmas in Asheville with a fellow who I thought might be a good prospect for an LTF. He was charming, but he later betrayed me in a very humiliating way, and Asheville is tainted by that memory. (Lord, this all sounds so Victorian. Please read charitably.) I'd like to ask that we defer Asheville and other mountain settings until we may - as I certainly hope - be more settled into our own LTF. Would some other place serve as well? Maybe somewhere between here and Maine, so you would not have to travel so far. Oh, I hope this doesn't sound too unbearably neurotic!

I can be away from here from 12/23 through your birthday, not returning until the 27th. That should give us ample time to see if what we are discussing is going to work.

I will dust and sweep the vestibule in anticipation.

Yours,
Faye

12/3/64

Dear Faye -

I understand. We'll put Asheville and the whole Blue Ridge up on a high shelf for later consideration. I do have a little apartment in Manhattan, overlooking Central Park. What would you think of a relatively urban setting? Certainly no lack of things to do, once the vestibule has been polished and decorated for the season.

I believe there is train service from Raleigh to NYC fairly regularly. If that appeals, send me your itinerary, and I will be there to meet you.

Yours,
Peter
(Peter A. Standish, MD)

***

From the Gabbro *Intelligencer* for Monday, 11/30/1964:

Mr. Morgan, Miss Lundy
Announce Nuptials

Intelligencer Managing Editor Forde Morgan and Miss Nora Lundy of Glasgow, Scotland have announced their engagement …

RATHBUN OPPOSES WYE PLAN

Sheriff Lyle Rathbun spoke out strongly against a Gabbro Garden Club plan to plant azalea bushes in the Wye, characterizing the idea as "numbskull," and dangerous in that vision would be obstructed …

THIS TOWN'S TIMES
by M. Faye Bynum
Associate Editor

… can't help thinking Sheriff Rathbun has a point about over-decorating the Wye with plantings. You wouldn't put a jungle of potted plants in your church vestibule without risking collisions between worshipers, and …

… On Thanksgiving afternoon, I stood with Editor Forde Morgan, his sister Annie Godfire, and Miss Nora Lundy of Glasgow, Scotland, and watched as Forde and Nora promised to marry and to love each other for the rest of their lives. It was one of the most moving sights I have experienced in my life. Forde and Nora complement each other's strengths and meet each other's needs, and I can only expect a marriage made in …

***

Faye placed this confection on Forde's desk with a wink and the gag-me gesture of a finger down her throat while he was on the phone with the administrator of the Charitable Action Division of the Textile Workers' Union of America. Forde read a few lines, blushed, and raised a finger to hold her there.

"Certainly. Yes, of course, we can do that. I'll speak to our editor … I think she can have a revised narrative in your hands by" - he raised an interrogative eyebrow at Faye; she scribbled 12/10 on his blotter; he crossed out the 10 and wrote 7 - "the eighth. Will that be good enough? … Good. Excellent. We certainly appreciate your interest and guidance in this. … Yes, of course. 'Bye now."

"What, we're not good enough?"

"No, in fact, they're very impressed. They want Nora to be a little more front and center, and they want a little more … lemme see … 'parallelism between our goals and their objectives.' Or was it the other way around? I never can keep those straight. Anyways, you can do that with your eyes closed. The thing about Nora, well, you could do an interview with her, and see how that works out. Make it sound like she's right in the thick of it, which she was, of course, before … well, before all this came up."

"'All this' meaning Forde Junior, and so forth."

"OK, yes. So?"

Faye let that go, but dropped her voice into a Gabbro drawl. "You two actually setten a date yit? First place, you don't want her showin too big, even this day and age, when she tosses that bridal boo-kay. Second place, Ol' Mist' Merrydown holdin that note, comin due first week a January, and we need to get the caish in his hands quick as ever we can, I think, and that means Mr. and Mrs. Nora gotta be one in the eyes a God an' man a good ways before that. Where are we on the bridge loan? ... Gosh, I almost typo'd 'bride loan.' Heh heh."

"Yes, yes, heh. The quicker you get that narrative revised, the quicker the pressure from Merrydown comes off. On the bridge loan, I got a positive nibble from Red Springs Building and Loan, with godawful interest, damn near twenty percent, but we can afford it and pay that out of our year-end renewals, if it's just for a month. Nora and I are working on the date, which is not a simple thing. There are plans and factors to consider."

Hand to cheek. "Och, land. Plans <u>an'</u> factorrs? Fordie!"

Forde rose and closed the office door, taking no particular care with the noisy blind. By the time he turned back to Faye, he was blazing red, but under control. "Faye, dang it, I begged you for years to marry me. So what the hell is all this, ... this sarcasm? It comes poorly from you to be snide like this, now I'm about to marry somebody else after you must of turned me down, I don't know, what do you think? About twenty separate an' distinct times? More? Certainly no less."

Faye had to concede - to herself - that he was right, which mollified no one, least of all her. Forde's dumping the rewrite of their funding pitch on her had irritated her out of all proportion. "Oh, Forde, Christ. I'm just ragging you a little. They play a lot rougher than this in '*Glahzgow*,' I expect. Sure you can handle her? Verbally, I mean."

"*Damn* it, Faye! I'm damned if I can see where you get off, with this so-called ragging. Nora is who I've gotten pregnant as it happens, so, yes, it's Nora I'm going to marry, you bet. For years, I'd have been more than happy to have fathered a baby with you, as you perfectly well know. Well, that's not the way it worked out. So now, all you're doing here is giving me a lot of hard-hearted, juvenile mockery that has no point except to make me mad. Well, fine, good going. You done it. Now, get out of here and revise that grant narrative like we discussed, or we'll all be looking for jobs come January, and you can see how funny that strikes you."

Faye bounced a hand from her forehead. "Jesus, Mary and Joseph. Really? Hard-*hearted*? About what? Are you sure you're not still hoping I'll say Yes to you, even now you've spawned a wee bairn elsewhere? Honest to God, Forde, is that how you see seventeen years of keeping you company and slaving away on this little rag, getting myself beat to a pulp and raped for my trouble, when I could have been, and looks like damn well <u>should</u> have been, putting my own interests first and moving up and out." She stamped her foot. *I have got to stop doing that.* "Is it?"

Forde pointed to the door. "It's not too late. If you think you got prospects elsewhere, you are always free to pursue them. Seems to me I recall a time where you done that, and it didn't work out all that well, compared to staying here and sharing your very considerable gifts with a little rag in a little town that both need 'em badly, but I guess could limp along without. So. Are you quitting, or are you going to do what I asked you to do in regard to this grant application?"

"You damn well know the answer to that." She left, to sit shaking at her desk. *Well, dang, the New Forde. Goodbye, Keeping Company. Why am I so mad about goddamn Nora? What, I want Peter in one pocket and Forde in the other?* She gave herself a shrug and a wrinkled nose. *What it is, I liked being the boss and now, guess what, I'm not.*

When she had calmed down, she picked up the grant manuscript and began to page through it. *Aw right, front an' center wi' ye, you suspiciously easily impregnated Missus Loondy-Morrgan. ...* Wait, <u>juvenile?</u>

She had the revision finished and on Forde's desk before he arrived on Thursday morning.

***

Saturday, December 6

Dear Peter A. Standish, MD:

An apartment overlooking Central Park? Oh, well, I guess. Does it have a vestibule? With a door-man? Or will _you_ have to, er, stand in?

Anyway, the Silver Crescent chugs into Penn Station with me leaping a-flutter from the step (vestibule, really, they call it, but don't try to picture that) and into your arms at 12:57 PM on Wednesday, Dec. 23 - 17 long days from today.

I guess I need not tell you how excited I am, and how hopeful that you will not find me, in any important aspects, less than you remembered.

Yours,
Faye

Dec. 8

Dear Faye –

Let's see. I remember a charming woman with dark eyebrows, a quick mind, a healthy body, a warm heart, and sore ribs. I'm sure all of those are still true, except, I hope, for the ribs. I will be at Penn Station at 12:57 on 12/23 (That was this year, right?). I'll be the ObGyn-looking fellow with the wilted bouquet that I've been pacing up and down the platform with for at least 6 hours.

Yours,
Peter
(Peter A. Standish, MD)

***

For the record, then:

- Forde and Nora's wedding was charming, if modest, executed at 2:15 PM on Saturday, December 19, at Gabbro Methodist with smiling Faye Bynum and solemn Annie Godfire as maids of honor in candleglow tee shirts, indigo bib overalls and work boots. A church-load of *Intelligencer* staff and Gabbro worthies attended. Some of the attendees toward the back may have been covert operatives from TWUA and Merrydown Industries, dry-eyed and stoically ignoring each other. The happy couple departed immediately for a five-day honeymoon in Asheville (Forde's possibly ironically chosen venue).

- The occasion was made all the merrier by the arrival the previous day of a letter from the Charitable Action Division of TWUA, awarding a grant of $60,000 for a 24-month campaign of support for workers' rights in general, and at River Mills in particular.

- On the strength of the award letter, the bridge loan was granted immediately, and drawn upon for a cashier's check from Red Springs Building and Loan in the amount of $51,847.63 that was handed over to Gabbro-Merrydown Prudent in full settlement of the *Intelligencer's* prior loan on December 21.

Faye boarded the northbound Silver Crescent at Fayetteville station at 6:12 AM on Wednesday, December 23, feeling that a number of loose ends had been well screwed down.

***

Peter's face was even more haphazardly carved than Faye remembered, but overlaid by such happiness that it seemed to represent a new standard of male beauty. The bouquet was only a little wilted by the fact of the train's 1:45 delayed arrival. They limited themselves to a cordial trackside kiss of greeting.

There was indeed a doorman in the vestibule of 904 5th Avenue, past whom Faye walked blushing with lowered gaze, to join Peter in a mirror-lined elevator. She sparkled at him in multiple reflections and followed up the sketchy trackside kiss with a detailed reprise while the elevator rose swiftly and at some length. In the mirrors, over his shoulder, the multiplication of Fayes appeared to her a little juvenile and spunky, like Margaret O'Brien in her ingénue phase.

Peter's "little apartment" certainly wasn't tiny, as Faye noticed while they molted coats, galoshes, her shoes and, amid a flurry of banter that popped from kernels of small talk, gliding like Fred and Ginger, spinning off textile impediments past dark paneling, a fireplace, books, and stately 21st-floor windows overlooking a sylvan blur that Faye took to be Central Park.

At the door to his bedroom, Faye stopped long enough to look Peter in the eye and ask herself if this panting fellow was the same as the wizardly gynecologist she had spent the late fall and early winter pursuing in memory; never quite capturing a full-length glossy image a person could take the measure of, but accumulating a scrapbook of wet clothing, large, capable hands, medical diplomas, garnet skarn, the semi-ruly lock of corn-silk hair, that linen voice, and tawny lean arms and legs. And the kind, killer eyes that she now saw were scanning her face in turn, with the same project of gauging reality to reminiscence.

"It's like no time has passed at all, isn't it remahkable?" His voice was faint with longing and anoxia. Facing now the joy in those eyes, the humming body pressed against hers, she nodded breathlessly, *Yes, here we are, it's us again,* and buried her face in his shoulder, kissing his neck and bringing him to a bosom that, she now saw, had been longing for this moment for an entire season of her life.

They passed the left-overs of the afternoon before the fireplace, discussing relational goals and strategies; establishing a few principles, but no final conclusions. It was a time for savoring each other without the sharp neediness that had driven their earlier collision; of polite explorations and revelation of attitudes, yearnings, taboos, likes and dislikes that seemed always to arrive at destinations richer than they might have expected. Faye's liberalism and love of language, Peter's ideas about women in science and politics, were noted as doorways through which they might walk together during future trysts that neither now doubted would follow and elaborate on the present one. They laughed a great deal, and it was the laughter of delight in the prospect before them. Even the tone and tenor of each other's laughter pleased them.

They shared dinner that first night at a little Andalusian place south of Houston Street where the manager knew Peter by name ("Ah, Do'tor Estandeesh, where you been?") and fawned urbanely over Faye while he tucked them into a booth with a pitcher of Sangria that started castanets rattling in Faye's blood. They returned to Fifth Avenue and fell back into bed, stunned.

Faye slept deeply, cradled within Peter's arms and legs. The demons, possibly still looking around for her in Gabbro County, were completely absent. At dawn, she whispered, "Lots better without the rib tape, don't you think?"

Peter had planned their time not to be overloaded. They did squeeze in some ice skating at Rockefeller Plaza on Christmas Eve (Peter swooping, Faye wobbling with cheeks afire), a bundled-up ride on the Staten Island Ferry, more meals in elegant dim eateries, and a matinee performance of "West Side Story" in revival (center orchestra seats, meaningful hand-holding during "There's a Place For Us"). Peter had the taxi detour by Spanish Harlem on the way home, and pointed out Rosa Mejía's building.

Faye acquainted Peter with the joy of morning sex ("Honest? Never?") followed by catered and discreetly delivered breakfast in bed; followed, and so forth. She breathed deeply of freedom, joy, privilege, and Peter's protection, and came within a hair of proposing marriage to him on the rumpled spot, after a delirious Christmas morning. Morgan and Lundy in Asheville, had they even crossed her mind, would have appeared as distant as the pyramids.

On Christmas afternoon, they walked arm in arm through the Park and greeted people as if they had fallen into a rom-com from 1950; they attended a ceremony of carols and readings at St. John the Divine; and over nightcaps between the stately windows and a crackling fire, exchanged gifts. Peter's package contained a charm bracelet containing cunning and apparently custom-made charms of a rubber float, a bikini (two charms); ceramic letters, joined between bars of gold: CPR, LTF, and WED; and five tiny firecrackers. Faye put it on at once, and offered him a laughing kiss. Then it was Peter's turn.

While Faye fretted and looked down on the sparkle and majesty of Manhattan fathoms below her tucked-up feet, he drew out two very small cordial glasses and a glass-stoppered and wax-sealed vial of a clear, pale blue liquid that Faye had begged from Annie. She offered Peter a sample, after pronouncing the Lumbee benediction.

"Eh?"

"Well. Maybe it is out of place here, amidst all this luxury and sophistication. It's a kind of cordial made by the local Indians by mashing and fermenting a berry that grows only in one place, deep in our local swamp. It is amazingly soothing and relaxing; the little bit of alcohol seems to extract some kind of stuff out of the berry seeds. It would be madly expensive if you could buy it, but it's not for sale. You have to be close to a Lumbee Indian to even know about it. Lucky for me, I have a very close half-Lumbee friend.

"You never drink it alone. If you're upset or in pain, it soothes you. If you're celebrating something, it transforms happiness to something even better, that I can't even think of a name for. What it might do for sex, I can't guess, but it might be fun to find out. The thing I said is what you are supposed to say, to get your mind ready, before you taste it. I'll teach it to you."

"You don't need to teach me the spell. I will only ever drink it with you."

"Well." She leaned over and nuzzled his ear to whisper, "Then I can only say, try it."

He did. They did. When he could speak again, Peter said, "Good heavens."

17.

W HAT'S THAT, NOW? ... OH, GOD IN HEAVEN! Forde put the phone down on the desk, followed by his forehead.

"Forde, what is it?"

"Wait a second, I'm still on with the guy. Yes, I'm here. And now what? ... Well, of course, to the best of our - ... All right, there's no need for - ... Yes. I will investigate and get back to you. We are as shocked as you, if not more."

Forde hung up and turned to Faye. "Oh, nothing much. That was Red Springs Building & Loan. The grant check we signed over to them bounced, that's all. We still owe them $51 thousand at twenty percent interest."

Faye sat suddenly in the least uncomfortable visitors' chair. "What? What about our checking account with the rest of the grant?"

"The whole check bounced, Faye, not part of it. Basically, we got no grant at all. Those wonderful folks at TWUA sent us a phony check."

"Oh, for ... wait, that can't be true! That's a big, reputable outfit. They're not going to hang fake paper on us. Are they?"

"Seems like they are. I'll get Nora to call them; I think she'll get better information than I could."

"OK, well, wait a minute. We're still clear of Merrydown, aren't we?"

"N ... Well, I suppose. Yes, sure. We paid him off with a good check, so he's got no problem. And we don't either, except that there's no way we can keep making payments on a 20 percent note, so we just swapped a vicious bastard for a miffed banker who's ready to turn vicious any second now. He said straight out, there's no way they would have made that bridge loan without the grant already a done deal; but they'll sit there and take their twenty percent until we go broke and can't pay it, and then they'll foreclose. We'd be smarter to stop paying right now, and save the usury, except when they foreclose, we'll have to declare bankruptcy, let staff go, cut to the bone and go back to being a neighborhood advertiser. Oh, God, Faye, I just can't do that."

"What about the pro-union articles? The first one is written and typeset, it was supposed to run tomorrow."

"Is it going to get somebody beat up for nothing?"

"I doubt it. It's very general and mild. I meant it as the thin end of the wedge."

"Let it run. I guess we can hold up our end for a bit. But that's all we're doing until we get some satisfaction on this."

"Well, Jesus, Mary and Joseph. Call Nora."

***

January 5, 1965

Dear Faye –

I do hope your Christmas was as magical as mine, and that you will want to get together again as soon as possible. I was thinking in terms of possibly as much as a week or so on one of the sea islands off Georgia or South Carolina. Do you like beach living?

I should also say that I would love to meet the person who produced that amazing blue – Oh, hell. Listen, Faye. I have to say this, because not to say it would damn me for a pusillanimous jerk in my own eyes and for all time. Faye, it turns out that I do love you, We are not talking here about, hey, what a fun girl, and what a fantastic lover. I just plain love you. I want to spend the rest of my life with you. Can we think in those terms?

Yours, really now,
Peter
(Peter A. Standish, MD)

***

Damn. Faye slammed herself into the glider, with a gimlet in her hand and turmoil in her belly. She looked back with disbelief on all the years in Gabbro when things just ticked along on their own, the School Board mismanaging in its comical, not quite harmless way, Forde rapping at her screen door with a bottle in his hand and hope in his heart; Rosie aging gently and loyally underfoot. Years of bland, manageable, undernourished options. *The only constant is change, yeah, stuff that.* What to do about Peter? What about the *Intelligencer*, dangling over a pit of foreclosure and failure?

OK. The *Intelligencer*: No good pretending that its problems were Forde's problems, and she just worked there; or that she could peddle her skills somewhere else as happily and profitably as she did in Gabbro. In seventeen years of sharing its ups and downs with Forde and his crew of more-or-less competent, reasonably loyal fellow non-travellers, it had worked its way under her skin. If the *Intelligencer* was threatened, then so was Faye.

Now, Peter: More than that, Faye felt that in some way she had <u>earned</u> the whole town of Gabbro itself, had created it from nothingness and chaos out of her moral imagination, as a stand-in for all that was unsophisticatedly human, dumb, dangerous, and more or less good-hearted; and paid for it in aggravation, blood, sweat, tears, and broken ribs. She was, in her terms, addicted to the South. How could she ever share that with such a one as Peter Standish? And how could she live without it? So now he "loved" her, and that would surely mean that he would push for something more substantial than an indefinite series of trysts in exotic settings. Did she love him back?

Oh, damn. She certainly did. In the setting, under the spell of New York and of first-class everything, certainly including sex, she had been worried only that she might not be good enough for him. That she might not, in some important sense, have <u>earned</u> a lover as expert, or a husband as kind, fascinating, and, Jesus, as wealthy as Peter Standish of Standish, Maine. Now, that first-afternoon feeling of wonder at this splendid affair had crystallized, inextricable from her very bones, an emotional commitment that she knew even now she would carry to her grave. But could such a man be imported into Gabbro, North Carolina, without detonating at the contrast? Marriage – if it meant cohabitation –was impossible no matter how you looked at it. And how could she manage this commitment without on the one hand, flinging herself into an impossible marriage or on the other, insulting and patronizing Peter by tactful management?

And for another thing: except for the bed interludes, where she had been more or less in charge of the large strategies while Peter filled in the tactics – God, did he ever – there had been a shadow. In spite of her bodily and intellectual delight in Peter, and her firm knowledge of his reciprocation, there had been a faint too-sweetness to the time, epitomized by the Andalusian headwaiter, that made her feel a little like a favorite niece being squired about the *haut monde* by a rich uncle. In Maine, she had initiated and managed the dinner date, right up to the point at which she braced her butt against the garnet skarn and invited him to herself, ready for whatever might follow. However fond one might become of being steered and taken care of by indulgent uncles, could one be her partner in a marriage she could respect?

If not quite, if she never managed to rid the confection of that undertone of inequality, could she really be happy and fulfilled as the ingénue wifey of a successful, sophisticated amalgam of Will Rogers and Jimmy Stewart? And even if she could give up on Gabbro, and go to Standish, Maine, with stops in New York, Hilton Head, and probably goddamn Paris or Biarritz, how could she not turn into an aging diva, getting face-lifts and boob jobs and butt tucks to keep Peter enchanted with her, keep him at the task of sending her into heaven with his charm and his gynecology. All the while not quite loving him rightly, and knowing that she would never, mind you, write another line of decent prose. She supposed she could probably write a "memoir," God help us, of life as an ex-person.

On Morgan's Eddy, a fish broke the surface to suck down a bug who'd probably had other plans. Faye sipped her gimlet and settled herself against the back of the glider. Frog divas trilled.

... Oh, shit. There was a path forward that might, played rightly, solve her problem, and the *Intelligencer*'s at one stroke. And restore to her the manageable poverty of options she'd been missing. What if she signed on to Peter's infatuation, responded that, Oh, God, she had been praying that he might find her worthy even to kiss his sandals, and *Of course I will marry you, darling, with my heart in my hand (not the one with the fingers crossed). But by the way, Honey, I have this ... this thing, such a stupid awful financial problem, but I bet you could probably clear it up easy. There's this debt, see, but I bet you spent that much on our Christmas in New York. Which I loved, by the way, specially the fucking part, which I will sure be in a mood to get back to, soon as we can get this little 51K issue off my mind.*

And Peter, his bluff called, would have to put up or shut up. And he would put up of course, what, a 48 year old guy in love with a woman young enough to be his ... well, his baby sister. He would write that check and she would give him a big lipsticky smooch and start fiddling with his buttons like a two-bit whore, and, with scales good and fallen from his eyes, he would turn around and go back to instructing his little dark-eyed charges in luffing and coming about.

All problems solved, except that it would be the end of Peter, their love, his baseless belief in her "clear honest intelligence," her "simplic-ity," oh, yes. *And what do you call it when a woman offers a man access to intimate parts of her body in exchange for value?* At least she would be free of the no-charge label.

She rose, put her empty gimlet glass in the sink, and fell into bed, baffled and heartbroken. She wanted Rosie, into whose fur she had cried so many times.

***

"Aye, that's the long and short of it. The very bahstard that signed your check absconded. Embezzled the place dry, an' not just the grant funds, but everything. The total loss is in eight or nine figures, and there's hardly one dime left to rub against another."

"Well, Jesus. Can't they track him down?"

"Oh, I suppose they will, eventually, and in a couple of years they'll try him and throw him in a dungeon. Meanwhile, the whores and the bookies and ... I don't know, pushers and Lamborghini salesmen he's throwing it at right the minute of now, they are fannin' through the bills and makin' plans for early retirement. The money is as good as gone."

Faye fell back against Forde's visitor chair, and gazed at Nora, who examined the floor at her feet. "So that's how ye hit it sa grand as to win bigger than ye were ever looking for. He knew ye'd never see a nickel of it in any case. The spalpeen." Faye could see a tear hanging from the end of her snubby little Scottish nose, and was slightly moved.

Forde cleared his throat. "What about some kind of insurance? And you've got dues income, I suppose."

"Oh, aye, some of each. Enough to light the lights, and pay a boss, a few staffers and a lawyer or two. They'll sell some assets that were too heavy to carry off to Singapore or wherever he is. But it'll be fifty years before there's enough surplus to give grants again. If ever. How long can you hold on an' pay that amazin' interest on your debt with Red Springs?"

"Maybe six months, if we cut expenses way back, get down to maybe three or four of us putting out a four-pager that nobody would bother to read, or advertise in. After that, I don't see ..."

Nora shook her head. "Just in time to welcome young Custis into the world."

***

January 9, 1965

Dear Peter -

What a pleasure it was to read your letter, following up on our Christmas visit. I, too, am in a "state" about our relationship, and I very much need to have you close, so that I can speak my heart to you.

... Well, I see that this first paragraph (what you see is the 7ᵗʰ 8ᵗʰ draft) is something short of blazingly encouraging. Do not be discouraged, dear Peter. I was in heaven every minute of our time together in New York.

I desperately need to see you and speak to you face to face. Is there any chance that you could come down here for a weekend, soon? I could hold out as an inducement that I will introduce you to my (honorary) sister, the source of the blue cordial. Also, of course, that your presence would fill an aching void in my life.

With love,
Faye

Tuesday, January 12

Dearest Faye -

Faye, is anything wrong? I would do anything to fill your aching voids. *I do hope and pray that nothing in my prior letter offended you, or pressured you in any way. I wish only happiness for you.*

I will be at your door by noon on Saturday, provided you send me directions before then.

*Oh, dear. I'm going to let that stand, with the plea that single entendres are as much as I can manage, most of the time.

Yours,
Peter
(Peter A. Standish, MD)

Dear Peter -
Directions to my house would involve things like, "Look for the live-oak with the lightning scar, then it's the second lane on your right."
Come to the Intelligencer office at 61 Church Street, and I'll meet you there at noon.

Love,
Faye

***

Forde put the phone back in its cradle with the care due nitroglycerin. "Let's continue. Faye, you manage the office and reporting staff. Where can you save us some money?"

Faye puffed her cheeks. "God, Forde. I will gladly take a cut. I can afford I guess a 30% reduction for as long as this crisis lasts. Beyond that, well. Rob Stoker is already gone, and Peter Maribel is filling in for him, with no salary increment. And doing a better job, at that. Replacing Sharon with Sedalia Baley has saved us some. Though in fact, a receptionist is a luxury we could probably do without, though I would hate, <u>hate</u> to give Sedalia a pink slip. The highest salary after mine is Jenny, and she's been here forever. Obits and social news sell ads and papers, so we could be killing an egg-laying goose to lay her off or lead her to quit. Golden eggs, I mean. Well, maybe silver." She tossed a hand. "Pewter. But still."

"Uh huh. The phone call was Naylor Oxendine at Red Springs B n' L. I sent him a letter asking if we could refinance that loan at a more reasonable rate, seeing it's going to be longer-term than we planned for. Long an' short of it, yah, maybe, down to around eleven percent. Still mighty stiff, but it would give us a few more months of life before we inevitably go belly-up. But here's the kicker: They been getting visits from Mason Merrydown, looking interested. He's just tendered a buyout offer that Naylor thinks is maybe twenty percent above their real worth, and the Board would be nuts to pass it up. Apparently, somebody informed Mister Merrydown of our problems, and he's making a move to get us back under his thumb. Maybe he wants to get us back on his side on the union thing. Or, I guess, he's just being a mean bastard who doesn't like to lose."

After a silence, Faye rose, shaking. "Give me a few days. I thought of something last night that might help."

***

"Faye, my word, this is just perfectly beautiful. What a delightful place to live."

"Uh huh. I guess I'm used to it by now."

Peter turned to her from his contemplation of the Eddy. "Faye. Would this be a good time to tell me what it is that's bothering you? That you needed to speak about face to face?"

Faye didn't answer, but continued to look at the Eddy. In days of worrying at her dilemma - that she could never give up living in Gabbro, but that the only way she could see to insure that - by rescuing the *Intelligencer* - would be to wheedle the money from Peter; and simply to acquaint him with the problem would amount to wheedling the solution, she recognized. And thereby expose herself as no different from a gold-digger trading sex for money, *you bet, soon as we can get this little 51K issue off my mind.* She shook her head slowly, and in the glow from inside the cottage, Peter saw a shine on her cheek. It hit him like a dart.

"Faye! Please, what is it? What, are you ill or something?"

She smiled. "No, I'm not. That would either make everything simple, or so completely ballsed up that I would simply give up. Look, Peter, my dear friend. I am just about deaf, dumb, and paralyzed with a horrible problem that seems to have only one solution, and that solution is even more horrible than the problem. And, worst of all, I simply cannot talk about it now."

Cruelest of women's weapons, even when wielded with no ill will: *Something is terribly wrong, but I can't talk about it.* But men relate to women, particularly now in 1965, by fixing things! How can they do that, one of the handful of ways they have figured out in 100,000 years of trying to please women, without knowing what to fix?

After a half-hearted supper, during which they spoke of Peter's sailing girls or of nothing, Faye turned down the sheet on the big, cool bed, and said, "Peter, this is nothing to do with you, and I'm not ... Oh, mad at you, or disappointed, or tired of you, or ill, or pregnant, or anything. In fact, I'm pretty sure I love you dearly, and that I will for all time. I've thought that before, and been wrong, so I'm a little wary ... but ...

"No! That is not what I mean to be saying now. This is just something that I have to figure out on my own. Thank you, thank you so much for being here; it's very sweet and helpful. But here's another thing: I don't dare sleep with you until I figure this thing out. I'm going to take a sleeping bag and sleep on the porch. You sleep here, and don't you dare come around in the night, because I won't be able to resist. In the morning, after we sleep on it, maybe I will be able to see things more clearly. Until then, can you please indulge me in this ..."

She fell on his shoulder in tears. "This extreme, world-class bitchery?"

"Of course, Faye. But, you know, sex is a language too, and one that you and I have spoken very fluently in the past."

"Yes, I know. I've loved our, our conversing that way, whether it was little chats, or whole three-act dramas. It's been like talking to … I don't know. A wise and funny philosopher. A mentor and a peer. But that's why I just can't talk to you right now, even that way. I would be a terrible partner, just like I'm being with words. I'd be like talking to the village idiot."

***

Surely by intervention, the evening of January 16, 1965, was the first night of full moon for that month. Fidgeting and frowning and twitching covers off and on again, Peter Standish dozed while the moon rose over Morgan's Eddy, until the dazzle reached him after midnight, as it had so often reached Faye in this same bed; and woke him like a thirsty two-year-old in the night. He lay, then, arms behind his head, and weighed his situation.

Here he was, physically, in his lover's bed; but no lover. Here he was, geographically, hundreds of miles from anything he had ever called home; dressed in boxers and a white tee shirt, stymied in what he had thought would be a straightforward renewal of their love affair, with Dixie overtones. Here he was, emotionally, in a vast wasteland – a phrase popular at this time – of puzzlement, helpless to offer Faye any of the four things male humans know how to offer females (fix things, copulate, earn a living, explain), none of which seemed to be what Faye needed now. He stared into the rafters overhead, seeking insight, finding only splintery puzzles.

He dozed again – and lo, now here she was with him in the small hours because, lying on the floor of the screened porch watching the moon rise out of the forest on the far side of the Eddy, it came to Faye, with the force of Saul's conversion, that she did in fact love Peter in such a solid, quiet way that she could not imagine not loving him, however long they lived; that it was the depths of unfairness to invite him here and refuse to tell him why she had; and that if she did not embrace him in the next five seconds, she would go screaming mad. Which increased her dilemma enormously.

But, dear Lord, his simple goodness! His awkward smile, his impossible eyes, his funny ways of speaking and thinking, his breathless boyishness and his kind, forgiving maturity in the face of her unfathomable bitchiness; his lean and muscular body and his enthusiastic sexual expertise, as if he had at last found a co-investigator and partner like Julie, who could share with him the elegant, earthy delights of transcendent neurophysiology. And that impossible mixture of laughter, worship, take-charginess, and calm protective admiration. That was like - Oh, God, no ... That was fatherly.

Chahming. I remind him of Julie, and he reminds me of my father. Well, I am not going to let that spoil it. She rose and went to him, breathing tears, touching his cheek, weeping quietly.

"My dear, dear Peter, what can I do? I'm so sorry, I love you so much. Please hold me."

"Faye?" *Stupid question.* "Faye, come here to me."

"Wait. Please, don't kiss me, or anything ... you know, gynecological. Just hold me."

"Fine. You bet."

"The full moon will last two more nights."

"Yes?"

"That's important."

"All right. Sleep now. I'll hold you. I will be here with you as long as you need me."

"That's exactly what I need."

***

When Peter woke at dawn, Faye, knowing what was good for her, was gone again. He rolled over, and re-woke to the sight of her in a tee shirt and shorts, doing something Yoga-like outside the kitchen door, her breath steaming in the morning chill. When she returned, he was puttering with cereal and milk in the kitchen.

"Good morning."

"Good morning, Peter."

"Faye, I -"

"Yes. I know."

"Ayah. Milk?"

"No, thank you. Peter, I clearly have some big apologizing to do. So, I apologize for bringing you here, and then -"

"No, you don't. Listen: I would rather be <u>with</u> you in whatever trouble and awkward silence like this, than in Maine without you."

"Well, that's ... Oh, Peter. That's so like you. It's so sweet."

"Not so intended, except, I guess, as the truth is sweeter than silence."

"Oh, God, I'm so sorry, Peter. All right, let me just try to... No, wait. I need to work up to this. You said you wanted to meet the person behind the blue cordial?"

"Well, yes. That doesn't seem terribly important just now, does it?"

"Maybe it will be. Anyway, it's something to do that needs done. Finish up, now. Do you want a shower? I'll need to show you how to turn it on."

"How to turn on a showah?"

"Everything in this house, including the shower, is enigmatic, Peter. Let me clear up at least that little mystery for you. Be quick, though, I have to go in to the office this morning, and we'll go out to visit Annie after lunch. You could come into town with me, and if you run out of excitement in Midtown Gabbro, go out to the College and try to make yourself understood."

***

If Faye were perfectly honest with Peter and with herself – and the pain of not having been so was astonishing – she would have admitted to both of them that she saw Annie Godfire's meadow and the Spirit Catcher as a venue in which dissembling and inscrutability were impossible; and that by taking Peter there, she would be letting herself fall into a pool of perfect honesty, wherein it would be impossible to conceal her hopes of a financial rescue at Peter's hands.

And thus, not her fault if she did, right? Preferably through the medium of Annie's no-nonsense reading of hidden motives. None of this did she admit to herself in so many words. Rather, thinking in images, she simply pictured the meadow, the Spirit Catcher, and Annie herself as a microclimate of complete clarity, unlike the swamp of debt, questions, emotions, and shameful motivations through which she now floundered.

Driving there in the yellow Volkswagen after lunch at the Terminal, she did her best to prepare Peter for the culture shock. "Peter, you know that Southerners are susceptible to talk of spirits, ghosts, arcane stuff like root conjury and witching."

"Yes?" Wary, bracing himself for something Gothic.

"Well, I don't mean to alarm you. Annie Godfire is not a witch or a root doctor or any of that. But she has a certain Gift, that I was as skeptical of as I'm sure you are. She helps people see themselves honestly, and without pretense."

"Uh huh. Does she do palms?"

"She doesn't have to. Notice, I didn't say that <u>she</u> sees the truth people are trying to hide, or not to see. She makes them see it. She's really quite amazing."

"Well. All right. Sounds like quite a gift."

"I won't try to convince you. You'll either see it for yourself, or you won't; and if not, nothing I can say will change that."

"Does it mean that she will help me see what it is that's bothering you so badly?"

Faye drew a breath. "Not exactly, I guess. Honestly, I'm hoping she'll see what's bothering me, and tell us both."

"Huh."

"Spoken like a skeptical male, and I can't blame you. Now, about the Spirit Catcher ..." But Faye did not have much describing to do, since by now they were jouncing down Annie's lane and into the meadow full of goats.

"Goats?"

"Yes. She has expenses, so she supplements her income with goat milk and fudge."

"Refreshingly mundane. But ... oh, my heavens! Faye!"

The Spirit Catcher was now forty feet high, and perched on top was Annie Godfire, wielding a brilliant torch and juggling an iron garden gate into place.

"Hey, Faye! Hang on, I'll be right down."

Peter craned his neck to take it in. "And as for whatever this is ... ?"

"Well, see. Let me start from the beginning. I told you about Annie's Gift. She is convinced – and she is right about so many things, I'm at a loss not to believe her on this too – she is convinced that her Gift is the product of listening to spirits, with which her world is crammed full. Her world, I say, though maybe she's just better at seeing them in our world. Anyway, I might as well plow ahead and say this: the structure you see before you is meant to be attractive to spirits, who will gather on, or around, it, and help her in her counseling."

Peter decided to let the crazy part pass, in favor of something familiar. "She counsels?"

"Yes. Couples, criminals, depressed and baffled people, crazies of all kinds, with which we are of course well supplied down here. She tells them things that are common sense counseling, but based on insights provided by her Gift; and says it's not her talking, it's the spirits." Faye sighed. "I'd be indulgently skeptical of it all, if it wasn't for the Gift, which I have seen many times with my own skeptical eyes. That's what makes her different from any other country herb doctor."

"Hm. What's ... my goodness, it's all made out of ... of things, isn't it? That's a lawn mower, and a ... a train coupler? And a fence. And ... oh, my lord, an auto transmission? How does she get all that up there?"

"Well, that's the other thing. She is the strongest person I've ever met. She slings around things that weigh hundreds of pounds as if they were made of styrofoam."

"Goodness. I do look forward to meeting her."

"Well, here she comes."

Peter looked up to see Annie stowing her torch and starting to descend. "And she's your honorary sister?"

"Yes, we ... " Faye sighed. "One afternoon, years ago, we each rescued the other from drowning in Morgan's Eddy. So you have something in common."

***

Driving back to Morgan's Eddy some hours later was a silent exercise. Peter, because he had, with Annie's guidance, climbed to the current top of the Spirit Catcher while Annie and Faye were in conference, and there had experienced something that had shaken him substantially. Faye, because during that conference she had as usual been brought face to face with herself by the Gift:

"Annie, you can't do this to me. Please, I need your help so badly."

"You're getting it. What I think you mean to say is, you need me to tell Peter that he should lend the *Intelligencer* money, so it can get out from under its load of debt."

"Well ... yes. Why does that feel so wrong?"

"What makes you think it is?"

"Because otherwise, you'd be fine with it."

"I don't think this is about my feelings, though, do you?"

"No. I suppose it's about mine."

"And what are they?"

Faye stared into the meadow; a goat looked up and stared back, and returned to its grazing; Faye plucked a stem of winter-dried clover and twirled it.

Annie smiled. "The fact that you don't want to tell me, tell you anything?"

Faye tossed the clover to the ground. "I'm ashamed of them."

Annie squinted into the sky above the Spirit Catcher. Peter was near the top, making careful progress. "Well. Why?"

"All right. Because sleeping with Peter, and then asking him for a lot of money feels like gold-digging."

"Not familiar with the term," Annie lied. "Explain?"

"A gold-digger is a woman who induces a man to spend a lot of money on her, in exchange for sex. Or the promise of sex. It's kind of slow-motion prostitution."

"Huh. So that would make you the slow-motion whore, and Peter the ... what is that slang term for a whore's client?"

"A john. Which is a pretty pathetic form of a human being. I would be making a decent, kind, very talented man, into a john."

"Land. You have that power?"

Faye opened her mouth, waited, and spoke. "I do, in the context of our relationship, yes."

"Must feel kind of odd ... Oh, gosh!"

Faye yelled in turn, because Annie had suddenly gripped her thigh hard enough to hurt, while looking up into the Spirit Catcher. Faye looked up and saw Peter dangling by one hand from a crowbar at the top of the Spirit Catcher. "Hang on, Peter! Annie, save him!"

"Get up there quick as ever you can, Faye. He's fixin' to fall."

Faye gaped at Annie, who pushed her toward the base of the Spirit Catcher. "You get up an' help him get another hand grip. I'll come on after to be sure he's safe. G'on, now! Do it!"

With her next breath, Faye found herself swarming up the first levels of the Spirit Catcher, hands and feet flailing at the steel rods and arabesques. After the first twenty feet, she lost a shoe, and the rough cold steel started hurting, but she climbed on past Peter's bicycling feet as they reached for footing. He had managed to get a second hand-hold by this time; but he still dangled toward the inside of the structure, which at this latitude had started its inward taper, so that he hung into forty feet of empty space. She let go with one hand, grabbed an ankle, and guided his foot onto a crankshaft from a Wegeman's Funeral and Furniture hearse.

"Ah," Peter gasped. "Faye! How did you get all the way up here?"

Faye looked down - a mistake - to see how far up she had gotten; and nearly passed out. At that moment, though, Annie Godfire came swarming up the interior of the Spirit Catcher, plucked Peter from his gut-straining backwards lean, and vaulted over the top. Chucking Peter over her right shoulder and Faye over the left, she eased the three of them down the Spirit Catcher to the ground.

On the way down, Peter and Faye gazed at each other across Annie's working butt. "Faye, you just saved my life." The words came out a little irregularly, because of the jouncing Annie's shoulder worked on his diaphragm.

"I did noth ... ing of the -"

Peter shook his head, mouthed "I love you," and held up a finger, indicating that he would pick up the discussion once they were on firm ground.

Hence, the passage from Annie's meadow to Morgan's Eddy in which the wheezing clatter of the Volks engine was not broken by dialogue. When they were parked at the foot of the cottage stairs, Faye circled around to the passenger side and took Peter's hand to lead him down onto the dock, while the sun kept its wintertime appointment with the forests to the southwest.

"Sit down, please."

He did.

"Peter, Annie showed me myself this afternoon, and as usual, I'm ashamed of myself. It's clear that the only way open to me is to be honest and frank about what's been bothering me, and throw myself on your mercy."

"My stahs, Faye -"

"Wait, OK? Let me get this over with."

"OK."

"OK. A little over five years ago, one of the *Intelligencer* presses broke down just as we were going into the holiday ad season ..."

18.

WHAT? <u>THAT'S</u> THE HORRIBLE DILEMMA THAT'S been chewing at you all this time?"

Faye swirled a bare foot through the waters of the Eddy. "Don't make light of it, Peter. I've been through hell on this."

"But, Faye ... well, I'm sorry it's bothered you so, of course. But my heavens, if we can't ask each other for help when we need it, what kind of future -"

"This is not as if I were asking you to run my zipper up. This -"

"Or down, alas."

The foot snapped through the water, sending an arc of silver drops through the early dusk. "Oh! <u>Can</u> you please take me seriously? I am talking here about very strong feelings of shame and disgust with myself, and you joke around about them."

"What? Shame and disgust about what? Asking a friend for help?"

"You're not a friend. Not <u>just</u> a friend, I mean. You are a man with whom I have slept, numerous times, beginning on our very first date. You're my lover, Peter. And I have just realized how enormously I love you. That makes it very different."

"And that disgusts you? Faye! Why didn't you -"

"No, of course not, <u>will</u> you pay attention! No, it's that I slept with you and loved you so completely. and I got you to commit yourself, all that, which I was fine with; very happy about, in fact. But then I turn around and say, 'Oh, by the way, sweetheart, I've got this little $50,000 difficulty, and could you be a *darling* dear, and bail me out of it,' like some gold-digging Damon Runyan chippie. And then I was sure that if I asked you anything like that, you would pony up, but be so disillusioned and disgusted that it would kill the relationship. And now Annie has half-convinced me that by thinking that, I was insulting you. And, OK, now I see that, but maybe that <u>will</u> turn you off, that I thought so little of your ... your devotion, or willingness, or something. And I'm so mixed up and miserable that I don't know where I am."

"Half convinced?"

"Completely. Annie doesn't do things by halves. So can you forgive me? For just the insulting part? On the understanding that forgiving me for that doesn't at all solve the rest of it?"

"Faye, for ... No, wait." Peter began to see a very attractive path through this thicket that might allow him to check off at least two of the big four male-female bonding channels. "Faye, my very dear friend, yes, of course."

She looked up at him beside her on the dock, and he looked so earnest that she began to think, for her part as well, that there might be a way out of this. "Yes. All right, but I need to actually hear you say it. You forgive me?"

"I do, I forgive you. With all my heart."

"For ..."

"Well, for, you know. I forgive you for when ... for the paht about ..." Peter snapped his fingers, and memory sprang to the rescue. "The insulting paht."

"I didn't mean to insult you, Peter. I love you."

"Well, of course you didn't. So do I. Love you."

"So you're not insulted that ... you know."

"Of course not. Fahthest thing from my mind."

"Because thinking you would be disgusted with me for asking you for money when we are lovers, is not a trivial matter."

Oh, that. "Well, look, Faye. Sometimes it's best not to over-analyze things, don't you think? Or look for trouble where it doesn't exist.

The fact is that I'm not in the least disgusted, or disgruntled, or even ... I don't know. Piqued. Peeved. Perturbed. Annoyed. Askance. Not one of those." He risked twinkling at her. "Not even miffed, or moody."

Faye softened, without twinkling back. "All right, Peter, thank you. Thank you so much. Now. The fact remains that you and I have an ongoing and profound personal and sexual relationship."

Hadn't noticed it, lately. "Yes, it does. Remain. Which means -"

"Which makes me very uncomfortable to be asking you for money. A lot of money."

"But look, it isn't you, I thought. It's your publisher, what was his name?"

"No, but I ... Well ... Forde Morgan. On his behalf, though." Faye paused a moment while this new perspective settled in. "Well, I suppose that is different. But you should know that in the past, Forde and I also had a relationship."

Christ, woman, so what? Peter put on a serious face and a gentle voice. "Perhaps we could deal with that separately, at a later time." *Or never.* "But listen: It seems to me that we're working on an unexamined premise here, which is that I have fifty thousand dollars lying around to hand over to bail you out. Your paper. This Morgan fellow."

"Well ... " The foot swirled the dark water.

"I don't."

"Oh ... You don't?" Faye peered into an abyss. *Then what was all this about?* Despair rose from the heart of the Eddy and contemplated her foot. She pulled it out and tucked it under her other leg.

"No, I don't. But look, how's this? I certainly would be open to a proposition from Morgan that I buy a share of the *Intelligencer* for, oh, somewhere between fifty and fifty-five thousand dollars. Do you think he might be open to such a proposition? We would need, of course, a competent third-pahty appraisal to determine the monetary value of the *Intelligencer,* so as to determine in turn what percentage of its assets - and thus its earnings - I would be buying."

"Yes? Yes." Faye's breath began to shorten. *But I don't think there's a house in this whole county that has three potties.*

"So I would not be doing this as a favor to you, Faye. I would have to sell some assets to realize the kind of cash we're talking about. But this would be a business arrangement between the *Intelligencer* and myself which, frankly, I would be going into with the expectation of making money in the long run. Because I understand that the paper is widely read in pahts of North Carolina for the sake of one particular staff writer, this Bynum person."

Faye laughed, and it felt like a sob of relief. "Well, ... " She fished a Kleenex from her shorts and blew her nose. "That is a very flattering and attractive offer in my opinion, and I will be pleased to refer it to Mr. Morgan for his consideration." *He always does what I tell him to.* "Let's go lay a fire."

And when they had laid and lit the fire, and held hands at the end of the dock and fallen backward together into the Eddy to bathe away the tension under the rising and still full moon, and hustled dripping and shivering to the cottage, bundled in Faye's for-the-purpose robes; and when they had used the robes to dry each other before the snap and hiss of the burgeoning fire, fumbling and kissing and skipping supper to repair in tearful celebration to the wide warm bed, and there exhausted each other, pending midnight hunger or dawn; and finally, when Faye's legs were pleasantly tangled with Peter's, and her head lay sleeping damply on his shoulder: when <u>all</u> this was done at last, Peter looked back on the sudden incident ... *phenomenon*, call it, that had made him lose his grip at the top of the Spirit Catcher.

Spirits, fiddlesticks. He could think of a dozen perfectly natural explanations for the voices of Faye and Julie whispering and singing together in the wind-crooning of a heap of scrap steel. In the first place, Julie ... Well, Julie aside, Faye was busy talking to this Annie when he heard it. And besides, look. You can hear anything you want to hear, out of randomly modulated white noise.

He looked into the rafters overhead and now saw in their slants and crossings a dozen variations on the numeral 4, and smiled. Fixing things, *check*. Sex, *check*. Earning a little money, maybe ... *check, anyway*. Explaining can come later. Thanks, spirits.

19.

A THIRD-PARTY APPRAISAL WAS OBTAINED, AGREED to by the parties of the first and second parts, and included in settlement papers. The round sum of $55,000 was found to correspond to the round percentage of 22.2% of the current value of the Intelligencer Company. Peter sold his part ownership in Camp Nokoma and took an equity loan on the Manhattan apartment for the remainder, and deposited it all in the Yankee Whaler's Thrift Society of Standish, Maine. The entire amount was signed over to skittish Red Springs Building and Loan with a cashier's check drawn from Yankee Whaler's in full payment of the *Intelligencer*'s debt, leaving a modest chunk of working capital.

Faye threw a celebratory cookout at the cottage for the *Intelligencer* staff on Saturday, February 13. Forde addressed the little crowd, slogging through the nature, history, and extent of the paper's financial straits (already well known to all of them); and then introduced the new two-ninths part owner and publisher, Dr. Peter Standish, who had driven down from Maine for the occasion.

Peter made a short speech in which he gave just enough selective background about his interest in the *Intelligencer* to leave them with the impression that he had been a long-time admirer of Faye's book, to which he might have been introduced by a Massachusetts-based editor friend (most Carolinians having only a rudimentary idea of the difference between Maine and Massachusetts in the first place.) No more than three ordinary English words in five, as rendered in his down-east accent, were comprehensible to them in any case. Forde then circulated him through the crowd, introducing Peter and distributing paychecks that included a small but noticeable bonus, courtesy of the excess working capital. Thus were the *Intelligencer* working stiffs conditioned to associate Peter with a pleasant surprise.

Peter then walked about on his own, being charming even to Rob Stoker, who had been invited in spite of his recent termination, and who attended, sulkily, because he was not in a position to pass up a free meal. Rob did not approach Forde Morgan, and in fact was shunned by all the women present and most of the men. He left early after hanging around drinking beer and eating pig-pickings with the press operators, who were not in the loop, and might not have seen in any case what was so transgressive about Rob's transgression.

Nora was there with a pretty good paunch on her now, and it made Faye laugh without a trace of irony at how pleased Forde was about that. Tipped in advance by Faye, Peter was particularly charming to Sedalia Baley, grinning and welcoming her as, like himself, a relative newbie, and leaving her awestruck in his wake. When the leftovers were cleaned up and most of the guests gone, Peter made sure to be seen departing in the Jaguar, but circled back to Annie's meadow. There he met Faye, who had walked up the river path, to settle down for a family welcome and counseling session with Annie, facilitated and joyfully solemnized by jots of blue cordial.

All very well; crisis resolved, Merrydown slapped to the background long enough for winter to succumb, and spring to reassert itself; and for the *Intelligencer* to recover its equanimity. A losing basketball season for Gabbro High's Quarrymen dribbled to a close and yielded to baseball, whose uncertain prospects were capably surveyed by Peter Maribel. The pregnancy of Nora Lundy Morgan ripened into its seventh and eighth months, with a date circled in the first week of July.

Forde busied himself with preparing a nursery and shopping for nursery furniture with Nora, and with being happy. He took pride in the burgeoning of Nora's belly into the very image of fruitfulness, ignored the tutting of the conventional who were numerate enough to subtract nine from July, and worshiped her as humans of old must have worshiped their big-bellied fertility totems. The mystic-messenger significance she had borne for him deepened, now that she indeed carried a message, not from the past but from a future that held his genetic immortality in the form of the child in her belly. When they made love, he felt himself joined to the line of his inheritance - and hers, to be sure; a link that joined two ancient lines of humanity. In that light, his earnest dalliances with Faye Bynum now appeared to him as no more than sterile distractions.

He bored the *Intelligencer* staff with rhapsodies on life, love, and reproduction; he even took some pleasure in needling Faye about, well, wasn't she just a little sorry that it was not she who waddled into the Terminal Café for lunch, big as a barn?

Not at all; because this spring also included several delirious get-aways with Peter Standish. Once on Hilton Head; once in Asheville, where the disastrous affair with Travis Wayland felt to Faye like an anecdote from grade school. Also, once each at Standish, Maine and Faye's cottage; and a memorable four-day weekend in New York.

But love and lover-ship, the easiest bases to touch, deepened into the only state that could overcome Faye's lonerism: intimate, intricate, fond and long-term friendship. They both loved nature, and proudly showed each other particular glories of their states. They competed in recommending books that each knew the other would admire. They amused each other by agreement or disputation about The Sixties and their politics, music, and notions of Love. They hiked, they swam, they cooperated to weave outlandish theoretical dreamcastles about Nature and her workings.

For all that, there was no drop in temperature along the bed axis, though the Maine interlude was nowhere near as giddily erotic as New

York, or even Gabbro had been. Something about the place inhibited both Faye and Peter, the scion of the founding family. It brought forth a visit from the night demons, with which Faye had thought she was quits. Her midnight cries in the alien darkness of Peter's second-floor bedroom gave her the opportunity to acquaint him with this feature of life with her, and gave Peter the opportunity to be manly and comforting, which he did not waste. On the second day of the Maine visit, Peter's sister Amy came down from Boston to meet Faye, whom Peter introduced as his "very good friend." Amy was amiable enough, and partly melted from guardianship of the late Julie's memory to sisterly indulgence when she saw how happy Peter was with Faye; but kept her distance.

For her part, Faye found Standish, Maine austere and barely civil by contrast with Gabbro County. People minded their own business, which Faye might have found refreshing and proper once; now, it seemed to mean that other people's joys, sorrows, and fears were for them to cope with as best they could. In reaction, her 'loving irony' style in regard to Gabbro doings and politics tilted toward warmth at their unvarnished humanity. Knowing that co-publisher Peter now would read everything that she wrote, she tried to keep to a tone of sober familiarity, without slipping in too many hidden messages.

Of course all the coming and going did not escape Gabbro County's corporate notice. Faye was absent often and long enough that even her former friends at the Salonnette noticed. When Faye encountered Mary-Deane Gaines outside the Piggly Wiggly, Mary-Deane pulled a meaningful face that said enough that Faye was sorely tempted to drop in to the Salonnette to stick out her tongue; but didn't, in loyalty to Sedalia Baley.

Nora, for her part, was a bit abashed, but pleased with Forde's delight in her blossoming. And not at all reluctant to contrast her melon-like fecundity to Faye's slenderness, which she did by mock self-denigration as a fat cow beside a body that could, as she said, hide twice behind her, fore and aft. She cut back a little on her unionizing, but she did not give it up entirely, driving from one mill to another throughout North Carolina in mild or sultry sunshine.

New leaves greened on bush and tree, as if determined that, this time, spring would last forever. Birds returned from the tropics and bickered over branches and nooks, or fattened themselves for more Northward-going; spring peepers took up their eponymous songs. Then Sheriff Lyle Rathbun walked into the *Intelligencer* offices one dewy morning in the first week of June, grim-faced and dismissive of Sedalia's greeting.

20.

FORDE, OH, MY GOD! OH, NO, YOU POOR MAN! POOR Nora! And the baby?" Not stopping to think what kind of miracle she was asking about. Forde said nothing, was capable of nothing but to shake his head. Faye, who had raced to Forde's office after his hoarse cry of disbelief, turned to a corner where Lyle Rathbun creaked and sighed.

"Doc checked. No heartbeat. Appeared she'd been there some time 'fore anybody spotted 'em."

Faye broke into tears, surprising herself. "Oh, no, God, this is ... Oh, Forde! How did it happen?"

Another head shake.

Rathbun shifted uneasily. "Early yet to draw no final conclusions. Seems like she went off the road where 74 crosses Gum Swamp Crick outside Laurinburg, comin' up t'the bridge. Left front tar rode up the guard rail, flipped the whole works upside down, inta the crick. Won't no blowout, so either she got distracted by somethin' and drove off the road, or some kinda mechanical failure." He shrugged helpfully. "Seems like she was knocked out when the car hit the crick upside-down. Either kilt her outright, or she drownt in two foot a water."

Faye started to imagine it, and her mind balked. "Where is she now?"

"Tooken 'er ta Wegeman's."

"Gone to Wegeman's" was a common Gabbro County euphemism

for death; Forde groaned and crumpled at the name; Faye took a slow breath and touched his shoulder.

"Gonna need 'im to come and identify Mrs. Morgan. Don't seem possible there could be much doubt, it was his car an' all, but the law requires it."

"No." Forde's voice was almost inaudible.

Faye and Rathbun exchanged looks. "Does it have to be right now?"

"Well. 'Fore the end of the day a'd be all right."

Forde drew a shaky breath and stood suddenly. "No, now. Let's get it over with. Can Miss Bynum come with me?"

Rathbun looked at Faye, met the level black eyebrows, and shrugged. "Law's fine with that."

Nora looked pale and upset, uninjured except for a small bloody lump on her forehead, the sort of thing you might get from running under an iron staircase. Annoying, excruciating even, but hardly fatal. Her auburn hair was dark, still wet-looking, though Faye could not conceive of touching it to check. Her belly, under the sheet, was nearly flat; the autopsy had required that the unborn baby be delivered by Caesarian, its sex determined, and verified dead. Forde was offered the opportunity to see it, which he began to accept and then simply could not do it. When the attendant got nervous about that, Faye shook her head.

"Oh, please. The man's surely suffered enough. Who else's baby could it be?"

"Law requires the next of kin or a designated representative to view and verify all deceased." Which was nonsense, but Faye could see no point in making a row about it.

"Designate me, Forde. I'll do it."

The gray, nearly finished fetus was a girl with abundant auburn hair, a snubby nose, and Forde's ears. Giving it a glance was all Faye could manage, but it was enough to satisfy the attendant.

***

The funeral, unbearably, was open-casket, because that is the Gabbro way. Wegeman's, inspired by the awfulness, bathed the baby and applied blusher, curled a pink ribbon into her hair, dressed her in a christening gown, and placed her in the crook of Nora's arm. When Faye saw people who barely knew Forde, and certainly did not know Nora, bursting into tears at the coffin, she opted not to advance to the front of Gabbro Methodist chapel and pay respects, knowing that she might never exorcise the sight.

June 7

Dearest Peter -

The enclosed clipping will tell you what has completely devastated the Intelligencer gang, and me in particular. I was not all that fond of Nora, but I certainly am of Forde. Life around the office has been pretty dispirited since Nora's death, and we need someone to step up and get things moving again. It is hard to see who that might be, other than me. Sorry to be such a droop - I send my love -

Faye

***

From the Gabbro *Intelligencer* for Monday, June 7, 1965:

Nora Lundy Morgan, Annie F. Morgan

Mrs. Nora Lundy Morgan, wife of Executive Editor Forde Morgan, was killed, along with her unborn child, a girl who will be named Annie Faye, in an unexplained one-car accident last Friday, May 27, when her auto …

***

```
                              Sebago Lake, Maine
                                June 8, 1965
To my new colleagues at the Intelligencer:
   Like all of you, I am sure, I have been devas-
tated at the news of the death of Nora Lundy Morgan
and of her and my partner Forde's daughter Annie.
   Even though little Annie Faye had only a brief
taste of life as a passenger in her mother's womb,
she is nevertheless an infinitely precious child
of God, whom we can hope to meet and cherish here-
after. Her mother Nora, precious already to Forde
and through him to all of us, was a vivacious and
yet serious worker for the rights of laboring men
and women. Her passing is a cruel blow not only to
Forde - though most cruelly to him - but to all
of us.
   Please know that my heart grieves for your loss,
and allow me, a newcomer still, to join you in
mourning.

Sincerely,
Peter Standish
Peter A. Standish MD
```

***

From the Gabbro *Intelligencer* for Friday, June 11, 1965:

Morgan Death Called "Suspicious"

The accident that took the lives of Mrs. Forde Morgan and her unborn daughter Annie Faye Morgan has been characterized by Sheriff Lyle Rathbun as "suspicious." Rathbun revealed to the *Intelligencer* that an examination by mechanics at Bypass Ford turned up what appeared to be deliberate damage to the steering linkages and the hydraulic brakes, making ...

***

"Either of you know anybody might have reason to want Mrs. Morgan hurt or dead?"

"Well, let's see. Don't I remember something about Nora being beat up, last fall some time? By a couple of thugs Mason Merrydown sent?"

"No evidence who actually done that, Miss Bynum."

"Really. What about the two thugs who roughed me up, probably because I provoked them in some way, according to you?"

Rathbun said nothing.

"One of them, I hear, showed up in Mr. Morgan's office *in company with Mason Merrydown*, with his arm in a sling from where I shot him, after he tried to help the other one - the one who I hear retired because he suddenly lacked depth perception - rape me."

"Very circumstantial, all of that. Shall we stay focused on Mrs. Morgan's accident? We do that, we can avoid getting into your discharging a unlicensed far-arm at a unarmed citizen."

Faye smiled. "By all means. You asked who might have wished Mrs. Morgan ill. Seems to me it would be pretty dumb not to mention the fact she was beaten to a pulp because she was a union organizer."

"We only have her word for that."

"Gosh, and now she's dead. Guess we'll never know, then."

Forde winced. "Faye, maybe we should calm down a little. Lyle, maybe for your part, you could stop trying to be Sherlock Holmes, and take some obvious facts at face value. My wife was a union organizer, and she was on union business when she was beat up, and again when she was killed."

Rathbun shrugged. "OK, fine. One of those obvious facts is that the car seems to've been tampered with so's it might could run off the road at high speed, which seems like the only speed Mrs. Morgan ever used. So there's some suggestion there, that it was anti-union activity. But another one is, it wasn't her car, that little AMC Gremlin, but your Fairlane. Why was that?"

Forde sighed. "Once she got to a certain point in the pregnancy ... " He clouded up and looked at the ceiling. Rathbun nodded and screwed the heel of his boot into the carpet. Faye blew her nose. Forde drew a shaky breath. "... she didn't feel safe in the Gremlin. She was always talking about selling it."

"Damn deathtraps, them little things, you ast me," Rathbun nodded. He glanced at Faye and shrugged. Faye smiled. "I drove my VW to Maine and back, and it never gave me a second's trouble." *Unless you count a butt-ache that took two days to go away and a love affair that hasn't gone away yet.*

"Anyway, point is, it was Mr. Morgan's car was tampered with, not hers. Maybe it was you, sir, was the target. Who had access to your car lately?"

"Nobody but me and Nora. Well, it got the oil changed a week ago."

"Where?"

"Mercer's, which is the same place I've took it for years, and every car since I started to drive twenty years ago. They got no reason to fool around with it now."

Rathbun made a noise close enough to "Ayuh," that it startled Faye. "Maybe I'll go chat with Mercer, see is he mad at you all of a sudden. Does seem unlikely, though."

Forde shook his head and plunged his face into his hands. "Don't see why he would be. I been giving him my exclusive patronage since 1947, dang it."

***

"Forde, I know you're hurting real bad, and it makes me hurt too. But we need to kind of get off our butts here, and stop acting like a Library Board meeting and Gabbro High baseball are reasons enough to put out a paper. Would you be willing for me to draw up a list of possible ... well, themes, we could be following as we get into summer?"

"You mean ways you can stir up trouble?"

"Has my trouble-stirring ever failed to make people buy papers?"

Forde smiled weakly. "Fire insurance goes up like a rocket every time you sit down at the typewriter. Sure, go ahead, but mind, we discuss the list before you start writing."

"Of course, Mr. Morgan."

"Oh, cut it out."

Thursday 6/10

Dearest Peter -

Well, what was already horrible has become almost unbearable. As you will see when yesterday's paper makes its way to you, it appears that Forde's car, which Nora was driving, was tampered with, and thus we are looking at not just a terrible accident, but deliberate murder. And, since that could mean that the target was Forde, and not Nora, we may not have seen the end of the horrors.

It is a pale, solitary pleasure to think of your strength and calm good humor in times like this. The only better thing would be to have you here with me. The Maine ladies don't know what a treasure they have right in their laps ... so to speak.

All my love,

Faye

***

From the Gabbro *Intelligencer* for Wednesday, June 16, 1965:

THIS TOWN'S TIMES
By M. Faye Bynum
Associate Editor

As the Decades Roll On

Eleven years ago this past May, the Supreme Court of the United States of America - you know the country I refer to, I think, the one that pulled together ("United") to survive the Great Depression and defeat the Nazis - decreed that racial segregation in so-called "separate but equal" school systems violated the laws and Constitution of that same country, the United States. Those who may wonder how I feel about Gabbro County's continued lawlessness in regard to *Brown v. Board of Education* can look up a series of articles that ran in May of last year. Gabbro Memorial Library has a full archive of the last sixty years of the *Intelligencer.*

I write this morning to mention that Gabbro County's lame imitation of the Ma Barker family continues a year and a month later, while at the same time we court (Ha) indictments on the grounds of criminally negligent working conditions at a number of Gabbro locales, including the County Jail, the kitchens at no less than three Gabbro County schools, and of course the Dickensian sweatshop known as ... Oh, wait. My health insurance premium is due; I'd

better wait to mention our local Inferno until I'm sure
I'm covered, and have a chance to reload.

***

Forde Morgan picked up the telephone. "Yes, Miss Baley?"

"Mister Merrydown and two associates are here, Mr. Morgan."

Forde shook his head. "Really? Did you tell him I'm in a meeting?"

"No, sir. Are you?"

"No. But that's a thing we use when we don't want to see somebody; and that is permanently true with regard to Mr. Merrydown."

Silence. Then, "I will need to speak to you about that."

"Fine. All right, send him back, then."

It was the same bodyguard menace as before. The sling was gone,
but the thug was identifiably the same, and he did most things left-
handed. Forde couldn't be sure about the other one, the one who stood
to the right of the doorway when Mason Merrydown came through
it. A kid, and kind of a pipsqueak, next to the other. Like the gunsel
Wilmer in "The Maltese Falcon," a movie that Forde loved, and rented
about twice a year.

"I see Bynum is feeling her oats again, with this business about
Nigras in the schools. She needs to take some care what she thinks
the public needs to know about that kind of stuff. In that connection,
I came to offer our condolences and congratulations, Morgan."

"How kind."

"The condolences are in regard to you having to sell off part of your
newspaper in order to meet your obligations, and for thereby having
acquired a powerful and relentless enemy in the form of myself."

"In the form of yourself? My. By the way, I would fire any writer
who put such a phrase in my paper. What about the congratulations?"

"That it was not <u>yourself</u>, Mister Morgan, who was driving
when your heap took a jump off Highway 74. That was a very lucky

circumstance that may not be counted on to repeat into the indefinite future. In my opinion, the person who apparently tampered with your car did not seem to care which of you, the union organizer or the troublesome editor, was injured. Would make a person reflect, seems to me."

Forde stood, staring at Merrydown; the thugs leaned forward.

"You filthy piece of slime. Take your apes and get out of here, and don't even think about speaking to me again on <u>any</u> subject." Forde tipped his head back and raised his voice. "Miss Baley, please call Sheriff Rathbun immediately. We have a dangerous criminal in here."

"Yes, Mister Morgan."

"Are they gone?"

"Yes, sir."

"Did they do any damage, or threaten you or anyone else on their way out?"

"The bigger bodyguard dumped a pile of papers off Jenny McCall's desk on the way out. I picked them all up. He called me a name."

"Yes? Would you be comfortable telling me what name?"

"No, sir."

"Very well. Miss Baley, I consider you a valuable employee, and I want to assure you that everyone else here does the same. If Merrydown or his gunnies ever insult you again, here, at home, or on the way between, please inform me immediately."

"Sticks and stones, Mister Morgan. Now, on that other matter?"

"Other matter?"

"Yes, about your being in a meeting when you are not. It places me in an uncomfortable position, sir. I can't tell lies for you, but I love this job so much that it would kill me to resign over it."

"Well, we certainly don't want that. The fact remains that I need to be able to avoid meeting people, when I'm busy, or just don't want to see them, as with Mr. Merrydown."

"Can't I just tell them you're too busy to see them?"

"People get insulted when you tell them that, as if their business is not as important as some other thing I'm doing. Even if that's true, we don't want to insult people if we don't have to."

Sedalia nodded, chewed her lip, and then brightened. "How would this be? I'll tell them you are at prayer, and cannot be disturbed. And if you will just be so kind as to tip me off by reciting the first few verses of the Lord's Prayer when I call about a visitor you don't wish to see, then ..." She smiled, pleased with her solution. "Then it would not be a lie."

When she was gone, Forde grinned in spite of himself, and then wept because Nora was not there to laugh with him.

***

Lyle Rathbun scratched his chin. "Who else was in the room?"

"His two thugs, that he takes everywhere. Though one of them isn't much of a thug. More like a mean little snake."

"No good."

"I'll say. But I suppose you mean, no good as witnesses."

"Uh huh."

"He as good as admitted he had my car sabotaged."

"He din't just admit it, he bragged about it. Still no good. I went after him on that, he'd just deny it, and his thugs'd back him up. Never said no such thing, no sir."

"Wait a minute. Forde lifted his chin. 'Miss Baley?'"

A chair scraped from the front office, and Sedalia Baley was with them. "Sir?"

"Miss Baley, did you happen to overhear Mr. Merrydown utter a threat to me this afternoon?"

"Strictly speaking, no, sir. He did say some vile thing about how you were not driving your car when it ... Oh, Mr. Morgan, I can hardly bring myself -"

"Well, save it, then. How about that, Lyle?"

"Confirmatory, but not strictly actionable. And besides, no ..."

"Yes?"

Lyle Rathbun sighed, and drew himself up. "Honestly? No jury of Gabbro folks is gonna credit hearsay from, well ..."

After a silence, Sedalia Baley spoke up. "He means nobody will value a Baley's word, Mr. Morgan."

Forde tossed a hand. Raised in Gabbro, he knew she was right. "Oh, that's just ... just - "

Sedalia nodded. "The way it is, yes. But be of good cheer, sir. The Lord assured Jeremiah that the wicked shall not prevail." She exited, gentle as always with the Venetian blind.

Forde tilted his head at Lyle Rathbun. "You got any idea what folks seem to have about Baleys, that a harmless little thing like that should be a pariah?"

"Goes way back. Never made much sense to me, neither, not that I ever give it much thought. But speakin' of pharaos, here's something to think about. B'lieve you had a bit of a run-in with Rob Stoker a while back. Shame, I always sorta enjoyed his stuff about the football team."

"Got a daughter, sheriff? Or a wife?"

"Yeah, I heard. I'd a plugged the sorry bastard. Anyways, for a while, Mr. Stoker was looking for a job worthy of his talents. Then, for a while after that, he'd of tooken about anything that paid decent. Got hungry enough, he finally landed something that paid next ta nothing, but happy to get it."

"Glad to hear it."

"No, you won't be. What he finally landed was, grease monkey at Mercer's Garage."

21.

THE OUTREACH INTERN

Chapter 8.

Mercy loitered by the riverbank, oppressed and moody. It had been two weeks since the last letter arrived from James; could a letter have been lost? Mercy knew how difficult it is to sustain a long-distance relationship by mail, with its crossed letters and failures to write clearly lovingly enough to bridge the aching distance. Worse yet, what if James had lost not just a letter, but interest in Mercy herself? The death of her Cousin Nora had affected Mercy greatly. She sat, at last, and threw twigs into the current, wishing each of them Godspeed and good fortune as they swirled away, knowing that she would never see them again in this life.

She felt a pang as they disappeared around the river's bend. Could even twigs have some elementary consciousness, that they could feel pain, or excitement at their new life? Would Mercy meet them again in the Afterlife, each of them angry at her, or eager to tell her what lay downstream? Indians certainly believed that all living things have spirits, so that even the cutting down of a tree required agreement and resignation by the tree to end its forest life and be dismembered to work or be burned for mankind. If all that, what about twigs? Mercy found the notion heartbreaking. At the sound of excited barking, she rose to greet her border collie Nell with affection. But Nell would not tolerate any delay on Mercy's part, but must immediately lead her to the house. Where, shining on the carpet amid the bills and flyers, lay at last a letter from James. Did it bring renewed assurance of his devotion, or the first hint of coolness? Or some weaseling suggestion that in view of their long separation, it might be appropriate for them to see other people? Accompanied of course by protestations of how "fond" he was of her. Mercy buried her face in Nell's fur and wept in anticipation of the heartbreak.

22.

FAYE OPENED THE LETTER WITH TREMBLING FINGERS.

June 18

Dearest Faye:

It has been a fairly humdrum week here, mostly consumed by a run of deliveries - couples somehow influenced by the turning of the leaves last fall to engender new lives. Or some such after-the-fact rationale. I know - and love - how you would puncture such phony psychologizing with common sense and a smile. I do love your smile, and I admire your common sense. But the thought of them together is just unbearably sexy. Isn't it time that we had our next get-away?

I will be busy with reopening the camp this week coming, right through the weekend. But how about the 4th of July weekend? Will you get some time off? Can we set off a few gentle fireworks of our own? How I have missed you!

All love,
Peter
(Peter A. Standish, MD)

Faye sat back in the wicker chaise and looked over the Eddy. *Very well. I am not Mercy, and Peter is not James. Thank God.* She felt that

"The Outreach Intern" had been going a little better recently, in fact since she gave Mercy a border collie as a companion - ignoring the question of fitting a dog into her "suffocating garret." Either the dog or, she supposed, her relationship with Peter had released a few flourishes of imagination. Meaning of course that it had been pretty lame in the early going, which in turn would require a re-write of at least the first chapters. And, she supposed, that would lead to re-writing the whole damn thing. Still, it must - mustn't it? - mean something, that she was so at home in Mercy's world that she would occasionally confuse it with reality.

Nor could she blame herself much for preferring the fantasy world of "The Outreach Intern" to sullen and dangerous Gabbro County. She had never particularly liked Rob Stoker - a macho idiot, as far as she had ever let him cross her mind. But she had not thought him capable of attempting murder in payback for a deserved firing. And wasn't it just The Way It Goes, just another Fascinating Vignette of Southern Life, that his sabotage had missed its target and killed Nora and unborn little Annie Faye instead?

There was no doubt of Rob's guilt; next to his body, hanging from a gas pipe in his apartment, was the note that confirmed it:

```
TO whoever finds me:
    (And I hope it's soon, I don't want
to stink up the place too bad!) You
probably already figured out, it was
me that wrecked the tie rod on Morgan's
car. I'd give anything if it didn't kill
Mrs Morgan and that baby instead. Also,
I apologize to the Forsythe girl, I was
full of anger. I am a corupt fool and
I hate myself and there is nothing else
I can do. I did it because I needed the
```

money and because I didn't care whether
it just hurt Morgan or killed him, I
wish it did. See you in Hell.
  ROBERT ALLEN STOKER III
   April 2, 1930 - June 22, 1965

***

Forde dropped the note on his desk as if it carried contagion. "Well. A shame and all, though I hope he's right about rotting in hell, the little shit. But what money? He left that part out."

"Well, that's the question, isn't it?" Faye raised an eyebrow at Lyle Rathbun. "Rob was forever leaving some important detail out of his stories, but now I can't send it back to him for a rewrite."

Forde sat up suddenly. "Are we perfectly sure somebody wasn't killing off a co-conspirator and making it look like suicide?"

Rathbun sniffed, and shifted around so his leather would creak, and remind them who was the Law in this county. "Not impossible, I s'pose. It's his typewriter, his fingerprints on the paper. No sign of violence or drugs, pre-mortem, except a kinda high blood alcohol. Dutch courage, I'd think. As for who paid him how much, you looking to make me say it, I know. I say somethin' out loud, you gonna quote me."

"No, I won't, I promise. Off the record, though?"

"Off the record, I don't have no more doubts than either of you. Still not gonna name 'im, 'cause you'll say 'A highly placed source close to the investigation,' some such crap, and ever'body will know it was me."

"Well, Sheriff Rathbun, you are a slick one. Is this nameless person beyond the reach of the law, then?"

"Never said that. First of all, you gotta recognize, it's ten to one the fella we're discussing never touched the cash nor talked to Stoker himself. He'd a sent them goons he walks around with, or maybe somebody else. I'm a-working that angle, try and catch one of 'em in something, see if I can turn him." He rose and opened the office door. "Meantime, y'all keep your eyes peeled. I mean, over your shoulders. Be safe, what I mean."

When he was gone - confirmed by Sedalia by phone as always - Faye rose also.

"Well, he did refer to 'goons he walks around with.' Pretty clear indication who he's thinking of."

"Uh huh. That and a Polaroid shot of the goon handing over the cash still wouldn't touch Merrydown."

When Faye returned to her office, she found an envelope on her desk, with a printed M. FAYE BYNUM on the front, and nothing on the back.

"Sedalia?"

"Yes, Miss. That was mixed in with the regular mail, as it come in the door."

"Huh. We got somebody that can mail letters for free?"

"No'm, I doubt. Could have been stuck in the slot ahead of time, though. Got mixed in when the rest of it come through."

"Uh huh, good thinking. Well, let me see what Mister Anonymous has on his mind."

```
Miss Bynum
Call SAndhills 1-5157 between 4 and 4:15 tomorrow
morning, for vital information re: Morgan death. Do
not attempt to identify the undersigned.
One Who Wishes Only Good
```

***

"Nuh uh. No fingerprints, paper or envelope. Paper an' envelope you can get in the Stationery section of the Rexall. Might could identify the type, if I impounded every typewriter in America. You figger out who it is, we could verify by checking his typewriter. No such number in the company directory at Riv- at the plant belonging to the fella we agree might be involved." Lyle Rathbun leaned back and examined his cigar, which seemed to Faye to be all too perfectly lit. "Did you call the number?"

Faye shrugged. "Of course. He claims he knows who ordered Nora killed, and has proof. I didn't recognize the voice, because for one thing, he was talking through some kind of squawky thing, like a kazoo, that made it hard even to figure out the words, let alone know the voice."

"What did he say?"

"That was about it. I don't think I could recall the exact words, it was so hard to guess what they were."

Forde sat up suddenly. "Wait a minute. He knows who ordered *Nora* killed?"

Faye thought back over the call. "Yes. God, Forde, I didn't even notice the implications. Oh, I am a dunce any more!"

"So the intended vic was <u>Mrs</u>. Morgan after all?"

"Vic?"

"Victim." Rathbun, a devotee of hard-boiled crime fiction, blushed, and turned to Faye. "So we got somebody that knows Mrs. Morgan was driving Mr. Morgan's car. Or else, just made a slip of the tongue because everybody knows that's who was kilt."

"Or, whoever ordered it, which you and I know who it was, didn't tell Stoker who the real target was. Could have been either one of them."

Rathbun made a dismissive motion with his cigar. "Maybe he didn't care, one of you's a union organizer an' the other edits a newspaper that's on his ass. What did you hear in the background?"

"Absolutely nothing at all. Not even the usual kind of mumbles and hisses. Maybe he put something over the phone."

"Huh. Did it occur to you to inform me, so's I could listen in on an extension, Miss Bynum?"

"Well. No, I guess not. Sorry." Which was not the exact truth; it occurred to Faye all right, but she didn't want Lyle Rathbun creaking and stomping and maybe making whoever it was hang up. She also didn't tell Rathbun about the next step required by the informer.

***

Faye sat on the glider with a gimlet and a nervous stomach, waiting as darkness, with frustrating slowness, overtook the Eddy. Checked her watch again; 8:18, only seven minutes later than the last time she checked. To force more time to pass, she imagined herself standing, opening the screen, descending the stairs step by step (*C'mon, Rosie, let's go for a walk.*) to the centipede grass, barefoot to the dock; to the end amid frog-song, holding hands with Peter; falling into the Eddy together to follow its slow gyration along the north bank, clockwise to the far side where the Gabbro River murmured in moonlight; onto the black gabbro outcrop in the river's current, then launching herself - Peter gone again - to follow the south bank back to the dock ...

And in that slow circling, exhausted by what her life had become, lost herself in sleep. So she was sprawled against the back of the glider, the empty gimlet glass dripping on the porch floor when a gloved hand reached through the steps she had not descended, and left there an anonymous manila envelope. A dark figure moved across the grass and disappeared into the forest by the river. The envelope glowed modestly in the risen moon when she woke a half hour later. *Sorry we missed you, lady. Anyways, here you go.*

Faye blistered herself for a numbskull idiot, and descended the steps (*Rosie, why didn't you bark, honey? Sleeping too, I see. Good girl.*)

The envelope was brand new, purchased at a Rexall, not necessarily the one in Gabbro, and contained only one thing: a low-resolution, low-light photograph of two men. One of them was recognizable - because Faye had seen him on some four thousand days in various characteristic slouches and slumps - as the late Rob Stoker. The other ... well, he might have been one of the Merrydown thugs; it was hard to tell in the light of her best gas-mantle Coleman lamp, but there was something unpleasantly familiar about him. She called SAndhills 1 - 5157; it rang and rang.

***

Lyle Rathbun was, if possible, even more dismissive and unhelpful about the photo. "Could be anybody, doin anything. What's it gonna take for you to start copperatin with duly authorized law enforcement on this? Somebody else to get killed? Sure would be a shame if it was you, tryna be Brenda Starr."

Faye looked him in the eye, and was suddenly tired of the plucky-girl-reporter business. "You're right, Sheriff. I should dump this in your lap and go about my business while you go about yours. I surely hope you get this wrapped up before anybody else gets killed. Best of luck to you, and I promise that I will contact you the minute I hear from this guy again, if I ever do."

When Rathbun was gone, Forde sat back in his worn Boss Chair and eyed Faye. "What was that?"

"What was what?" Sulky, knowing what.

"I never once knew you to ... well, give in like that. Most of the time, you find a nice way to tear their heads off. Make some kind of sassy back-talk."

"Getting old, I guess."

No.

Well, maybe; slowing a little with the effects of age, starting to make waves that lapped the shores of her fifth decade of life before they died out. But other factors outweighed her age: First, being beaten up and nearly raped did not stop hurting when her body healed, no matter how faithful her adherence to Sister Immaculata's body-toning exercises, no matter how Peter's loving attention soothed it. Faye was chastened by how being beaten up, first of all, just plain hurt; and how it humbled and oppressed her, and sent demons into her sleep; particularly the experience of complete helplessness, before Rosie's saving intervention when rape seemed inevitable. Pluckiness - in contrast to courage, she now saw - is made easier by ignorance of the consequences and retaliations available to its target. When she nearly drowned in Sebago Lake, one of the final thoughts that raced through as the sunlight faded overhead was, *I had this coming.*

Next, and on the other side, for the first time in her life Faye had someone who offered her something to care about beyond whether she was being demeaned and intimidated for being a woman. Peter Standish had opened a landscape and a way of life that was not a competition, but a celebration in which she was an indispensible actor. As such, she had less need to show the world a spunky, no-bullshit exterior. If anyone wants to conclude that Faye was truly growing up at last, fine. But, really; half of humanity "grows up" without learning these lessons.

23.

FAYE, RESPONDING TO PETER'S LETTER, EXPRESSED A wish for some kind of old-fashioned 4th of July celebration, preferably in a small town, maybe in the North or Midwest, since Gabbro did not celebrate the Union. So they met for the weekend at a car rental counter in the St. Louis airport to drive north to Quincy, Illinois, chosen by the dart-in-the-map method. (Faye had been sort of aiming for St. Louis.)

Quincy sits on a bluff over the Mississippi between St. Louis and the Illinois - Wisconsin border. They drove –laughing and chattering the multi-entendre language of lovers long parted – the hundred or so miles up the Mississippi to a bridge from the Missouri to the Illinois side. Following signage, they found themselves driving into Quincy on Maine Street, which Faye took as a good omen right off the bat.

"Bet we can find a cozy New Englandy motel here that will make you feel at home and they'll serve us some kind of a drink that's special for the 4th. How about that one?"

Riverman's Rest Motel proved to be full up. "Honey, you'd about have to drive to Pittsfield to find a vacancy, this weekend." The clerk gave them an appraising eye. "Wait, though, my sister'n-law's got a little apartment over her garage, might be available short term, seems like she told me her tenant skipped out last week. That sound good? You two <u>are</u> married, ain't you?"

"Oh, ah -"

"On our honeymoon, Ma'am. Now, don't you tell nobody, or they'll be settin' off fireworks outside your sister's all night, hear?"

"Won't say a word, Honey, bless your hearts. Second time around for you?"

"Yes'm. Five whole years later, we are still in mourning for Bruno and Sylvie, who was a brother and sister we married, was kilt in the same accident left Peter with scars you cain't believe, and me with a awful limp, of a cold morning."

"Way-ell! Bless your hearts, both of you. Helped each other through a tough time, did you?"

"Yes, Ma'am, that's exactly right. The whole love thing just snuck up, an' about mashed us flat, didn't it, Honey?"

"Ayah."

"He means yes." Faye summoned up a hoarse whisper. "A little hard for him to talk about it, still, Ma'am, if you didn't mind. Could you maybe call your sister-in-law, see if she's interested in helpin' out a couple middle-age honeymooners?"

Truthful Faye, the girl who could not lie. But once the thing was started, she felt it better to remain true to the story, than to the world as it was. It had to do, she supposed, with the arbitrary way they had settled on Quincy, Illinois; if there was no real reason beyond the flight of a dart that they were here, then there was no rhyme to reality, either. But the sister-in-law was, it turned out, tickled pink at the thought of these two sad but resilient lovers who had fallen into each others' arms, and said to come right on over.

The drove their rented Dodge according to directions straight west on Maine Street, and when they had passed 36th, watched for, and found, Blarney Lane at the second right. Talking their way past Lena Melton, their hostess, fell to Peter, because Faye was still struck dumb at her own mendacity; she stood smiling shyly at the embroideries Peter came up with to the basic fiction. For her part, Mrs. Melton seemed welcoming enough.

Faye spent the time dimpling at the linoleum and inventing a name

— other than Lying Their Asses Off — for what they were doing. She thought of something that had a kind of intentional and scientific sound to it; while Peter signed the register - "Dr. and Mrs. Peter Standish / Standish, ME" - she considered how to spin "Applied Field Fiction" out to the acronym AFFAIR. She came up with "Imitation Respectability" for the end, but was dissatisfied with anything that presented itself for the second A. Affordable, Artificial, Anonymous, Arranged ... they all refused to fit smoothly with the AFF and IR already in place.

When they were safely into the oddly angled over-garage unit, a collection of nooks and polygons and hallways stifling in the July heat of the Midwest, they turned on the exhaust fan that was all there was to cool things, and stripped. Faye was reminded, not too unpleasantly, of her first blazing-hot apartment over the Five and Dime in Gabbro, and told Peter the story of the courthouse worthies who had spied on her with field glasses on hot afternoons. When he'd snorted appreciatively, and they'd found the shower, they shared it, lathering and laughing. Uncooled, they turned the handle all the way to C, which produced something well short of cold. Parched by their long exile, they took each other standing in the tepid cascade. It was like drowning in bliss, Faye thought, but without the danger and the CPR. Afterward, draped Maja-like over the bed and already starting to sweat, Faye acquainted Peter with the problem of AFF_IR.

"What's wrong with 'And?'"

"*Applied Field Fiction And Imitation Respectability.* Well, heck. I like that." Faye beamed and stretched, sinuous in the glow from the bathroom. "Peter, you are a gem of Yankee ingenuity. Come, give me one more kiss."

He loomed over the bed and did so, which led to one more, and ended in an old-fashioned Midwestern afternoon rooming house boff on nubbled chintz, in an atmosphere of slather, sweat, and hot wallpaper; and the need for another shower. When the towels had no further power to dry them, they dressed damp. Faye stood languid before the mirrored dresser and brushed her hair.

"Let's go find supper, and then spend the next, oh ..." she looked at the late sun outside the window, and at her watch ... "say, 26 hours sleeping and screwing. They ought to start the fireworks pretty soon after that, I'd think."

***

Forde Morgan, at Sedalia's gentle urging, called up Virgil Barnett, using as cover his long-ago promise to Mason Merrydown to give positive news coverage to River Mills.

"Seems to me, y'all could use a little boost. I keep hearing in town here, folks grumbling about work conditions, and about what was the deal anyhow with Rob Stoker's death, which there was a rumor involving Mr. Merrydown. Rob was pretty popular in here, with his sports coverage."

"Reckon so. Why the change of heart all of a sudden? What I heard, you were convinced yourself, Merrydown had something to do with your wife's death. Condolences on that, by the way."

"Thank you. The *Intelligencer* does not deal in inference and speculation. I have personally found that to be a good way to get through life, which is my biggest priority right now. The question you implied is still open, and I can barely stand to think of it. I am going to give anyone who is mentioned as a suspect the same benefit the law gives any accused person: innocent until proven guilty. Meanwhile, I have this unkept promise on my mind."

"Well, that is mighty white of you, Mr. Morgan. How can I help? We have a fact sheet about the mill that might be a starter for you."

Forde smiled at how easily Barnett swallowed it. "I need to see for myself, Virgil. I can pick up your fact sheet when I come out to tour the mill, if you'd be so kind."

***

The fireworks were in the best Midwestern tradition, launched from the river's edge out over the broad Mississippi. The best viewing was from the bluff on the Illinois side, giving them the full spectacle in mid-air and reflected, wrinkled and silent, in the flowing river. Faye and Peter stood for a while at the edge of the crowd, then sat in the grass and held hands while the crowd celebrated in chorus. After the empty-the-tank finale, Faye and Peter collapsed backward onto the grass to watch the smoke clear and reveal again the distant fireworks of the galaxy.

"Word got out." Faye whispered. "They're cheering for us." Peter had brought to Quincy a copy of the Kama Sutra; Faye had barely heard of it, and was a little *(Come on, a lot.)* shocked at the thing. He of course wanted to start with the first illustration and work their way systematically from beginning to end over the course of a year; and had figured out a quota of positions for this weekend based on an estimate of likely occasions. Practical Faye pointed out that they could probably check off several as already accomplished, and was more inclined to browse with an eye to what might be fun. Either way, she was confident of a good outcome; and they did check off a couple of new ones, including how they had managed inside the skimpy little shower. Her limberness exercises had been a help with that one.

Now back at the garage apartment, they considered checking off one more toward the weekend's quota; but they were tired. They looked at each other over the page, laughed the laugh of the sated, and fell tangled into bed and sleep.

When they knocked next morning on Lena Melton's back door to pay up and head back to St. Louis and eastern reality, they found Lena and her sister from the Sailor's Home, along with a couple of grinning guys in leisure suits and comb-overs. On the kitchen table was a curious pineapple upside-down cake, on which each pineapple ring was plugged through with half of a peeled banana, topped in turn by a dollop of whipped cream. It struck Faye as kind of obscene, but Peter seemed unbothered. Professional callousness, she supposed.

"What ...?"

"Honey, set down, we got a nice little surprise for you lovebirds. See, folks in the Hospitality business here in Quincy have a little competition we run ever' month. Bear in mind, we're the first town in Illinois you come to when you cross the river, means we get a good deal of interstate traffic from folks like yourselves that's looking to get away on 'honeymoons' with somebody they just got married to. Or surely might yet, one of these days, see what I mean."

"Yes?"

"Uh huh. Well, we get a lot of funny stories from these folks – to which we wish only happiness, by the way, and long may it last – when they check in. So we started a little competition with six or eight other motels, for the funniest story of each month. June was a little slow - lots a legitimate brides, understand, kind of crowded out the funny-story folks - so we didn't make no award in June. We're fixin' to submit your story retroactively, even though you come in July. So 'Doctor and Mrs. Peter Standish of Standish, Maine,' — pause here for a giggle — we are pleased to announce that you Take the Cake for June of 1965 as our entry in the Greater Quincy Honeymoon Competition. Frankly, we think you'll win in a walk."

Faye started working up tears. "B-But ..."

"Oh, mind now, it wasn't the story about the car wreck, kilt your exes, that done it for you. Land, we get that one so often, we just check a box on the entry form for it. No, tell you what done it, was the name. 'Doctor Peter Standish of Standish Maine,' honest to God, honey, it was all Axel and me could do to keep straight faces when we read that, ain't that right, Hon?"

"Yup." Sheepish grin. "Figgered it come to you, drivin' out Maine Street."

"So, to show our appreciation, we are cutting your bill in half, and offering you a nice slice of what we call 'Honeymoon Upside-Down Cake.' Y'all travel safely, now, and may your Peter always be Stand-ish."

"Now, see heah ..." Peter began hauling out his drivers' license.

Faye put a hand on his arm. "No, Honey, they got us dead to rights. Listen, y'all, 'Doctor Standish' and I can't think when we've had a more delightful getaway weekend, what with the fireworks and now this. We do appreciate your hospitality and your sense of humor. So pay up, 'Peter.' And thanks, but you can keep the cake, freeze it, give it to your next winners; I'm inclined to be a little careful what I eat from the hands of such funny folks. 'Bye now."

The standees in the kitchen, peeking through the curtains, saw her doubled over with glee next to stiffly striding 'Doctor Standish' on the way to their car. When the Dodge had pulled out of the drive, Axel Melton snorted. "Good enough sports about it; her, at least. Set down, folks, have a piece a cake. I got the print back from One-Hour, and you ain't gonna believe the shower footage we got."

24.

FORDE MORGAN PULLED HIS NEW FAIRLANE TO THE side of East Church Street and mopped his face. It was hot, as it is in Gabbro ten months of the year, but he was used to that. It was the recent vision that had him sweating now. How on God's Earth could anyone run an operation like what he'd seen at River Mills? Or, given the usual answer to that, what on that Earth would drive a person to work there? Well, Forde was damned if he would be complicit in perpetuating that Hell on Earth. It was time for an editorial rampage.

***

The return through Quincy to the bridge that would take them back across the Mississippi was accomplished in near silence.

"Looks different in the daylight."

"Ayah."

Seven blocks of silence.

"Oh, there's that lovely old house we saw yesterday. I didn't notice, it has a widow's walk on top."

Three more blocks.

"Peter, is anything the matter?"

"No." *Yes, but I can't talk about it. See how you like that.*

Three more; seeing Peter about to speak, Faye turned toward him.

"I don't happen to enjoy people making fun of my name."

"Well, why be huffy with me? I didn't make fun of your name."

"Strictly speaking, they did, of course, but you thought it was just hilarious."

"Oh, come on, Peter. So they made a stupid joke about your name, because they thought we made it up. It's a perfectly wonderful name, and it never occurred to me -"

"They desecrated it, but that's not the thing."

"Well, what is?"

"You laughed along with them. I will never be able to say my own name, that I've carried happily for almost a half century, without thinking of a partial erection and you laughing at it."

Faye looked out at the Mississippi passing below them. "Not that there's anything partial -"

"Faye, damn it!"

"All right, OK, I get it. Fine, I apologize for laughing. ... No, really. But I wasn't laughing at their dumb joke. I was laughing about their contest, that I bet was all made up on the spot. And I was laughing because I was embarrassed at how they saw through the 'Field Fiction.' I got us started on that, so that was my fault. But also, I didn't think it would be such a bad thing for them to think it was a made-up name, seeing that they never got any other from us."

"Yes. It also bothers me to lie to strangers."

Oh, good for you, you upright Yankee. "Huh. Well, you had a chance to say something about it at the time." *Mister Doctor Peter Stand-ish.* Faye couldn't suppress a smile, but confined it to the side of her face away from him. The little pop of guilt led her to try to soften things.

"Look, if things worked out that I totally lost the name I've carried for my whole life and I became 'Mrs. Peter Standish,' I would be nothing but glad about it."

"Yes, well, that's another can of worms that I don't think we should get mixed in with this."

Faye pictured a can of worms, dumped and wiggling on top of the Honeymoon Upside-Down Cake, like live pubic hair. "No, you're right. We've stumbled into a big enough mess, right here in the Middle West. But, Peter, come on. It doesn't have to spoil what we had this weekend. It doesn't have to come between us … I mean –"

"See, there you go again. I'm telling you, Faye, it's going to take me some time to get over this."

Well, good grief. "Well, honestly, Peter, then I have to say …" She stopped and stared out the window.

"Yes?"

"I have to say you're acting like … like a humorless j - dope about it."

"Ah." (*A half mile of silence.*) Well, maybe I am one, is that what you think?"

"I said, you're <u>acting</u> like one. I said it because that's the way it looks to me right now. You're standing on your very considerable dignity because of a stupid joke made by a bunch of yokels. And, you're bashing <u>me</u> about it because they aren't here to bash."

When they parted at the St. Louis airport, at the gate to Peter's plane, it was at the end of an hour of silence and scattered tersenesses between them.

"Peter, don't let's part this way. I love you."

"Yes."

"I'll write to you."

"Yes. I suppose."

"You <u>suppose</u>?"

"I mean, I suppose I will be glad to see your letter come. Well, of course I know I will. I'm trying not to stay mad, but I'm not very good at it. This whole thing has hit me like a freight train, Faye." He smiled on one side. "Snuck up and about mashed me flat, I guess I should have said. I can't begin to explain it, but I can't seem to get over it, either."

"I can see that. I hope you will, Peter. I have apologized, and that's all I can do. Goodbye. … Well. Kiss goodbye?"

He did; It was a kiss that Faye could not read; a kiss of impenetrable Down-East dignity.

Late that evening, sitting again on the porch over the Eddy with a kerosene lamp and a gimlet, she listened to the night sounds and interviewed the moonlight. *So the Yankee gem is a bit flawed. Now what? What if he stays mad? What if he doesn't? Am I shocked that he is human after all? All too?*

As if a page had turned, Faye saw that the affair with Peter had been wonderfully easy; too easy, impossibly so. Whatever sharp corners there might have been were nicely rounded by Peter's money and charm, by their gloating enjoyment of each other and by the sexual harmony that underlay it. She took the charm bracelet from her wrist and laid it on her lap: a lot of gold baubles in a circle around nothing. *Hey, that's kind of literary.*

Twelve hours ago she believed, and would have told anyone, that she was solidly in love with Peter, her body still glowing with the weekend's achievements. But, she pondered, within the gaudy circle of sex, what was there?

Are they partners in any worthwhile endeavor? No.

Do they share a cause, a danger, or even a hobby not described in the Kama Sutra? Not really.

Are they simply so entangled with each other that there is no other reason needed for immolating herself in the flames, etc.?

Well. Their love is a strange mix of indulgence and worship. Peter is older and more sophisticated, but endearingly boyish. His mind is full of surprises, quirks, gynecology, and New England. She supposes that she is as much a new world to him as he is to her, once you factor out the things - largely neurophysiological, no doubt - that she may have in common with departed Julie. It occurs to her again that he is like her father, and yet is nothing like him at all. Every time they meet, she is ravished anew - as was, she had thought, true for him too.

She might once have said that they make each other better (stronger, sexier, happier) than they are in ordinary life. Now she is not sure that was not simply hormones and her lonely body talking.

Shouting.

She had already considered, and despaired of, the notion of marrying Peter and moving to Maine. What would she do among that frigid tribe, but serve as a useful ornament to him? Or bringing him here to parboil in Dixie. Misery either way. She supposed — always assuming he could be jollied out of this current snit — they could just go on as they had, gaudy interludes punctuating separate lives, aging without commitment or prejudice until he was in a nursing home, ninety years old and incontinent, and she well on her way.

So maybe, if no future sounded other than sad, she should end it now, while the pain would be a little numbed by her irritation at his prickly prickishness this morning. End of the AFFAIR.

***

Faye walked into the *Intelligencer* office on July 6th with some cheer in her step. She knew she had been tired and upset last night, and she should probably think again about the Peter Problem. Meanwhile, she would be good and distracted with Forde.

"Well, Forde, didn't I warn you about it?"

"Yep, OK. Knew you'd say that. I also think it was you, said you had to see it to believe. Well, I went to see it while you were on vacation with Peter. Have a good time?"

"Yes."

"... So anyways, while it was quiet around here, I went to have a look for myself. Jesus, Faye, how could anybody -"

She put a hand on his shoulder. "I tried to stop you from looking, Forde," completely mistaking his meaning, because she'd been thinking about the Quincy Tiff while Forde was talking.

He covered her hand with his. "You did? I just thought you were being bossy and insufferable, nosing into where you had no business. But I went out there. Lord!"

"Wait, what? Out where?"

"Well, River Mills. What were you thinking about?"

"Oh. Yes." For no reason she could fathom, she thought he'd been talking about the sight of tiny Annie Faye in her mother's coffin. "Yes, well ... so much for the power of words, I guess. 'Hell on Earth' didn't make an impression?"

"That was before they murdered my wife and daughter. Changes how you see things, I guess."

"In any reasonable society, knowing they'd been murdered would bring down some legal trouble on the 'perps,' as Rathbun likes to call the likes of Mister Merrydown. Has there been any movement at all out of him?"

"Rathbun?" Forde shrugged. "Such as?"

"Oh, gosh. A press conference with hints about arrests being imminent. Persons of interest. That kind of stuff."

Forde gave that a half smile. "No, looks to me like somebody else is gonna have to step up. Some citizen, like."

"Such as?" Knowing.

"I was thinking of you and me, Faye. We're injured parties, both of us. We have one weapon, the *Intelligencer*."

"Well, I guess it's better than nothing."

"Huh. Sounds like one of those desert-island stories, where they make a tower out of, you know, driftwood and underwear, and use it to signal a passing tramp steamer."

"I never did like steamed tramps."

They looked at each other, curious, smiling. "You've changed."

"You too, you know."

"Who could blame us?"

"Change or die."

"They say. But I like you as much as ever."

"Me too. Take care."

When Faye had left, Forde looked at the picture of Nora on his desk. One of her eyebrows was a little lower than the other, he noticed for the hundredth time. She seemed to be about to wink at him about something. God, how he missed her.

***

From the Gabbro *Intelligencer* for Friday, July 9, 1965:

This Town's Times
-by-
M. Faye Bynum, Associate Editor

Managing Editor Forde Morgan and I sat down recently for an editorial conference. You might think that just about every conversation we hold could be called that, but in fact it was the first chance we'd had to talk journalism since the tragic murder of Forde's wife and child in an act of criminal vandalism by ... oh, Persons Unknown, I suppose we must call them, though they are known to themselves, to God, and, honestly, to anyone who is willing to pay a little attention. And nearly the first since I was subjected to a severe beating, by maybe the same Persons Unknown, as punishment for describing River Mills as "ripe for unionization," because it is a hot, noisy, exhausting, and dangerous place to work. Our editorial conference was about the role of labor unions.

Unions are not popular here or throughout the South, I understand that. Yet, for some reason, other civic associations are: the Jaycees, the Rotarians, the PTA, the Baptists. (Oh, I'm going to catch it for <u>that</u>.

Of course, the Baptists are devout members of the Body of Christ. But they are also an important civic association, or what should we call their generous support of Gabbro Memorial Hospital, their summer camp for city children, and their outreach programs for the poor?)

Labor unions have come into being because they serve an important civic role: they represent the economic and worklife interests of people, your neighbors and mine, who work together to make the things we buy and use. Individual workers are powerless to improve dirty and unsafe manufacturing practices. Why should these neighbors of ours - people we live and worship with, whose children learn beside ours, who kneel beside us on Sundays, who practice anthems with us on Wednesday evenings after supper - why should they not group together to multiply their voices at work as they do in church? Why should they not have the right and power to earn a decent living in a safe and healthy environment? That is what unionization promises to these hard-working neighbors. Sure, this promise may or may not be kept in any given case; but without unions, they are left at the mercy of owners and managers not to subject their workers to the dangers and miseries of unregulated workplaces.

What miseries? What dangers? Anyone who cares to visit, can see them on full display at merciless River Mills.

***

Peter's letter - smilingly delivered to Faye's desk by Sedalia, along with an assortment of what looked like hate mail and indignation

in response to her **"Town's Times"** column - arrived on Monday the
12th. Faye sorted through the bundle and started with the hate mail,
as being easier to deal with:

To M. Faye Bynum:

Any fool knows that unions are communist-inspired organiza-
tions, and nothing like the Baptists. "Workers of the world unite, you
have nothing to lose but your chairs." Do you know who wrote that,
Miss Bynum?
R. McLeod
Gabbro

Miss Bynum:

God love you, Honey, but my Daddy mined copper in Arizona for
17 years before he died in a mine accident, and he never once signed
on to a union appeal ...

To the Associate Editor:

"When the union's inspiration through the workers' blood shall run
There can be no power greater anywhere beneath the sun!
Yet what force on earth is weaker than the feeble strength of one,
But the union makes us strong."
Solidarity Forever! Bless you, Miss Faye Bynum!
- A Union Maid

Faye stared at the quotation, and puzzled at why it should look
familiar when in fact she had never in her life seen it. Well, it scanned
nicely, except that the third line was a little awkward to get going right.
She could quote it next time, hoping to smoke out the writer for an
interview. She shrugged and opened the rest of the letters, ignoring
still the stiff envelope from Standish, Maine. Rants, most of them, with
no sense and no grammar, and no kindness or love, except the phony

love that is spoken of by people who want to patronize and own you. *God love you, honey.* The one with the poem praising unions was the only exception. Faye's heart began to sag under the burden of all that unhappy anger, and when it had settled into a dull rhythm of acceptance, she slammed the letters into the trash, knowing she would have to recover them and pass them on to Forde.

In the Ladies, peeing in a sulk, she heard a small drum begin to tap in the rattle of the vent fan:

Tap a rappty tap ta-rappty tap
Ta rattle-y tappty tap.

Faye ignored it, because to pay any attention would be another distraction when she was already distracted beyond bearing. She re-assembled herself and walked back to her desk, heels tapping on the inky floorboards:

Rap a rappty tappty ... greater anywhere beneath the sun.
Ta rattle tap ta rappty tap ... strength of one? ... Yes!
But the union makes us strong!

Of course the words looked familiar, though she had never seen them; their rhythm was the Battle Hymn of the Republic, the song one must never whistle or hum south of the Mason-Dixon. The righteous, forbidden, smug, triumphant song of such power that it hummed in the blood of those hundred dead boys from Massachusetts, and the million men from the North who marched with it to fight in Dixie. She retrieved the letter with the poem, and sang under her breath, knowing the tune now,

When the union's inspiration through the workers' blood shall run,
There can be no power greater anywhere ...

There was no chance of forgetting the words; the music lined them up like a column of infantry and marched them through her brain: ... *But the union makes us strong.*

Unions, that alien European notion, sinister craziness brought to America by a bunch of Polaks and Hunkies, but not to <u>our</u> America, no sir; up there to <u>Yankee</u> America, to the mills of New Jersey and the mines of Pennsylvania and the factories of Connecticut from which, decades before, came the guns that rammed Union down the throats of outgunned rebels.

That's why they hate the idea. It's Union. It's too selfless, too mobbish, not Beau Geste enough, not Lost Cause enough, and it puts the good of many poor folks against the privileges of the Masters. It's just too damn Yankee.

***

Friday, July 9

Dear Faye –

I know that you were going to write to me with your thoughts about our discussion earlier this week, but I wanted to pick up on something you said then. Paraphrasing and shortening, it went something like, "If it should work out that I become Mrs. Peter A. Standish, I would be nothing but glad and proud." Now, I know that the context was your sense that I should not be in a huff about the joke perpetrated by those cretins in Quincy. But the statement carried so much more meaning, and I keep hearing it now in your gentle voice. Well, what do you think? Shall it so work out? Will you consider it? I am so very sorry that I blamed you for my injured dignity. It was completely wrong of me.

Yours, still –
Peter
(Peter A. Standish, MD)

Faye rested her forehead on the heap of hate mail. *Why don't I dump this on Forde's desk, along with the rest of it?*

Forde leaned back in the Boss Chair. "And will you?"

"I rather think not."

"Why not?"

"I can't answer that. What shall we do about Mister Merrydown?"

"Kill him if possible. Otherwise, at least annoy the shit out of him. Why can't you answer that?"

"What, about Peter? Because first of all, I don't know, and second, it involves matters that I would rather not talk about."

"You don't have to get huffy. You had plenty to say about Nora and me in the early going."

"Don't let's do this, Forde. We need each other."

Forde shook his head. "Don't I know it."

"What about a vote?"

"On what?"

"On unionization. I think there's a law of some kind. Look, let me go up to Chapel Hill, spend some time in the library. I'm almost sure there's some law that guarantees workers the right to vote on a union."

"Really? Seems doubtful to me, but OK. You got this week's column done? All your other stuff?"

"On your desk by five."

***

On Tuesday, having slept on Peter's letter, and with an unsupervised day ahead in Chapel Hill, Faye took some time on the porch glider to reply to him:

7/13

Dear Peter -

It is, of course, a cliché for a reluctant maiden to tell a suitor that a proposal of marriage is 'flattering.' I hate clichés, so I will not insult you with that one. I am still waiting for my feelings in regard to our Quincy Tiff to settle into some recognizable form. But I have to say, Peter, that I was some considerably shaken by it. Though I am no maiden, I yet remain reluctant in regard to marriage.

Which is not to say that, at the same time, I do not love you other than dearly. (Damn. I was never good at multiple negatives.) Look : I love you. Dearly. I cherish our times together. You are some terrific lover and a fascinating, complex, lovely man. I definitely do not <u>like</u> the side of you that I saw last week. When I have a chance to consider that in the context of all that you have meant to me over these months, I can give your question the serious consideration it deserves.

Best I can do for now-

Faye

Faye left it in the drawer with the reloaded roscoe, figuring to get back to it when she returned from Chapel Hill. All through the two-hour drive there, she ransacked her memories of Peter, from the CPR awakening at Camp Nokoma through the garnet skarn, the fairy-tale Christmas in New York, the seclusions at Morgan's Eddy and the various getaways down to the erotic shower stall in Quincy, as well as his letters. Winnowing grains of recollection for some pattern that would tell her whether that prissy, pissy outburst in Quincy was a revelation or simply an aberration. Was it the accidental slip of a mask of endearing vulnerability, revealing the priggish schoolmaster beneath? Or was it only a fleeting megrim triggered by ... well, what? The bumpkins who'd made a joke of his patrician name? Sleep deprivation? (They'd napped in Quincy, but pretty actively for the most part.) Boredom with the Midwest? Or – uh oh – with Faye Bynum? And did it mean anything that he always signed letters, "Peter A. Standish, MD," even intimate little handwritten billets-doux and proposals of marriage? *So much easier to ask hard questions than to answer them. Thank God some bratty reporter isn't asking.*

***

"Forde, honest to God, you'll never believe it. Thirty years ago this month, this law was passed that - get this - it <u>guarantees</u> workers the right to vote on whether to form a union, and forbids employers to interfere with the voting. Thirty years ago, mind."

"Huh. Where'd you find it? Don't tell me you went to the law library."

"Yes, I did, but it was too arcane by a mile. I was just finding that out, trying to ask the librarian an intelligent question, when this guy in a tweed jacket and horn-rim glasses comes by and says, you know, 'Couldn't help overhearing,' blah blah, obviously seeing a pickup opportunity. But it turned out he's a professor of labor law, and he gave me the complete run-down in exchange for a beer and my phone number. Which I had the presence of mind to reverse two numbers, so I don't think I'll hear from him, since he also never got my full name."

"Man. No wonder men keep women oppressed. We let you loose, you'd be in charge of everything. This law have a name?"

"The Wagner Act. Don't ask me who Wagner was. I actually have a brochure about it in my purse, and it spells everything out. It was kind of watered down later on, the professor said, but not in a way we're going to care about. So listen ..."

She pulled out a gray and black, Federal-looking pamphlet with a flaring eagle on the cover, and began paging through it.

"... blah, blah ... OK, here: 'Section 7. Employees shall have the right to self-organization, to form, join, or assist labor organizations, to bargain collectively through representatives of their own choosing, and to engage in other concerted activities for the purpose of collective bargaining or,' here we go, 'other mutual aid or protection.' How's that? That's the law of the United States of America which, last I looked, included the State of North Carolina, kicking and screaming."

Forde rubbed his chin and shrugged. "What's 'mutual aid and protection' about? Protection from what?"

"How about from brown lung? Or passing out from the heat? Or getting your hand cut off?"

"Huh. So if we ..."

"Yep. Funny coincidence, huh? Signed into law by Mr. Roosevelt in July of 1935, thirty years ago on the dot." She squared up her fingers in the air, outlining a headline. 'Three Decades of the Wagner Act: Labor in Transition.' We'll talk about how working folks have all these rights to organize to improve wages and working conditions. Maybe some stories from other places, where workers actually organized. It'll drive Merrydown nuts."

"All I need to hear. Knock yourself out."

***

At the Salonnette, Pearlene Skinner was left alone to clean up after the departure of the Regulars. Pearlene didn't think much of the new Regular, a Gabbro High graduate named Mitchie Malkovits who had dropped out of UNC after a dean observed her attending a fraternity Halloween kegger dressed as Venus de Milo in marbled paint, long black formal gloves, and a sheet. Mitchie found being back in Gabbro a letdown after Chapel Hill, and let no opportunity pass to comment on the contrast. And besides, she always seemed to have something nasty tangled in her hair, that it would be Pearlene's job to wash and comb and finally pick away with her fingernails. Pearlene missed Faye

Bynum, whose hair she had trimmed every two weeks for almost eighteen years, and who never failed to have a cheerful word, a decent tip, and something snippy to say to Ginnie Freeman.

Besides, Pearlene had been troubled about that Baley person that Faye brought in ... well, first of all, what was she <u>thinking</u>? Brought in, anyway, on the theory that all God's children were infinitely valuable, and thus deserved a hairdo just as much as Mary-Deane Gaines, the ranking Regular now that Ginnie Freeman was talking about moving out to Sunset Acres. It was a notion that Pearlene wished with all her being might be true. Because if it was, then chubby, permanently single Pearlene Skinner, the least and lowest of the Salonnette ladies, in the scrappiest no-account little country town in Christendom, might herself be valuable. The idea about made Pearlene cry.

***

Back at the cottage, Faye took her letter to Peter out of the roscoe drawer, read it through, and put it in an envelope to take by the Post Office in the morning. She realized that she was tired of the whole business; it obviously had no plans either to resolve itself or leave her in peace. She could not find in herself the enthusiasm, or gumption, to take on a battle with Peter on top of what she was already engaged in with River Mills, the School Board, and advancing age. Nor was kissing him off thinkable. He was a wonderful lover, a swell person whom she actually loved, and a companion that she could either have, or have not, as it suited her. Why couldn't that be enough for him, too?

And she felt old suddenly, or at least older than her age. Thirty-seven years, she had read somewhere, was what human evolution had decided was a good enough life span to keep the species going, and anything beyond that was superfluous gravy. In the <u>old</u> old days, when men made a living by killing mastodons, a woman that old was pretty much a crone, about done with life after breeding herself half to death for twenty years.

Faye had for years, like Mercy in her novel, generally been happy enough with what she saw in the mirror. Now her *body* had become something worrisome and apart from her *self*, who had never had to make the distinction. Something to be watched warily as it turned middle-aged before her eyes, day by day. She knew that she was in terrific shape, for a woman of her years; but never before had that hateful qualifier slunk into the equation. She found more gray hairs this morning that pretty much added up to a gray streak now, and a new frown line.

She pulled a bowl of tomato soup out of the fridge, garnished it with a dozen Ritz Crackers, and settled on the chaise. By the time she'd finished, she was cooler, but too sleepy to resist, and laid her head back.

..........*do you think? Shall it so work out?...* I do not love you dearly. No, wait, I cannot fail to question the serious consideration..... some terrific lover's **huff about those damnable cretins in Quincy** and a reluctant maiden tapping on the screen door, and Annie Godfire was there, smiling and smelling of acetylene and welding flux.

"Hey, Faye, you forget what night it is?" Annie's head tipped toward the Eddy, beyond which an enormously pregnant full moon was extricating itself from the swamp, the topmost trees a clinging black filigree, its upper edge a silver rim for the highlands and maria; the Man therein winking and clearing his throat, in company with a bullfrog and three dozen crickets. Faye jumped from the chaise, making the wicker shudder and creak.

"Annie! Oh, thank God."

"Something wrong?"

"No, does something have to be? I'm just thanking God you're here in the world. You ready?"

And the cannonballs and the glides, the stripes of golden light on chilled ecstatic bodies; the embrace of the warm air, the drowsy naps side by side on the dock under fireflies, until a breeze stirred the pines and drove them back into the water. And when the moon had climbed and silvered and shrunk to a vertical searchlight at midnight, they drifted downward, held hands and looked up through six feet of lunar phosphorescence at the rippled surface above, while the fool's-gold Confederate bones danced in silence far below.

And Faye was horribly afraid, gasped in water, and clung to Annie hard enough to about drown them both. When they were back in the shallows, Annie gently pounded Faye's back and held her in the air like a newborn, to expel the Eddy she'd inhaled. When Faye was breathing normally again, Annie held her over the broad knoll of her shoulder, her hand holding the back of Faye's head, rocking in a comforting pivotal motion.

"You OK?"

"Ye - No. I'm not. It was like I fell asleep under water, and didn't know where I was when I woke up. All of a sudden I felt like I was drowning, and I'd never get back to the air."

"You did about drown in Maine, didn't you tell me?"

"Yes, but it wasn't like that. This was like some kind of horrible magic, and the bones were coming up after me, and I couldn't get away."

Annie said nothing, but waded ashore and wrapped Faye and herself in the robes. They walked back to the cottage, hand in hand; sat on the screen porch and sang Lumbee songs that Annie had taught Faye, while they sipped at thimble-size jots of the blue cordial. And at last, they collapsed onto Faye's bed to share the wide pillow while the tick of the Grandmother Clock faded into moon-dusk; whirred; and struck once, unheard.

25.

THE OUTREACH INTERN

Chapter 9.

Mercy lay in her solitary bed and considered what she could say in reply to James' puzzling and worrisome letter. What on earth could he have meant by "cherished friend?" My God, you might say that of a favorite niece or a school pal. Were James' feelings beginning to cool? Had he found someone new, someone close by who had regular access to him, to charm and tease and ... Ah! It was too awful to contemplate. She buried her face in the pillow and wailed.

26.

F ROM THE RALEIGH *OBSERVER* FOR FRIDAY, JULY 23, 1965:

Guest Editorial:

The Wagner Act and River Mills
- M. Faye Bynum-

Three decades ago this summer, President Franklin D. Roosevelt signed into law a bill titled "National Labor Relations Act." Also known informally as the "Wagner Act," after its author, Senator Robert Wagner (D-NY), the law tosses a lifeline to workers who, like those in many North Carolina textile mills, are drowning in an ocean of brutality, danger, and stingy pay. It offers a mechanism by which workers can get together like good American neighbors, to solve their problems jointly and collectively.

The writer is quite aware that the word *collective* will raise "red" flags. There are some who fear that to consider the welfare of those who make the goods of our commerce is to embrace the evils of communism. There are also some - many of them owners and managers of factories - who exploit this fear in order to stand in the way of citizens who are entitled to bargain as a group ("collectively") with factory management and owners to improve wages and working conditions. But in fact, their right to do that is the Law of this American land.

My paper, the Gabbro *Intelligencer,* has carried stories about the hellish working conditions at River Mills, a Merrydown Industries mill in Gabbro County: workers fainting in the heat, coughing with the early symptoms of Brown Lung Disease; workers maimed by the dangerous and unsecured machinery that they use. The *Intelligencer* now employs a former River Mills worker who was badly injured by a machine, and - if you can believe this - billed for the fabric that her blood stained while she lay wounded on the factory floor. We understand that the Textile Workers' Union of America has been active in trying to encourage the workers of many North Carolina mills to embrace the right that the law guarantees them, and to vote on establishing a union to bargain on their behalf, with the aim of improving their pay and working conditions.

There is nothing subversive or communistic about that aim. It is enshrined in the American Declaration of Independence as "the pursuit of happiness." Allowing workers to vote on whether to join a union, does not guarantee that they will do so. A union election simply gives workers the opportunity. The *Intelligencer* joins the *Observer* in calling for union elections throughout North Carolina's textile industries without delay.

M. Faye Bynum is Associate Editor of the Gabbro, NC *Intelligencer.* She can be reached at *The Intelligencer,* 61 E. Church St. Gabbro, NC 27352

***

Some days after this editorial appeared in the *Observer,* Pearlene Skinner rinsed her sink, swept her area, and hung up the broom. "Ladies," she said to the Salonnette Regulars. "I have a piece of urgent business downtown, and I will be away from my chair for the next hour or so. I have done some studying on this matter, and I have been able to reckon that nobody's hair will grow more than a thousandth of an inch in that time." She unsnapped her apron, hung it with the broom, and exited the Salonnette, stumping down Church Street the three blocks to the *Intelligencer* office.

Once there, she was not sure how she was going to manage it, but her errand was three-fold: First, to quiz Faye Bynum as closely as she could about this "infinitely valuable" business of which - and she had studied hard on it - she could find no mention in her Bible. She was confident that Faye would know exactly where it was written. Second, to beg Faye on bended knee to come back to the Salonnette and put Ginnie Freeman in her place, who badly needed it before she went to Sunset and was seen no more; and third, while her knee was bended, to apologize to the infinitely valuable Sedalia Baley. To invite Sedalia back to the Salonnette was beyond Pearlene's authority, and would surely lead to something unpleasant; but she would go to Sedalia's home - however humble it might be, and in whatever godforsaken quarter it might be found - and give her the wash, trim, and set she so plainly needed. As a valuable child of God herself, she could do no less.

***

Forde Morgan raised a delaying finger at Lee Forsythe, and picked up his phone.

"Mr. Morgan, Mr. Merrydown is here to speak to you."

Sigh. "Our Father who art in heaven ..."

"Yes, sir. Thank you. I beg your partin." Sedalia turned to the trio at her desk. Mason Merrydown and his bodyguards were all wearing white fedoras in some kind of porous mesh, evidently intended to ward off the hot sunshine of a Gabbro August. "Mr. Morgan is at prayer, and cannot be disturbed."

The larger thug chuckled, the smaller one smiled nervously, and Mason Merrydown snorted. "Good idea, but too late. Shoulda started it a couple years ago." He pushed past Sedalia and started down the hallway, trailed by the lesser thug.

"Sir? *Sir*! Mr. Morgan is at -"

The larger thug brushed her aside roughly enough to slam her hip into the corner of the desk, bringing tears of pain. In a distorted hobble, holding herself upright with the maimed right hand, she made her way back to her chair, where she picked up the brass nameplate from her desk and polished it with the hem of her dress. Her hip was painful enough to make her a little nauseous.

The larger thug hustled to catch up with the others, and opened Forde's office door, banging it into Lee Forsythe's heel. Lee - there to get a time sheet initialed by Forde - jumped and managed not to scream, but turned, paled, and shrank against the wall. She goggled at the smaller bodyguard, who shrugged and smiled nervously while Mason Merrydown snarled, "Where's Bynum?"

In fact, Faye Bynum was at that second doubled over the washbasin in the Ladies', retching, trying to keep her voice out of it but not really succeeding. Hearing the voice of Mason Merrydown at the reception desk, and his footsteps in the hall, she had been on the point of rallying to Forde's side, hoping to continue their campaign of driving Merrydown nuts.

When she cracked open her office door, the larger thug, passing, smiled and winked at her, wagging a promissory finger. He wore black leather gloves. He was the Assistant Thug who'd held her up for the Boss Thug to slap and punch, and held her down for the aborted rape; and whom Faye had wounded with her last bullet. His body and walk were those of the demon of her night agonies. Faye ducked back, heart pounding and fear ripping at her belly. She sank to a squat inside the door, sure that she was going to vomit on the doormat. When she heard Forde's venetian blind rattle to mark the thug's arrival, she darted across the hall.

Forde shook his head. "She's on an assignment."

"I want her here."

Forde looked at him without speaking for a time, and shrugged. "I want you gone. I thought I told you never to come in here."

"Free country to them as makes free. Where's this assignment?"

Forde lifted his phone. "Miss Baley?"

"Yes sir?"

"Please call Sheriff Rathbun. That criminal is in here again."

"Yes, Mr. Morgan."

Mason Merrydown turned with a grunt of impatience, spat on Lee Forsythe's shoe and strode back toward the door. Passing Sedalia Baley, Merrydown went out of his way to push her against her desk again. Before the bodyguards could react, her right arm shot out and flicked the white fedora from his head, while her left hand slammed the brass nameplate into his skull, not all that violently but cutting his scalp and releasing a sheet of blood.

Sedalia recoiled, white-faced at what she'd done. Jenny McCall, passing, screamed, and the larger bodyguard drew a pistol and shot. Sedalia cried out and lurched into the junior bodyguard, who caught her and lowered her roughly to the floor. He turned, snapped, " 'Tcha think you're doin, Dumbo?" and sank a fist into the belly of the larger. The thug's breath abandoned him and the pistol dropped to the floor, where the smaller bodyguard scooped it back down the hall toward Forde Morgan and Lee Forsythe, just emerging from Forde's office. Lee, more flexible and quicker on the uptake than Forde, stooped and picked it up.

In the Ladies', Faye was gathering herself to get out there and face the menace when the shot sent her whimpering to her knees again, her forehead pressed against the cool porcelain of the washbowl. *Shit, what is this?*

On Church Street, Denny McLeod, a Gabbro High dropout with an interest in Mitchie Malkovits, popped a wheelie on his Harley and gunned it, planning a maximum noise level as he passed the Salonnette with Stetson waving. Beginning two blocks ahead was premature, but he had spotted Pearlene on the sidewalk, and couldn't resist the chance to rattle her, because her attitude toward Mitchie sucked. The racket was loud enough to distract Pearlene and cover the sound of the scuffle and shot inside the *Intelligencer* office.

Pearlene rolled her eyes. *Infinitely valuable, really? That'll take some God-ing.* Faye had better be able to point to some verse that said all that, plus *Yea, even unto the worthless riff-raff that maketh noise on thy streets.* A God that long-suffering would be pretty interesting, and certainly worth worshipping. Pearlene sniffed, turned back, and reached for the *Intelligencer* door.

Mason Merrydown, yelling about lawsuits and hopping in circles, could not see well with blood streaming down his face, so tripped over Sedalia and fell toward the front door. The door opened to admit Pearlene just in time for the heavy brass inner handle, backed by the weight of the door and the bulk of Pearlene Skinner, to rendezvous with Merrydown's forehead; it struck him above the eye and snapped his head back, nearly breaking his neck. He collapsed to the floor and lay with his arm in the pool of blood seeping from beneath Sedalia.

The larger bodyguard rose to his feet, clutching his solar plexus, and came eye to eye with the pistol still shakily held by Lee Forsythe. Lee screamed and jumped back, flourishing the pistol in Forde's direction; Forde redirected it to the bodyguard, where it was needed. Lee, with a finger stuck in the trigger guard, couldn't let go, so they held it jointly. The larger bodyguard considered rushing them, and then shrugged, grinned, and raised his hands.

Lee gathered her wits and yelled, "Somebody, call the Sheriff." The smaller bodyguard snatched up the phone from Sedalia's desk. "Doing it right now."

"Good for you. Tell him get a ambulance." She eyed the small thug over the gun "How come you punched his breadbasket just now? You one of his thugs, or not?"

"Uh uh, not no more, I'm not, since he spit on your shoe. Soon's he wakes up, I'm giving my notice."

Lee sniffed, and extracted her finger from the pistol. "About time, Tucker Pardee."

An ambulance came and went, bearing Mason Merrydown and his former employee to Gabbro Memorial. Sedalia was judged to be the more urgent case - Merrydown was by now conscious, if not exactly lucid. She was whisked off to surgery, where the usual team of cut-and-stitchers did what they could in regard to a bloody but really minor wound, and tossed the result into God's hands with their usual shrugs.

When Faye was encouraged by the silence to emerge from the Ladies', a damp paper towel to her forehead, she found the little collection of shocked people mopping up blood and asking each other, Now what?

***

"I'm a wreck, Annie. I'm biting people's heads off -"

"People?"

"Forde, today. I'm having bad dreams, I think I'm out of love with Peter, and today I had a ... a whatchamacallit. A hysterical attack."

"Panic attack?"

"That's it."

"What triggered it, do you know?"

"Of course I <u>know</u>, whadda you ... Oh, damn... See? Anyhow, it was Merrydown's thug, one of the pair that beat me up. He came past my office on his way with Merrydown to see Forde. He had on his black gloves."

"Hardly seems hysterical, does it? He wears black gloves, beats you up, hurts you badly, he's never caught or punished for it, you got upset when you saw him and his black gloves. What am I missing here?"

"Upset? <u>Trembling</u>, like some character in a romance novel. Vomiting in the Ladies' instead of kicking his balls out the window. Then he shot Sedalia, and that set me off again. Lucky I was already hiding in the Ladies', so I was close enough to the potty that I didn't shit my panties. Annie, I'm just completely a wreck. It's hurting my work, and making me worthless." She scuffed a foot in the grass and flopped against the first layer of the Spirit Catcher. "Plus, now Peter decided he wants to marry me."

"Huh. Put that aside for a minute. What about the dreams?"

"Black gloves. Something grabbing me out of the dark with black gloves on, and I know they're going to hurt me, and this time they won't quit, because Rosie's dead, and can't save me. That time we were swimming, that was what I saw, we're six feet under water, I'm wide awake looking at the moon, and all of a sudden those bones are coming after me, they're going to hurt me. I took in a breath to scream, which you saw what came of that."

"I did. Come here."

"Annie. I'm turning into a neurotic old maid."

"Come here."

Annie put down the bottle of blue cordial and looked out the screens at the Eddy. Dusk, frog songs, an aerobatic bird skimming the surface and scooping up water beetles, leaving a vee of silver on the dark surface. "Now. Do you want to marry Peter?"

"I don't want to marry anybody. I just want people to leave me alone, for a change."

"I won't."

"Well, good. That isn't what I meant, you know that."

"I do. Yet you say you love Peter."

"... Yes. I do. I love you too, Annie, but I don't want to marry you. I'm not sure I'm the marrying kind, and I don't want to get into a situation where ... Well. Where I'll be trapped."

"Oof. Trapped?"

"Well." Faye surveyed the teeming bug life of the Eddy, and turned back to Annie. "Yes, trapped. I love Peter, but when it's a matter of Peter day in and day out, in Maine ... Well, that's different. That's a terrible thing to think, isn't it?"

"I gave up on trying to decide whether things people think are bad or good. Come to find out, it's what they do, pretty much every time, not what they think."

"Well, I'm going to have to <u>do</u> something about Peter."

***

Gabbro, August 1

Dearest Peter -

Again, thank you for the honor you do me in asking me to marry you. I am afraid that the answer will have to be, No.

I love being with you. Hell, I love <u>you</u>, Peter. But I simply cannot understand how a marriage between us could possibly survive the strain to either of us, of living in the other's home environment. Nor, to be honest, can I ever picture myself as anyone's wife, responsible for decades of meals, laundry, peace-keeping, children, and, of course, love-making. I recognize in this a failure of courage on my part.

If you would be at all interested in picking up our LTFWED where we left it, I am finally and completely over the Quincy Tiff. I hope you are as well, and I am here for you if you want me. We have whole chapters of the Kama Sutra to get through yet.

If it should be the case that you are determined to settle down in marriage to someone, I will bitterly regret that I simply cannot be that someone, but I will understand and bless you and your someone from afar.

Your loner lover,
Faye

This letter, like many before it, sat cooling with the roscoe in the bedside table while Faye slept beside it, rose to her morning rituals of exercise and bath in Morgan's Eddy, always after scanning the woods for intruders. Solitary breakfast. Dressing for work, with parting examination of her reflection for presentability and new signs of age.

These rarely fail to appear now that the beating and the demons it woke have broken the spell of youth that held her for twenty years. *I will be 38 next week, and 40 soon enough after that. I am becoming middle-aged and mortal. And a fool to shun a safe harbor of love and affection and a lover who will overlook my wrinkles and flab. A scout who will go ahead of me into age and senescence.*

But a loner is a loner; all the more when the prospect is gloomy. She knows that she can never run to anyone – Peter, Forde, Annie, or ... well, that's pretty much the list – for comfort and protection from demons that in the end are herself. The streak of gray in her black hair has become the flag under which she marches into the slow chaos of a Southland that has marked her for its own.

***

It was the same plain white envelope, coming in with the rest of the mail on Saturday the 7th:

Bynum –

    Nice editorial. Look, if you don't want to do anything about Morgan's wife and kid, just tell me, and I'll shut up about it.

    SAndhills 1-5157, between 2:00 and 2:10.

True to her promise, Faye took it to Lyle Rathbun and tossed it on his desk, where it skidded against a snow globe that said *Souvenir of Lake Placid,* rousing a small plastic flurry. "OK, here. Don't tell me I'm not cooperating."

"When'd you get this?"

"An hour ago."

"You call the number?"

"Nope. Thought you might want to be on an extension, like you claimed one time."

Rathbun looked at his watch. "It's after three."

"Last time, he meant AM. The thing came with the afternoon mail, about two. I figured he meant it this time, too."

"Two in the <u>morning</u>? Jesus."

"Don't be scared. It can be nice at that hour. So what's the plan, Mr. Sheriff?"

27.

FORDE SLUMPED ON AN IRON TRACTOR SEAT 35 FEET above Annie Godfire's meadow, watching the gathering dark and listening to the dusky voices of the breeze in the Spirit Catcher, and to Annie. Annie's voice was gentle, but clear in the dusk; amplified somehow by the scrap steel, or by the life it had witnessed.

"Fordie, you know I really learned to like Nora before the accident. She was so full of life already, and then when the baby started to grow, she was twice as full. She came out here one Saturday toward the end of April, and she really understood about the Spirit Catcher. Told me stories of how they talk to spirits in Scotland, when the wind is off the ocean, and it's all fog and smoke, and -"

"Annie, stop, please. I still haven't got over her."

"OK, sorry. Did you want to get over her?"

"Ye ... I don't know. Why not?"

"What does 'get over' mean, do you think?"

"Get on with my life. Forget Nora so I don't feel so sad all the time." He shrugged. "And the baby."

"But why would you want to forget them? They haven't forgot you."

"Annie, they're dead, damn it all. Dead ... " He couldn't finish, but shrugged. "Just don't talk about them like they ain't."

"Well, all right. But ..."

"Spirits, is that it? Well, Annie, that's always been your business. I guess I gotta tell you, I'll believe in spirits when I see one."

"Fordie. You've been seeing spirits all your life. You look at me, or

Faye, you're seeing a spirit. Is it so hard to see them when their bodies aren't there too?"

"You bet. Impossible, you ask me. Sure, I see Faye's spirit when she's there in front of me. How could I not, it's unavoidable. But when she's not there ... well." Forde had to stop there, because he was unwilling to say what was true, which was that something of Faye had always been present to him, even when she was not, even when she was off in Maine with Peter. That thing, that under-the-skin presence that had become part of him some time during their apprenticeships in Charlotte, and had never disappeared, is that what Annie meant by a spirit? And, starting soon after her appearance as flotsam in the Gabbro River, so had something of Nora become a larger and larger part of who he was, or could be. He shrugged, stubborn. "It's not the same thing."

That a snowy owl who'd been hunting voles in the goat meadow all week chose just that moment to soar over the Spirit Catcher and land soundless on a manhole cover opposite where they sat, was certainly caused by some predator's necessity that no human could conceive, far less understand. Forde knew that; still he couldn't help staring at the great bird, white in the dusk, and asking it, " ... Nora?"

***

Faye was baffled at first. Here came a pair of headlights lurching down her lane half an hour early, blazing off one pine tree after another, sweeping across the dock, picking out a blizzard of small moths circling at the foot of the steps. She rose from the glider and retreated into the living room to monitor from its darkness whatever the hell the Mystery Informant thought he was doing, coming in a blaze of light like that. Early, sure, he was being cute about getting in and out before she could set up some kind of trap. She took the roscoe from the bedroom and laid it on the mantle beside the Grandmother Clock. After picturing things for a moment, she took a flashlight out of kitchen drawer, tested its weak but adequate light, and stood it next to the roscoe.

On the far side of the chimney, a window no larger than a tea-tray had been sawn into the log wall as an afterthought. It looked awkward and ill-fitting, and it hadn't opened since the day it was shimmed into its opening, but it did offer a means to vet newcomers as they arrived. Through this, she surveyed the lawn and the fringe of forest, hoping to hell Lyle Rathbun was out there where he said he would be; he should have checked in by this time, and of course had not. "Everybody's got a plan 'til they get smacked in the chops," Rathbun had once opined, another insight he owed to crime fiction, and now seemed likely to illustrate.

The headlights came to a stop at the foot of the steps, and in the glow reflected from the stone footings of the cottage, Faye could see that they were attached to a rust-orange pickup truck, shit, like the truck the thugs had driven on the day she had been beaten mortal. The door opened, and a shadowy figure emerged. Faye squeaked at the sudden taste of fear at the back of her mouth.

***

The call to SAndhills 1-5157 had gone smoothly. Lyle Rathbun arrived at 1:30 AM, to Faye's surprise; brandishing a tech-ish looking box bearing a pair of hollow cylinders. He unscrewed Faye's phone line from its wall jack and passed it through the cylinders. "I can listen, but it don't put nothing out itself," he said. "No way your fella will know nobody's on the line." He re-attached the phone cord, and stood.

Anybody. But, as far as Faye could tell, so it had gone. She dialed SA 1-5157 at 2:05 AM. It was picked up before the first ring was finished.

"*Don't say nothing.*" It was the kazoo voice again.

"I ... OK"

"*Di'n I tell you, shut up? Just listen.*"

Faye said nothing. The voice sounded like somebody trying to start a car with an empty tank; words emerged from the garble only in retrospect.

"*That's better. You want no-shit dead certain evidence about Morgan's so-called accident, stay on the line. Otherwise, hang up now.*"

Faye said nothing, stayed on the line.

"*I'll come to your house tonight, yet. Be there around four. Don't have no witnesses or cops, or you'll never see me or hear from me again. I mean it. I won't be leaving nothing on your steps, neither. It goes straight from my hands to yours, you hand me $5,000 cash, we're done. So long.*"

"Wait! How -"

Dial tone.

"How are we supposed to put our hands on five thousand dollars between now and four o'clock in the morning? Who does he think he's jerking around?"

Lyle Rathbun exhaled reluctantly. "Got a bunch a counterfeit we confiscated last week, in the evidence locker. I'll run in, pick it up, be back here by three, latest."

"Five thousand?"

"Prob'ly not. More like forty cent worth of scrap paper anyways. Worst counterfeit I ever seen, some of it ain't even printed on both sides. It'll be dark, he ain't gonna count it. He give us that photo for nothing, so what's he thinking now, shakin' us down?"

∗∗∗

Peter Standish gave up on sleep and padded downstairs for some Pepto-Bismol to quiet a nagging ache in his belly. He had slept no more than three or four hours since he had rescued Faye's letter, with its uncompromising No to marriage, and its talk of Erotic Dimensions, from (Border Collie) Julie's uncompromising hostility to all mail and its carriers.

Well, what about another little tryst?

The trouble was, Peter felt that he had been seduced - not sexually, of course, that was a *fait* long since *accompli* - but morally, civically, by Faye's damn silly Applied Field Fiction, in which he had cooperated because he could see out Lena Melton's kitchen window the neatly erotic little garage apartment, the outside stairway threading its way from a bed of gladioli to an apartment that would surely be as unlike a dreadful Midwestern motel room as ... well, as Standish was unlike Gabbro.

And, Lord, he'd been with her since meeting her plane in St. Louis and sharing one decorous greeting kiss, and then endured – through the humming tedium of a two-hour car journey – the taut perfection of her body, the warmth of her voice, and her electric delight in being with him again on this crazy pilgrimage. Even the beginnings of the gray streak in her hair was sexy; he simply couldn't wait to get her alone. If he'd had to swear that Adam's rib had bred all womankind last Wednesday to accomplish it, he'd have done it without a murmur. But when he'd been slowed enough by post-coital lassitude for his conscience to catch up, he'd been a little ashamed.

Peter Standish had been raised by Boy Scout standards of abhorrence for lying, cheating, and stealing, and in fact to see those as in fact three faces of the same ugly thing. When you lie, his father had instructed him, you are stealing something – the Truth – from the one you lie to; when you steal, you are lying about whom the thing belongs to, that you stole; and when you cheat, you are both lying and stealing. So lectured Dr. Colwell Standish, MD, with a pince-nez on his nose and a used willow switch in his hand, and so believed from then on, the tearful boy with the stinging fanny. In fact, it was the centrality of that belief to the character of Dr. Peter Standish, MD, that shaped his interactions with patients, campers, and ladies rescued from drowning, and had pleased and captivated Faye Bynum.

Peter of course outgrew his awe of his father and his belief in the absolute truth of any moral teaching; as in the humane practice of medicine, much depends on circumstances, he knew. Peter certainly didn't think of creative fiction, or even good natured yarn-spinning, as the same as lying; but when it was Applied in the Field, well. Somewhere in the background stood Dr. Colwell Standish, with his hand on the switch. Peter rinsed his Pepto-Bismol spoon and went to the side porch to contemplate the streak of moonlight on Sebago Lake. He felt compromised. On the one hand, there's Faye. *God, you know I love her. On the other, there's Dad, fearful old grump, and yet the most kindly and admirable man I ever knew. And yet ...*

And yet Faye Bynum was no liar, in any reasonable sense. She was too honest, for example, to equivocate about his proposal of marriage. Her letters in response had been painfully honest, warm, and loving. He took the last one from where it sat next to Julie's photo on the piano, and read it again by moonlight (no great trick; he had read it seven times since it arrived two days ago).

I am here for you if you want me.

Peter smoothed the rumples from Julie's rough treatment. *Who do I think I am, anyway? Diogenes? George Washington?* He kissed the paper and climbed the stairs to bed, rubbing the little sore place.

***

"Jesus, Terry, what are you doing out here at this hour? Get that truck out of here, now! And where'd you get it, anyhow?"

"Easy does it, Little Princess. I got something for you."

"Easy does it, crap. Listen, first thing, you just drove into the middle of a police operation. Well, sheriff."

"I know all about it. Rathbun told me, tell you he can't make it. Three-car pileup out at the wye, two dead, baby in critical. But he give me this for you." He held out a paper bag that looked like it might hold a pound of worthless paper.

"Well, Christ, what am I supposed to do with that? I need backup!"

"Whaddya call me?" He started up the steps.

"Really? You're it? What, you got deputized or something?"

"Nuh uh. Listen, babe, it's only a little after three. Whyn't we go share that big wide pillow, get ourselves a little relaxed for the big rondy-voo. You sound like you could use some R an' R."

"OK, look, Terry. First place, no. Not a chance. Second place, get that goddamn truck out of sight. Pull it down the river path or something. And third -"

"Your command is my wish, yer Maj. Here, take this bag of queer cash. Back in a secont."

Faye sagged against the wall of the cottage, and tried to imagine innocent scenarios by which Terry Morgan could be driving the unmistakable orange pickup that Merrydown's thugs had used. It had the starred hole in the driver's window where one of her shots had landed. Maybe it was his all along, and they borrowed it. But Terry didn't seem a likely owner of two working trucks, even as ragged as this one and the white van he'd used when he worked on her roof. Well, maybe it was theirs, and he'd borrowed it because the white van had expired. But that would mean Terry was some kind of buddy of the Merrydown thugs, not a good thought.

When he returned, she quizzed him through the latched screen door. "Where'd you get the truck?"

"Bought it. You gonna let me in?"

"In due course. Bought it from who?" *Whom.*

"Bypass Ford. Set me back $250, but the van ... Oh, wait, you know that truck from somewhere?"

A little too innocent. She unlatched the door, reluctantly. "The thugs that beat me up drove it."

"So <u>you</u> put that hole in the winda? You did, didn't you? My stars, I'd a given that pirate another hundred, I'd a known that cute little hole come from my own roscoe, held in your hot little hanny, instead of tryin' to jew them down about it. But speakin a cute little -"

"No. The answer is still no, Terry. You and I are no longer on that footing."

He looked stricken. "Babe! After all the great times we had? We don't have to do the foot thing, you don't want. Aw, come on, you gone prissy on me? Not the way I remember it. C'mere."

"Terry, no! I mean it!"

"Just a little snuggle, how about? You know you want it."

Faye turned and walked in the cottage door.

"See, I thought so. C'mere, baby, I been missing you so - Hey, shit! Put that thing down."

Faye pushed off the safety. "Now, Terry, here's how I see it. In twenty minutes, a guy is going to come by here with evidence about a murder. He says. If he's not lying, well, fine. But there's a chance he is, and that he's coming here to shut me up permanently. I don't like how he's trying to shake us down for cash, in exchange. There was no question of that, the last time around. How do I know it's even the same guy? He could be coming here to kill me; so the very last thing I need is you, sleazing around trying to get me into bed. On the other hand, I do need backup, and it looks like you're it, damn Lyle Rathbun to hell. So I need you somewhere out of sight, and ready to jump the guy if he so much as lifts a finger at me. Got it?"

"Yuh, OK."

"I mean this, Terry. This is life and death, so if I can't count on you, or if you're still thinking of getting me into bed, tell me, and I'll shoot you right now. As it is, you make one move when the guy is here, that isn't clearly directed at backing me up, I'll shoot, and since I'll be nervous and scared, I can't answer for shooting carefully. I'll aim at the middle of you, and what happens next is your problem, not mine. Clear?"

"Jesus, I said yes."

"All right, fine. Where will you be?"

"OK, back in the living room here? In the shadows?"

"No good. I might want to bring him in there to get at the roscoe."

"OK, hell. Kitchen?"

"Fine. Quiet. Let's have a signal word. If I say ... what?"

"Uh ... *Nookie.*"

"<u>Will</u> you be serious? Life or death, didn't I say? Jesus!"

"OK, Babe. *'Jesus'* it is."

She waved him off. "Fine, *'Jesus.'* Get back there. And leave the roscoe where it is. Jesus, Mary and -"

He spun, pointed at her, winked, and clicked his tongue. "Yup. To the rescue, on *'Jesus.'* Pow!"

28.

THE OUTREACH INTERN

Chapter 13.

Mercy gasped with fear when the gloved hand clamped over her mouth and nose.

"Quiet, you little bitch," the voice muttered. "You got my money?"

Mercy nodded hard and quickly, her heart and diaphragm lungs pumping, terrified she would vomit into the glove and drown. "Yes," she gasped when the gloved hand was removed. "It's in here, on the mantle ... Oh, don't, please! Jesus!"

No help from the kitchen. One of the gloved hands pinned her arms behind her back, while the other began to invade her body, roughly attacking fondling her breast. Mercy's heart went into overdrive, and she groaned with pain and fear. And, as if a switch had been thrown, she was through with fear and its demons, with being beaten and mauled. She spun and brought a knee hard into her attacker's groin. When he cursed and doubled over, clutching his himself, she dashed into the living room and snatched the "roscoe" from the mantle. Quickly, she pushed off the safety and switched on a flashlight.

"All right, my friend, let's have a look at you. Don't move, and take off that ski mask."

Sullenly, the intruder looked about himself for a path of escape; but Mercy was vigilant, and kept him covered. "Off with it, scum! Now, or I'll shoot. I may be a lousy shot, but I can't miss at this distance, can I?"

The thug laughed, nervously; his gloved hand rose, and pulled off the mask. Mercy gaped, and nearly forgot to keep the gun level. "Barney Virgil?" she gasped. "Jesus!"

From the darkness of the kitchen came a stumble and the crash of a chair. "Ow, shit! Coming, Babe," Randy called.

29.

VIRGIL BARNETT CLAIMED TO BE IN DISGUISE AS A thug, to avoid detection by the real thugs that, he claimed, prowled the streets and byways of Gabbro County, vigilant for defection and unionism, as he delivered what he referred to as "the clincher:" a blurry photo of a ledger, with an entry of $2500 to "Agent, c/o Mercer;" for: "Morgan."

"Yes? Pretty good disguise, the black gloves, the assault, trying to shake me down for five thousand bucks."

(The laugh) "I apologize. I guess I figured you'd never expect it of me, a professional man and an upright citizen. It was just part of the dis -"

"If that got you upright, good for you. It's the last thrill you'll get out of me. If you ever touch me or anyone I know again; if you ever so much as offer to shake my hand, you lying piece of crap, I'll refer the matter to my associate here, with a recommendation against mercy. Got it? Got it, Terry?"

Terry Morgan, spinning the roscoe on his trigger finger, spoke lazily from the rustic couch. "Oh, yeah. Not sure I'll wait around for no referral. Faye Bynum is my lady friend. Anybody gonna assault her, it's me, so you best stay out of my line of sight, now on, got me?"

Barnett shrugged. "Don't promise what you can't deliver, little man. I got resources too."

"Can we cut the pissing contest? Barnett, I don't see that this alleged le - this thing you claim is a ledger from River Mills clinches anything. You could have faked it with a ledger book from the five and dime. It could be talking about the price of a used car."

"It's probable cause for Rathbun to seize the real ledger, first place. And to subpoena the bookkeeper to explain the entry, for another."

"Well, gosh, Virgil. Wouldn't that put <u>you</u> in a kind of a tough spot? You're the manager out there. You'll be in the spotlight, not the bookkeeper."

"I think I told you once, I am not a free agent. Both I and the bookkeeper act under orders from Mason Merrydown; in this case, only the bookkeeper, without my knowledge. The coy language was supposed to hide it from me. This page is from the second set of books, the real set. It's not in the set he gives me to read, which is all about bales of cotton and 37 cents times 40 hours a week."

"Hm. What about the $5000 shakedown?"

"I never expected you to be able to come up with it. It was part of the disguise. Like the voice disguise."

"Well, here. You've earned it." She tossed him the bag of coun-terfeit, and watched him struggle. After a couple of uncompleted gestures, he opened the top and looked in, eyebrows at half-mast. He pulled out a fistful of bills, and his face gave him away.

"Hell, Bynum, what's this junk?"

"It's an indicator."

"Some of it's not even the right size. A what?"

"An acid test. It's litmus paper, but it turns <u>you</u> pink if you flunk, which you just did. Terry, call Rathbun. It'll be sunrise next thing, and I need a nap. I'll hold the gun on him while you dial."

Terry Morgan handed over the roscoe like a lamb, and picked up the phone. Faye gestured Barnett to kneel. After Terry had left a message with Verna May, the County dispatcher, he turned to Faye.

"Well, now, a good night's work. I like the idea of that nap, I gotta say. C'mon, Babe, we could prob'ly get it done by the time ... Aw, come on, dang it."

Faye pushed Virgil Barnett to the floor, put a foot on his back, hiked her skirt to mid-thigh and kept the roscoe centered on Terry's chest. "You wanted to see me looking like Wonder Woman. Look your fill, and then give me a hand with this creep."

"Wait, give you a hand with what?" Barnett's voice was muffled by the rug.

"Pinning you down, Mister Barnett. We're going to let you try your disguise story out on the sheriff, see if he bites. Take him out and tie him to a pine tree, Terry. Cut a piece off the clothesline."

"Don't need no tie-up. Rathbun give me cuffs, which I was gonna try out on you, see if that'd get you going. Kind of a waste on him, you ask me." He pulled a pair of handcuffs from his back pocket.

"Hey!"

"Shut up, Barnett. Didn't ask, Morgan. Out you go. I'll keep him covered. <u>And</u> you."

An hour passed in which Faye struggled to stay awake and repulse Terry Morgan's pestering - *Come on, Baby, just a little cozy rest, I wouldn't be up to no tricks, heck, I respect you more than that* - and ignore first Barnett's fulminations about wrongful confinement without cause, and then his snoring, when he gave up and got comfortable against the Eddy-side pine. She was glad when Lyle Rathbun's cruiser at last jounced down her lane. The sheriff's first course of business was to reclaim his bag of counterfeit, and the second, reluctantly, to take Virgil Barnett under his wing.

But Barnett started complaining again about unlawful confinement, which was a mistake because Lyle Rathbun never liked his elbow jogged about crimes he had not personally detected. His gingerly treatment of Barnett inverted to gruff, and he re-snapped the cuffs to stuff Barnett into the back seat of the cruiser.

When they were gone at last and the shot-up orange truck had followed it at gunpoint, Faye dragged herself up the steps to the porch, not neglecting to greet Rosie in her deep and sandy sleep. Incapable of another step, she lowered herself into the arms of the chaise; it welcomed her to its wickery comfort. She let her head fall against the summer-mildew-smelling cushion. A breeze looped the Eddy and fanned her through the ragged screen. The Carolina Wren began its song about cardinals and teakettles. Faye smiled, it felt like the first time in a year. *I did all right, didn't I? I dealt with two nasty customers - three, counting Rathbun - and I didn't puke or faint. That ought to be worth ...* But she was asleep, the cocked and loaded roscoe across her belly, before she could decide what it might be worth.

After a time, a church bell sounded, rousing her enough to survey the entirely benign surroundings, click the safety on the roscoe, and stumble into her proper bed.

***

From an "EXTRA" edition of the Gabbro *Intelligencer* for Tuesday, August 10, 1965:

RIVER MILLS WORKFORCE WILL VOTE ON UNION

In a surprise move, River Mills manager Virgil Barnett announced Sunday afternoon that workers there will vote on whether to organize to be represented by a labor union, and if so, by which union. The canvass will take place on Saturday, August 21 at the River Mills plant. "This concession to our workers is being offered as a tribute to the late Nora Lundy Morgan, in recognition of her tireless efforts on behalf of Gabbro County workers," Barnett said. He added that River Mills management and ownership could be "presented with a serious dilemma" if workers should OK the union's ...

Azaleas Blamed for Wye Tragedy

Gabbro Garden Club Chairwoman Berrit ("Bertie") Lang dismissed as "sheer nonsense" Sheriff Lyle Rathbun's opinion that the screen of azaleas on the knoll at the "Wye" was responsible for the three-car accident killed two and left little Amy Sue Benson clinging to an orphaned life. "Drivers should be watching the road, not (Cont'd on P. 2A)

***

"Huh. The heck got into Barnett?"

"Well, there were discussions, Forde. Mister Barnett got himself into a compromising position last Saturday night at my house, and -"

"Wait. What kind of a compromising position?"

"Now, see, that's exactly the sort of question you have no business asking. However, I will tell you that it's not what I suppose is on your dirty mind. He tried to sell information to us about your ... about Nora's accident, and -"

"What?!"

"Calm down. He had a copy of a journal entry that might have ... well, probably did, show a payment to somebody at Mercer's for, quote, 'Morgan,' unquote."

"Well, Jesus, did it look real? Is somebody following up?"

"Hard to tell, about real. It was blurry and sort of ad-hoc looking. You'd have to subpoena the original, which Rathbun will talk to the Prosecutor's Office about. But the whole thing was a kind of a farce. I told you I got one of those mystery messages, call this number for the 'clincher' about the accident. Like I promised I would, I took it straight to Rathbun. We agreed that it looked fishy enough that there was no reason to drag you through it, when it's a painful subject for you. For one thing, this mystery informant asked for money for his information, which was a new feature. He didn't do that before. Plus, it was absurd, because he asked for it in a two AM phone call to be ready for him at 4 AM the same night. He later claimed he knew it would be impossible to come up with, but it was a way of 'disguising' himself. But he couldn't keep himself from grabbing at the lame counterfeit that Rathbun came up with. And locked him up on Sunday, just to teach him a lesson.

"I offered to drop the assault charges, and intercede with Rathbun, in exchange for this civic-minded gesture of cooperating with a union election at River Mills. I am aware that in doing so, I compromised my journalistic objectivity. I am prepared to accept any reasonable reprimand on your part in that regard."

"Forget it. When you do good, you do excellent. When you go nuts, you exceed expectations there, too. What do you suppose Barnett was up to, giving us all this evidence about Nora's accident?"

"I've been thinking about that. Either Merrydown's antisocial deeds finally pushed Barnett over the line, or ..." She ruefully ruffled her hair.

"Or?"

"Or he was the union organizer all along, and wasn't ready to show himself until now."

"Either way, bet we've seen the last of him in this town." Forde was silent for what seemed a long time, and then frowned. "Assault?"

"He assaulted me, claiming it was part of this disguise, which was to avoid detection by Merrydown operatives."

"You mean, he ... well, he -"

"Yes. He placed his hand on my breast aggressively, while otherwise mugging me."

"The son of a bitch. I knew it. If he'd just slugged you, you would have said so. How was that supposed to be a disguise?"

"He figured I would never guess that a gentleman like Virgil Barnett would do such a thing. He was wearing a ski mask and leather gloves, like one of Mason Merrydown's thugs."

"And you somehow penetrated this disguise."

"I made him unmask, at gun point."

Forde shook his head. "Jesus, Faye."

"I agree. This business has been a madhouse. There's no joy, no generosity, no ... no charm. Nothing but pain and sorrow. I'm sick of the whole mess. Bring back the Gabbro Hunt and the School Board." She smiled, suddenly. "You know what I would just love? My birthday's today; it's been a year since our last date. Would you be interested in sharing dinner? I don't necessarily mean, you know ..."

"I'm still in mourning."

Turned down by Forde Morgan, dang. "Well, exactly. I'm just talking about a quiet dinner between friends. Old friends. Look, we'll have Annie over, just to keep it kosher. Maybe have a swim before. No presents or candles, just supper."

"Well ... OK. That sounds pretty good, actually."

"Good. About six? I'll stop by Annie's on the way home."

I'll bring the Blue Nun."

***

At Raleigh-Durham Airport, Peter Standish stood in line at the Hertz counter, rubbing the nagging little cramp under his diaphragm. He drew a deep breath, but it didn't help. Peter tried to decide whether it was getting worse or easing off. It was too high for appendicitis, and too localized for simple indigestion. Besides, indigestion doesn't sit there for weeks. It felt like the textbook description of gallstones, but Peter's mastery of internal anatomy tapered nearly to layman level when it came to the equatorial latitudes of male subjects. His shirt was wet with sweat; the rental office was hot, air being agitated but not cooled by a floor fan that more than anything made it hard to understand what people were saying.

Never mind; he was within 100 miles of Faye, and in two hours he would be with her, maybe already in bed. The thought overrode the pain and cushioned it, like the million tiny pearls. Peter allowed himself to think of Faye's breath, her smile, her immaculate and exemplary vestibule ...

And now he stood at the counter, and nodded his way through the questions and card-showing and disclaimers and form-filling, while the little ache rose and fell, and seemed sometimes to fade to nothing, and then come back in some other place, or in some other shape; now dull, and now jagged.

***

"So, Annie, what do you know about Faye's career as a gunslinger?"

Annie Godfire smiled. "I want the gun. Lot of my stuff is either full of happy spirit, or mostly just routine. Like the barber chairs and the train couplers. I need a few things, people handling them were scared and mad, so I'm hoping she'll chip it in, when she's done slinging."

"Well, you're out a luck on that one. I never knew nothing that scared her."

A lot you know. Faye spoke up from the kitchen, over the noise of frying chicken. "I'm done with it right now, but it doesn't belong to me. You'd have to talk to Terry Morgan."

"Guy that fixed your roof? How's come you got his gun?"

"He lent it to me last year, when the first articles started coming out about River Mills. He thought they might send goons around to teach me a lesson."

Forde grinned. "Smart fella. He looking for a job, political prognosticator?"

"Oh, boy. The *Intelligencer*'d be out of business in a week. He's smart enough, but he's got no sense of journalistic vocabulary, to put it mildly. First time he referred to some librarian's hooters, we'd be done for."

"Maybe we'd sell enough copies at the college to, um … You expecting company?"

"What?"

"Somebody coming down your lane. Better throw in some more chicken."

"Well, crap. I already got all the company I want, thanks. Why can't people back off a little? Could you guys see who it is? I'm covered with grease and flour."

The drive from RDU to Gabbro took more than two hours, because Peter stopped twice to use fast-food bathrooms, trying to get rid of the pain in his belly; nothing seemed to help. Finally, at a Pik-Kwik outside Fayetteville, he bought a packet of Goody's and a Pepsi. The pain cut back from 6 to 3 on the physicians' scale of one through ten *where-ten-is-the-worst-pain-you-can-imagine*, Peter could recite it in his sleep. Being a physician not about to heal himself, as well as his own worst patient, he allowed himself to be encouraged by the temporary relief.

He arrived in Gabbro at 5:30, and bumbled about the back roads for a good twenty minutes before he found East Church Street Extension, figured out from the sunset which way was east, and followed the growing dark to the head of Faye's lane. By that time, the pain was back up to 6, or maybe 7. The ride over the pine roots to the foot of Faye's lane was torture. He pulled to a stop at the porch steps, and looked up, wondering if he had what it would take to climb them. But while he pondered, a human shape appeared in the shadows behind the screen door.

"Faye?"

"Nuh uh, Annie Godfire. Who's there?"

Peter emerged and began to climb. "Hi, Annie. Petah Standish. I came to talk to Faye. Is she … ?" He broke off, not rhetorically but because getting out of the car made the pain leap to 8 or 9 territory, and he needed the breath for a gasp.

"In the kitchen. C'mon up, Peter ... you OK?"

Peter took another step. "Little stitch in my - Nnngh!" He turned white and reached behind himself for the railing. As his hand was fumbling for it his eyes rolled back. He vomited, and tumbled backward to the lawn.

30.

ALLSTONES. I GUESSED AS MUCH, BUT I WAS IN TOO much of a hurry to get down here. I needed to talk to you, Faye."

"Well, goodness, Peter. Of course, I'm glad to see you, but you came all this way without telling me? You could have called. What if I'd been gone?"

"I know. I just wanted to see you so badly. I only made up my mind last night; wait, what day is this?" He looked at his wrist, but his watch was in a "possessions" bag at the nurses' station.

"Thursday. The 12th."

"Damn. Night before last, then. I missed your birthday, because we were at an impasse about ... you know."

"About marriage. Peter, I hope you understand how much pain it gave me to turn you down."

"You were right to say no. A Long Term Friendship is probably the most we can achieve, for now. And that's a very great deal. Maybe some day, things will change enough to make a difference, and then all you have to do is say the word. The offer remains on the table, but without pushiness. Meanwhile, I look forward to our continued WED. Specially the 'E' paht. Now: there is another matter."

Jesus, now what? "Yes?"

"While they were hacking around in there, they found ... well, they ran across what they call a suspicious formation."

"What's that supposed to mean?"

"Well, I know what it means when I say it to a patient. They think they saw a cancerous growth. It was operable, so they cut it out and took a sample for biopsy."

"I see." Faye sat abruptly in the bedside chair. "Oh, Peter, what -"

"Now, Faye, let's not jump to conclusions. It's only a biopsy; though I would guess from what they told me, that it's better than fifty-fifty it's some kind of neoplasm. If so, given where they found it, chances would favor malignancy. So it's very lucky and timely that I had that gall bladder attack, or things could have progressed to the point where ... well, beyond hope of survival. As it is, there are many new drugs against cancer, and a good deal of evidence that a positive attitude on the patient's part helps. That's the part I plan to contribute. As soon as I'm out of here, I want to sit down with you and make plans for our next tryst. Are you up for that?"

"Oh, of course! But Peter -"

"Good. Fine. Stop right there with the But Petah's. If you'll be my long term friend in this, we'll lick it together. They say that a regimen of ahgasms, in the presence of a trained associate, works wonders."

"Yeah? 'They' who?"

"Well, other researchers. Or they will, after we publish. We'll be famous."

"Do we have to get a grant? And will there be, you know, tables and figures? Illustrations of the vestibule, with letters and arrows? A list of publications cited?"

"I'm afraid it will be lonely work, at first. We'll be in unchahted waters."

"Long as you don't call them 'unchartered.' Anyway, who needs a chaht? Seems like the Kama Sutra has enough of those to last the rest of our lives."

"I knew I could count on you."

"You just wait till I get you into another shower stall."

The buoyant mood lasted until Faye passed through the lobby, where fear caught up with her. A mosaic on the floor read, *Duke*

University Hospital. "Gone to Duke" was another Gabbro euphemism; it was often enough followed within a year by "Gone to Wegeman's."

***

Sedalia Baley, evidently one of God's favored handfuls, was recovering well enough from her gunshot wound that she could have visitors. The first to cross her doorway was Faye Bynum, with a bouquet of bachelors' buttons she'd found on the rarely visited far side of Morgan's Eddy. Admiration was expressed, and a nurse provided a plastic water pitcher to hold them.

When Faye was seated on the visitor chair, and polite commentary on returning health and queries about what the patient might need from the world outside Gabbro Memorial were rendered, she asked, "Do you still know enough people at River Mills that you could recommend someone I could interview about the union election?"

Sedalia frowned. "You know, Miss Faye, most of them ladies didn't have much truck with me. Me and one other Baley worked there, kep' pretty much to ourselfs. And he's left, what I hear."

Faye sat back and looked at the ceiling. *The Mind of the South. Such as it is.* "So there you were, every one of you in that madhouse like souls in Hell, and instead of comforting each other, or seeing you lying there bleeding to death, or God knows standing together to push back against the pitchforks, they still found a way to put themselves over somebody even lower?"

"Well ... reckon. Never thought of it that way, exactly."

"OK. Well, was there one of the non-Baleys that seemed like, I don't know, kind of a leader? Somebody folks were friendly with, looked up to?"

"Oh, that 'ud be Nancy. Let me think ... Nancy, Nancy ... Roseboro?" She nodded. "Roseboro, that was it."

Faye scribbled it on a pad. "Do you think she might be willing to talk to the *Intelligencer* about it? The union vote?"

"I reckon you'd have to ask her. Don't go down to the plant, now, you know that. It'd get her fired, they saw one of the workers talking to a reporter."

"Oh, no, of course not. 'What force on earth is weaker than the feeble strength of one,' the song goes."

Sedalia blushed. "You wasn't offended, was you?"

"Of wh- ... " Faye's face lit. "Oh, wait, did <u>you</u> send that letter with the union song in it?"

"Yes'm. I hope it didn't offend. I didn't mean no -"

Faye leaned over the bed and gingerly enfolded her. "Bless you, Sedalia, certainly not. I didn't know that song before, but it sticks with you, doesn't it? But you didn't include the chorus. You know, the part that goes *Dumpty, dumpty-dumpty <u>dump</u> dump*, and so forth. I've been going nuts, having to cut it off, not knowing where to find the words."

"Well, it's just 'Solidarity forever,' three times. Then the last line's, 'For the union makes us strong.'"

"Come on, join in, then." She sat down again and softly sang, "*Solidarity forever!...* Then it's just *Solidarity forever* again?" And Sedalia nodded, twanging along,

"Solidarity forever.
Solidarity forever,
For the union makes us strong!"

Faye sidled a hip onto the bed and threw her arm around Sedalia, who cautiously reciprocated; and with Faye supplying an alto harmony she'd learned long ago in the Mount St. Anne Glee Club, they sang the whole song, verse and chorus, as quietly as they could; nearly whispering, but still drawing mixed notices from nearby beds and a scowl from the nurse's station:

When the union's inspiration through the workers' blood shall run,
There can be no power greater anywhere beneath the sun.

Yet what force on earth is weaker than the feeble strength of one?
But the union makes us strong!

Solidarity forever,
Solidarity forever (Tears appear on Sedalia's cheeks.)
Solidarity forever
For the union makes us strong!

Faye fetched a box of Kleenex from the sink, and approached the bed carefully.

"Sedalia, what is it?"

"Oh ... Nora Lundy taught me that song, that I thought was one of God's own soldiers. I near crossed over when I lost my hand, but if I done, and that was a chorus of angels, it could not of been beautifuller, and I could not be happier to hear it. I just wisht she was here to sang it with us."

Leaving, Faye looked up *Roseboro* in the lobby phone book, and found only one such in Gabbro County, north of town on the Fayetteville road. Back at the *Intelligencer,* she called, intending to leave a message, and found Nancy Roseboro at home.

"We're doin' trick-work this week, cotton harvest comin' in, and I just got home from the four-ta-noon. You'd be welcome to come on out, I hate talking to folks on the phone."

"Well, I don't want to disturb your chance to rest."

"Naw, now's when I get a little peace 'fore the kids get home from school. We're the next place after the barn with the Mail Pouch sign."

Which turned out to be an immobilized Airstream on cement-block footers, with an assortment of more or less rusty tricycles and a brown-spotted hound running back and forth on a wire and greeting everything that moved. Nancy Roseboro was stout, permed, and amiable.

"Let's set out and see if there's a breeze, you mind? I'm hot as a fox. Wont some lemonade?"

"Well, that'd be nice, if it's not too much trouble."

"Open you up one a them lawn chairs under the oak. I'll be out directly."

When they were settled, Faye said, "Ma'am I know I'm taking up some of your leisure time, so I'll get right to it. The *Intelligencer* is curious to know how the workers out at River Mills are likely to be thinking about this chance to vote on a union."

"I doubt ...Well, wait a minute. I know you ain't from management nor ownership, I been reading your columns ever since they started. Still, I hope you understand that if my name gets in the paper in connection to anything at all about a union, I'll lose my job the next day."

Faye nodded. "How about 'A representative of the workforce?'"

"Nuh uh. 'Representative?' We ain't supposed to be represented. Six of us'd get fired until they figured out who it was, and like as not, they'd figger it was me. Or one they'd fired would drop my name, so they'd hire her back."

"Land. I have to say something, or folks will think I'm making it up. How about 'a source close to the Mill who spoke on condition of anonymity to discuss sensitive personnel matters?'"

"That's a mouthful. What's wrong with letting them think you're making it up?"

"Oh, well. Nothing, I guess. They think I make stuff up all the time as it is. All right. Are you looking forward to collective bargaining?"

Faye took a drink of her lemonade, and was startled to hear, "No, Ma'am."

"No? Um ... wouldn't you like to have better working conditions, higher pay that's in line with what folks are making in Illinois, Ohio?"

"I don't know what they're making in them places, and I know you don't know what we're making here, 'cause it's a firing offense to talk about it, even among ourselves."

"Well, see, that's one of the benefits of a union shop. All that comes out in the open, and when it does, I think you'll find that you're making way less than half what they do, even in little rural towns, where they've got a union. You tell him you're ready to go out on strike for fair pay, and watch what happens to your pay envelopes."

Nancy Roseboro looked at the Airstream and the tricycles, lame and halt. She sighed, and shook her head. "Ain't you supposed to be neutral on things? Journalists?"

"Yes, Ma'am, when it's a matter of debatable questions, like the Garden Club. But if I see a guy in a ski mask push over a little old lady and snatch her purse, I don't have to be neutral about that."

"Ski masks are kind of a thing with you, I hear, and I don't blame you. But you never asked me how come I don't look forward to working in a union shop."

"OK, why not?"

"'Cause I been talking to folks - off the premises, mind, I'd be fired for doing it on - and I don't hear no great enthusiasm for handing over our business to a pack a Yankees up in Washington DC. They got our interests at heart, you think? Way off there?"

"Mrs. Roseboro, excuse me, but just now you were talking about getting fired for discussing your pay, and getting fired for talking about the union. This is supposed to be a free country, where we have freedom of speech." Faye could see that Roseboro was getting tense, but she wasn't finished. "Look. I've visited your factory and seen your working conditions. They are hot and noisy and unhealthy and dangerous, but I bet you'd get fired for talking about that, too. You're talking about a life that you'd expect to read about in Russia or Red China, somewhere. Finally, not meaning to contradict you or insult you, but I do know what some employees of River Mills make. It's ... well, pretty small, don't you think? For how hard and uncomfortable and dangerous your work is? The point of a union is to let you get together and bargain for better conditions and better pay."

Nancy Roseboro leaned forward, shaking her head. "Is that the school bus I hear? I think maybe it's time for you to leave, Miss Bynum."

Faye rose. "Yes, Ma'am. I'm sorry if I upset you."

"Don't think nothin' of it."

***

From the Gabbro *Intelligencer* for Wednesday, August 18, 1965:

Union Vote Delayed

James Diamond, acting Manager at River Mills, has announced a delay in the scheduling of a union election at the plant until mid-September. "So many of our good folks off on vacation, it'll be hard to get a good representative vote till kids are back in school and things settle down a little after the cotton harvest ...

"If that isn't the biggest crock of ... Next thing it'll be October, and Halloween coming, and this Diamond will figure folks will be too spooked. Who is he, anyhow?"

Faye slumped against the window and examined the alley that skirted the *Intelligencer* offices. A feral cat with one eye looked back at her. "I dunno. Somebody in the Merrydown outfit they promoted, I suppose, in place of Virgil Barnett. Who's probably on a train to Siberia by now."

Forde Morgan leaned back and sniffed. "Nothing we or nobody can do about it, I guess?"

"How would I know?"

Forde blinked. "You a little bit on edge, Faye? Needing a break?"

Faye shrugged. "I'm fine." Tears sprang up to contradict her, and she reached for a Kleenex from Forde's box. "Thanks for not getting huffy, Forde. I'm tired, and I'm frustrated and upset about River Mills. I thought we'd made some progress, got them to actually obey the law and facilitate a union vote. And now look. They could keep this up forever."

"Uh huh. Pretty bad, but it don't seem like something to shed tears over, which — aw, Faye, honey, really. Come here, OK? This'll take care of itself, or not, but ... there, now. What is it, really? Can't you tell me?"

She nodded, wiping her nose. "Something's come up with Peter. He's getting radiation and chemotherapy for a 'suspicious growth.' If it's melanoma, which they seem to think, he's basically got six months to a year, according to what I read."

"Oh. Jesus, Faye."

Faye tried to breathe past the knot in her throat. "You know he wants to marry me. Well, I turned him down a week before I found out about this. But probably not before he suspected it. Like he was reaching out for a hand, and I slammed the door. Now I can hardly go back and say, 'Oh, well, you should have told me you have cancer,' like I would marry him out of pity. God, Forde, why does life have to be so cruel? You didn't deserve what happened to Nora, and neither do I deserve this, I swear it." She crossed the office and laid her head on his shoulder. He smelled like dry cleaning. "And, of course, our bad luck is nothing like Peter's and Nora's, is it?"

He began to embrace her, and then backed off to fatherly back-patting. "Go up there and be with him. It'll help, but even if it doesn't, you have a chance to say goodbye, and I'll tell you, that's something."

She blew her nose. "I know, Forde. I could never go through what you did without breaking down. But I'd just be in his way. Plus, school's starting, we've got the structural problems in the junior high and the chuckle-head school board to report on. What I'll do is, I'll write to him about vacation plans for when he's past his chemo. Maybe that will cheer him up some. And me."

***

And so again August passed, and much of September. The biopsy of Peter's tumor confirmed a verdict of melanoma, but the surgeon was confident that they'd rooted it all out during the gallstone operation. Faye drove him back to the airport when he was discharged from Duke. While he sweated out radiation and an experimental kind of chemotherapy in Portland, Faye kept in touch by letter and telephone, and kept her mind as much as possible on business. After James Diamond announced a second postponement of the union vote to October 21, Faye called him and requested an interview.

James Diamond was a considerable upgrade on Virgil Barnett in size and directness, an athlete gone just slightly to seed who sported a salt-and-pepper crew cut, a tight jaw, a tailored suit, and an air of let's-get-this-over-with. Faye met him in his office at River Mills, where the hum of air conditioning went some way toward masking the clamor of cutting, weaving, and shipping on the other side of the wall.

"How do you do, Mr. Diamond. I appreciate your taking time to talk to me. As you may know, the *Intelligencer's* mission is to keep Gabbro County informed about -"

"About things that are your business. I'm not exactly sure what part of the management of this plant is your business. With that understood, Miss Bynum, I'm happy to talk to you."

"Our business is information and the welfare of the people of Gabbro County. A good number of those people work at River Mills. Do you see the connection now?"

"Is that a hostile question?"

"Certainly not. I'm asking so that if you need further information about our mission, I can supply it, to the best of my ability. Not a hostile stance, I'd think."

"Let's talk, and find out if it is, OK? What aspect of <u>our</u> mission here, which is to produce useful materials from bales of raw cotton, can I assist some of your readers with? I expect the Gabbro citizens who work here, already know all there is to know about it."

"Maybe not quite all. On August tenth, your predecessor Mr. Barnett announced that River Mills would sponsor a vote on whether to organize a union local, on August twenty-first. You then postponed that to an unstated date, but implied that it would take place after Labor Day, maybe mid-September, when school was back in session, and the cotton harvest completed. School has been in session for over three weeks, and now you have postponed it again for another month. Aren't you afraid of running up against the holiday season, or the Senior Prom?"

Diamond smiled. "People told me you could be abrasive and smart-mouthed, Miss Bynum. It's probably good that we got that confirmed right off the bat."

"I do apologize if I hurt your feelings, Mr. Diamond. Let me rephrase my question, if you will. Do you intend <u>ever</u> to allow your workers to vote on whether to organize for collective bargaining, as the law of the land requires?" She raised a hand. "Oops, sorry, strike that last phrase. I did not intend to abrade you by reminding you of their legal rights."

"Mm-hm. And what gives the Gabbro *Intelligencer* the standing to advise workers of a completely separate enterprise about their legal rights? Are your workers union?"

"In fact, they are; but if they were not, were you intending to advance an argument that if any workers are entitled to organize, all should be entitled to? If so, we are in complete agreement. But, look. I'm not here to argue labor law with you, Mr. Diamond. I am here as a simple reporter, in search of information important to our readers."

Diamond put on a look of baffled good will. "I'm trying, but I fail to see why that information is important to the majority of your readers - such as they may be. My information is, almost none of our workers are readers of your paper."

"Really, you have access to your employees' reading habits? I didn't know that power existed outside the Soviet Union. In fact, I did meet one recently who claimed they had read my editorial column since I began writing it seventeen years ago."

"Yes? Who was that?"

"I don't believe I should share that information, do you? It sounds to me as if there might be danger in it for that person."

"Suit yourself. Are we finished here?"

"Only if you mean by that, that you have no intention of fixing a date for the union vote."

"A date will be fixed when it suits Merrydown Industries to fix a date."

"May I quote you?"

"Oh, please. Good afternoon, Miss Bynum."

Back in the yellow Volkswagen, clattering past the guardhouse, it occurred to her that one could read "Oh, please" as dismissively sarcastic - as it surely was intended - or as "Oh, please be my guest."

***

From the Gabbro *Intelligencer for* Friday, September 24, 1965:

River Mills Chief Hedges on Union Vote

Acting River Mills manager James Diamond says that the plant workers will be permitted to exercise their legal right to vote on union representation "when it suits Merrydown Industries." Mr. Diamond was dismissive when ...

Faye knew she was being hostile to Diamond and Merrydown with this, but when Forde questioned her on it, she snapped at him about toadying to censorship, and cried on his shoulder again.

"All right, Faye. This does it. I am <u>ordering</u> you to take a vacation.

You can use it to sleep for a week, or plant a garden, or take piano lessons. Or you can fly up to Maine, which you know you want to, and should. I don't care. You're relieved of duties until a week from tomorrow. I can give next week's "This Town's Times" to Lee Forsythe, 'cause the Gabbro Hunt is next week, and she's a nut on the subject; if you object to any part of this, I will give it to Jenny, so you better not."

31.

PETER WAS SKINNY, BALD AND RADIANT WHEN FAYE came down the rolling staircase from a prop-jet at Portland Airport.

"There you ah, Faye! You look great, I'm so gluh ... " - cut off in mid-word by Faye's mouth pressed against his, her hug throwing him backward a step.

"Easy does it, you Doberman! I'm still getting my strength back from that damn chemo. But listen! Blood enzymes down to the detection limit! X-rays negative! I'm clean, and all I need now is rest and somebody to work with me on that regimen we talked about."

"Regimen. Oh, the one with the - " She broke off to look around the tarmac; nothing there but bustle and airplane noises. Still, she breathed it into his ear: "The ahgasms? That one?"

He stepped back. "That's the one, but let's not start it out here on the runway. Give me that case." She did, and could see how taxing it was for him to carry it; but knew better than to intervene.

They drove to the lobster place in Falmouth; by unspoken agreement, they spared the captive lobsters and stuck with pasta and greens. Over which, Faye recited the Merrydown arrogations and treacheries, and let Peter jolly her out of her frustration by means of charm, irony, and topics of universal interest like nautical safety regulations, birth rates in Cumberland County, Maine, and Position 147.

"What? Why wouldn't I – why wouldn't the woman just fall completely on her ass?"

"That paht seems to be up to the man, the way he's using his knees. And feet, probably; the illustration is not terribly clear. Probably something to try in zero gravity, if we ever get there. I suppose at this stage, we'd need to stick to things that keep us more, you know. Secure."

"Fine with me. Let's go home. I bet there's a lot of things we can do where we can doze off afterwards without falling in a heap."

And there were. Peter's debility proved not to be limited to his muscular strength; but Faye loved simply being in bed with him, caressing and smiling, running her fingertips over his egg-smooth head, and comforting him when his prowess did not match his will.

"Oh, Peter, don't let it bother you. I'm just fine, and I love being intimate with you, whatever the physical details are. Come here, just hold me."

"Well, you are a very loving and generous woman, Faye. Maybe that's why I love you so ... so thoroughly. I was thinking about it this morning: loving you is like the love just penetrates all the way through. As if I'm transparent to love rays. Does that make sense?"

"Yes. And pretty poetic for a gynecologist. What sends out the love rays? Do they dazzle and scatter after they pass through? Do they make rainbows?" She ran her fingers down his neck to make rainbows across his body.

He shivered. "Well, see? It's a very mysterious area, on which fah too little research is being done."

"We'll do what we can with the means at hand."

"Severely underfunded, and a little short on means, just now. But Faye -"

"But not on hands."

"No, true. But Faye, listen. I have a serious mattah to discuss with you; or, I suppose I should say, to tell you about, since I don't think there's much room for discussion."

"Yes?" Faye fought down a clench of fear and pulled the sheet over them.

"Yes. I hope to live a good, long life yet, in your company as much as possible ... no, now wait, this isn't about marriage. You already know my position on that, and I know yours, and we're both right. No, this came to me when I was doing the chemo, and thinking I had maybe six months. I started thinking about my estate. I have a sister, as you know, and she has children and expenses and debts. So I can't -"

"Peter A. Standish! MD! First of all, I don't know about you, but I consider us married in fact, if living at a distance, as many married couples do. I am completely committed to you, your happiness, and our LTF. That said, I have exactly zero expectations and needs in re-gard to your estate, except to be able to care about you and for you, for as long as we both last. The very last thing -"

"Yes, yes, I knew you'd say that. But this is — Well, wait. That was very sweet. You express my beliefs to a T, and if I stop to relish what you just said, I will break down in tears, so allow me to push on, and reciprocate your declaration in a moment. So, in regahd to my estate: this is a special case, and it involves my part ownership of the *Intelligencer*. I'm leaving that to you, and I think that makes all kinds of sense. My sister would have no interest whatsoever in owning a piece of a newspaper in North Carolina. You, on the other hand, do."

"Well. What about just giving it back to Forde?"

"Well, yourself. Forde's a lovely fellow, but I don't love him nearly like I do you. I want to do this, it's already changed in my will, and, Faye, dahn you, I'm dahned if I'll listen to a lot of push-back from you about it. All right?"

"OK, yes sir, all right, then. And it's <u>very</u> sweet of you, Peter, so thank you, and ... Oh, will you look at that. When you get stiff and bossy, it happens all over."

Peter laughed. "I'm glad we could get this straightened out. Come here, then, let's not waste it."

The visit in Standish passed in bittersweet intimacy that recog-nized Peter's good medical news as possibly of limited term, that could be followed by reversal as easily as by continued improvement. Melanoma is a persistent opponent, unlikely to be conquered as easily as it had yielded ground in Peter's case. Talk, laughter, bed time, pleasure in the autumnal beauties of Maine lake country were all built over a shaky ground of fear, borrowed security, and humility in the face of such an enemy.

Peter apologized for the Quincy Tiff by referring to himself as more "Stand-*ish*" than ever. Further cheering Faye was a telegram from Forde the same day; River Mills suddenly switched policies and announced that balloting for a union election would take place at the plant between 6:00 and 7:00 AM on October 1 - a Saturday. Faye was amused at the transparent maneuver to keep participation down, but was confident of the outcome just the same.

They observed the year anniversary of their CPR meeting by writing and exchanging vows of intimacy and fidelity to the LTFWED, followed by a two-party reception aboard Peter's catboat. After mussels aux herbes, plums, a local baguette and a heady little Pouilly-Fumée, they napped, lulled by the gentle slap of waves against the hull. Peter stayed under a floppy coachman's hat to keep from broiling his unprotected head. When they woke, they stripped and swam to cool off. Diving and splashing, they bantered and dared and tussled each other like newlyweds into a precarious semi-aquatic mating in mid-lake, where there was 360 degrees of privacy around them, and 300 feet of water below; Faye more or less anchored to the taffrail, floppy-hatted Peter anchored to Faye. The open air and the gentle water acted as tonics and seducers and a near enough zero-gravity environment. Everything went, as Faye remarked, swimmingly. She nominated the giddy mess for inclusion in the Kama Sutra as Position 146-And-a-Half (hat included), refusing to picture the black void below, or to entertain metaphorical notions about it. But she clung to Peter long after they had emerged and dried.

When they were ready for society again, Peter sailed them to a little mill town on the north shore where they strolled hand-in-hand, Faye flushed and languid among the leaf-peeping tourists and townsfolk, two of whom greeted Peter by name and beamed approvingly at Faye. Peter's obvious pride in being seen with Faye surprised her by pleasing. She had never in her life cared to be part of a publicly acknowledged couple, unless you count "keeping company" with Forde; but it was a small liberation from being only herself. And it made her think again, wistfully, of the forsworn upsides of married cohabitation.

In a second-hand book store a block or two from the lakefront, she found an ancient first-edition Agatha Christie to take home to Forde, and a treasure: a leather-bound 1937 edition of *Spiritual Sojourns in the Near East*, by the Right Reverend Austin Mayfair, M. Div., whose 314 numbered pages were completely blank. A printer's error, unless Right Rev. Mayfair was an utter cynic. Faye loved the softness of the calfskin binding and the texture of the dove-white paper that cried out to be used as a diary or journal, to be written on with trenchant intimacy and existential humor. She vowed to use only her best fountain pen, and to mean with all her heart every word she placed in it. The first entry was a heartfelt, if not terribly trenchant, paean to the happiness of this day.

When Faye left at the end of a six-day rejuvenation, she took with her a key to Peter's house and the surprise of a firm sisterly hug from Amy.

***

"Oh, for God's sake! You're kidding me, and it's not in the least -"

"Nope. Eighty-three to five against the union."

"Oh, you're ... What is <u>wrong</u> with these people? Are they a bunch of masochists? They <u>like</u> brown lung? Sweat getting in their eyes and ... and in the cuts from the knife machine? Getting paid what a shoeshine boy would spit on?"

"OK, take it easy. I mean, I don't blame you. Thing is, it was a secret ballot. And -"

"Who counted it?"

"Getting to that. A lady named — " Forde ruffled through some loose paper. "Yeah. Nancy Roseboro."

"Huh. I interviewed her, and I thought she was a sympathetic interview for a while. Then she clammed up and hustled me out of there. But I can't imagine she would cheat."

"Huh, indeed. Anyways, I was going to ask: I just did the math and the vote was 94% No, 6% Yes. What's that make you think of?"

"... Well. Russia."

"Close enough. I was going to say East Germany. Anyhow, someplace where it's risking your life to go against the boss. Question is, what can we do? We can't go accusing them of a fake election, on no evidence."

"Let me get at Roseboro again. I think she chased me because she lost her nerve."

"And you think she'll get it back now? She'll admit that she faked the vote count?"

"I don't think she did. But who took care of the ballots between the vote and the counting? Maybe somebody stuffed the box."

"Well, you watch yourself. We just got you back from Maine, and I'm not going to send you back up there again so soon. How's Peter doing, by the way?"

"Pretty well. His latest blood test and x-ray were both good, so we're just keeping fingers crossed."

"Huh. Is that one of the beginner positions?"

"N – Mister Morgan, really!" She turned in the door to stick our her tongue, wondering if Peter would laugh too, or get on his dignity. Better not to test those waters.

On the way out the door to catch Nancy Roseboro before her kids got home from school, Faye was thumped into by Lee Morgan, who was skipping backwards toward the front door, waving a carefree goodbye to someone in ... oh, damn, no ... an orange pickup with a starred window that made it impossible to be sure of the driver's identity.

Oh, come on. Surely Terry Morgan wouldn't stoop to messing around with a high-school kid? After all, ... well. He's early twenties somewhere. Sixteen is a lot closer to 20 than 37 is, isn't it? And Lee Forsythe: growing like cotton, her suddenly lovely face blushing hard when she turned around to see who she'd hit.

Oh, boy.

***

"Hi, Mrs. Roseboro. Hope you don't mind my dropping by like this."

Silence; a civil nod.

"Well, I just wanted to ask how you felt about the union vote. I guess a lot of folks in the county were a little surprised it came out so strong on the 'No' side."

Silence, then: "Did these folks tell you about their surprise?"

"Yes. Yes, they did."

"Could you name me a couple?"

"Well, there's where you raise a problem. Often, folks would rather their opinions not be spread about by name. For example, I have not mentioned your name since we had our first conversation. I can say, none of the people I'm talking about were River Mills employees."

Not current ones, anyhow. When Sedalia Baley was apprised of the result, she said, "That's a flat lie. People didn't talk to <u>me</u>, mind, but I listened to what was said. That was part of my job, far as working with Nora. Most of the machine workers couldn't wait to see what a union might bring, in the way of conditions and pay. Maybe a vote would be close, one way or the other. But it would never of been so lopsided against."

Nancy Roseboro scuffed the dirt and moved one of the tricycles against the wall of the Airstream. "Good, then. That's better."

"Well, Ma'am, would you be willing to share, in strictest confidence, mind, how you yourself voted?"

Silence, but a considering silence. "Well. You know it was a secret ballot."

"Yes, Ma'am. But I also know there were some votes each way - of course, more against than for, by a long shot. But I mention that, only to say, there's no way to connect any one person's vote to the over-all outcome, see." Faye wasn't sure she saw herself what she was getting at. Just talking, to prevent the sort of silence that leads to mandatory departure.

"I voted ag'inst."

"I see. Would you be willing to share why you voted that way?"

"No."

"... I mean, for example, was it what you said before, that you don't trust a bunch of folks in Washington to look out for your -"

"No."

"Because, you know, I had a chance to look up some pay levels in union shops in Pennsylvania."

"Don't care about that."

"I understand. Expenses here are less than up north, anyway. So $2.16 an hour is good enough for you?"

"I don't make no - " Sudden silence.

Bingo. "Really?"

"Nobody on that floor makes no $2.16 an hour."

"Well. If you say so. I can see I've leaked something that I should have kept to myself. Well, I'd better be -"

"Who makes $2.16 an hour?"

"I'm afraid I ... well, see, I thought you must be making that too, one of the leaders of the workforce and all."

"So there's somebody makes more'n me?"

"Well, I don't know what you make." In fact, Faye had no idea what anybody made at River Mills, beyond the pathetic 37-cent side-liners. But she had been pretty sure $2.16 an hour - a little over $4000 a year - would be well over what any of the suffering souls could be bringing in.

"Well, I'll tell you, Miss. I make a dollar seventy-seven, and that's top draw on my shift or any other. Somebody's making $2.16, I need to know about it."

"Oh, I couldn't possibly. Isn't that a firing offense for you, discussing somebody else's pay?"

"Not for you, though."

"No, Ma'am, that's true ..."

"You tell me, I'll tell you why me and ever'body else just about, voted No."

"Gee, Mrs. Roseboro, I'd sure love to help you out with your question. But -"

"All right, then, damn it. I'm mad enough, I'll tell you anyways. I'll tell you once, so listen good. That Mister Diamond got up on his little balcony with a bullhorn, and told us, we vote for a union, Mister Merrydown a'd shut the plant down."

"What? Why would he do that? River Mills makes him a ton of money, and it's the biggest employer in Gabbro County."

"What's he care? Mister Diamond says he'll move it to some little town in Texas that he's already talking with, make a ton a money there. None of us can afford to find out if he's bluffin', but they raise a sight of cotton in Texas. So the vote was a honest vote. We just about all of us voted against, and I can gar'ntee that's why."

***

"Sure, it's probably illegal, Forde. But I can't publish that, because I can't protect my source, and she'll be fired."

"Why can't you protect her?"

"Because River Mills will know without my telling them, who it was bound to be, who would know why folks voted how they did."

"What if some ... I don't know, third party, found out about it, and it did turn out to be illegal. Maybe you could find out from TWUA."

Third potty. "No, wait. Maybe I'll try and dig up that guy from Chapel Hill."

"The guy who tried to pick you up."

"Yes. I don't suppose you'd be willing to call him? Tell him I'm on assignment in Scotland, or something? You could give me an assignment in Scotland County, so it wouldn't be a lie."

"Okay. I'll tell him you admired him so deeply, and were a little puzzled that he hadn't tried to get back in -"

"Never mind, I'll call him myself."

Back in her office, Faye dug through drawers and came up with a card:

> **The University of North Carolina**
> **School of Law**
> **FRANCIS X. DUBER, J.D.**
> **Associate Professor, Labor Law**
> **TArheel 1-5501**

Yeah, Frank Duber. She'd heard "Doober," which sounded about right for the guy. She dialed the number.

***

.... *and he was just completely no help whatever. I could have crowned him. It is possible that he was peeved with me for giving him a fake telephone number. In the end, he told me I should have called the Textile Workers Union, which I will, first thing.*

Well, my dear fellow scholar of the odd-numbered byways

of Kama Sutra; my rescuer, my rib-cracker, Knight of the Vestibule, Captain of my Catboat and my lawfully WED-ed long-term friend : my thoughts are always with you, from your rising up until your lying down and through the peaceful watches of the night that we are about to enter together, vast latitudes apart. How I pray for your continued recovery and your happiness! Even when I am not by your side, I am with you.

All my love,
Faye

***

"*Textile Workers.*"

"Good morning. My name is Faye Bynum, with the Gabbro *Intelligencer*. I would like to speak with whoever has taken Nora Lundy's place." *Whomever.*

"*Nora Morgan?*"

"That's right. Thank you."

"*How may I direct your call?*"

"… Well, I'm calling on the premise that TWUA may have given Nora Lundy Morgan's work to another person by this time."

"*Case load, we call it.*"

"Very well, thank you, yes." Faye gritted her teeth and thought of the peaceful watches of the night. "May I speak to that person, please?"

"*One moment, please.*"

A pause of a dozen minutes was followed by a different voice:

"*Textile Workers, who were you holding for?*"

"Whom. Did your previous receptionist take early retirement?"

"*Pardon? No, she was laid off. We're having tough times here.*"

"So I understand. I'm calling because I would like to speak with whoever there might have taken over Nora Lundy's - Nora Lundy Morgan's - case load. My name is Faye Bynum, and I'm calling from Gabbro, North Carolina, about an attempt to unionize workers in a towel factory here. Is there anything else you'd like to know?"

"Goodness. There's no need to be short with me. The person you seek would be I, Naomi Briskett, at your service, Ma'am. And you would be ... ?"

"Faye Bynum, Gabbro, North Carolina. Your case load includes River Mills, in Gabbro?"

"I'm sorry, but we have not yet established your basis for wishing to access that confidential information."

"Oh. Well, good for you. I'm with the local newspaper, the *Intelligencer*, and I was Nora Lundy's sister-in-law, somewhat. Our editor is Forde Morgan, her widower. Forde has asked me to follow up on developments at River Mills, particularly since this landslide vote against the union. For which, by the way, I have discovered the reason. It is possible that management committed an illegal act in connection with the election, and I am calling to ask about it."

"I see. May I have your permission to record the remainder of this conversation?"

"Well. I suppose ... Yes."

"Thank you. This conversation between Naomi Briskett of TWUA and Faye ... Sorry, not sure I caught it?

"Bynum."

"And Faye Bynum of Gabbro, North Carolina, is being recorded on fourth October, 1965, with the agreement of both parties. Miss Bynum, are we discussing River Mills, a subsidiary of Merrydown Industries located in Gabbro County, North Carolina?

"That's the one."

"And you have information regarding a possibly illegal interference of management in an election whether to organize workers under the leadership of this union?"

"That's right. They -"

"Excuse me. Is the possibly illegal act something like threatening to close the plant if a union is formed?"

"Um. Well, yes. Mister Merrydown had it announced on the evening before the election that an affirmative vote to organize would result in the plant being shut down and moved to Texas. You already know about it?"

"Not in this particular case. It is a very common maneuver when a union election is approaching. It would appear to run afoul of Section 8a(2) of the NLRA, and there are dozens of suits filed about it, all of which are making their way through the courts."

"I see. Do you have an opinion yourself on the question?"

"Of its legality? Yes."

"... And?"

"I believe such behavior could constitute an unfair labor practice under 8a(2). That is not my belief alone, but that of virtually every union governing body, and we expect to be vindicated in court."

"Of course. Some time in the 1970's I suppose."

"It might not come that quickly. Thank you for your assistance; I will add this instance to our file of similar such management actions. This conversation is no longer being recorded."

"Oh, my. And meanwhile, our poor damned souls labor on in a living hell for pittance wages with no contract, except when they contract brown lung, and whatever physical contraction results when unsafe machinery slices pieces -"

"Stop, you're breaking my heart. Do you have any idea how many workplaces you're describing?"

"Miss Briskett, I challenge you to come down here and see for yourself. What we have here is something special, that you won't find the like of outside of Alcatraz."

"Miss Bynum, all I can say is, as at the corner bakery: Take a number, and you will be assisted in turn."

32.

So WE'RE SMALL, ROUTINE POTATOES TO THE TEXTILE Workers. Small doughnuts, I suppose I should say. She told me 'take a number.'"

"Get that a lot in towns like Gabbro. It's got to be the Boston Massacre of Philadelphia Lawyers in a New York Minute before it's a crime worth thinking about for big outfits like TWUA. Ask me what they've done about Nora's death, either."

"Well, I suppose they're still broke after their big embezzlement. This Naomi Briskett told me as much."

"Poor things. They sure got my sympathy, you can bet. What say we go out and see Annie? She's awful good for my mental health. Yours too, I'd guess."

Faye sighed. "The fact that I'm not that enthusiastic about it is probably proof enough that I need to see her. But Forde, wait, I need to say this: you are being so generous about me and Peter. I'm pretty depressed these days, so I might not show it very well, but I'm certainly not oblivious to how admirable I find your, your … well, your loving patience. I don't think there's a word for it, exactly. But thank you."

"Aw, hell."

The Spirit Catcher did not seem to Faye to have progressed much since her last visit which … she had to think back. Good God, had it been the August night Peter fell down the cottage steps with his timely gallstones? No wonder she was cranky and rebellious about losing the union election – and so she thought of it, not the union voted down, but Faye herself humiliatingly, cheatingly defeated. She needed Annie's healing word and touch. She decided to slow her thoughts by walking up the river path to Annie's, rather than drive the long way in the clamoring Beetle.

The river was slack with a dry season; equinoctial rains a bust, the water dark with tannin. Yellow and brown leaves lined the bottom and piled against snags of brush left against the banks by the last rain, weeks ago. Strings of algae waved under scant inches of water that smelled of vegetal decline and decay. Dragonflies hovered and darted, ignoring the gnats and mosquitos that pestered Faye. *How the South gets under your skin, hey?*

Annie was not welding when she arrived, but walking about her piles of iron treasures.

"Taking inventory?"

"Hey, Faye. Nope, I know what I got, and what I need ain't here. Thought I had a Pullman leaf spring over here somewheres, a'd be about the right curvature for where I'm at. But the dang weeds grow up so fast, stuff gets lost in 'em."

Faye looked at Annie, and at the piles of rusting junk, and saw not the potent young mystic she'd known since arriving in Gabbro, but a haggard and feckless back-country dame with tangled hair and premature wrinkles, sorting through piles of scrap iron, hoping for gold. Faye half expected her to spit tobacco juice.

***

Dear Faye –

Thinking of you so much these days, since your beautiful letter of last week. Particularly in the "peaceful watches of the night" when I would love to reach out and find you watching alongside.

I had a session with Renfro the oncologist this morning. Enzyme levels are up a bit unfortunately; but Renfro says this is very common and tells us nothing yet about the long term. I take him at his word and continue to regain strength. I believe that my hair is starting to grow again at least in the form of a kind of curly fuzz.

I have begun to see patients ...

***

Spiritual Sojourns in the Near East

-4-

10/6/65

I had intended to commit nothing to these pages but wisdom and joyful matters, but both seem to be in short supply these days. The union "election" farce at River Mills was followed by a glum and disappointing evening with Forde and Annie, during which no one had anything joyful to say. The Spirit Catcher is bogged down somewhere about forty feet high (out of 110), and Annie is fretting. Forde is depressed, as the shock of Nora's death fades and the reality of his likely middle age as a frustrated bachelor sets in. I must do what I can to comfort him, short of going back to sleeping company with him.

Peter's recovery may be such in name only, since the latest news is not encouraging, though he does his best not to upset or alarm me ~ which is all the more upsetting.

The mess in Vietnam grinds on, more deadly and grotesque with every.

***

When Faye walked into the *Intelligencer* lobby on Monday morning, Sedalia Baley was back in place at the reception desk, her flyaway black hair done up in a tidy French braid. It was staggeringly chic for Sedalia, and when Faye was finished greeting her, she commented on the transformation.

Sedalia smiled. "Well, thank you, Miss Faye, but, see, that's not the end of it. Could we just step back to your office for a secint? I got something else to show you, just between us."

Faye extended a hand, ready for whatever Sedalia thought was worth seeing in confidence, between us girls. When they were alone and private, Sedalia winked at her, reached behind her head to undo some pins, and removed the French braid bodily, leaving a cap of dark hair that she then brushed forward into bangs and a close-fit swirl down her neck.

"I wanted to try the kind of hairdo that you used to have, before you quit the Salonnette. You don't think it's too ... " Sedalia shrugged. "Too fast for the likes of me?"

"Sedalia! Oh, it just looks completely elegant and very flattering! Who did you get to ... " *Oh, dear.*

"Hit were a flat miracle. That Pearlene, from the Salonnette? Come around an' knocked my door Saturday after I got loose from the hospital, an' says Jesus come told her, go an' do my hair, which she then said she got down own her knees an' ..."

"Pearlene? Wait a minute. Jesus ... you know, of Nazareth? That Jesus?"

"Yes, Ma'am, you just bet; I don't doubt it for a minute. His eye is own the sparrow, an' I reckon he's got some attention left for the likes of Pearlene and me."

"Uh huh. Funny, I never got the feeling of that, when I was going to the Salonnette. That, you know, Jesus gave much of a hoot one way or the other about hair styling, you look at those paintings. And also, who was it, washed his feet with -"

"Well, there's where you missed the train, with all respect, Miss Faye. Pearlene says she about fainted when she realized that he done give a considerable hoot, and she thanked him for the guidance. Own her knees, she said."

"Well, she certainly did rise to the occasion. That do is just as cute as the dickens, and makes you look like you just stepped out of *Cosmopolitan*. Or something. It's a lot smarter on you than it ever was on me."

"Well, I beg respectful leave to doubt that. But Pearlene told me tell you, whoever's doing your hair any more, it ain't near as good as her, and for you to please come back to the Salonnette, and bring me along, any time you wonted. She said tell you Ginnie Freeman don't come there no more, since she's moved out to Sunset Acres. And Mary-Deane or nobody else, turns out, don't care one way or the other." She brushed her hair back, pinned the braid into place. "She was real friendly, Miss Faye. All I could do not to cry too much." She was, Faye saw, having the same trouble now; her eyes were brimming. Faye gave her a Kleenex and went to stand behind her desk.

Sedalia blew her nose and smiled. "She said we was like sisters, bein lowly handmaidens, both of us. That was what just got to me, but good. Anyways, turns out, she seen that whole business with Mister Merrydown, which I never knowed, being shot an' all. She said we had something in common, see, we both banged Mister Merrydown in the head, and she told me she heard - cause, you know, she hears everything, it all gets talked out in the Salonnette."

"So I understand."

Sedalia blushed. "Yes'm. But she said, anyways, he has not been out of the hospital yet. I do hope I didn't hurt him too bad. I would hate to think I was the source of any true evil."

"Well." Faye's knees sank her into her chair. "Well, I guess that's something you and Pearlene will have to share. According to Forde, the door handle was a much harder hit. But you're awfully forgiving of a man who banged you around, and got you shot. Not mention, as good as chopped your hand off." *You may think Grace is gone forever, but it will reappear …*

Sedalia walked to the window and spoke to the alley view. "Miss Faye, I would of cut my arm off at the shoulder if I'd knew it would get me out of that mill and into a job like this. Ever night I go home, I about cry with gratitude to you and Mister Morgan for that day's pleasant work. Ever morning, come in the front door here, I see that name plate with my name on it, sitting on my own desk, I hold you both up to my Lord an' Savior in blessing." She tossed the maimed arm dismissively. "I have got far more than I lost."

***

At noon, Lee Forsythe came in to collect her paycheck for filling in while Faye was in Maine. Faye encountered her exiting the Ladies', wiping her nose on a length of toilet paper.

"Oh. Hey, Lee. Nice job on the Gabbro Hunt. That whole topic just seems to be magical for you."

"Hey, Miss Faye. I find it a touchstone to entire sectors of the Gabbro County relatedness nexus."

"Ain't <u>that</u> the truth. But listen, there was a different subject I was wondering if you'd listen to a little advice about. The other day I couldn't help seeing Terry Morgan's truck -"

"Yes, Ma'am, Miss Faye. I know what you are fixing to ask about, and you should know that I have … I h-have …"

"Whoa, Honey. Come on in my office, get yourself a fresh Kleenex or two."

Lee followed her in and helped herself from the box on Faye's desk. "I got to be back for Fifth Period."

"Which is?"

"Study Hall." Lee blew her nose and poised with the used tissue in her hand, pivoting to look for the wastebasket. Faye took it from under her desk and held it out. Lee looked into it, deposited her Kleenex and smiled. "Got some company in there, I see."

"Investigative journalism, good for you. It's been a tough week, I admit. But how does this sound? I'll call and get you excused from Study Hall if you'll let me chat with you about ... well, things. Have you had lunch?"

"Yes, Ma'am. Don't worry about Study Hall. Plus, you know, my mother has already lit into me for going out with Terry, so if that's -"

"Well then, you don't need me to, do you?"

"No'm, not exactly." Lee's face collapsed. "But, God, he is just so ..."

Faye nodded, remembering the gleaming torso on the roof, the wit and banter, the lyrical clatter of the moonlit dock. "Oh, is he ever. Listen, Lee. I suppose you consider me pretty much middle-aged, and all. This time last year, I was completely infatuated with Terry Morgan for about five minutes. I had to yank myself up by the scruff of my neck ... don't try to picture that."

"Yes, Ma'am. I know."

"You know?" Faye strolled to her office door and closed it; and then realized how futile a gesture that was. "What say we take a little drive, I'll drop you at school in time for Fifth Period. When does that start?"

"1:30."

"Over an hour. Come on."

In the Beetle, parked in Annie Godfire's meadow, they watched the flicker of Annie's torch as she welded something that might have been the lost Pullman spring onto a section of park fence.

"I just wanted to say, Lee, that you seem to be maturing rapidly, and you are already an attractive young woman. Men and boys are going to buzz around you like sweat bees."

"I suppose."

"You will have a lot of choices, most of which will be way less sexy than Terry Morgan. Hell, all of them, probably. I realize that I am speaking out of turn here, in that, as you say, you already have a mother, who seems to be on the case. However, I kind of doubt that your mother knows Terry like I do."

Lee snorted. "Reckon <u>not</u>!"

"Uh huh. You said before that you know about my dalliance with Terry. Did he also imply to you that we had become intimate?"

Lee sighed and fidgeted. "You have been so kind and frank with me about exactly this kind of subject. What you discussed with me last year about selling access to intimate parts of my body, and about virginity, were very valuable and have influenced my thinking a great deal, to say the least. So I have to be frank with you. No, he did not <u>imply</u> anything, Miss Faye. What he done, he described it in some detail. He said -" Lee's eyes dropped, and she skidded to a stop.

Faye drummed the steering wheel, blushing. "Go ahead."

"I ... I had better not, Ma'am. It was extremely intimate material indeed, and I was shocked."

"Material. Lovely. That low-down son of a bitch." She looked out the window until she had her voice under control. "Well. I am surprised that you continue to treat me with a shred of respect, or as anything other than a hopeless libertine sex addict. So have you drawn any conclusions from hearing that ... material?"

"Yes, Ma'am. I concluded that if I agreed to have sex with him, he would be pretty likely to describe it to the next girl he takes a fancy to, in similar terms." Lee fished a spare Kleenex from under her belt and blew her nose again.

"Very good for you, Lee. I'd have never figured that out in a million years, at your age."

Weak smile. " 'Course, you would be a million and sixteen by that time. You'd of probably figured it out along the way somewhere."

"Ha. But also, please take a memorandum to your older self: *There is no such thing as 'old enough to know better.'* But since you did figure it out, why the Kleenex?"

Lee shrugged. "Don't make sense, does it?"

"I'm not going to insult you with a cliché about how love never makes sense. But maybe I've lived long enough to be able to say that sex doesn't make any more sense than love does. You want him anyway, is that it?"

Lee doubled over in the cramped passenger seat, nodding. "It's real bad." She opened the door and wandered across the grass to a little knoll, to stand scuffing the dirt with her saddle shoe. Faye followed and sat in the grass at her feet.

"He told me about you the day you ran into me outside the *Intelligencer* lobby. The next afternoon after school, under the influence of certain aspects of that conversation, I rode my bike out to where he was fixing old Miz Stephenson's porch, and I dared him to meet me down at Riverbend after sundown."

"Good Lord, Lee! Why on earth?"

"I don't know. I was the most crazy worked-up I have ever been in my life. And regardless of appearances, I do have some previous experience with sex."

"Are we talking about your bargains with Tucker Pardee, here?"

"No, Ma'am. I had a regular boy friend, Timmy Summerton, and we fooled around some, so I got some idea. Well, a good enough idea that Timmy got sent off to military school over it. But Terry is nothing at all like that. Terry is like the difference between ... well. Between Jesus and a communion biscuit."

"Theoretically, no difference, you heathen. So you went through with it, the Riverbend date?"

"Didn't have to, not quite. He said Miz Stephenson was in town getting her hair done, and wouldn't be back till six, and why didn't we just go inside and have a chat right there."

"Oh, boy."

"Yes, Ma'am."

"A chat."

Lee nodded. "We did chat, for a while. He's a very entertaining talker."

"I know. And chat led to banter, one thing led to another. That's his style, and I have to admit, it works. And now, you are worried about ... what? Pregnancy?"

"Oh. No, Ma'am. Not this time. We got pretty far along, but I fended him off by telling him I needed time to get used to the idea. I will say, he respected that, though just barely. He went outside and kicked a piece of two by four back and forth while I recovered my ... my grooming."

"Good for him, I must say. Good for you both. So the Kleenex is about ...?"

"How sorry I am I fended him off, I guess. Or no, I'm not sorry. I'm just very upset about the whole thing, including how I feel about him." She sniffed and blew her nose. "Look. I'm very young, I realize that. I'm also smart enough to know I can make something of myself. I am beginning to think about college, and a career. I can't do that, and fall in love with Terry Morgan, can I? But, oh, God, he is just so ... "

She sighed. "Anyway, we agreed to cool off for a couple of days, and maybe meet again at the end of the week. That's today. Tonight. Just thinking about it makes me go all crazy. I don't see how I can possibly stand to not meet him, but Faye, Jesus, he's a high school dropout that lives in a trailer and scrapes a living bangin' nails."

"Not that there is anything dishonorable about physical work, I have to remark."

"No, of course. But ... it's Terry that's dishonorable. If I give in, he will spread it all over town, and it will kill my mother, and probably ruin my chances of a scholarship to Chapel Hill. My daddy will ground me to a corner of the basement and make me wear a chastity belt. And if I <u>don't</u> have sex with him, he's just as like to lie about it and spread <u>that</u> around. So I am just going to have to grit my teeth, face the music, and get over him. You could help with that, if you wonted to."

MORE THAN I LOST

"Gladly. How? But first, look, I think I know Terry fairly well, and I don't believe he would lie about having sex with you. There is some decency to him, in spite of his behavior with respect to me. For example, kicking boards around, instead of insisting forcibly. Raping you."

"Well, that's pretty generous of you, I must say. And I'm glad to hear your good opinion. But I'm such a coward, please, could you talk to him and get him to leave me alone? I know sure's sin, I couldn't do it myself, without, you know. Giving in."

Lee looked around the meadow; Annie was climbing down the Spirit Catcher with a box of tools on her shoulder. "Listen. I just have to say this to somebody or I will go crazy holding it in." She blushed, ducked her head over Faye's lap, and gritted, "I am flat *dying* to fuck him." She pivoted her head upward. "Please, please don't tell nobody I said that, will you?"

"Of course not, Lee. First of all, I'm flattered that you trusted me to say it to. Bravo, for coming right out with it; <u>and</u> for expressing it in the active voice, ha, bravo twice!" Faye put an arm around Lee's shoulder and pulled her close. "When I was sixteen, nobody thought a woman could say such a thing without the Seven Seals of the Revelation going off like volcanoes. I might have said it myself last year. But even all this time later, with a, um, friend who is miles more loving and mature than Terry, I can still sympathize with the sentiment. Now, where were you going to meet him?"

"At Riverbend. But -"

"What if he went there and found me instead?"

"Well ... with respect, Miss Faye, you're quite attractive and all, but I think he'd be -"

"No, no. Don't worry, I don't flatter myself that I would be competition in the way you're thinking. I have an item of his that I need to return, and I think that might aid the discussion. But even if he never bothers you again, what about you?"

"I will just have to stop thinking about him."

"Just like that?"

"I was going to pray on it."

"Mm hm. Well, good, do that, but - " Faye nodded to the Spirit Catcher, where Annie was cleaning and putting away tools. "Have you met my honorary sister, Annie Godfire?"

***

It came out of the blue in the form of a press release:

MASON MERRYDOWN TO STEP DOWN
-For Immediate Release-

Merrydown Industries announces the retirement of founder and CEO Mason M. Merrydown "to pursue new horizons," the industrial behemoth announced today. Since the company is a closely held family enterprise, this effectively means that control and policy will devolve to Alice Fernwood Merrydown, Mr. Merrydown's wife and partner of twenty years. "Properly speaking, the real head of the Corporation has become our son Steven," Mrs. Merrydown clarified. "Stevie is a very bright and capable boy, but rather young to be managing a corporation just yet. I will have the honor of serving as Principal Advisor to him, under the condition that all matters of large policy are to be discussed between us as equals, while day-to-day execution of such policy will remain in my hands for now. The Corporation invites all interested parties to join me in wishing my beloved Mason well in his new endeavors."

***

Tucker Pardee spread his open palms. "When I went into Mr. Diamond's office to give my notice, he was on the phone, real mad about something. He didn't hardly look at the letter, that I spent a half hour typing out, just snatched it down on his desk, initialed it, and waved me out. But I had a couple questions about severance, so I set down on a chair outside his door and waited for him to get off the phone. Couldn't help overhearing some of what he was phoning about."

Faye smiled. "Ah, 'couldn't help overhearing,' the reporter's best friend. We'll make a journalist of you yet. So, give. What couldn't you help overhearing?"

Tucker blushed. "Not that I meant to eavesdrop, now, but -"

"Of course not. I didn't mean to tease, either. What you may have overheard may be a matter of vital importance to the whole Gabbro community, which we will consider whether to pass on or not, and in any case we will thoroughly protect our source. So go on."

"All right. Seemed like he was speaking to Miz Merrydown. You know, Mr. Mason's wife?"

Faye nodded. "Go on."

"Well, seems like Mr. Mason never was quite right after that scuffle we had in your lobby, where Miz Baley whopped him, and then he banged his head on the door handle. Gabbro Memorial cleared him to go home, but ... well, he'd changed. He'd started yelling at the TV set when the news come on, and talking about helicopters and Citizen Freedoms, bearing arms, what-all. Kind of thing you hear these radio commentators yelling about. She'd try and get him to settle down and think about business, but it would never last."

"Wait, you overheard all this from Mrs. Merrydown? Were you on an extension or something?"

"Course not. He put her on speakerphone, reckon so he could go ahead and work on other things while she talked. He shut the door, but it's got a little ventilator in it, and it come through pretty clear. Anyways, Mr. Diamond got pretty mad, and said how it would be necessary to get Mr. Merrydown out of the way, how he put it, if he wouldn't settle down to business."

"Lord. They were going to 'rub him out?'"

"Hard to say. Miz Merrydown told him, no, don't do nothing drastic, that she'd work on him, and if she couldn't get him settled on business, she'd set him up with some kind of Foundation, and take over the business herself, with the kid, Stevie, to take over when he come to be twenty-one."

"Gosh, a regency. This is pretty exciting, in a small way. I have to wonder what little Steven's feelings are in regard to unions."

"Huh. Bet he don't have none, yet."

33.

RIVERBEND IS THE NAME OF A PLACE WHERE THE Gabbro River, having loitered at Morgan's Eddy and plunged into three miles of shaded wetlands, pulls itself together to emerge from forest and swamp, and pools against a dike of black gabbro. Over the centuries of human habitation, this pool has been a source of pretty good fishing, particularly below the waterfall where the accumulated water spills over the natural dam of gabbro. The spring-fed swimming hole above the dam has always been more popular with children than with their elders; the water there is very cold, which affects parents and grandparents more than it does their hyperactive children. It is reached by a silent pathway, deep in pinestraw, that leads down from a roadside meadow into the woodland.

The forest setting makes the sound of the waterfall, echoing from a hundred cypresses, spooky; particularly at dusk when the impressionistic mélange of babble, hiss, and murmur can sound remarkably like the lamentations of children. Those so inclined hear in the blather the cries of Indian, settler, and town kids who have cramped and drowned in the freezing water, or slipped on the gabbro dam and fallen to the rocks below. And it was at dusk that Terry Morgan stole down that quiet pathway and, passing a larger-than-average gum tree, felt a quarter-inch circle of steel on the back of his neck.

"Whoa, there, easy does it, Jesus. Faye? Scared the crap outa me. What you doing here?"

"I have been needing to return your roscoe for months, Terry. Which I will, as soon as we have a discussion about a couple of things."

"What things?"

"Oh ... they both involve your new girl friend, Lee Forsythe."

"Yeah? Thought I heard you had a new boy friend. What, you gettin' upset all of a -"

"Don't be silly, just listen. Thing number one: What did you tell her about our little fling last August?"

"Noth - " Faye drew back the hammer with a practiced thumb - "Hey! Damn, put that thing down. Is it loaded?"

"You keep lying about what you told Lee about us, you'll find out."

"I didn't – All right! All right. Yeah, I bragged a little about how, how you enjoyed my technique in, you know. Taking care of a lady. Was that so -"

"Yes. If we pump that back up to something like the truth, you tried to impress her with your skill as a lover, and with what transports she would be missing, by giving her a detailed account of my response. Would that be a pretty close approximation?"

"Aw, Faye, now, come on. It wadn't like that. What did she say?"

"She said a couple of things. The first was, that you described my behavior 'in some detail,' you little snake. 'Extremely intimate' was how she described it, in refusing to repeat it to me. She also said she quickly realized that, if she went to bed with you, you would do the same to her with the next girl.

"So that brings me to the second purpose of our little meeting tonight, which is to say, leave her alone. I have some embarrassment coming to me, because I'm old enough to know better. She's only sixteen, and isn't. Which means, by the way, if you take her to bed, it's a criminal offense."

"Faye, there ain't gonna be no next girl. That girl is *it*."

"Really. Wouldn't it be more realistic to say, That girl is one of *them*?"

"No, Ma'am. You referrin' to how I said one time, I had a lot of ladies on the string?"

"Well, don't you?"

"Naw. At the time I said that, there was a lot of ladies I kind of liked the looks of, but far as actually f - as far as any actual, you know, action, you were it. And that was for maybe a week or two."

"Yes, thank God. Anyhow, I'm here to deliver a message. You have succeeded in charming Miss Forsythe, hooray for you. Now let her alone to grow up and make something of herself. And the same to you. Grow up. Make something of yourself besides a handyman and a hick Lothario. I'm not going to run some sort of line about how she's too good for you, or she's in another world. I try not to think in those terms. But she needs time without being in a sexual relationship, to grow up and become an adult. That will be a matter of a few years, I'd think. If Lee Forsythe really is 'it,' you can wait that long. It will give you time to grow some morals and integrity. And a little more income. How old are you, anyhow?"

He shrugged and looked over her shoulder at the dark pool by the dam. "Twenny-one."

"Oof. So last year when you and I were howling at the moon, you were twenty? Jesus."

"I was too young for you? Didn't sound that way to me."

"No, I actually did enjoy our carrying-on, at the time. Since then, I've met an actual adult who shows me how dumb that was."

"Gee, thanks."

"All right, sorry. I mean how wrong I was to take advantage of you like that. That better? But now I see, I didn't know the half of it."

"Hell, you can take all that kind of advantage you want. I got a couple blankets in the truck. Wanta screw?"

"Yeah, well, see? So much for 'that girl is it,' huh?"

"Naw, I was just raggin' you."

"Well, don't."

The darkness was thickening, and voices of the waterfall began to clamor and lament, raising hair along Faye's neck. She backed up the path toward the parking area, keeping the roscoe leveled at Terry. "Are we finished here?"

"You said your piece, and I will think about what you said. No, I really will give it some thought, 'cause it made some sense. You gonna give me the roscoe?"

"I guess maybe I'll hang on to it for a while, yet. You can't be too careful any more. The next I want to see or hear from you is, you sent Lee a note, dumping her. Make it gentle, but unmistakable. When she's of age, you can try your charms on her and see if you're good enough to fool a grown-up."

He grinned. "A'ready seen that last summer, wouldn't you hafta think?"

***

From the Gabbro *Intelligencer* for Friday, October 15, 1965:

River Mills Will Stay, Expand Product Line
"Do -over" on union vote?

Rumors of imminent closure of River Mills are no more than that, according to a release from parent Merrydown Industries headquarters in Raleigh. The textile giant plans expansion at River Mills to a line of industrial cordage and canvas to meet demand created by recent escalation of American military commitments in Viet Nam ...

"... thus in view of plant and hiring expansion, ownership concedes that the expanded work force may be entitled to consider again whether to organize to bargain collectively with management and owner-ship." according to Mrs. Merrydown. "This view has been advanced very strongly by our son Steven, now the titular CEO of Merrydown Industries. Though he is young, he is capable of being very persuasive. His father and I are determined to consider and respect his better ideas whenever feasible in accordance with our Christian principles and sound busi - (continued P. 3A)

***

"Really? What ..."

Forde shrugged. "Well, the kid got sent to Sunday School, probably to get him out from underfoot on Sunday mornings, and something somebody said stuck. He did come in here one time with the old man, and he sat next to me in that Labor Appreciation parade while you were gone, read a comic-book Bible the whole time."

"So you charmed him, I guess?"

"He paid no attention to me, except to drip ice cream on my pants. I might have looked a little peeved about it, except I didn't bother to put on good pants for the GLAD nonsense. He didn't seem all that repentant."

"Well, he's what? Ten? Twelve?"

"Or so. This announcement that young Stevie would have the ruling vote on matters of large policy obviously backfired. Mason, of course, would veto the whole thing, but he might not be in his absolute right mind, seems like. Well, more than that; he'd never agree to step down like he did, unless our receptionist and our door handle have left him more or less permanently concussed."

He snorted. "Instead of just cussed. Jerk kept laughing about Steve and his comic book Bible, and his drippy ice cream. I got him, though. The Bible comic was on Luke, so I showed Stevie where Jesus said,

'The laborer is worthy of his hire.' Maybe he looked a little thoughtful about that, I suppose."

"Forde! You knew that out of thin air? Honest to God, the Methodist Sunday School saves the day! That's got to be it, don't you think?"

"No, I think we're kidding ourselves. But let's wait and see."

34.

THE OUTREACH INTERN

Chapter 15.

Mercy folded the farewell note from Chad - good, patient, unassuming Chad - and turned the key for the last time on the stifling, poky little garret. Awaiting her were the Chevy with the once elegant upholstery, and her faithful Nell. She walked with a bounce in her step, in company with Nell, who barked to be allowed to ride in the front seat. Mercy boosted her in, and admonished her not to jump around and cause an accident.

Mercy carried within her the soreness of her failed romance with James, and the eager gladness that she was at the beginning of her new life in St. Louis Chicago. The weather was crisp and blue, a booming wind bringing chill from Canada. Well, she supposed, at least from Ohio somewhere. Mercy pulled away, turned north, and opened the little vent window to direct the cool flow down her into her face.

A sweet note from Chad, she thought; I probably judged him too harshly. She imagined inviting Chad to Chicago, after she was settled; show him around the town, open his Greensboro eyes and his Southern mind. Maybe he would be a lifelong friend; even a discreet occasional lover. As the crippled hairdresser Mabelene had told her, "I have found much more than I lost."

"Haven't I, Nell?"

Well; why wouldn't that be a good title for her novel? Much More Than I Lost, A Novel, by Mercy Greylock. Which now consists of an ambition, an opening sentence ('Faith Blackstone, recent graduate of Johnstown High School, stands before a mirror on the top floor of a rooming house.') and a ream of paper on the back seat; five hundred clean white pages hungry waiting for the words that would make people smile, or nod, or maybe cry a little. So many things were possible now, weren't they?

"Aren't they, Nell?"

"Arf," said Nell.

THE END

35.

November 15, 1965

Dearest Faye:

Good news this morning from Renfro, in that my blood enzymes are down again, <u>almost</u> to the detection limit, not quite. I am feeling quite a bit stronger, though, and my appetite is much better. So all in all, some promising developments. I am quite sure that your visit - it already seems years ago - and your letters have been the tonic.

Christmas is on the horizon again, and I hope you will be able to join me in New York, as last year. I have a few ideas for entertaining things we might think of doing - they have made a musical of Don Quixote, if you can imagine such a thing, but people say it is very intriguing. Or, perhaps I should order in a half-cord of firewood and a bearskin rug, if that sounds more appealing.

Please write and let me know what your availability might be over the Holiday, and what you fancy in the way of entertainment.

Longing for you -

Peter
(Peter A. Standish, MD)

Nov. 17

Dearest Peter -

You can just bet that I will be there with you at Christmastime. I would be up for a musical about the Book of Deuteronomy, if you are there with me. Rug and firewood, heck, yes. As long as the bear was good-humored and fuzzy, I'm game - no pun intended - but I think those rugs with teeth might be a little hazardous for some of the Positions.

My patient, generous boss Forde appears to believe that I need regular visits with you, for the sake of my mental health and productivity; I am not about to contradict him in that, so I will be able to take the Wednesday afternoon train, December 22, and not have to be back here until after New Year's. Can you put up with me for that long? As the Beatles are singing these days, "We Can Work It Out."

All my loving -
Faye

36.

12/21/65

Off tomorrow to see Peter in New York, and step again onto the shaky ground of his health and happiness. It's lucky that I love him so thoroughly, given what a fearful thing it is to be with him. (But the whole notion of loving someone 'thoroughly' is an idea that came from Peter. Thoroughly and transparently, he said, and I can only smile, knowing what he means ... saturated with it, pierced through by it. Dying of it.)

So I have no choice but to molt my self-sufficient loner-hood by sharing in his struggle with cancer, though I already half-know that it cannot end but with his eventual death, this year or years from now. It is hard to be with him in its presence; but how dead I would be myself, if I were so self-contained as to leave him alone with it. And how hard it must be for him, not only to fear for himself, but to fear for me, as I know he does when he sees my fear. So that must be my part of the fight: I cannot be afraid. I will show neither fear nor blithe optimism, the two responses that would hurt him most. As long as cancer is part of him, then I can only - God help me - embrace the cancer too.

Epilogue:

From the Gabbro *Intelligencer* for Friday, October 4, 1974:

Intelligencer Partner Peter A. Standish, 57

Dr. Peter A. Standish, 57, of Standish, Maine passed away October 2, after a years-long struggle with complications from melanoma. Dr. Standish was co-Publisher of the *Intelligencer*, and as partner of Editor in Chief and Publisher Forde Morgan, owned a 22% equity position, which will revert to the newspaper.

"Peter Standish was a good friend and supporter of the *Intelligencer* for almost a decade," Morgan said. "He saved our bacon when we needed a boost, and he will be very sadly missed around this office."

Dr. Standish's long-time friend, Associate Editor M. Faye Bynum was unavailable …

***

After the years of scares and reprieves, surgeries, chemo, remission, radiation, health, discouragement and hope; after the weeks and weekends spent in joy and in anguish, in struggle and in bed, but never for poorer, Faye parked a Chevy at the front door in Standish, Maine at dusk on October 1. Entering, she passed the hall to the garnet-skarn kitchen, and the sleek piano with its portrait of Julie, whose look had evolved from haggard to pensive over the decade of Faye's watching. She found Amy Standish emerging from the office that had become a sickroom.

"Bless you, Faye. This is how he wants it, and I'm all for it. I'm upstairs if you need me." She kissed Faye's cheek and left.

Faye walked to the side of the bed: an assembly of bones, sallow in the lamplight. Three or four machines for sustaining life beeped and dripped around the bed. Peter's eyes opened, and he spoke in a whispered rasp.

"Well, Faye, my love. I'm afraid -"

"Hush." Faye took off her driving gloves, her eyes locked on his.

Peter raised a hand. "Wait. I feel lousy, and half of it is all this crap sticking into me." He shed the oxygen tube, pinched off the IV and eased it out of his arm, reached under the sheet and came out with a catheter. She popped off his EKG leads, and a machine at the top of the bed began to whine. "Ayah. Here, now. That feels much better. Thank you for coming all this way for one more tryst."

She turned off the EKG and the light, shed her shoes and raincoat, and climbed onto the hospital bed. "Uh huh. Scootch over, dope. You want me to fall out on my butt, like Position 147? Which we never attempted, by the way."

"I guess this is Position 147 for us. Just hang on to me, I'm not going anywhere."

And when she was settled against him, their legs pleasantly tangled and her head sharing his pillow, he sighed. "I truly thought I could lick this. I hate to lose."

"Silly." She stirred against him and was pleased to feel a response. "We <u>won</u>, you know. Ten years ago almost to the day. Don't you remember?"

"Of course I remember. I was scared silly. Much more than I am now."

Her voice became a purr of contentment. "Now, let's just think about that, shall we? How many women in the whole history of the world have been seduced by CPAh and a kitchen full of gahnet skahn? One, maybe, and lucky me, I'm it. Fit yourself against me ... oh, that's good. Now, close your eyes."

"Meet you at the Spirit Catcher." It had become a joke of theirs.

"We'll have a cordial to relax us, and I will hold you. I will be here with you as long as you need me."

"That's exactly what I need."

"Ayah." She was as gentle as the word, holding his head up to sip at the cordial while she pronounced the Lumbee benediction, watching them restore to his skull the face she loved. The raw angles, the tender mouth, the kind, killer eyes.

The window was open a hand's width. Faye heard the rain that had dogged her from New Haven pass northward in darkness; swell, peak, and taper to the drip and flutter of bright, exhausted leaves. Light came and went with clouds that raced across the moon. In the direction of the lake, a night bird keened. Medical diplomas and Latina campers watched from the walls while Faye murmured and whispered about their years of delight in delighting each other. Reviewing the Spirit Catcher they had built together out of sex and love and spare parts. Climbing it with him, pausing at one story after another to admire, weep, and laugh; a reverse Scheherazade spinning a thousand nights into one. Peter nodded, breathed, smiled. Stopped breathing; started again.

In the early dawn she felt him go. A caught breath; a shuddering sigh that might have been no more than a shiver of happiness, in which the names of Faye and Julie seemed to mingle and toss inaudibly. She laid her head on the stillness of his chest and wept for a time that was long and too short. She rose, dressed, considered the stairway; but wrote a note for Amy to find when she woke.

Outside, she leaned against the roof of the car, tears flowing while she watched the stars fade one by one until there was just one left, steady against the pale sky. When it too dissolved in light, she took a last breath of Maine, unlocked the Chevy, and settled in for the long journey South.

About the Author

Tom Blackburn has published short fiction in *Exquisite Corpse, The Saint Andrews Review, Cairn,* and *Crucible.* He is the author of nine novels centered on the fictional town of Gabbro, North Carolina, and of two texts in chemistry and a how-to book on securing grants for scientific research. Blackburn holds a PhD in chemistry from Harvard University.